FROM FIRST BULLET TO LAST,

THE FOUR KILLINGS TOOK
SEVENTEEN SECONDS.

The killer whirled. His gun arm locked straight out while his eyes scanned the world beyond the black shark fin gunsight. He saw her staring at him from the bottom of the ramp, staring at the four bodies on the floor. He saw her start to move, scared rabbit but not stupid, not wasting time screaming, moving as he squeezed off two quick shots. She lunged forward so the slugs whizzed into the darkness behind her, then dove back up the ramp, her form flying through the sunlight as he popped two more rounds her way.

The killer pressed against the edge of the brick entrance. Strained his ears. Noticed the round curved mirror mounted high on the opposite wall. The mirror showed an empty ramp, no gun-drawing copy waiting at street level. And no scared rabbit.

Without looking back, the killer walked up the ramp and out into the city winds.

JUST A SHOT AWAY
by JAMES GRADY
author of Six Days of the Condor
and Razor Game

JUST A
SHOT AWAY

JAMES GRADY

BANTAM BOOKS

TORONTO • NEW YORK • LONDON • SYDNEY • AUCKLAND

JUST A SHOT AWAY

A Bantam Book / February 1987

ISBN 0-553-26268-8

Published simultaneously in the United States and Canada

Bantam Books are published by Bantam Books, Inc. Its trademark, consisting of the words "Bantam Books" and the por-
trayal of a rooster, is registered in U.S. Patent and Trademark
Office and in other countries. Marca Registrada. Bantam
Books, Inc., 666 Fifth Avenue, New York, New York 10103.

PRINTED IN THE UNITED STATES OF AMERICA
KR   0 9 8 7 6 5 4 3 2 1

For Rich Bechtel

Just a Shot Away is a work of fiction, and any similarity to real persons, places, or things is purely coincidental.

The author gratefully acknowledges the assistance of the Baltimore Police Department, radio stations WRQX and WHFS, Hoang Minh, Don Goldberg, Dennis Hill, Michael Yockel, and Bonnie, all of whom helped make this novel possible.

1

Until the killer's day, Baltimore bragged about the Ward Building, a black glassed skyscraper rising from the worn streets of a resurrected city. The Ward Building symbolized that rebirth—so had said many a politician in speeches celebrating the building's grand opening less than a year earlier. Until that day, the only smudge on the building's polished image was the Blake Fund controversy, a paper-shuffling financial scandal spawned in one of its suites. Few Baltimorians cared about such an esoteric matter. They gazed upon that triumphant ebony mirrored tower and felt proud.

On that winter Saturday afternoon, few cars filled the yellow-lined slots in the Ward Building's underground garage. During business hours, an attendant in a glass booth controlled the wooden crossbar that blocked the garage entrance. After hours, the attendant—a pensioned-off steelworker whose left leg had been mangled at a now boarded-up mill—limped to the corner bar, had a shot and a beer, went home to his wife and three kids. Then tenants needed a plastic card to raise the crossbar.

The killer looked like just another man in blue jeans and an old army parka hiking through weather-deserted concrete canyons. No one noticed him walk down the garage entry ramp.

The killer turned left at the bottom of the ramp, followed yellow traffic arrows until only two concrete columns separated him from the gray steel elevator doors. His rubber-soled shoes made no sound on the concrete floor. He stopped, carefully considered the terrain. A parked car screened him from anyone stepping out of the elevator. He was close enough to the entry ramp for a quick retreat, close enough to the elevator for his job. He leaned against the nearest column. Staring straight ahead into the cavernous garage, he could almost see both the elevator and the entry ramp with his peripheral vision.

Not much longer, thought the killer. The concrete column seeped through him. His bones ached for the coming moment. His skin burned, his spine was tense. Magnets pulled at his sandy hair. His stomach was hollow and quiet, his loins tight. His black-gloved hands hung empty at his sides; they didn't tremble, and inside those leather sheaths, his palms were dry.

Soon, he thought. *Very soon.*

The darkness was like a mist. Bare fluorescent tubes glowed in the maze of overhead pipes. A shaft of winter light filtered down the entry ramp. The garage was deserted.

He breathed in: musty concrete, oil dried on a cement floor, the ghosts of exhaust fumes, and the basement dampness tinged the frigid air he inhaled. The garage was eerily silent. A car horn's blare in the street echoed through the garage. Apart from occasional traffic noises, all he heard was the slamming of his heart.

He breathed out: his exhale formed a fog that floated before his eyes, then vanished. Those clouds couldn't be seen by anyone emerging from the elevator until it was too late.

No need to check the watch. The target was due any second. Backlit floor numbers cut through the brass plate above the elevator doors showed which floor the elevator was on. The killer could see number 9 glowed. That hadn't changed since he'd taken up his position. But it would. Any second now. He unzipped his parka, ignored the icy draft that swept over his shirt. He became still, at one with the shadows, at one with the moment.

The light behind 9 went out. Ten glowed. Then 11. The sequence continued upward.

On time, thought the killer as he checked the entry ramp again. *On schedule.*

The killer sidestepped around the column until he faced the ramp, his eyes alert for any form walking down into the garage through the shaft of sunlight from the outer world.

His empty, black-gloved hand moved up inside the unzipped parka, emerged full. He held that heavy hand against the back of his thigh, waited.

A bell dinged; the elevator doors slid open.

Suddenly a truck in the street outside blared its air horn long and hard. The blast reverberated down into the garage.

Keep it up! thought the killer. The blaring truck horn would mask the sounds of his work. The horn also drowned out any heels clicking on the concrete floor. He'd planned to use footsteps and other sounds to key his move, but so what? He counted to five instead.

Hands tight against his side, he spun off the concrete pillar, whirled around it . . .

Found his target.

Found a problem.

But all problems had long ago been worked out, with solutions plugged into him. His business allowed no luxury of hesitation. He'd made himself into the perfect tool for his work, which he thought of as *profitable assertion of ultimate power.*

He moved like a dancer, with rhythm, fluid grace, and orchestrated precision.

Those black-gloved hands rose from his sides to meet at chest level as he took his third step toward the target, bent his right leg, and firmly planted that foot. His stance leaned forward, yet gave him perfectly braced balance. The right-gloved hand cradled the left, which held the long-barreled, black automatic.

Fifty feet in front of him were four human beings strung out in a casual grouping as they walked toward their cars; as they walked toward him.

The woman lagged at the back of the group, so he shot her first: she was farthest from him, had the best chance of fleeing. The hollow-point .22 slug punched through her forehead and plowed through nine centimeters of brain matter. She wore her thick black hair parted in the middle; it hung free, over her cheekbones and her soft brown flesh, down to the Christmas gift tartan scarf bundled snugly up to her dimpled chin. The slug's impact shook her head enough to loosen the scarf's wrap and make her beautiful hair sway. Inertia let her body complete its last step.

The second victim, a squat, pale man in a tan overcoat, was daydreaming happiness as he walked toward his car. His eyes reported *strange motion* to his brain as the woman behind him crumpled. He instinctively turned to his left for a better look. The blaring truck horn in the street outside stopped the instant before the killer fired his second shot. The squat man's brain didn't register the pistol's *crack* before the slug smashed through his right temple. His arms flew wide, a wounded goose spinning to the earth. He died before his body hit the floor; died before even the woman's corpse settled on the concrete; died before he realized he wasn't dreaming.

"No!" screamed the third victim. He wore a leather trenchcoat and Italian loafers. He was handsome. Anxiety made his hands tremble; that morning he'd cut himself shaving. The third victim had time to see the man wearing an old khaki parka. Time to wonder why the guy crouched. Time to blink at the first shot, time to register that the man had a gun, and time to hear the *crack* of the second shot. Time to stutter step and throw his hands up in the air. The handsome man had time to scream.

Then his time ran out, and the killer shot him through his open mouth. The slug blew out the back of the handsome man's neck, severing the spinal cord. He fell on his back. His left arm draped across the head of the woman, who'd collapsed face down behind him. His right arm lay palm up on the concrete; those fingers flexed once. The dead goose of a man lay curled on his right side almost at the handsome man's feet.

Those three shots played out with a steady beat: *One*. *Two*. *Three*. The fourth victim broke that rhythm.

He'd played high school basketball. That athletic history combined with his rekindled passion for physical fitness plus the fact that he was the last person targeted gave him a chance. He'd recognized *man with gun* as the killer fired the second shot. The athlete had been to the right of the other three targets. He spun away from them, ducked as he raced toward the shelter of a parked car.

He never made it. The killer took three beats to shift his aim from the handsome man's mouth to the moving target, acquire that target, then fire. The slug tore through the athlete's neck. He tumbled head over heels, crashed on his back, his wingtip shoes thumping the concrete. Blood squirted into the air from his severed throat artery, crimson geysers that flecked the ceiling and the car parked 10 feet away. The red cloud rained back down on the flopping, gurgling man and the gray cement floor. His heart pumped furiously three times while the killer zeroed his bull's-eye, then shot him in the head. That strong heart pumped twice more; was forever still.

Start to finish, the killing sequence took 17 seconds.

The killer heard her just as he realized something might be wrong.

She knew better than to make any noise, but couldn't help whispering, "Oh shit!" as she saw the four bodies on the floor and the man in the parka as he straightened up from his crouch; as the athlete's heart sent one last spurt of blood toward heaven.

The killer whirled. His gun arm locked straight out while his eyes scanned the world beyond the black shark fin gunsight. He saw her staring at him from the bottom of the ramp, saw her and her familiar brown uniform. Saw her start to move, scared rabbit but not stupid, not wasting time screaming, *moving* as he squeezed off two quick shots.

She fooled him: instead of bolting up the ramp, she lunged forward so the slugs whizzed into the darkness behind her, shattered the windshield of the building superintendent's midnight blue '66 Mustang. She planted her foot, threw a head fake, then dove back up the ramp, her form flying through the sunlight as he popped two more rounds her way. He lost one round in the darkness, heard the last one chip brick off the edge of the entryway and ricochet somewhere into city.

Last round in the chamber. As he ran, he ejected the empty clip, dropped it in his pocket and slapped in a full one, his eyes locked on the shaft of sunlight.

He pressed against the edge of the brick entrance. Strained his ears. Noticed the round curved mirror mounted high on the opposite wall so entering drivers could see anyone coming their way around the blind corner. The mirror showed an empty ramp, no gun-drawing cop waiting at street level. And no scared rabbit.

Without looking back, the killer walked up the ramp and out into the city winds.

In the garage, all was silent, still.

2

Captain Goldstein lumbered toward the two police cruisers blocking the mouth of the Ward Building's garage. Their spinning blue lights cut through the sunset, made the two detectives hurrying to catch up with him look like aliens in a science fiction movie.

"What took you so long?!" he yelled as the three of them started down the sloping ramp.

"Less than a minute from the uniformed cruiser's call-in," answered Detective Perry, businesslike and defensive in her short tan leather winter coat and black pants. Gray streaked her close-cropped black hair; her face had few laugh lines.

The other detective wore a blue topcoat and said nothing. The new guy on the squad. Brown hair and an eager, handsome face. For a moment Goldstein forgot the kid's name: Harris, that was it: Gary Harris.

Guess I am getting old, thought Goldstein.

"How many?" he asked as they walked down the ramp.

"Four," answered Perry as they ducked under the crossbar.

A uniformed sergeant waited at the bottom of the ramp. He nodded to the captain.

"How long we been here?" asked Goldstein.

"About four minutes," replied the sergeant. "Two units plus me, more on the way. Technicians coming too."

"Who phoned it in?"

"Some kid lawyer who was putting in his Saturday slave time. Rode the elevator down to go home, saw the mess, punched the button to get the hell out of there and back up to his office phone. A uniform has him upstairs now."

Goldstein nodded, led the group around the corner. Stopped them three steps into the view lit by the bare

6

fluorescent bulbs and flashlights held by two uniformed officers.

They looked like well-dressed winos passed out in the park, or maybe costumed dancers pressed against the floor of the stage, awaiting the crowd's applause before they rose to take their bows. Only the four figures were too still for winos or dancers, and instead of grass or the bare boards of a stage, they lay in a lake of blood.

"Holy shit," whispered Harris, who'd only seen 15 homicides in his seven years on the force.

"Not exactly what you wanted to ease you into retirement, huh captain?" muttered the sergeant.

"I'm not gone yet," he muttered. He felt the others waiting on him as he considered what he saw.

"What's been done?" he finally asked.

"Outside of securing the scene, not a—"

"Keep it that way," the captain interrupted the sergeant. He looked at the two detectives. "Where's Rourke?"

"Off duty," replied Perry. She shrugged. "He hung around the squad room for a couple hours killing time. Next Monday he—"

"So what?" said her boss. She interpreted his gruffness as a rebuke and pulled back inside herself to grow cold as the weather and hard as the .38 tucked in her waistband. The captain had no time for her emotions. He focused on the pay phone by the attendant's glass booth. Probably would be okay, but this one had to be letter perfect and the lab team hadn't dusted the scene.

"This is the way it is," announced Goldstein.

"Button this place up *tight*! Nobody—no cops, no technicians, not the fucking press or the mayor or the commissioner —*nobody* does anything down here until I say so. Make the rounds outside—all the places somebody might have seen something happening here. Get the plates off the parked cars. Knock on all the doors. You know the routine. And nobody says nothing to anybody. Got that?"

"Yes sir!" snapped brand new Homicide Detective Harris.

His boss grunted again, turned, lumbered up the ramp to the street and the coming night.

3

"Really," insisted Julia Simmons to Devlin Rourke as they talked on the phone, "we have more important things to talk about than my breasts!"

"Like what?" he demanded.

Devlin Rourke sat at the roll-top desk in his apartment's bay window. He wore a long-sleeved, arctic underwear crew-neck top and faded jockey shorts. His bare feet were beginning to chill. He was precisely six feet tall. Wiry, muscular. His black hair was barely an inch long; after showering, he used his long-fingered hands to brush it flat. Lately he'd noticed silver glints among the strands. He told himself that his forehead had always been that high, just as his eyes had always been blue. He was too hungry-looking to be commercially handsome. His snub-nosed Smith and Wesson in its worn leather holster, his handcuffs, the leather wallet containing Baltimore Police Department badge number 47 and a picture I.D. lay on the desk. As Julia and he talked, he tipped back in his chair, gazed out at the light fading on St. Paul Street, wondered if it would snow.

"Like—" began Julia, but he interrupted her.

"They're so beautiful! I love your breasts."

"I know."

"I didn't even think much about them. . . ."

"*Much,*" she repeated.

"Much," he continued, "until that night I took off your shirt."

"When you finally got up your nerve. Now stop it: you're embarrassing me!"

"Why? Who'll know what we say besides us?"

"Dev, this isn't the time, . . ."

"Of course it is! It still amazes me how far you had the hooks in before I realized how beautiful—"

8

"I didn't put those hooks in, dear," she said.

"You make sure they're snug."

"Do you blame me?"

He laughed.

"Now," she said, "about—"

"About your breasts," he said, heard her sigh. "They're so beautiful, perfect! Just big enough that I can't completely cup one in my hand. Smooth. Solid. High, no sag, no marks. Your nipples, God, Julia, your *nipples*! So big! Symmetrical. That beautiful brown aurora or whatever it's called, the way they bud up, get like marbles when I rub my fingers on them, when my lips—"

"Devlin!"

"Come on," he said. He heard her smile behind her protests.

"You're sweet, dear."

"So you've said."

"Devlin! We've got more important things to discuss!"

"Like *what*?!"

"Like what you're going to wear to dinner tonight."

"You're kidding?"

"Seriously, Devlin, Frank and Janet Mathews are not just another couple."

"Really?"

"None of that. They are my friends. A little stuffier than you're used to, but with this promotion, they're the kind of people you'll be meeting. You have to look your part."

"I always do."

"And act it! I'm not sure they'd like your crazy cop stories."

"They'd probably like my crazy cops less."

"They'll never meet them. Now, what are you wearing?"

"Probably what I've got on."

"What are you . . . Oh darling, never mind. You know I adore you and trust you completely."

"I know."

"Are you picking me up?"

"I hope so."

"God, I can't wait until you get rid of that broken down wreck! Why anybody would want something that old and beat up . . ."

"Call me sentimental."

"You are that, Dev, but—"

A loud *beep* cut through their conversation.

"*Will the party on 555-4729 break for a phone call from Captain Goldstein, Baltimore Police Department?*"

"Yes! Hang up!" Devlin shouted into the telephone, doing so himself without waiting to hear Julia's response. The phone rang ten seconds after he pushed the receiver button down.

"Rourke," he answered. He walked to the sofa where the jeans he'd discarded lay in a heap, pulled them on one-handed while the torrent of words poured out of his receiver.

"I know who the hell it is!" growled Captain Goldstein. "And where the hell you're going to be in 10 minutes. You got your ass kicked up the ladder and you're a hot shot new lieutenant, but somebody turned the Ward Building's garage into a slaughterhouse. I got four gunned-down citizens floating in their own blood. I need a goddamn detective, and until you get transferred or I get retired, your ass and the badge pinned to it belong to me! Get them down here now! You got that?!"

"Got it," said Devlin.

4

"Where you been?" growled Captain Goldstein as Rourke nodded his way past the shivering uniformed cops standing guard at the top of the ramp.

"Car wouldn't start," said Devlin. "I had to badge some high school kid picking up his girl, commandeer a ride. Scared the hell out of them. Their first date. They'll be late for the movie, but now they've got something to talk about. What the hell has you so bent?"

Goldstein sighed. The two men ducked under the cross-bar. Sirens wailed toward them through the night.

"I don't know, Dev." Goldstein sighed again. "I've been barking all day. Chewed Perry for nothing."

"Don't worry," said Devlin, "you'll be out of all this soon."

"Yeah, guess I will." The older man shook his head, smiled. "You ought to get that car fixed. Fix it or junk it."

"So I keep getting told. Why did you call me for this?"

"You'll see," said Goldstein as they reached the bottom of the slope. "You'll see."

Devlin turned the corner, took four steps, stopped. Blinked.

"This is how it was," said the captain to the lieutenant. The cavernous room echoed their voices, squawks of police radios.

"I've got Perry ramrodding the neighborhood check and license plate detail," said Goldstein. "The evidence technicians are holding. We haven't even taken the pictures. I kept it this way until you got here."

Rourke held out his hand. Ken Urtz, the head civilian evidence technician, gave him a flashlight. Rourke flicked it on, started toward the red lake.

"Kenny," he said, and that man fell in step behind him. As they walked, Rourke swept the flashlight beam back and forth over the concrete floor.

"What do you figure?" said Urtz. "Hold-up boys berserk on PCP? Drug rip? Gang shit? Another psycho?"

"I don't know," answered Rourke.

"Look," he said, spotlighting two clusters of ejected cartridge cases a little more than a yard apart. Their brass gleamed in the flashlight glow.

"Automatic. Probably a .22," said Urtz.

"Two clusters."

"Two shooters?"

"Maybe," said Rourke. "One guy would have grounded himself, blasted away. No reason to shift. Even if the cartridges rolled, they all ejected from the same side of the gun. The two groups aren't close enough for that, unless . . ."

He swung the flashlight beam into the darkness on each side of the elevator shaft.

"The place been checked out?" asked this lieutenant.

"Just enough to be sure the shooter's gone," said Urtz.

Rourke swung the beam in an arc. The light played over the wall, past the corner, to the captain and the others waiting at the bottom of the ramp, to—back to the corner. There, on the floor next to the wall's edge, pebble-size pieces of brick and mortar. Devlin raised the beam along the wall's edge, found the jagged break.

"What . . ." asked Urtz, then: "Why the hell would he shoot behind him?"

Rourke swung the flashlight 180° from the bodies. The beam faded into darkness before it reached the far wall.

"Let's find out," said Rourke. He yelled a command. The other evidence technician and a uniformed officer switched on their flashlights, fanned out as they searched their way toward the far wall.

"Get pictures of all this," said Rourke. Behind them, more lab technicians and cops were walking down the ramp. "And forget about those budget directives. Don't miss an angle, don't blow a shot."

Urtz nodded.

The red lake had cooled, congealed. An undisturbed rusty stain surrounded the four bodies. In some places, the stain still looked sticky; in others, the flashlight's glow sparkled off frozen ice crystals. Devlin made his light linger on each corpse, then swept the beam over the stain's smooth surface.

"Who checked to see that they were dead?!" His shout echoed through the garage.

"First officer on the scene!" bellowed a grizzled uniformed sergeant. He and the captain moved toward Rourke—who yelled at them not to disturb the shell casings. A uniformed cop ran down the ramp.

"Yes sir?!" yelled the cop, his face pale in the fluorescent light, his panting breaths turning to clouds.

"You the first officer on the scene?" said Goldstein.

"Yes sir. My partner and I got here at—"

"Did you check the bodies?" asked Devlin. "Touch them or anything close to them?"

The 24-year-old cop looked from one superior's face to another, trying to guess what answer was wanted.

"Ah . . . we . . . we looked around the garage to be sure nobody was . . . We didn't want to disturb . . . Jack was sick over there in the corner and I . . . Ah, check them for what, sir?"

"To see if they were alive," said Devlin quietly. "It's been almost half an hour since you got here, since 'help' first arrived on the scene. There are no tracks in the blood. Who checked to be sure they didn't need an ambulance?"

"Oh shit!" whispered the young cop. "I . . . We . . . I'd never seen anything . . . How could they be alive? Look at them!"

They all did.

"I mean . . . all that blood! And you can see . . . the holes. How could they be alive?"

"Never mind," said the captain who commanded homicide. "They're dead."

"Should . . . should I call for medics?" asked the young cop.

"Call the morgue," said Devlin.

"And next time," said the grizzled sergeant, "make sure they're dead."

"Next time?" asked the young cop.

"Hey!" yelled the evidence technician in the darkness behind them. "Somebody shot the shit out of an old car back here!"

"Pictures of that too," said Rourke.

Urtz nodded.

"Get this first," said Rourke. "Then I'll check them out."

"You want me to do it?" asked Urtz, nodding toward the four corpses.

Rourke shook his head.

"We got some overshoes in the station wagon," the evidence technician told the homicide detective. "Keep your shoes clean."

"They been dirty before," answered Rourke.

The sound of running feet turned them around.

"Hey captain!" called Detective Harris.

"Stay there!" yelled Rourke, pointing to the spent cartridges scattered on the floor a few steps ahead of the detective.

"Ah, right," answered Harris, halting. He raised his eyes from the floor to his commanding officer.

"You still bossing this?" he asked Goldstein.

"Rourke," said the captain.

"Perry sent me to get whoever's in charge. We found something weird out there."

"It'll take us 20 minutes to shoot this up and sketch it like you want," said Urtz.

"We'll be back," said Rourke.

"Not me," answered the captain. "I'm going home."

"Here," he said, handing Rourke a set of car keys. "I've got a deputy commissioner's cruiser. It's radio-equipped."

Rourke nodded. Few Baltimore police cars have radios; each policeman——detective and uniformed——normally carries a radio or wears one mounted on his utility belt.

Rourke walked away from the carnage with his captain. Harris hesitated before turning away from the four bodies to join them as they strode toward the exit.

"Who were those people?" he asked. "What happened to them?"

"Yeah," said Rourke.

5

"Cops," grumbled the fat man as he faced the three of them from behind the lunch counter. "All day long, I'm up to my ass in cops. Can't run my business. Can't earn an honest living. You *cops*."

"What about us?" said Perry.

The fat man didn't answer her.

"Tell it all to me," said Rourke.

"I already told it to her."

"Now tell it to *me*," said Rourke, steel slicing through his words.

The Empire Coffee House and Cafe was sandwiched between a men's hat shop and a shoe store two blocks from the Ward Building. The yellowed, hand-lettered sign taped to the cafe's glass door promised "fast delivery three blocks." The Empire had a brown ambience of stale time.

The fat man leaned on the lunch counter beside the cash register. He had black, oily hair, wore a grease-stained white shirt and white pants that strained against his massive gut. His arms were hairy and short. The veins were broken on his bulbous nose, his saggy jowls needed a shave.

"So what makes you different than the other cops?" snarled the fat man.

"I have no patience," whispered Devlin. "Cut your crap or I'll break this garbage pit on the law."

The cafe's only customers were two retired men who had nothing better to do that cold Saturday afternoon. They sat in the middle booth, their coffee mugs empty, their eyes downcast as they tried to be invisible.

The only waitress sat slumped on a stool at the far end of the counter, smoking and reading *People* magazine. Her name was Mavis. She had peroxided hair whipped and sprayed into a beehive, a clown's pink makeup over her half century of wrinkles. She wore the brown smock and pants uniform the boss insisted all the waitresses buy and wear.

Mavis wouldn't wear glasses, although she had trouble with images more than an arm's length away. So much trouble she couldn't get a driver's license (though she still drove the Buick). That made her a bullshit witness. So she'd told the cops. Besides, she hadn't noticed anyway. She smoked as she read, a long cigarette; the butt was smeared red from her lipstick. She ignored the ashtray, ignored the cops and the two old men with empty coffee mugs.

"You didn't need to get nasty," said the fat man, his scowl switching to a whine.

"I get what I need to get," said the cop. "What happened."

"Like I said," the fat man told him, "I've been up to my ass in cops all day.

"The first one was . . . I don't know. Maybe 15, maybe 20 minutes before I heard a bunch of sirens up the street.

"Big guy—well, tall anyway. Six feet, six one. Wore one of those puffy blue parkas. Noticed him standing outside across the street. Finally he walks in, flips out the badge, starts asking questions about Rachel."

"Who's Rachel?" asked Rourke.

"Good question," answered the fat man, trying to be buddies with the law. "The other waitress. We work at least two, in case we get a call for a delivery. She started here two, three weeks ago."

"Three weeks," intoned Mavis from the counter. She didn't look up from her magazine. "Right after Jenny quit."

The fat man glared at her, but she never saw it; didn't care.

"The lazy bum is never here!" protested the fat man. "I warned her: no personal breaks on company time, 'cept to go to the facilities."

He jerked his thumb toward the back rooms.

"You can't get dependable help these days. I always make 'em hang their coats there," he said, nodding to a row of garments dangling from hooks on the wall, "so I can keep my eye on them. Dumb bitch, she fuckin' snuck off without her coat in the middle of winter. That's it there."

He pointed to a worn leather flight jacket with bulging chest and side pockets.

"Anyway, this guy flashes his badge and describes this broad who sounds like Rachel, and—"

"Does this Rachel have a last name?" asked Rourke.

"Dylan," said the fat man.

"Like the singer from Minnesota," monotoned Mavis, still reading her magazine. "Dylan is just his stage name."

"What does Rachel look like?" asked Rourke.

"Tough," said the fat man, nodding his head. "Dirty blond hair, chopped short. Big face. Blue eyes. Maybe five-five, maybe a little more. Husky, but not fat. About like 38, 40."

"About 35," said Mavis.

"Why don't you mind your own fuckin' business?!" yelled the fat man.

Mavis slowly turned her eyes toward him. She flicked the ash off her cigarette, then went back to reading.

"This Rachel," said Rourke. "She's wearing a uniform too?"

"Yeah." The fat man sneered at Mavis's unwatching form.

"Go on," said Rourke.

"This cop—"

"Did he give you his name?" asked Rourke.

"He flashed a badge," answered the fat man. "That's all the name you guys need."

"What did he look like?"

"Like a cop. White guy. Brown hair. Mustache. One of those give-me-no-shit faces. Blue jeans. Black gloves. Oh yeah: he wore them glasses that the lenses change color with the light, kind of gray and don't show you the eyes."

"What did he want?"

"Rachel. He flashed his badge, ran down her description. I thought she was in the can. He went back there, comes back, says she's gone. I say 'No shit,' and he tells me to watch my fuckin' mouth. Says he's part of some narcotics bust and they want to talk to her. He asks for her address, name, all that jazz. I ain't the kind of guy to bullshit cops. I give him what I got and away he goes.

"Then the Sonny-and-Cher cops come in 'bout half hour later, I tell them their buddy's already been here. The next thing I know, I'm talking to you and taking shit from everybody who thinks they know everything—which is a fine goddamn way for a good citizen *and* a taxpayer *and* a voter to have to spend his working Saturday!"

"And that's it?" asked Rourke.

"That's it," said the fat man.

"Where does this Rachel live?"

"London Hotel, fleabag joint on Lamont."

Rourke stared at the fat man for a moment, then walked down to the end of the counter where Mavis sat.

"You got anything you can add?" he asked her.

She took a last drag on her cigarette, didn't look as she dropped it to the floor beside her white-shoed foot, ground it out. She licked her left thumb and used it to turn the magazine page.

"I didn't see nothing," she said. "You can ask the Department of Motor Vehicles about that. I was busy, too."

Mavis's hairspray smelled sticky-sweet. She turned her cosmetic raccoon eyes to Devlin.

"Besides," she said, "I don't scare cheap and easy like some people. And I don't talk to cops."

The fat man cursed, but no one cared.

Perry met Devlin between Mavis and the fat man. No one could hear the cops whispers.

"I called narcotics," said Perry. "Nobody is looking for a Rachel Dylan for anything. They're still checking with the feds, but I don't think we'll hit anything with them."

"How do you figure it?" she asked Devlin.

"Plainclothes cop shows up looking for somebody who disappeared the same time four people get gunned down two blocks away. No one knows who this cop is," said Devlin. "How the hell can you figure it?"

Rourke walked back to the surly owner.

"This Rachel," said Rourke, "does she have a phone?"

"At the London? Lucky if she's got a toilet."

"Do you expect her back?"

"She comes in, she goes out again—just as quick as I can tell her she's fired. She knows that."

"What about her jacket?" asked the cop.

"What about it?" said the fat man.

"From what you've told me," said Rourke, "it may be abandoned property. You could ask us to take custody of it. Should she come in, you can tell her we've got it and to contact us."

"You want her jacket, take it. No skin off my back."

Harris lifted the jacket off its hook. A bulky sweater was stuffed inside it.

"Be a smart," said Rourke. He handed the fat man a business card. "If you see Rachel or hear anything about her, call me right away."

"I'm smart enough," said the fat man.

"Un-huh," said Rourke. He led his two associates back into the cold night.

"Did you get anything else out here?" asked Rourke as they hurried toward the Ward Building.

"Lot of license plates," answered Perry. "Lot of locked doors, empty stores."

Rourke halted at the top of the garage ramp, where whirling red and blue lights atop the emergency vehicles lit the night.

"Let me see that," he said, taking the leather jacket and sweater from Harris. The sweater was a blue cable knit crew neck. The jacket had no label. Rourke pulled heavy gloves from the side pockets, found a Graham Greene paperback in one chest pocket, along with 44 cents and a red-handled, folding Swiss army knife with 10 utility blades. The other chest pocket yielded two pens, a bus schedule from Cincinnati, an uncanceled stamp ripped off an envelope, matches, and a map of Baltimore.

"Not much," he said.

"Hey lieutenant!" one of the uniformed cops called out from the bottom of the ramp. "The building superintendent is here and Urtz says you can move the bodies now!"

Devlin stared into the night.

"Okay," he finally said, "you two hustle over to the London, try to find this Rachel Dylan. I'm betting she's scared, wants to run, but if she's staying there, she can't have the bucks to get far. Not right away. Not in this weather. She'll go to ground. If she's not in her room, stake out the building. Park out front—not too conspicuous, but be there. Keep warm. And keep your eye out for anybody matching the description of that cop. If you see him, brace him."

"Could be a hundred guys in town like that," said Harris.

"You're looking for the one who carries a badge," said Rourke. "And be careful. Four down already."

"What about this Rachel?" asked Perry.

"I think she was supposed to be number five," he said. "Our boy shot up a lot of garage behind him down there, but all he hit was a car. I think he was trying to hit Rachel Dylan. Maybe she made herself into an accidental witness."

"How?" asked Perry. "What the hell was she doing down there?"

"That's what I want to ask her," said Devlin.

"Our cruiser is almost out of gas," said Harris.

"Here," Rourke said, handing them the captain's keys. "Give me one of your radios. I'll have somebody take care of your car if I don't use it. You two use the D.C.'s car. Ride in style."

"One more thing: Don't use the radio more than you must. There's a pay phone in the garage. Soon as I know it's been dusted, I'll radio the number to you. When you got something to report, call me."

"Who don't you trust?" asked Perry.

Rourke didn't reply.

6

"Do I have to do this?" the building superintendent asked the detective lieutenant as they stood at the bottom of the ramp. The super kept his back toward flashing strobe lights as two evidence technicians photographed the dried lake and its four crumpled islands.

"Legally we can't compel you to," answered Rourke. "But it would be a big help to us."

The superintendent was a chunky man wrapped in shirts, sweaters, sweatshirts, and a coat.

"Got to be a good citizen, huh?" he said.

Devlin didn't answer.

"Sure as hell ain't easy," said the superintendent.

"Seldom is," answered Rourke.

"Okay." He sighed. "Might as well get it over with."

The lieutenant led the way. Urtz brought up the rear. They stopped at the shore of the dried lake: Would it soak into the concrete? How could he ever clean it up? The super felt the gaze of officialdom. *Do I have to walk out in that?* A uniformed cop accidentally scraped the edge of the lake with his shoe: The crusty brown stain flaked; frozen crystals glistened. The super took a deep breath—not *too* deep, in case . . . He raised his eyes.

"Oh shit! Not her!" gasped the super.

Rourke flicked his flashlight beam to the woman's head, spotlighting her tangled ebony hair, its tresses stuck to the concrete floor; her features pale except for the jagged and hollow red third eye punched in the middle of her forehead and the crimson tendrils running down her cheeks like the legs of a spider.

"Oh!" sighed the super. "In this light, I thought it was . . ."

"You know her?" asked Rourke.

"Not by name, though she's been in the building a couple years. She works on the eighth floor, wholesale office products. Butwin's Office Supply."

"But you don't know her name?" asked Rourke. Urtz stood behind the super, pen poised above notebook.

"It's Chinese," said the super. "They all sound alike."

"Know anything else about her?"

He shook his head.

Rourke shifted the beam to the athlete. Dried blood from the red rain covered his face like a scarlet mask.

"Do you know him?" asked Rourke.

"Who did this?" was the whispered answer. "Who in the hell did this?"

"That's what we'll find out," said Rourke. "Do you know him?"

"Not . . . not really. We used to nod, say hi when we saw each other, though lately . . . Haven't seen him much. Should have taken more time just to—"

"What's his name?"

"That's the hell of it, isn't it? I've seen him regularly for half a dozen years. And he knows my name—'Course, most of the tenants do: I'm their super. I don't know his name. He works—worked—for a commercial art company up on 11. Nice guy.

"*Nice* guy," he said again.

Rourke shifted the flashlight beam to the man who'd been shot through his mouth.

"Holy shit! I don't believe it!" exclaimed the super.

"What?" asked Rourke.

"That it's him! That he's dead!"

"You know that guy?" asked Rourke. Urtz was ready with his pen on the pad.

"You mean you don't?!" said the super incredulously.

Devlin stared at the face illuminated by the flashlight beam. He had no idea who the man might be.

"Hell," said the super, "even . . . even like that. . . . His face is everywhere: billboards, ads in buses, on TV. You must know him! He's Johnny Curtis!"

"Who?" asked Rourke.

"Johnny Curtis! The radio deejay!"

"Hey, I know him!" said Urtz. "He and this other guy—"

"Gordy Miller," interjected the super, nodding.

"Yeah," continued Urtz, "Gordon Miller. WBBX. They're the weekday drive-to-work show. 'Curtis and Miller, the Men in your Morning.'" Urtz shook his head as he scribbled in his notebook. "Damn!"

"Truth is," said the super, "I never listen to that rock 'n' roll crap, but he's *somebody*! And a great guy too! Every time I see him, I wave and he shoots me that finger, you know? Snaps it right out there, right at you, like he's pointing a . . ."

The garage fell silent.

"What would he be doing here?" Rourke asked.

"Their studios are on the top floor," said the super. His tone implied Rourke had asked a foolish question. "That's their antennae on the roof."

"He works a morning weekday show, right?" Rourke said. They both nodded. "What would he be doing here on a Saturday afternoon?"

Neither of them had an answer. Rourke shifted the flashlight beam to the last body, the goose of a man curled up on his right side.

"Do you know him?" asked Rourke.

The super frowned.

"I've seen him around," he said a moment later. "He works on 14 for Dix Beverages. He's not the kind of guy you pay attention to."

"Not anymore," said Urtz.

Rourke's glare drew an unspoken apology from the technician.

"You don't know his name," said Devlin.

"Right."

"Thanks, you've been a big help. If you'll go back to the ramp, one of the uniformed officers will walk you around the garage. See if there's anything you notice—"

"Not more of this!" cried the super.

"No," Rourke assured him. "No more dead people."

"Thank God!" said the bulky man. He retreated toward the ramp as fast as he could.

Rourke and Urtz were rolling over the deejay's body to get his wallet when they heard the super scream:

"Oh my God, *no*!!!"

"What is it?!" yelled Rourke as he raced to the back of the garage where the super stood with a uniformed patrolman.

"Look at it!" moaned the super, throwing his hands wide; his gaze fixed on the midnight blue Mustang with the bullet-shattered windshield. "It was fucking *perfect* and now look at it!"

"Nice car," said Devlin.

"*Nice car?*" replied the super. "Nice car! It was a classic, and now it's ruined!"

"Doesn't seem so bad," said Devlin.

"Ha! 'Doesn't seem so bad.' Just look at it!" He reached toward the machine, but Rourke grabbed his arm.

"Don't touch it yet," said the detective. "The lab team hasn't finished."

"Oh, great! I spend months getting this thing ready, pay artists an arm and a leg—*artists*, mind you, guys I had to go all the way to Pikesville to find, and now a bunch of eggheads are going to rip it apart!"

"Come on," said Urtz. "It won't be that bad."

"It's already that bad," said the superintendent. He shook his head, walked around the car.

"The windshield is kaput. I'll have to get it replaced. Look there: glass blown all through the passenger compartment, scratches on the black leather upholstery. The bullets probably hit the dash, shot the shit out of the brand new stereo tape deck and radio—"

"Doesn't look like it," said Urtz.

"Yeah, but you can't ever tell, right? And look there: a goddamn star punched in the rear window! You can't find rear windows for these babies anymore. The windshield, yeah, I got one in an old junker I cannibalized, but . . .

"Who the hell's responsible, that's what I want to know! The son-of-a-bitch!"

The pay phone on the wall behind them started to ring.

"We're here for murder, not vandalism," Devlin told the super. One of the patrolmen waiting at the bottom of the ramp answered the ringing phone. "Somebody will call you when we're done with your car."

"Hey, Lieutenant Rourke!" yelled the policeman holding the pay phone. "It's for you."

"Rourke," he said into the phone.

"It's me," said Harris. "I lost the flip to call you from the pay phone on the corner by the London."

"Yeah," said Rourke, picturing his fellow detective standing in the freezing winds.

"Remember the London?" asked Harris. "Smells like a bathroom and looks like a garage sale. They *nail* the guest register to the counter."

"What about—" began Rourke, but Harris cut him off.

"Rachel Dylan's registered here. Street-side room with a window: 307. I pried the desk clerk away from his space heater in the back room. He says she's been there about a week—which matches with the guest register. No home address. He said he hasn't seen her since this morning and doesn't care about seeing her again until tomorrow. They make you pay your rent in advance every day, or they chuck you out by noon. She hasn't gotten any mail he can remember.

"He says nobody has asked about her. No phone calls about her either. He's got the building's only phone in his room. The pay phone kept getting busted up, so the phone company took it out.

"There's a passed-out wino and some kid on the nod huddled on the bench next to the radiator in the lobby, trying to keep from freezing to death. Desk clerk says they've been there a couple of hours. He says he'll throw them out soon, but his heart is too golden to toss them into the streets before midnight."

"He said that?" asked Rourke.

"Almost verbatim. He's a swell fellow. The wino wants to be left alone. The junkie just stared at me. He's out of bucks, waiting to come down from the last fix."

"The desk clerk offered me the key," continued Harris. "I told him no, went up and knocked. No answer. The lock is cheap. We don't need to bother the desk clerk if you want a quiet look-see. We parked the cruiser at the corner where we can see the door. Anybody with half a brain left in their head can make us."

"And be deterred by you," said Rourke. "Is there a back door to the place?"

"It's chained shut," said Harris. "We should tell the fire inspector."

"Any other way in or out?"

"Fire escape in the rear alley. Seven feet off the ground, but there's garbage cans under it."

"Stay put," said Rourke. "I'll be there soon. Don't holler if you see me. I want to check out the place before they know I'm a cop."

"Down here they *smell* cop before we even drive on the block."

Devlin glanced at his hastily donned ancient buckskin winter coat, torn and stained; his blue jeans and scruffy hiking boots. "I'm not official fashion."

"When I transferred to the squad, a lot of the guys mentioned that."

"Yeah, yeah, yeah," said Rourke, smiling for the first time since he'd entered the Ward Building garage. "Do me a favor?"

"What?" asked Harris.

"Keep Perry from freezing to death."

"Then you better get over here quick, or we'll need to move in with the wino and junkie, and we can only stay there till midnight."

Urtz walked over to Devlin as the detective hung up the pay phone and passed him a handwritten catalog of the victims.

"You'll have the complete inventory in the morning," he said.

According to the athlete's wallet, he was Peter Maxwell, Vice-President of Creative Designs, Inc. He lived at 7953 Open Sky Lane, Columbia, Maryland. Columbia is a carefully planned suburban city created on the drawing boards, then constructed between Baltimore and Washington, D.C.

Peter Maxwell's wallet contained: a driver's license; seven credit cards; social security card; plastic health insurance card; 24-hour-banking card; blood donor card; picture of a smiling woman standing behind a little girl; family membership card for the YMCA; half a dozen business cards with other people's names on them plus four business cards of his own; the plastic key card necessary for after hours use of the Ward Building's garage; $57 in bills; and neatly folded and tucked in the plastic envelope behind the driver's license, a piece of blue-lined school notebook paper. The writing on the paper was smudged, a single line printed with what the lab later identified as eyebrow pencil. The line looked like a series of numbers; the first and the last few digits were smeared. Between those smudges were the numbers 389.

In the right pants pocket of deejay Johnny Curtis, Rourke found a small glass vial of white powder, which, pending lab tests, Urtz catalogued as "?cocaine? −/- 1 gr." Curtis's wallet yielded gold credit cards, club membership cards, and an expired driver's license. His address was Berkley Towers, an expensive condominium high-rise in Towson, one of Baltimore's affluent suburbs.

The dead woman was Le-Lan Nguyen. Besides the $43 and change in her handbag, she carried five $100 bills in an envelope tucked inside her underpants. The lake of blood had soaked through her clothing, stained the envelope, but the money was still clean.

The goose man's wallet named him Hershel Bernstein, gave his address as the Harborview Apartments, a building miles from any body of water.

"Sergeant," said Rourke, and the ranking uniformed officer joined him. "Send officers to notify the next of kin at the home addresses."

"What if nobody's home?"

"Then have them leave a card with instructions on it to call me at homicide immediately. Have somebody get that detective's cruiser back to headquarters, it's about out of gas."

Rourke looked over the sergeant's shoulder to where ambulance technicians were lifting the bodies onto stretchers. He watched for a moment, then walked out into the night.

Harris hung up the phone, scurried over the sidewalk toward the idling cruiser parked three doors from the London's entrance. Perry sat behind the wheel, her eyes moving from the London's door to the rearview mirror; to the sidewalk across the street with its closed stores and grimy apartment buildings. Occasionally someone would pass the car, note its running engine, the antennae on the trunk, think *cop*, and sink deeper into his winter coat. No one looked directly inside the cruiser. In the mirror, Perry saw her partner hurrying toward the car, so she leaned across the front seat and unlocked the door.

Across the street from the parked cruiser was a bar that catered to those who'd scrounged up enough money to hide from their demons in cheap booze. A broken but lit blue neon sign hung inside the bar's window. On that indigo night, the blue neon sign read:

Nat o l

B emian

* * *

National Bohemian is the local beer. Baltimore, the self-proclaimed All-American City, is one of the few American towns that still has its own brewery.

A man stood inside the bar next to the neon sign's blue "l" and "n." He wore a gray wool overcoat over a customized work vest and no glasses; had a mustache, longish sandy hair. He wore black gloves and ignored his glass of beer. The man watched the cops park, go into the London, and come out again 21 minutes later. He saw the male cop make a call from the pay phone at the corner. He watched the two detectives shivering in the parked car, watched the London Hotel. His black-gloved fingers drummed on the window ledge, a rhythm steady, patient, and sure.

7

A bare bulb lit the London's third floor hallway. Devlin heard a radio playing behind one of the brown wood doors—Big Band music from before World War II. The music helped the worn strip of carpet muffle his footsteps.

He'd taken a cab to within five blocks of the London, then walked. Rourke glanced at the idling cruiser as he hurried past it—everybody was expected to. Just as they should, Perry and Harris checked him out: a shabby soldier of the night in a town where changing times had put thousands of honest citizens out of yesterday's man-powered factories and into today's computer-controlled streets. With his muted police radio stuffed down the front of his jeans and his .38 hidden on his hip, Rourke looked as anonymous as any of progress's refugees.

The wino at the London didn't stop snoring when Rourke walked through the front door. The junkie's eyes pointed at Rourke, but that glassy gaze recorded nothing. The desk clerk was nowhere to be seen.

The lobby radiator hissed, clanked, fell silent as Rourke

glanced over the counter to a wall box of pigeonhole mail slots. Once they'd held room keys. Now they held dust.

Why did I come? he wondered rhetorically.

Because you needed the scent, he answered himself. *And you didn't want your badge in the way*.

He went upstairs.

The jazz radio station played Duke Ellington behind door 304. Devlin was five steps from 307's door when metal rattled in the alley behind the hotel.

He ran to the back of the hall and peered out the window. A figure in a long coat was climbing the fire escape. The figure stopped at the second floor landing, tried the window, and found it open. Stepped inside.

Devlin drew his .38. Footsteps climbed the stairs. He put his gun-heavy right hand in his coat pocket. Shooting through a coat pocket is risky, but at least he was half ready, gun hidden enough to not scare an innocent citizen. Or an already frightened witness.

The footsteps climbed closer.

Rourke pressed his back against a closed door, tried to melt into the shadows.

The footsteps reached the top of the landing, reached the carpeted strip, took two steps, turned the corner into the hall.

She didn't glance his way.

Mistake, he thought.

The long gray overcoat fit her like a cloth-covered bird cage. The Empire's brown uniform pants showed below the hem of her coat. Her walk was weary. She didn't hear him as he walked softly over the thin carpet. She pulled her key from inside her wrap, glanced ahead.

Saw his reflection over her shoulder in the hall window's dirty glass just as he spoke.

"Rachel Dylan." His voice was firm but unthreatening.

She froze. The radio inside 304 played a lively, blaring horned song.

String of Pearls, thought Devlin.

Slowly, carefully, she turned to face him.

She had a solid face with fine cheekbones, a strong, slightly bent nose. Her blond hair was mussed and uneven. Her wide mouth was her most feminine facial feature, with full, well-shaped lips. In the dim hallway Devlin couldn't see the color of her eyes, but he didn't miss the intelligence shining through them.

"There's two cops parked outside," she said. Her voice was husky, her tone tense but steady. "They might be dumb, but they aren't deaf. You try anything, they'll hear it, come running."

She slowly raised her right arm, the long sleeve of her coat falling back to reveal her clenched fist.

"I know about the cops," said Devlin. He let go of his gun, felt it tug down his coat as he took his hands out of his pockets, showed her they were empty. "I'm their boss."

"Sure you are," she said.

"I'm going to get my badge and I.D.," he said, reaching inside his coat. He saw her flinch.

Devlin eased his black leather badge and I.D. case from his rear pocket. He flipped it open, held it in front of him.

"Great picture," she said. "Obviously genuine."

A languid, sultry, muted jazz horn piece played on the radio in 304. Slowly, step by step, Devlin closed the gap between them, his badge and I.D. held out like a talisman. He stopped when his extended arm was a foot from her, waited while her eyes scanned the badge and I.D.

"So why all the cops?" she asked.

"Why the fire escape when you've got a key?"

"Maybe I like a challenge. Any law against it?"

"We want to talk to you, Rachel."

"Tell me something I haven't figured out."

"What's wrong, Rachel? Why are you afraid of us? Why did you dodge the officers out front?"

"Who says I'm afraid?"

"You do. Your voice, your act in skipping from the Empire, leaving your coat there. Why didn't you go back for it?"

"What do you want?"

"What did you see in the garage, Rachel?"

She blinked.

"What garage?" she said.

"What were you doing there?"

"Like I said, what garage?"

"This is getting us nowhere," said Rourke.

"Fine, then let's drop it. You go sit in the car with your buddies, leave me alone. Better yet, go chase some bad guys."

"That's what I plan on doing, Rachel," he said. The sultry jazz ended on the radio in 304. An up-tempo, Glenn Miller–sounding song started. "And you're going to help. We can do it the best and easy way, or we can do it the hard way."

"Suit yourself," she said. "But I'll tell you straight, I don't have much use for cops."

"Who else can you call when you got trouble like now?"

She glared at him.

"Listen, . . . Whatever your name is," she said.

"Rourke. Detective Lieutenant Devlin Rourke."

"Listen to me, *lieutenant*. I learned not to count on anybody being there for trouble except the trouble boys. I clean up my own shit."

"That's so tired and lame I'm surprised it could climb the stairs."

She shook her head, walked toward her door. Devlin followed her.

"You guys and your badges," she said. "You think you can do it all."

She put her key in her lock, then glanced at the floor.

"This is so damn typical!" she said, bending to pick something off the floor.

"What?" asked Devlin.

"Cops. Never there when you need them."

She straightened up, turned, and handed Devlin a stamp-sized piece of a magazine page.

"You're so busy watching for me you don't do the job you're supposed to. Or maybe you guys are playing it cute."

Devlin frowned at the piece of paper.

Rachel put her key in the lock, turned it until it clicked.

"Catch up to the parade, lieutenant," she said, her hand on the doorknob. "I stuck it in the door crack. Found it on the floor. While you heroes were parked out front or haunting the halls, some junkie picked his way into my room. What little I got is probably gone. That's what the report will read, right? Unless maybe it was you guys snooping."

She turned the doorknob.

The door swung open.

Devlin grabbed her collar with his left hand, jerked her away from the door. He jerked her past him, stumbling and sliding along the wall, too startled to scream. He hadn't let go

of her coat, and he spun with her, fighting to keep his balance
and pull his gun from his pocket.

The bomb blast tore the door off its hinges and broke it
into flying chunks of wood. The concussion knocked Devlin
and Rachel off their feet. They crashed in a sprawl as dust and
smoke billowed over them. The cloud swirled, then rained
debris on their tangled heap.

The blast blew the windows out of Rachel's room: glass,
frame and all flying to the street in a roaring orange flash.

"Jesus!" yelled Harris. He bounded from the car before
the last of the glass hit the frozen street. Perry grabbed the
radio's microphone.

"Signal 13! Signal 13!" she screamed, jerking open the
driver's door with her free hand, demanding it all God please
let it be unnecessary but damn damn damn get it here quick!
"Explosion, 1432 Lamont! London Hotel! Officer down! Repeat, officer down! Ambulance! Signal 13!"

Then she was gone too, microphone dangling out the
open car door as she ran toward the hotel.

Behind her, the car radio crackled as the dispatcher
ordered a primary response team and a backup unit to the
scene. He needn't have bothered.

From Mt. Vernon Square to the highway, from Federal
Hill to the shadows of Memorial Stadium, from the red light
district of the Block to the quiet neighborhood called High-
landtown, where flat-faced townhouses with three-step marble
stoops stretch for miles, everywhere in the city, cops heard
Perry's "Signal 13!"

"Officer under fire, officer in trouble, officer needs help!"
And, "Officer down!"

Baltimore keeps a tight rein on the cops cruising its
streets. It is the only American city to forbid its police officers
to engage in hot pursuit of ordinary criminals. When answering emergency calls, Baltimore policemen must stop at
red traffic lights, proceed with extreme caution. To chase most
criminals fleeing the scene of a crime, Baltimore relies on
teams of police observation helicopters that cruise over the
city in all but the emptiest of hours just before dawn. The
copters are code-named Foxtrot; the hoods call them the Buzz
Fuzz.

Baltimore's police regulations say that Signal 13 calls are
to be handled efficiently and minimally. On a Signal 13 call, the

regulations provide for the dispatcher to send a primary response unit and one backup car. Foxtrot chops its way through the sky until it hovers over where a cop needs help.

Cops all over Baltimore ignored the regulations and their dispatcher's commands. They hit their sirens, blue lights, raced their compact economy-sized cruisers toward the trouble spot. Half of them hadn't heard Perry say anything about the explosion. The intensity of her voice cutting through routine radio traffic grabbed their attention. They heard "Signal 13" and they'd heard two words that meant the hell with everything else: *Officer down*.

Officer down.

No breath, then coming back slowly as Devlin realized he was jammed around, groin-hurting, knees sore, forehead bumped. Somebody groaned underneath him. He pushed himself up on his hands, looked at the body between his knees.

The body groaned again, shifted.

"Are you . . ." Devlin started to ask.

The door to 304 flew open. A hot radio jazz song blared from the room. A fat, hysterical woman with rollers in her dyed brown hair, white cream smeared on her face, and wearing a red and white Hawaiian moo-moo over wool long underwear ran screaming into the hall.

"Oh my God! Oh my God!" she yelled. Her eyes were open so wide her pupils looked like periods on a blank page.

"Oh my God!" she yelled again, then screamed wordlessly, a scream that turned into a gurgle as she clutched her right hand to her massive chest, staggered two steps, then fell on her back with a floor-shaking crash just as Harris raced around the corner.

"Dev—" yelled Harris.

"I'm okay!" he yelled back. He pointed to Rachel as he stumbled toward the fat woman. "Check her out! Call an ambulance!"

"On the way!" yelled Harris as he hurried to Rachel.

The sirens in the street grew closer.

Feet ran pounding up the stairs: Perry, who'd finally freed herself from the grasp of the crazed wino in the lobby. As she came through the door he'd grabbed her screaming, "I didn't do it, Martha! I didn't do it!"

The junkie never even flinched.

Devlin found no pulse in the fat woman's neck, tilted her head back, covered her gaping mouth with his, gave her four fast puffs, and started CPR. Perry dropped to her knees next to the woman's head, took over the breathing treatment. They kept at it until the ambulance crew relieved them even though they knew it was too late. The two detectives paid no attention to Rachel as Harris helped her stand.

"Wow," she said. She blinked. Heard the sirens, smelled the smoke and plaster dust. Saw the man and the woman laboring over the woman in the terrible Hawaiian dress. Rachel blinked again, memory and understanding coming slowly through her fog. "What happened?"

The explosion rattled the window glass of the bar across the street. The neon sign swayed. The watching man saw the flash, the hotel glass flying into the night, the two cops run inside. He ignored his fellow bar patrons who swarmed into the street. He stayed in his window as more people poured out of the dark buildings, as police cars roared to the hotel. He watched the fire truck arrive, the firemen milling around with nothing to do. He stayed until the ambulance came and two attendants unloaded a collapsible stretcher, slowly carried it inside. He walked out of the bar, turned his back to the city chaos.

Five blocks later he climbed into his parked car, then drove to an all-night drugstore. The pharmacist, cash register clerk, and two security guards were playing bridge by a space heater in the back. They watched him drop coins in the pay phone on the front wall, then went back to their game.

The number rang four times, then a man answered: "Yes?"

"Do you know who this is?" said the killer in the drugstore. His mustache rubbed against the phone receiver.

"I thought you would never call me at this number!" hissed the man on the other end of the phone.

"There've been some difficulties with our arrangement."

"What 'difficulties'?"

"I expect you'll read about most of them in tomorrow's paper."

"Most of them? If you've screwed up—"

"I do my job!" said the killer, his voice harsh, threatening.

And didn't phase the man he'd called, who said, "You don't ever want to play games with me."

"I'm a businessman. I don't—"

"Our contract was for a job to be done within a certain time period," interrupted the man he'd called. "If you've screwed up my schedule—"

"I said there were difficulties," snapped the man in the drugstore. "I didn't say you'd be disappointed!"

The killer in the drugstore slammed the receiver on its hook before his client replied.

8

Baltimore Police Sergeant Liam McKinnon sighed as he sat in his cruiser, waiting for a traffic light to change.

Why did all the guys on the force call him the Duck behind his back?

And why did he have only special assignment detail?

And if his father had been such a great cop, why didn't anyone respect his memory?

The light changed from red to green. Liam eased his cruiser over the icy pavement. He stopped at the top of Baltimore Street's hill, carefully looked both ways before proceeding down Carson Street. As he drove he uncramped his six-foot-four frame. His belt creaked. He readjusted the .44 Magnum holstered on his hip. Mirror sunglasses poked him from inside his shirt.

A woman's voice blared from his police radio:

"Signal 13! Signal 13! Explosion, 1432 Lamont! London Hotel! Officer down! Repeat, officer down! Ambulance! Signal 13!"

Liam pulled his cruiser to the curb. Carson intersected with Lamont 14 blocks ahead at the top of a hill. The London was six blocks from that intersection. He was only a minute away from the scene, even driving over icy streets while obeying Baltimore's laws.

And there he sat.

Because of Baltimore's rules.

Not the ones forbidding officers to respond randomly to Signal 13 calls. Even the Duck knew that was just a law, a regulation, not a rule. In the sirens cutting through the night, he heard other policemen defining the distinction between what was on the books and what went on in the streets.

The Baltimore rule that prevented the Duck from responding to Perry's frantic Signal 13 gave the Duck no duty other than to drive his cruiser. The rule let him drive in parades, though not as lead cruiser, not since the year he led the Daughters of the American Revolution's annual Harbor City Float Festival down a garbage-strewn dead-end alley instead of the banner-hung main street. The Duck Rule forbid him to answer any calls—and applied to the department's dispatchers, who under no circumstances assigned any mission to the Duck.

Responding to help to the Signal 13 would violate the rule. But couldn't he see what was happening?

Slowly, carefully, the Duck drove to the intersection at the top of the hill. To his right, six blocks away, blue lights pulsated in front of the London Hotel.

The Duck leaned across the seat, his size 12 shining black regulation shoe pressing down on the brake pedal as he wiped the passenger window clear. The glass immediately fogged over again.

Perhaps I shouldn't get any closer, he told himself. *A rule is a rule. But what harm would it do if I just got a good look?*

The Duck took the cruiser out of gear, braced himself for the cold, and opened the door.

The wind pushed against him. He held his hat tight on his head as he shuffled around the front of the car, past the hood, along the passenger's side until he stood beside the window. He looked down Lamont Street.

The Duck saw half a dozen cruisers, blue lights spinning; two unmarked cars parked nose-first to the sidewalk. In the middle of the street a policeman frantically waved a flashlight. Klaxon blaring, red lights spinning, a fire truck roared into the crowd. Firemen in yellow slickers jumped off the truck, raced into the hotel.

The Duck felt a surge of pride: *We take care of our own!*
He turned around.

His cruiser was rolling backward down Carson Street.

He'd taken the car out of drive, but forgotten to put it in park or set the hand brake.

The Duck lunged toward the slowly receding machine. He slipped, flayed his arms as he fought for balance on the ice-slick street. The wind snatched his hat from his head.

"Halt!" he yelled. "Stop!"

The car rolled faster.

"Stop!" he yelled as he ran after the rolling white cruiser. "Please stop!"

The car gained momentum.

So did the Duck. He slipped and slid and stumbled as he ran downhill, 241 pounds of panicked policeman, arms flapping madly.

At the end of the first block, the cruiser led the race by 10 feet.

At the end of the second block, the gap had narrowed so that the Duck could brush the car's hood with his fingertips.

By the third block, the Duck was abreast of the front wheel on the driver's side.

"Stop!" he yelled again.

But the cruiser kept rolling, past the donut shop, past the men's clothing store, past the building where lawyers specializing in accident claims kept offices. The buildings were dark, the sidewalks empty. Carson Street was deserted this wintry Saturday night.

Except for the empty police cruiser being chased by a frantic cop as it rolled backward down the slick hill.

Huffing, puffing, propelled by adrenaline and his extreme sense of duty, the Duck drew abreast of the driver's door in the middle of the fourth block.

The door was unlocked.

The door was half open, ajar enough so the interior light illuminated the front seat where the Duck's radio lay next to the white paper bag of leftovers from the restaurant for his dog Sam's dinner. He heard the radio squawk; some official on the scene at the London Hotel reported that everything was under control.

Less than a mile away, the Duck yelled, "Help!"

No one heard him.

The cruiser and the Duck raced into their fifth block. Carson Street slopes through downtown Baltimore to the edge of the harbor. The pavement stops at a six-inch curb. Next comes four feet of brick sidewalk. An inch-thick, white wooden rail fence rises from the sea wall to keep pedestrians from stumbling over the edge. Into the harbor. Into the sea.

The sea was 14 blocks away when the Duck reached for the door handle, trying to jerk the door all the way open so he could dive inside his cruiser, stop it before . . .

Before.

He grabbed for the chrome handle.

Missed.

Grabbed again.

Missed again, his fingers brushing the cold steel but closing only on the night air.

The runaway cruiser and its pursuer flew through the sixth block, 12 more to go before the sea. A janitor coming out of a stationery store saw them fly by; he blinked, didn't believe he'd just seen a giant cop chasing an empty police car rolling backwards down the middle of Carson Street. Besides, even if *he* believed what he must not have seen, who would believe *him*? He turned his back on his vision, walked up the hill to where he'd parked the pickup.

Ten blocks from the sea the Duck grabbed for the handle. His hand slammed against the car door, . . .

And pushed it shut. He heard door latch *click*. Shut. Firmly, neatly shut.

"Shit!!"

Can't grab the handle, make the latch go loose, swing door open, run around it and dive in, he thought. *No way.*

Could shoot out the tires, he thought. *Make them go flat, car won't roll. Maybe. What if I miss? .44 Magnum slugs whizzing around Baltimore.*

Again.

Besides, shooting his own car seemed too much like the mortal sin of suicide.

Only one thing left to do.

The Duck sucked a huge breath, lowered his head, and charged with every ounce of energy he could muster.

He ran past the back door.

Past the back wheel.

The cruiser and the Duck sped through another intersection. Nine blocks between them and the dark sea.

The Duck ran past the trunk. Slipping, sliding, triumph in his stride, he raced five, ten, twenty paces ahead of the rolling car.

Stopped.

Slid on the ice, but didn't fall as he whirled to face the cruiser, spread his feet as wide as he could, fought for—found his balance. Took a deep breath. Locked his arms straight out from his chest, his palms aimed at the cruiser's trunk.

The Duck swallowed hard.

"Stop!" he yelled one more time.

The cruiser kept coming.

The Duck gritted his teeth, leaned forward.

The rear end of the cruiser smacked into the Duck's hands with a *boomp!* Man and machine shuddered.

Stood still.

For seven seconds.

Then, slowly, the ton-plus of Detroit-engineered automobile obeyed gravity. And rolled down the hill, with the Duck leaning at a 45° angle against its trunk, his palms pressed against the cold steel, his size 12s sliding over the ice on the street.

Half a block.

Through another intersection.

Eight blocks left before the cold sea.

Through the middle of downtown, cruiser pushing cop.

Until those size 12 shoes hit a patch of dry pavement. Their soles grabbed. The cruiser kept rolling, buckling the Duck's legs beneath him. The cruiser rolled over the Duck, ran a red light, rolled into the next intersection, . . .

And rammed into an orange Volkswagen minibus from St. Ignatius. The minibus whirled like a dreidel. It's side door flew open immediately after impact, and inertia threw the seven classically habited nuns into the street like so many bowling pins.

The cruiser crunched to a stop against a parked Cadillac.

Father Callaghan—who'd been driving the nuns back to their cells after their nursing shift at the hospital—braked the minibus, scrambled outside to help.

The seven nuns bobbed to their feet, disoriented, but unhurt. They scurried around like dazed penguins.

Sergeant Liam McKinnon lay sprawled on his back in the middle of Carson Street.

The police Foxtrot helicopter returning to routine patrol after responding to Perry's Signal 13 flew overhead, spotted the confusion on the ground: the smashed cruiser, the minibus, the priest running to where a policeman lay on the cold pavement, the nuns darting hither and yon in the streetlight's glow.

"What do you call that?" the observer asked the pilot as he picked up the radio microphone.

The pilot recognized the officer in distress.

"Duck soup," he laughed.

9

"This is going to make us real popular," Rourke whispered to Captain Goldstein as they entered the outer office of Baltimore's deputy police commissioner that next morning. Their arrival brought the total of men waiting there to eight— not counting the D.C.'s aide, who sat behind his desk reading reports.

Goldstein laughed quietly, and without humor.

His laughter elicited a nervous smile from Liam McKinnon, who sat against the wall to their left. He was the only man in uniform; the others wore badges or plastic I.D. cards clipped to their suit coats. He was also the only one with a Bandaid on his forehead and two black eyes. No one had spoken to him since he'd arrived at headquarters. The Duck's smile faded faster than the laughter's echo.

Rourke recognized all men, including the department accountant and Greg Sonfeld, a wispy, balding man with thick glasses who wore a pinstripe blue suit like a suit of armor. Sonfeld habitually pushed his finger against the nose piece of his gold, wire-rimmed glasses. His prominent Adam's apple bobbed up and down above his sternly knotted tie. When

Rourke and Goldstein entered. Sonfeld left his chair and met them in the middle of the room.

"Watch it!" Goldstein whispered needlessly as the mayor's man approached them.

"Captain," said Sonfeld, smiling and shaking the older policeman's hand. "And *Lieutenant* Rourke. Congratulations on your promotion."

"Thanks," said Rourke.

"Although," said Sonfeld, with a practiced conspiratorial smile, "I don't think anybody should be congratulated for having to spend their Sunday morning here."

The two cops smiled politely.

"You know the police," said Goldstein, "always on duty."

"Politics doesn't keep hours either, captain." The mayor's assistant kept his tone casual. "Something extraordinary must have brought you two here today."

"Just a glitch in the routine," said Goldstein.

"Really," said Sonfeld. His cold eyes lingered on the captain for a moment, then shifted to Rourke. "Is that what you'll be handling now, *lieutenant?* Glitches in the routine?"

"Sure," said Rourke.

"Ah." Sonfeld nodded. "Then you and I will get to see a lot more of each other, won't we?"

Rourke forced a smile.

The politician shook his head, smiled broadly again. "Well, gentlemen, be sure to let the mayor's office know if we can help. And keep us fully advised."

He walked back to his chair without waiting for a response.

As soon as Sonfeld was seated, a homicide detective waiting with two FBI agents crossed the room to shake Rourke's hand.

"How you doing, Dev?" asked the city cop.

"Been better, Paul," answered Devlin.

"This bring you down here?" Paul McKee gestured with the folded front page of the Baltimore *Star*: a bold headline proclaimed, "Brutal Mass Murder at Ward Building."

"Sort of," answered Rourke.

"Why? You made lieutenant. You're supposed to leave all of us lowly homicide detectives tomorrow."

"We're still sorting that out. You know the department."

"Tell me about it," said McKee. His sandy hair, twinkling

eyes behind his gold-rimmed glasses and boyishly-40 face, plus his bow ties and tweed suits made him look like a teacher, not a murder squad detective who'd once had the fastest fists in the middleweight division of the East Coast police boxing league.

"What about you?" said Rourke, trying not to show how anxious he was to change the topic. "Some other citizen buy it last night?"

"Beats me. I've been backing up the feds' play for some guy who became smoke when his fancy investment firm started to shake. He left his BMW at the airport, a couple of his assistants holding a bag full of bullshit upstairs from your mess."

"So the feds think he's still around?"

"Nobody knows. And nobody wants to yell 'crook' yet."

The two men went to their chairs. Sat down. Waited.

A buzzer sounded on the aide's desk.

"Captain Goldstein?" he said. "You two can go in now."

"Did you see what's out there?" The D.C. scowled as Rourke and Goldstein settled into padded chairs before his desk. The D.C.'s ebony skin had an unhealthy hue.

"That mayor's boy Sonfeld is trying to carve out glory for himself using the city as his knife. He claims he's after civic corruption, but what he wants is to hang a few cops' scalps on his belt and grab some good press so he can run for the legislature. The little shit. You saw him out there, didn't you?"

Goldstein and Rourke nodded.

The D.C. leaned across his desk. "What did he say?"

"Nothing much," said Goldstein.

The D.C. looked at Rourke; Devlin's nod confirmed his captain's answer.

"Huh," grunted the D.C. "I'll bet. That little shit. Watch him. He wants to nail my— He wants to nail the department."

The D.C. leaned back in his chair, ordered again: "Watch him!"

His two junior officers nodded.

"And if Sonfeld ain't bad enough," said the D.C., "I got your buddy the Duck!"

"I wouldn't call us buddies," said Rourke.

"You know why we're stuck with him?" interrupted the D.C. "He's our legacy.

"His old man was the crookedest cop I ever knew. Took a

heart attack to get rid of him. But before he dies, he levers Liam into the department, rabbis him up to sergeant."

Devlin interrupted his commander's tirade: "The Duck . . . he's not a bad guy, sir. He's totally honest, wouldn't hurt a—"

"He's too goddamn dumb to be crooked!" said the D.C. "We can't give him normal duty—he fucks it up! He's Daffy fucking Duck! So we gave him a squad car, right? Keep him out of the way. We let him pack that stupid .44 Magnum, the only out-of-policy thing he's ever wanted. Keeps him happy.

"We never thought he could draw the thing, let alone hit anybody with it."

Nobody spoke for several seconds.

"So we're stuck with him right? Because all the hotshots know his damn father paid a lawyer to hold an affidavit to be read should his son ever lose his job or rank with the department."

The D.C. shook his head: "I'd *love* to know what's all in that affidavit!"

He sighed to Rourke: "You know what your buddy did last night?"

"No sir," answered Rourke.

He told them.

No one spoke for a full minute.

"What are you going to do?" Devlin finally asked.

"What the hell can I do?!" said the D.C.

"Beats me," said Captain Goldstein.

"So," said the head of Baltimore Police Department's Operations Bureau, "what do you want from me?"

"Four victims shot to death in the garage," said Rourke. "We have one key witness, one other death from the bombing who—"

"Bombing? What bombing?!" said the D.C.

"Who," continued Devlin, "may or may not be legally counted as a homicide victim. We'll get a prosecutor's ruling on that later.

"I think what we have is a professional killer—or killers," said Devlin.

"Why a hit?"

"The technique is too smooth and brazen for much else. It doesn't have the feel of a psycho or a holdup."

"What about this bombing?" said the D.C.

"The kicker," said Devlin, ignoring his boss, "is we may have one or more police officers involved."

"What do you mean, 'involved'?" asked the D.C.

"On the shooter's side. Maybe as a triggerman."

Silence took over the room.

Finally, the D.C. sighed.

"Give it to me from the top," he said.

Rourke began at the beginning, told it through the bombing.

"And you think—" said the D.C.

"I think the man with the badge took the information from the fat man in the cafe, either passed it on or went to the London himself, found Rachel Dylan in the register, rigged the bomb, . . . Blamo! No more witness."

"I'd be worried about the cafe guy's health."

"Good point, sir."

"And your witness who isn't dead?"

"We're okay with her," said Rourke. "So far."

"How do you figure?"

"Page 6, today's *Star*: 'Woman dies in explosion at London Hotel, identification withheld pending notification of next of kin.' That I.D. won't be released. With four murders of solid citizens to cover, the press doesn't care about an accident that kills anybody who'd live in the London."

"Does the killer know he missed?"

"Nope," said Rourke. "He got a woman—the newspaper says so. Hell, the ambulance took a woman's body away."

The D.C. thought for a moment.

"Where you going with this, lieutenant?" he finally asked.

"We want to take it outside," said Rourke. "Let me run a shadow show—under Captain Goldstein. The four homicides have to be handled officially to make it work, but we'll control that. For the books, give Goldstein the homicides, with the detectives who answered the squeal. Off the books, it's my case and I'm under the captain. I'm supposed to be transferred out of homicide. Bury me somewhere nobody will notice or care about what I'm doing, and we'll hide the real investigation from everybody. Keep it safe—in case."

"Where's this Rachel Dylan now?" asked the D.C.

"Sir," said Lieutenant Rourke, "with all due respect, I haven't even told Captain Goldstein. If anything happens, we'll need to backtrack, find the leak. The fewer badges that know—"

"The fewer you'll need to suspect. So you jump over the chief of CID. So you cut me out."

"Best that way, sir."

The D.C. drummed his fingers on the desk.

"Why not turn the woman over to the feds' witness protection program?"

"One, too many people would know," answered Devlin. "Two, I want her close. At least for a while."

"If the shooter is a pro," said the D.C., "and if he's not a Baltimore policeman, then he's probably from out of town. And he's probably long gone."

"That's our bet too, sir," said Rourke. "The way I figure it, one of those four people in the garage was the target. The others just got in the way. One of those people was worth killing. We find the motive, we find who could have hired the killer. We nail that person, he'll lead us to the triggerman."

"You're talking 'bout building quite a chain."

"Yes sir," said Rourke.

"The department is like a family, Rourke," said the D.C. "You can only keep secrets so long. If we got a shooter—which I doubt—and if we got a dirty badge—which I doubt even more—then the rogue cop has his eyes glued to the investigation. Pretty soon, he'll figure out that the on-the-books show isn't what's real."

"I realize that, sir," said Rourke.

"How long do you figure you can keep your secret?"

"A couple weeks," said Rourke. "Maybe more."

The D.C. grunted.

"You're going to have Sonfeld watching you like a hawk," he said. "He'd love to see us botch a big one. You're going to have the press breathing down your neck. Mass murders generate political pressure."

"That's not our problem," said Rourke.

"It's my problem so it damn well is your problem!" snapped his superior officer.

"Yes sir," said the lieutenant.

The D.C. drummed his fingers on his desk.

Rourke started to speak, but Goldstein shook his head.

"It's Sunday," said the D.C. after a minute of drumming. "I'm drowning in work. Statistics show two, three times the average number of shootings in the streets these last few months. Everybody has a gun and wants to use it. This keeps going, forget about Detroit or Miami, we'll be the shoot-'em-up city. Last week, the commissioner created some new squads to handle it. Gonna call them Violent Crimes Suppression Units, issue them shotguns. They respond to all gun incidents. A lot of it is PR, but . . ."

The D.C. paused, stared out his window. From his ninth floor niche he could see the glint of the sun off the cold gray harbor.

"Monday morning, Lieutenant Rourke will be officially assigned to develop those shotgun teams under my direct command. The Ward homicides—booked and worked like you said. The bombing stays lost in paper. As for the real show . . ."

His fingers stopped drumming; he pointed at Rourke.

"I keep it off the books, you keep it clean so it looks good when it gets written up."

"Yes sir."

"I expect to be fully informed."

"Within the limits of security, sir."

The D.C. smiled at him, slow and sweet, like a cobra. "Don't you trust me, lieutenant?"

Rourke carefully considered his answer.

"Sir . . . The only was to keep suspicion off of you is to keep you free of any involvement."

"That puts me in a bind, lieutenant," said the D.C., his smile hardening. "I have to pick up the chit for whatever you do, and you don't want me to hold any cards."

"I can't think of any other way to work it, sir," said Rourke.

The D.C. drummed his fingers on the desk.

"You wrap a tight package, lieutenant," he said. "What if I don't buy it?"

"Then we'll probably lose this one and you'll be blamed."

"And you'll see to that, won't you?" said the D.C.

"Sir, I'm just a cop who wants to do his job."

"Remember this, lieutenant: you don't *ever* want to play games with me!"

"Yes sir."

"You got one week to bring me something," said the D.C.

"One week!" yelled Rourke.

"And if you don't bring me something by then," added the D.C., "you're going to take all the heat if this case doesn't get made."

"What if one week isn't enough?" said Goldstein.

"Then we work it on the books and by the books," said the D.C. "After Sonfeld gets through lynching our new lieutenant."

Goldstein and Rourke held their tongues.

"Even if this works, this is going to fuck up your retirement, Ted. And your promotion and real transfer, Rourke."

"I'll take it as it comes," answered Rourke.

Goldstein shrugged, smiled slightly, then quickly grew somber once more.

"What do you need?" asked the D.C.

"What don't we need!" said Goldstein.

"Undercover cars," said Rourke. "Detectives from a couple squads. Money for the outside expenses . . ."

"Cars," said the D.C., "Yeah, okay. There's some seized drug dealers' machines the courts just turned loose. You can have a few. Radios are no problem. As for detectives who ain't already on this with you, forget it."

"Sir . . ."

"Rourke, you said yourself that the more badges that know the more unsolved murders we'll probably have."

"But—"

"I don't *have* extra detectives, lieutenant! Don't you read the newspapers? This is the era of *fiscal conservativism*, of lean and mean government machines!"

"Tell you what," interjected Captain Goldstein. "I'll get the routine legwork out of other commands and cover it my way. You ask the captains for it officially, they'll say no. I ask them my way . . ."

"Can you keep it secure?" asked Rourke.

"Can you get it?" asked the D.C. "Tell me how, because I need it, too."

"Yes," said the captain to his lieutenant. To his superior, he smiled, said, "No."

The D.C. sighed.

"Ted," he said, "we'll miss you around here."

"I'm not gone yet," grumbled the captain.

"What about money?" asked Rourke. "We're running this on the outside. It's an expensive world."

"You'll have to figure a way to cover that yourself."

"That's outrageous!" said Devlin, then quickly added: "Sir."

"Money leaves tracks, lieutenant. We've got ledger books."

"There are half a dozen ways to juggle—"

"Juggle *what*? We're four-point-five *million* dollars short today, lieutenant!"

"You mean if somebody kills you outside of the budget, they walk?" snapped Rourke.

"What do you think? Justice is free? Rourke, this morning you came to my office with lieutenant's bars on your shoulders. They're suppose to replace any chips you carry up there, and you're supposed to be dry enough behind the ears so you don't fog up their gold finish!"

"I can't believe this!" said Rourke. "We come to you with a problem and you add to it! What are you doing?!"

The D.C. leaned across his desk, jabbed his forefinger toward Rourke.

"You don't *question* me, lieutenant! You don't criticize me! You dealt this hand, and now you're going to play it!"

"The issue," interrupted the captain, defusing the situation, "is feasibility. We need to be able to function. That's all we want."

Rourke and the D.C. turned their eyes to Goldstein. After a moment, the lieutenant and the second highest ranking Baltimore police officer eased back in their chairs.

"Look," the D.C. said to Rourke; stopped, began again. "I don't have any advances or petty cash. Zero. Zip. Keep receipts. You foot the bills, I'll figure a way to get you reimbursed. Do we understand each other?"

Rourke blinked: "Yes."

Goldstein sighed.

"One more thing," smiled the D.C. "Since I've done so much for you, you guys are going to do something for me."

"What?" asked Devlin.

"The Duck," answered the D.C. "He's yours."

"What?!" shouted Rourke and Goldstein at the same time.

"Sgt. Liam McKinnon is officially assigned to your secret unit. As soon as I get through chewing his ass to shreds."

"You can't do that!" said the Captain.

"Of course I can," said the D.C.

"This . . ." sputtered Devlin. "Sir, this is serious."

"So am I."

"We're working murders and he's a loose cannon!" The D.C. cut Devlin off:

"You claim you need more men."

Rourke swallowed, said nothing.

"You won't tell us what to do with him?" asked Goldstein.

"The Duck?" said the D.C. "As long as he's out of sight and out of trouble, I don't care what you do with him. Now get out of here and let me wade through the rest of the shit in my waiting room."

"You got one week!" the D.C. called after them as they walked out. "Don't screw up!"

The door slammed shut.

"Got to give him credit," said Captain Goldstein as he and Rourke walked past the main lobby's museum display. "He gave us something."

"Yeah," said Rourke as he opened the heavy glass door, "and wasn't it great?"

Both men braced themselves against the weather. The Arctic front had moved out to sea, but the wind off the harbor and the clouds hiding the sun held the temperature barely above zero.

Goldstein shrugged. "This isn't the city of perfect dreams, but it's ours."

They walked down headquarters steps, looked at the vacant block across the street where hulking yellow and orange bulldozers, graders, and earth-moving machines sat motionless. The dirt field beneath their wheels had been a black-topped parking lot until these machines chewed it up. Skiffs of snow danced through that herd of silent monsters, frozen pellets stung their unfeeling steel skin. Traces of diesel and oil tainted the wind.

"He also figured that cafe owner angle," said Goldstein.

"I should have thought of that," said Rourke.

"Yes, you should have," said his boss, without anger.

"It's been so much, so fast," said Rourke. "Whirlwind."

"Sometimes it's like that," said Goldstein. "You do the best you can."

"You think we got a chance on this one?"

"Crooks might have more money and fewer rules than us, Devlin, but we always got a chance." He frowned, kept his eyes focused on the earth-moving monsters as he asked, "Where you got the Dylan woman?"

Devlin blinked, answered: "Motel out on the Beltway."

"How do you want to work it?" asked the captain.

"Not the way I have to." Rourke shook his head. "Ideally, we should have two cops as bodyguards all the time. If we do that now, that only leaves one of us on the streets."

"Plus me," said Goldstein.

"Hell, captain, you spend nine hours a day keeping the homicide squad together. People aren't going to quit getting murdered just so you can do legwork for us."

"You got the Duck."

Rourke shook his head. "He might be worse than nothing."

"You never know."

"Believe me," said Rourke, "I wish that were true."

"Anyway you work it, you'll be worn ragged." Goldstein shrugged. "Maybe the D.C. is right. The shooter did his job and thinks he's eliminated the witnesss. He's probably hit the road."

"I don't know whether that's good or bad," said Rourke.

"Both," said the captain. "What do you want me to do first?"

"Come meet Dylan, let her see you so she knows who to trust."

"Just looking at me going to do that?"

They laughed.

"Not for her," said Devlin.

"What did she say?"

"Not much," answered Rourke, remembering.

She'd been scared, shaking as soon as she'd realized what had happened. Rourke hid with her in an empty room on the London's fourth floor while they waited to retreat. She sat on the bed, her back pressed against the wall, her arms hugging her chest. He leaned against the locked door. The only light came from the night outside the shadeless window: street-lights' glow, blue and red pulsations from emergency vehicles parked outside. Devlin and Rachel were dark forms to each other. They didn't speak. Their hiding place smelled of must, mildewed bedding. They listened to the firemen and ambu-

lance crew, other policemen clomping about on the floor below
as they worked their routine on the heart attack victim in the
Hawaiian dress and Rachel's bombed room.

Finally, Harris knocked quietly.

"Now," he'd said, and they'd moved, in darkness, in
silence.

Down the hall, down the stairs to the third floor, through
the rubble in the hallway. She carefully stepped around the
empty space on the carpet where the woman had fallen.
Devlin led her into her blasted room. She stopped, blinked at
the chaos as the cold night air rolled through the shattered
window.

"Get your things," he told her.

Without replying, she went to the closet, took out a
canvas suitcase, opened it on top of the rubble. From the
closet to the bag went a pair of worn hiking boots. The bureau
lay on its side. She jerked open the drawers. A pair of jeans, a
pair of corduroys, four shirts, a red cotton sweater, a gray
hooded sweatshirt with the maroon letters "U.M." across its
chest, a pair of blue sweatpants and two handfuls of underwear
and cotton socks went into the suitcase. From the tiny
bathroom she brought a hairbrush and a draw-stringed cloth
sack used in the 1950s for marbles. She dropped to her hands
and knees, rummaged through the debris under the bed.
When she stood, one hand held a 1980s belt tape player with
a set of earphones; her other hand held a diarylike ledger,
three tape cassetes, and two more paperback books. She
packed these items; shut her bag.

"That's it?" asked Devlin.

"It's enough," she said.

He led her to the fire escape.

She'd asked no questions and he'd given her no answers
as they drove through the city, cruised on the interstate
looping around Baltimore until they found an acceptable and
unquestioning motel with anonymous, brightly lit gold decor
rooms containing shower-tubs, bad landscapes, dirty movies
for $2.50 extra, and no surprises.

"You're absolutely okay," he told her when they were safe
in the room. Harris and Perry were in the next room.

She sat on the edge of the queen-sized bed.

"I've got your word on that," she said, more an accusation
than a question.

"You've got the best I can do. That's all there is."

"Then it'll have to do," she said.

"It's late," he said: 2:15 AM, and he still hadn't reported to Goldstein. "We got a lot to talk about, a lot to do, but not now. You need some time to collect yourself, rest, feel safe."

"How about a century?"

"How about tonight."

Her cheek twitched. She lowered her eyes.

"Try to sleep," he said. "I'm going next door, but I'll be right back. One of us will be in the room with you all the time. Awake. Ready. The other two will be right next door. Nobody—*nobody*—knows we're here. Do you have anybody you need to call who'd be worried about you?"

She shook her head.

"Good," he said, "that makes it easier, better."

"Think so?" she said.

He'd left her, conferred with Harris and Perry, called Goldstein, and had him set up an 8 AM meeting with the D.C. Rourke took the first shift sitting in a chair in Rachel's room while she lay beneath the sheets, fitfully dozing in the darkness while the detective fought to stay awake. Perry relieved him at 4:45. He napped next door in the bed beside the one where Harris slept. The detectives slept in their clothes, their unholstered guns on the nightstand. Rourke's digital alarm watch woke him at 6:45. He tiptoed from the room where he hoped Harris still slept, checked on Perry and her restless charge, then drove back into the city.

"What are you going to do about the fat man from the cafe?" asked Goldstein as they walked through the wind.

"Send someone to get him," answered Rourke.

10

Nick Stavadopolis pondered the cops who'd interviewed him at the Empire Cafe as he drove home from work that Sunday morning. The cafe was closed Sundays, but, while the suckers sang for their souls in some church, Nick swabbed out his place and paid himself the time-and-a-half he would have needed to pay anybody else.

Stupid cops, thought Nick. He'd answered all their dumb questions, told them his name and address, told them about that dumb broad Rachel. Stupid cops. Had to come back for a second round, go over it again.

Nick got lucky, parked in the same spot in front of his row house that he'd left earlier that morning.

No lights shone behind the shades in his windows. Why pay for electricity he didn't use? So what if it was dark in his house when he came home, even during the day? The sun didn't shine so bright on Nick's street. He didn't need the sun to watch TV, which was what he was going to do just as soon as he could pop a brew, fire up a cigar, settle down in that big red overstuffed chair in front of the living room's color Sony. All the Jesus shows would be off soon. Sports would be coming up. 'Til then, one channel showed old movies.

His new lock turned smooth and easy. It ought to. He'd bitched about the old one enough to his landlady next door. She was his aunt. Nick hated her. Nick had been 11 and his sister 14 when the car wreck killed their folks.

Nick remembered how his aunt raised them. His sister ran away from "home" as soon and as often as she could. The damn cops caught her every time. Brought her back to the aunt who put a lock on her bedroom door and the uncle who believed in the evangelical powers of his razor strap. At 17, his sister found refuge in marriage to a boy too young to vote but old enough to plant new life in her belly. Nick's aunt and uncle

thought him a weakling because he'd cried for six months after
his parents' car wreck, no matter how often his uncle gave him
the solace of the strap. They also thought him stupid.

But I wised up, didn't I? Nick thought. *I got to be a smart
guy. It was smart of me not to move away. For me to bide my
time.* Other than his sister—who wouldn't blink if the aunt
dropped dead at her feet—he was the only living member of
the family. The older bully of a cousin, who'd been favored
over the orphans by his mother, stepped on a land mine in
Vietnam and was history. Last year, her husband coughed
himself to death with emphysema. Nick was his aunt's heir, the
only one who'd be there to look out for her when she got too
old to do so herself.

Which will be soon, thought Nick. *Which she's finally
figured out*. He smiled as he opened the door to the place he
already thought of as just *his* house.

He stepped inside.

Shut the door.

Locked it.

Walked through the curtained doorway and into the dark
living room to turn on the Sony, let it warm up while he took a
leak in the bathroom upstairs, grabbed a brew from the frig in
the kitchen. The Sony didn't need to warm up, but Nick liked
television's friendly chatter. He flipped the wall switch, turned
on the lights in the living room.

"What the hell!!" he yelled as saw the guy sitting in the
overstuffed armchair.

"Hello, Nick," said the man.

"Holy shit!" said Nick. He closed his eyes, sighed. When
he looked again, the guy was standing only a couple steps
away, watching. Waiting.

Nick's right hand touched his chest.

"You could scare a guy to death surprising him like that!"
he said.

"Sorry," said the visitor.

I'll bet, thought Nick: *Goddamn stupid cop!*

"I thought I was through with all you guys and your crap,"
said Nick.

"Not quite," said his surprise guest. "We want to be sure
you told us everything about what you saw."

"Of course I did! I told all you guys!"

"All of us?" The man frowned, then slowly smiled. "Yes, I forgot. Who else talked to the other officers?"

"You mean Mavis? Ha! That blind old broad. She only looks at her magazines."

"So nobody paid her any mind?" asked the man.

"Na, why should they? She didn't tell them any more than she told you," said Nick, "and you didn't talk to her."

"That's good," said the man with the badge. "I thought not, but I wanted to be sure. That's why I looked you up."

"What now?" asked Nick, his eyes narrowing.

"Just a few more routine questions. You can relax. And don't worry: I hate remedial work as much as you do."

"Yeah? Well that's easy for you to say! You don't have people popping in and out of your life all hours of . . .

"Hey!" said Nick, suddenly: "How'd you get in here?"

"I'm good with locks," said the man. He stepped closer.

"Don't you need a warrant for that?!" asked Nick. He put his hands on his hips, took a wide stance and wrinkled his brow with indignation, and said, "What is this? Some kind of burglary?"

"No, no," said the guy, waving his hand to pooh-pooh Nick's concern.

He waved his gloved hand high, by his forehead. Nick's eyes locked on the motion.

The man wearing black gloves kicked Nick in the groin.

Nick's mouth gaped open but no sound escaped. White fire engulfed him. His eyes rolled back in his head. He sank to his knees as his hands reached around his trembling gut to cup the pain.

Nick's attacker wondered how much the fat man would weigh; if it could be done.

Of course it could, he concluded. A glove reached out, grabbed Nick's lips. Nick fought the new hurt, tried to think but couldn't, could only crawl on his knees and one hand, his other hand feebly pawing at the vice that held his mouth. Nick crawled where the black glove pulled him, out of the living room, to the hall. To the stairs.

"No," said the man as he led Nick upstairs, "this isn't a burglary."

11

"So this is how the regular world lives," said Rachel, shaking as she watched Rourke and Susan Perry unpack styrofoam cups of coffee and plates of cooling eggs and bacon, plastic silverware. "If only I'd known what I was missing."

Harris sat in the corner chair, where he could watch the motel room's door, the color television playing a black-and-white Humphrey Bogart movie, and Rachel. She sat on her unmade bed wearing a blue hooded sweatshirt, gray sweatpants, and the sneakers in which she'd waitressed at the Empire Cafe. She'd brushed her short blond hair. Her blue eyes were puffy, swollen, and bloodshot from lack of sleep.

In the TV movie, Bogart was confident.

"You two want to go next door and clean up?" Rourke suggested to Perry and Harris after they finished eating.

When the door closed behind them, Devlin pulled his chair next to the bed. The room was on the second floor of the motel. From the highway outside came the blare of a truck's air horn, the faint hum of traffic. The maid's cart rattled over the concrete balcony. A room door opened, the cart rattled, the door closed. Bogart told somebody to shut up.

"How are you?" asked Devlin.

"Scared, sore from where you fell on me, tired, mad, and anxious as hell for this to be over," answered Rachel.

"I understand," said Devlin.

"Do we have a plan or is this trip to the country just a whim?"

"We're working on it," he told her.

"You and who else? The guy with the bomb?"

"He thinks you're dead."

"Don't set the record straight on my account, okay?"

"Don't worry. We won't."

She blinked.

"You know," she said, "all night I tried to figure what your next move would be. I decided you were going to let me 'volunteer' to be a decoy for the killer."

"That's stupid," said the cop. He nodded to the flickering screen. "That's what they do on TV. Stupid. Like tasting suspicious white powder to see if it's drugs. Great way to end up dead or sick from whatever shit the powder is. We aren't stupid."

"That's good," she said, "because I won't pay for your mistakes."

"I hope not. But you signed the tab for this, like or not."

"What do you mean?"

"You were in the garage, Rachel."

She didn't reply.

"We know it. So does that killer. . . ."

"Who is he?" she asked.

"We don't know."

"I never saw him before in my life," she said.

"But you saw him."

"Tell me something we both don't know."

She took a deep breath, held it; exhaled and closed her eyes. When she opened them again, she said, "What do you want me to do?"

"First, relax. Second, trust us."

"Those sound like lines from a bad teenage date."

"We're a long way past adolescence."

"No American ever gets far from adolescence."

"We're the police."

"I told you: I don't like cops, don't trust them."

"We're the chance you got."

"I could take off. You've never seen anybody disappear until you've seen me go."

"Wouldn't work. We need you, so we'd look. That would drag you being alive out in public, and pretty soon your pal from the garage would hear about it. Maybe you could hide from him. But you'd never hide from both him and us."

"I know a lot of places."

"I know a lot of ways to look."

"Okay," she said after staring at him for a moment, "I'll stick around. For a while. But no promises about forever."

"Tell me what you saw," he said.

"Not much. I turned the corner in the garage, saw some bodies and blood . . ."

"Four. He shot four."

"Swell. He had his back to me when I came in. He heard me, turned. I ran and he shot at me."

"Could you recognize him again?"

"Yes," she said, "I'm pretty sure I can."

"You were under a lot of stress," cautioned Rourke. "That was a rough situation."

"It wasn't my first 'rough situation,'" she told him. Met his stare with her own.

"Could you help an artist sketch up a likeness?"

"Probably."

"Great," he said.

"My turn," she said. "Tell me what's happening."

As much as he could, he did.

"How long before this is over?" she asked.

"We don't even know what over will be," he told her. "But as far as you're concerned . . . Plan on sticking it out at least a couple weeks, maybe as long as a month."

"You're not going to catch him, are you?"

"Right now," said Rourke, "the important thing is that he doesn't catch you."

Rourke stood, asked her, "Do you mind being alone for a minute?"

"Mind? I'd *love* it!"

He put on his coat, walked to the door.

"Don't use the phone," he said before he went out.

"I don't have anyone to call," she said.

In the television movie, Bogart laughed.

Rourke knocked on the door of the room next door. There was a pause, then the door swung open. Perry stood deep in the shadows, close to the cover of the bathroom. Her hands were at her sides, and he was sure she held her gun.

Harris will be off to the side of the door, thought Rourke.

"We need a conference beyond these thin walls," he said.

They walked to the end of the balcony. Devlin looked in the corner room's window, saw it was empty. The wind whipped around them, and they could smell the exhaust from the cars whizzing by.

"They bought it," said Rourke. "The D.C. approved our plan."

He told them about the deadline, about the money. But not about the Duck.

"The next of kin have all been notified," he told them, "except for Hershel Bernstein's family. The resident manager at his apartment building said he hasn't seen the wife or son around. The uniforms left a card stuck in their door, but so far nobody's called in."

"Mother never said it would be easy," said Perry. "What's next?"

"We'll keep her here for the night," said Rourke. "One of us always babysitting. If we have to move tomorrow . . . Can she stay with either of you?"

"Forget it," said Perry. "I'm not putting her up, sticking by her, guard duty only—just because we both happen to be women!"

"Nobody said you should," said Rourke. "The question was, could we stash at your place?"

"I've got a studio efficiency, ground floor, lots of windows and nosy neighbors. Two cats. My mother says she's coming to town this week because she's sick of Florida."

"In other words, Susan," said Rourke. "Probably not."

Perry shrugged.

"I'm not exactly set up for company," said Harris. "My house has a bed, an easy chair, a couch propped up with a couple bricks, a TV, one set of towels, and some personal junk. It's one bedroom."

He shrugged.

"I'm not an elegant guy," he said.

"Did you get anything from her?" asked Perry.

"Some," answered Rourke. "How about you two?"

"Not a thing," said Perry. "She woke up early, took a long bath. Didn't speak except to ask the time. She pretended to read, gave that up for the TV. She plays it tight, our Rachel."

"What about Goldstein's for her?" asked Harris.

"The captain's is out," said Rourke. "His wife has a heart problem. The extra stress . . ."

"Jesus," said Perry. "No wonder. . . ." She didn't finish; shook her head.

"What about your place?" asked Susan. "Does Julia live there?"

"Not officially," he said.

They all laughed.

"We've got another option, but it's less practical than Harris."

"I don't get it," said Perry.

"Well, the D.C. assigned us another man."

"Who?" asked Harris.

"In fact," said Rourke, "he insisted we take him."

"Who?" asked Perry.

Inside the motel room, Rachel heard Harris and Perry yell, *"What??!!"*

Devlin led them back into Rachel's room a minute later.

"So," he said, his tone flat and humorless, "is everybody happy?"

Rachel nodded toward the glum faces of Harris and Perry.

"They don't look so hot," she said.

"It's the weather," said Rourke.

To Harris, he said, "Time to go."

On their way out, he told Rachel, "Take care."

The door shut.

"See you around," she said.

12

The winter Sunday weighed heavily on Devlin.

Harris drove him back into the city. They passed a billboard with the smiling faces of two men and the words, "Curtis & Miller, The Men in Your Morning, Baltimore's *hottest* station, WBBX, FM86." Harris double-parked next to the money machine at Devlin's bank. The machine greeted Devlin. Devlin punched in his code. The machine asked him what he wanted. Devlin said money. The machine told him he could have no more than $50. Devlin took it all. The machine told him to have a nice day.

Harris left him at headquarters, went to find the fat man

from the Empire Cafe. Rourke scrounged file folders, note-books, pens, report forms, paper clips, other office items. He put the supplies in a brown paper grocery sack he got from a garbage can. Pictures of two missing children decorated the grocery sack. Rourke didn't recognize the kids' names, though he'd seen their look before.

The lieutenant bent regulations and had two on-duty uniformed cops give him a ride home. Once there, they hooked jumper cables from their sleek white patrol car to his lifeless blue '67 Camaro. The two cops sat in the double-parked cruiser, engine running, cables hooked to the Camaro, while Devlin ran up to his third floor apartment, made instant coffee. The three of them drank it inside the warm cruiser before they tried to start the Camaro. The old car's engine turned over once, gave no other sign of life.

"Do you want some advice, sir?" asked one of the patrolmen as he and Rourke unhooked the jumper cables, shut the cars' hoods.

"I want my car to work," answered Rourke.

"If you ask me," said the uniformed cop, "that ain't going to happen."

"That's why I don't want to ask you," said Rourke.

He thanked them. Shuffled to his building door with the "Apartment for Rent" sign taped inside its glass panel. He checked the mailbox in the hall, found nothing. Trudged up the three flights of stairs to his apartment. Sat at his desk and stared out the window.

All I want is a little warmth, a little peace, he thought.

The phone he called rang four times before it was answered.

"Hello?" said the voice he knew well.

"Julia!" sighed Devlin. "Am I glad you're—"

"Don't you ever do that to me again!" she yelled.

"Ah . . . What?!"

"You hung up on me!"

"Julia, I didn't. . . . There was an emergency phone call."

"I know that! I heard! You didn't have to be impolite!"

"Julia . . . one second can mean life or death. The world doesn't wait, so there are priorities. That's the way it is. It's not personal, or directed to or against you or—"

"It's personal to me," she said. "I thought I was personal to you, too."

Devlin closed his eyes, cupped his forehead between his thumb and forefinger while he pressed the phone to his ear.

Must be because I'm tired, he thought. *She just doesn't understand. I'm too tired so I didn't explain it right.*

"Julia, honey," he swallowed, said: "I'm sorry. I didn't think there was time. I'm sorry if you didn't understand. We weren't the issue. The world was. I didn't mean to be impolite, or to offend you."

"Hmph." She thawed.

"It's been rough," he said.

"I've missed you, too," she said. "I had to go to the Mathews' alone. I made up an excuse for our hosts."

"That's good. How was it?"

"Fine. You should have come. There were some very important people from one of the banks there, and—"

"Did you read about the murders in the Ward Building?"

"Oh my God, yes!" she said. "That's all that place needs. J.B.," she said, referring to her hallowed boss at the Better Business League, "J.B. said Friday that everybody is nervous about the Blake Fund thing, what the rumors will do to the investment community, . . ."

"Four people shot to shit in the garage," said Devlin. "My case."

"Oh, no!" she cried, exasperated. "I thought you were through with all that murder work!"

"Not yet. This one's special."

"Why?" she asked.

He told her as much as he could. At first, he tried to skip over the bomb.

"So we had a little trouble at the hotel when I went to pick up the Dylan woman," he said.

"What kind of trouble?"

Why not? he thought. Besides, he needed her to care.

"The guy tried to bomb us."

"*Bomb?! Us?!!* What bomb?!"

So he told her right up through the deputy commissioner meeting; told her about having to work the case outside.

"Oh my poor, sweet Devlin, I'm sorry! I didn't know! Are you all right?! I'm coming right over!"

"No, hey, I'm okay. Just a few bruises. Occupational hazard."

"Occupational hazard! That's why I'm so glad you're getting out of the streets! I can't stand it, knowing you're out there with bombs and bullets and . . . and occupational hazards!"

"Don't worry about it," he said, feeling warm because she cared.

"What do you mean, 'work it outside'?"

"We're not completely sure yet."

"When can you transfer?"

"This case will decide my next move—one way or another."

"What about this woman who almost got you killed, this what's-her-name?"

"Rachel Dylan. What about her?"

"What does she look like?"

He laughed. "Is that jealousy?"

"Devlin! Don't be silly. And don't get cocky! I just . . . What does she look like?"

"She's blond."

"Un-huh."

He laughed.

"And tough," he said. "Shorter than you. Older, my age."

"And pretty?"

"If you look for it. If she tried to be."

"Well, don't plant that idea in her head. Let her keep thinking she's a street person or whatever you call them. And you take care of yourself. I don't want any bombs or blonds knocking you off."

"Oh yeah?"

"Yeah. I've got plans for you, Devlin Rourke."

"What kind of plans?"

"How tired are you?"

"Pretty tired. But I've been drinking coffee."

"Do you plan on staying up for a while?"

He laughed.

"Depends on what there is to do," he said.

"Well," she said, her voice, soft and low, husky. "How would you like it if—"

A loud *beep* interrupted her:

"Will the party on 555-4729 break for an emergency phone call from Detective Harris?"

"Hang up!" he yelled, doing so himself before she could reply. Ten seconds after he depressed the receiver button, the phone rang.

"Yeah!" he yelled when he answered it.

"Devlin?" Harris's voice soft, hesitant. Nervous.

"Yeah?"

"I found Nick Stavadopolis."

"Who?"

"The fat man from the Empire Cafe."

13

Nothing looked unusual on that grim street. The flat-faced townhouses stretched for blocks without distinction. Devlin waited on the three-step marble stoop until the taxi drove away.

Harris opened the door.

"In here," said the young detective.

"Nobody answered when I knocked," he said as he led Devlin through the hall. The lime green curtain at the entrance to the living room was tied aside. A frail old woman wearing glasses and a faded red cloth coat sat timidly on the living room couch.

"I checked the back door," said Harris as Devlin watched the silent woman. "Locked too. She lives next door. Our guy's landlady. And his aunt. I I.D.ed myself, asked her if she knew where he was.

"She thought something was funny: she didn't hear the TV." Harris nodded to the television set in front of the overstuffed easy chair. "The walls are thin in this neighborhood. You know about your neighbors. She says the first thing he always does when he comes home, day or night, is turn on the TV. He's got one in every room of the house. We looked through the front window, saw the lights glowing in the living room. The TV wasn't on. She let me in with her key."

"How are you, ma'am?" Devlin said to the old woman. She stared back at him.

Harris whispered: "She's been like that ever since . . ."

"Since what?" asked Devlin.

"Come on," he said. "I'll show you."

He led Devlin up the stairs. As they neared the second floor, Harris flicked on his flashlight.

"All the fuses on this floor blew," said Harris.

"Why don't you just tell me . . ." said Rourke.

"I'd rather show you. So you can tell me."

Rourke followed Harris's shadowy form and the glow of his flashlight down a narrow hall. The house had a musty smell, old and uncleaned. Stale cigars. And something foul.

"In there," said Harris, nodding to a closed white door. "It's a tight squeeze."

He handed his flashlight to Devlin.

The bathroom was cramped, the sink to the left of the door, a closet opposite it. The bathtub stretched along the far wall. The room was clammy. Devlin raised the flashlight beam to the tub.

And found the fat man.

His eyes were open, glazed and dead. He was naked, slumped in a bathtub full of water, a portable TV set submerged at his feet. A black electrical cord stretched from the TV to a socket in the wall above a crooked shelf.

"Shit," whispered Devlin.

He snapped off the flashlight.

"Classic home electrocution accident," said Harris in the darkness. "Right?"

Devlin closed his eyes, leaned against the sink to steady himself. A moment later he followed his flashlight into the bedroom. A TV sat on a stand at the foot of the bed. A pair of shoes and two socks waited for feet on the worn carpet. A rumpled work shirt and a pair of pants, the tops and bottoms of a long underwear set, lay in a heap on the unmade bed.

"I haven't called anybody," said Harris. "I haven't used the radio. I haven't let the old lady do anything either. I didn't want to tell you on the phone because . . ."

In the darkness, he shrugged.

". . . because I wanted you to see it."

"You did good," said Rourke. "You did right."

"This is one of ours, isn't it?" said Harris.

Rourke shined his light on the clothing pile. The order in which the garments were stacked signified nothing.

"Did you see any puncture wounds, bruises, or abrasions on the body?" asked Rourke as he held the pants up, shone the beam on them.

"I, ah . . . I looked, but . . . It's so gruesome . . ."

"Don't worry," Rourke told him. "I didn't even want to look. Goldstein will make sure the morgue does a thorough job."

Rourke put down the pants, picked up the shirt, spot-lighted it with the flashlight.

"A button is missing," he said. He squeezed the shirt, put it down, squeezed the pants. "And they're damp. So is the underwear."

Rourke went back to the bathroom. He swept the floor with the flashlight beam, slowly, thoroughly; found the small white button in the corner by the toilet.

"Make sure they get a picture of that," said Rourke.

"What happened?" asked Harris.

"I can write you a dozen scenarios," said Rourke. He let the flashlight beam roam over the body in the bathtub. He snapped off the flashlight, talked to Harris as they stood in the humid darkness.

"Nick let the wrong somebody inside, somebody who somehow got Nick upstairs. Maybe Nick is already undressed and ready to take a bath. Maybe the killer has to scare Nick into undressing. Maybe rip off a button in the process.

"But he gets Nick naked. Gets him in the tub of water. There's some fighting, splashing. Maybe that's why Nick's clothes are damp—the killer used them to mop up the floor after he was done.

"So Nick's in the tub. If he's been hollering . . . well, through these walls, screams can sound like TV.

"The killer reaches up, easy as you please, knocks the TV into the tub with Nick. *Zap!* Another problem solved."

"But why?" asked Harris. "Why would he worry about Nick?"

"He covers possibilities," said Rourke. "Our guy is smart. He stays safe by being a perfectionist. Vulnerabilities are eliminated."

"That's extreme!" argued Harris.

"That's effective," said Rourke. "Give me your car keys."

Harris passed them to him in the darkness.

"Where are you going?" he asked.

"I'll get the name and address of that other waitress from the old lady downstairs," said Rourke.

"That waitress told us she didn't see anything," said Harris. "And she obviously turns her back on any trouble. She'd have done that for our guy, too. He'd have noticed."

"Probably."

"So he won't kill her," said Harris.

"I'm not going to wait around and see if you're right." He handed the flashlight back to Harris.

"Call Goldstein, tell him what happened. Tell the ambulance people, anybody who asks, that this is probably an accident. Anybody pushes you, dodge them, let me know.

"But *you* handle this as a homicide. All the paperwork stays with us. Pick up the lab report from the morgue yourself."

"Do you think the lab will turn up murder?"

"The only thing that would help would be if they turn up something about the killer," said Rourke.

He shook his head. In the dark, Harris sensed rather than saw the gesture.

"I'll take your radio in case I run into somebody we'd like to know," said Rourke as Harris passed him the hand-held lifeline between a policeman in the field and all the help in the world.

Rourke walked to the head of the stairs, turned, and looked back. Harris saw his shadowy outline, imagined the hard expression on his face.

"Watch your back, Harris. Somebody out there means business."

14

"By now, most of you out there know what's happened," said the man in the soundproofed room that Monday morning.

Devlin watched him through the window in the wooden door. Devlin and Harris stood beneath a red ON THE AIR sign. Their escort, a red-headed woman named Terry, stood behind them.

The man in the soundproofed room spoke into a microphone that angled up from the horseshoe control console surrounding his chair. The control panel in front of him was a baffling array of sliding colored switches, needle-jumping dials, knobs, red and green lights. Soft yellow light filled the room; it was cold: even in the winter, this man kept the temperature in the sixties. The cold kept him from falling asleep. His face was pale, covered with two days' worth of stubble; his eyes were bloodshot. His wispy black hair was plastered down with its own unwashed oils.

"You know what they did," the man said into the microphone. "They gunned him down. They gunned him *down*. King, the Kennedys. John Lennon. And now Johnny Curtis. Our Johnny Curtis. *Your* Johnny Curtis. My partner. My friend. Your friend. They blew him away with three other innocent people, right here in Baltimore. Our town. Our bloody, damn town."

Lights flashed behind the 10 plastic buttons of the console's telephone. The man glanced at their flashes, then Devlin.

"We don't know why they did it yet," the man said into the microphone. Today's and Sunday's Baltimore *Star* lay sprawled on the counter in front of him. Sunday's paper had a front-page picture of the Ward Building's blood-stained garage floor. "We don't know who they were, what . . . what twisted thing they wanted or thought they were doing. Charlie

67

Manson. John Hinckley. Who can understand the crap they've
got between their ears? But we know what they did. They and
all the creeps like them. The creeps who came to Baltimore.
To our town. They killed our Johnny Curtis.

"What the hell more do we need to know?"

The man pushed a button with his right hand. The red
light went out, and from the two giant speakers suspended
from the ceiling in front of his console came the sound of The
End sung by The Doors.

The man beckoned for Devlin and the others to enter.

"I'm Gordy Miller," said the man surrounded by the radio
booth's console. He watched his visitors with wary eyes,
nodded as the cops introduced themselves.

"What do you need, Gordy?" asked the woman. She was
in her midthirties. Tall, lean. She hugged her chest. She wore
a dark gray sweater and faded black cords. Her amber eyes
were bloodshot.

"You have to ask?" he said.

"We're sorry to disturb you now, Mr. Miller," said Devlin.

"Gordy," corrected the man. "Everybody calls me Gordy."

"What we wanted—besides to talk to you—was to get a
feel for where Mr. Curtis—"

The man everybody called Gordy interrupted him: "Call
him Johnny. Dead or alive, everybody calls him Johnny."

Harris spoke up:

"I just want to say, . . . I've always liked your show."

"Thanks."

"We'll need to talk to you after your show," said Rourke.

"What else do I have to do?" replied Gordy.

"You been here long?" asked Devlin.

"Since 3:30, 4. Couldn't sleep, couldn't sit around home
anymore. Usually we got here at 4:30. Nowhere even to have
breakfast then. Signed on at 5. Today . . . It was so eerie.
Parking in the garage . . . walking over, looking down
where . . ."

He shook his head.

"It was like I wanted to puke. Only I couldn't."

"Did you work that Saturday?" asked Devlin.

"Nah. You know us: the men in your morning, 5 to 10, every workday. We bargained our way out of Saturdays after the six-month probation period."

"Coming up on 30 seconds, Gordy," said the woman, her eyes fixed on a red-numbered digital clock set into the control panel. The numbers flashed toward zero: 31, 30, 29, . . .

"We'll have to . . . I'm not really concentrating, you know?" said Gordy. "After we . . ."

"Sure," said Rourke. "After."

Gordy pushed a button. The red ON THE AIR glow flashed before the song was over.

"The End," said Gordy.

On the roof of the Ward Building, twin antennae beamed his words out with 50,000 watts of FM power.

"This is the end," he said. "The end for Johnny Curtis. You know who he was. He was America's best deejay. He was your deejay, Baltimore. Yours. He died here, at your studio. A rock 'n' roll story—no! A legend, a rock 'n' roll *legend*. And we're all part of it, all of us and all of you. Eighty-Six-X. Maybe we should call it the death ship, huh?"

Terry frantically sliced the side of her hand across her throat.

"Yeah, well, rock 'n' roll," continued Gordy. "Lotta death there. Jimi and Janis and Buddy and Jim Morrison from the Doors singing about the end, man, he knew and he bought it. Just like our Johnny, our own sweet Johnny. What do you think about that, huh?"

Terry frantically waved her hands, tried to get him to stop, but he punched one of the flashing lights on the phone.

"Yeah, Eighty-Six-X."

The disembodied male voice sounding through the speakers was startled.

"Wha . . . Wha . . . I got through!"

"You're on the air," said Gordy.

Terry moved into the horseshoe with Gordy. Her fingertip rested on a button as she strained to listen to the caller.

"Oh, wow, I . . ."

"Yeah," said Gordy. He made a hurry-up motion with his hand that the person calling from the world couldn't see.

"This is too much," said the caller. "I mean, they killed you. One of you guys. It's like they can do anything."

"Maybe they can, brother."

"Yeah, but . . . *you guys!*"

"We put our pants on just like everybody else."

"But it's like . . . Your voice floats out there in the air. One minute you're everywhere. Then, suddenly, you're nowhere at all."

"Know what you mean. Thanks."

Gordy jabbed another phone button.

The girl's sobbing echoed through the speakers. Gordy turned a knob, and her anguish grew louder.

"Oh, Gordy!"

"I know, babe. We all know."

"It's so awful!" She sobbed again.

"How does it hurt?"

"It's so bad!"

"We all loved him," said Gordy. He listened, but the girl merely sobbed.

He punched another button.

"Eighty-Six-X."

"You're next, Gordy, we're going to—"

Gordy punched another button before Devlin could stop him.

"Come on, sucker! Come on creep! No, it wasn't you. You're just some ghoul, some creep with no guts and no class. You want to whine on the radio and feed off our pain. The hell with you, buddy. Not today, not tomorrow, not ever for you. Not on Eighty-Six-X."

The deejay pushed another button.

"Gordy?"

"Yeah, man?" Gordy told the teenage boy.

"Look, bunch of us over at Clairmont High?"

"Yeah, man, we were there, Johnny and I did your dance 'couple weeks back."

"We don't forget," said the boy. He tried to sound tough, but tears strained his words. "This is Baltimore, man, and we don't fu— fu—" he stutter-chopped the prohibited word short: "fuhning-forget!"

"You got it, brother!"

"Johnny Curtis, like man, he'll live forever!"

"Right on!"

"He'll live forever out here in the streets!"

Terry perked up, waved to get Gordy's attention, then raced to a record bin behind three racks of tape cartridges.

Her finger slid along the spines of the filed records and she pulled a blue-gray album from its slot. She put the record on one of the two turntables, cued it, and spun back to face Gordy; nodded.

He'd kept the boy on the line; was saying, "That's right, brother, you got it right," when he saw Terry nod. He wrinkled his brow, and she mouthed the words, "out in the streets." Gordy shrugged, frowned in concentration.

"You got it brother," he said again. "Ah . . ." He strained, worked the words out. "You got it. Where they going to remember our man Johnny?"

"Here, man!" shouted the teenager, overflowing with emotion.

"Yeah! Where?"

"Baltimore!"

"Everywhere in Baltimore?" asked Gordy. He glared exasperation to Terry. She motioned for him to continue; her face showed encouragement. Gordy touched another button on the phone, but her waving hands stayed that execution.

"You got it. Clairmont High, man, we—"

"Never gonna forget, right?" shouted Gordy over the kid's frantic, *you got it!* "Where we gonna shout his name in Baltimore!"

"In every damn street!" yelled the teenager.

Terry chopped her hand.

Gordy pushed a button; the record on the turntable spun. Bruce Springsteen singing, "Out in the Street" blared over the speakers. The red ON THE AIR light went out.

"That's smooth, Terry," he said. "Couldn't figure out where you were going, but—"

"You can't do the call-ins live," Terry hissed. "Even with the cut-off button, it's too—"

"Just a few more," said Gordy. He held down a button on the control panel, looked into the engineering booth.

"Harold," Gordy said, "start making tapes from the call-ins. Use contest carts. We aren't giving money away today—"

"We're making it!" said the engineer over the intercom. "The other stations aren't even getting call-ins for their contests. The whole city is listening to us! The station manager is going crazy. He said to use the commercials on your log, but he's calling the big accounts and telling them if they want airplay on this show for the next few days, they gotta buy bonus rates."

"Bloodsucker," said Gordy.

Nobody replied.

Gordy moved the song and commercial log to where he could see it better. He fed tapes into a six-slotted tape deck.

"None of the scheduled stuff. You keep me hopping with music, okay, Terry?" he asked softly.

"Sure, Gordy." Her reply was flat.

The engineer cut in with the intercom:

"What do you want from the call-ins?"

"Hell!" yelled Gordy. "You know what. . . . Honesty, damn it! Let them say what they want, ask them about Johnny, how they feel, stuff we can use a general lead-in to. We'll edit them around."

"Right," said the engineer.

Springsteen ended abruptly. Gordy punched a phone button.

"Eighty-Six-X."

"Gordy?" said the girl.

"It's me. We're all here."

"Look, I just . . . We're all so sorry!"

"Thanks."

"You know what a bunch of us decided to do?"

"Keep it cool, dear."

"Oh no, nothing like . . . Nothing bad!"

"Johnny wouldn't have wanted it any other way."

"We'll miss him so much!"

"All of us," said Gordy, encouraging her, involving the audience.

"What we're going to do, we got a bunch of black crepe paper streamers left over from our Halloween dance. We're going to give out long pieces of it to all the kids in the halls today, and we're all going to fly them like banners from our car antennae."

Gordy covered his face with one hand.

"That . . . Thanks. Thanks for that. Thanks for Johnny."

"We'll fly them forever! All year!"

Gordy shook his head.

"Maybe the kids in other schools will do it, too," said the girl.

"I hope so." Gordy's voice was hoarse, a strained whisper. "Listen, honey, what's your name?"

"That's not important," said the girl. She sniffled. "I'm just a fan."

She hung up.

"Ah," said Gordy. He wiped his cheek. "Ah, we'll be back, we gotta . . . We'll be right back. Don't go away."

He punched a button. The commercial jingle for a soft drink filled the speakers.

"We'll wait for you," said Devlin.

Gordy nodded.

Earlier that Monday morning, winter ended in the streets of Baltimore. The wind stopped at midnight when Devlin drove the waitress named Mavis to the airport, put her on a plane for Las Vegas.

"I don't mind leaving this town alive," she'd said.

Devlin watched her pack, made sure she left no tracks.

"I'll call you when we're sure you can come back," he said.

"Do that," she said, snapping a match to light a cigarette. "I'll be hanging around waiting for your call."

As long as you don't die, too, thought Devlin. He drove back to the motel, slept in the room next to Rachel's.

When he woke at six, the temperature was below freezing but rising. Dawn lit the city by the time Harris picked him up. Steam rose from ice patches in the gutter as they drove through the outskirts of town. The air looked clean, smelled of life and days to come.

The detectives stopped twice on their way to the radio station: first for carry-out coffee and donuts at a early hour convenience grocery store, then at a high-rise apartment building Harris had visited before.

"Is the Bernstein family in?" Rourke asked the sleepy security guard who opened the door to their badges.

"How should I know?" said the guard, a retired plumber in a shoddy gray doorman's uniform. He shuffled back to the sports page.

A policeman's business card was still wedged in Bernstein's apartment door. No one answered Devlin's persistent knocks.

"We'll give them until this afternoon," he told Harris as they walked away.

"It's two days since he was shot," said Harris as they walked down the hall. "Where's his family been?"

"Be sure to ask them," said Rourke.

WBBX's studios filled the top floor of the Ward Building. The elevators opened to a reception room with a glass back wall and a high tech desk with a bank of ringing phones. The receptionist was 20, well-dressed. Crying. While Rourke and Harris waited, they stared at the signed poster of the voluptuous, Cupid-lipped, henna-haired L.A. model who'd become a Baltimore celebrity for the husky-voiced television commercial she'd starred in for the radio station.

"Damn!" Harris whispered to Devlin, nodding toward the poster. "All my life I've been looking for someone like her."

Before Devlin could answer, Terry Cassidy came into the reception room, introduced herself, and led them back to the studio.

WBBX was a labyrinth of carpeted blue corridors and clean white offices, walls with smiling photos of disc jockeys, station-sponsored community events, famous stars who'd visited the studios. They walked past a glass case of trophies for the softball teams, for raising the most money for a community charity, for news and feature competitions. Framed replicas of gold and platinum records hung from one wall, with plaques thanking WBBX for "making another hit possible." Gordon Miller's broadcasted voice flowed over Devlin and Harris as they followed Terry Cassidy's black-slacked, thin hips toward a windowless white door with the ebony X-86 monogram. They passed half a dozen people in the halls, all of whom were crying or red-eyed.

Devlin glanced into an open office, saw an executive desk, a potted rubber tree, and, scotchtaped to one wall, a white papered briefing poster with black magic marker lines of instructions:

1. Energy, Excitement
2. Sell Music
3. Concise, to Point
4. Imagination
5. Fun on Air

The detectives met with Gordy Miller for the second time in a windowless conference room with a round table for 20.

"Sorry I was abrupt in the studio," Gordy said after they sat at the table. "I hope the wait wasn't too bad."

"We're used to waiting," said Harris.

"Besides," said Rourke, "that let us talk to a few people who were here Saturday."

"Did you get anything?" asked Gordy.

"Everyone was cooperative," answered Rourke, *though no one told us anything useful*.

"Right up front," said Gordy, "let me tell you where I was."

"Fine," said Harris. He clicked his pen over his notebook.

"My next door neighbor's," said the deejay. He spelled the man's name for Harris. "His pipes froze. We spent the day wielding a butane torch. My wife ran over to tell me about . . . about Johnny."

"Would you say you two were friends?" asked Rourke.

"Friends isn't the word for it. We were partners. You guys ought to understand that!"

"We do," said Harris.

"There's maybe 50 people work here. Ten people for one job, man, knives in your back like you wouldn't believe. The only person I trust is the guy who sits with me—and he ain't there no more."

"Could you explain how your show works?" asked Devlin.

"Don't you listen to us?"

"I want to get a feel for what goes on behind the scenes," said Devlin, who hated get-up and get-going, screaming deejays' shows.

"Just the basics," he added.

"So you can figure out who might have whacked my buddy?" said Gordy. "Sure. I'll explain it to you."

"He had enemies?"

"About a million," said Gordy. "Anybody and everybody who works in this business who wanted a piece of our pie. Who wanted to ride our coattails, who . . ."

The deejay shook his head, closed his eyes, and pinched the bridge of his nose.

"You gotta understand," he said, in a softer voice, "I'm real strung out."

"Sure," said Harris. "We understand."

"Like, my best friend is dead, right? And I feel shitty about that. But the show has to go on, right? We got an audience, we got responsibility."

The man who'd lost his partner shook his head.

"Johnny *was* a star. He had talent like you couldn't believe. Put a mike in front of him and he could con the world. If he had the right back-up. Now maybe last few months he was—"

The deejay cut short his ramblings.

"He was what?" asked Devlin.

"I don't know. Just me, maybe."

"You were closer to him than anybody," encouraged the detective.

"We want it all," said Harris.

"Think I should have my lawyer here or what?"

"Why?" asked Harris. "Have you done something wrong?"

"Me? Hell no! It's just . . . I don't know if, you know, when a guy knows something and talks to the cops, sometimes he lands in the trouble even if he hasn't done anything wrong."

Devlin guessed:

"We know all about Johnny using coke," he said.

The dead man's partner sighed.

"So, big surprise, huh?" he said. "A rock 'n' roll legend dusted with drugs. Hell, you should have been surprised if there *weren't* drugs in Johnny's life."

"And yours," said Harris.

"Now wait a minute!" said the deejay. He leaned forward, shook his finger at Harris while he addressed Rourke.

"That's just what I was talking about! I try to be honest with you, and right away you put *me* up against the wall and—"

"We don't really care about a crime that's immaterial to the investigation we're presently pursuing," said Rourke.

No one spoke for several seconds.

"Why should I buy that?" Gordy finally said.

"Because we can play the same song another way, and you won't like that at all," said Rourke.

"Okay!" said the deejay. "Okay! Maybe I do a little blow at parties now and then.

"But never—and I mean *never*, man!—never on the air. Gotta keep cool if you want to be hot, and that means a clean nose! You use that shit to put you up there, it's gonna bring you down all the way when you can't afford to fall."

"Had Johnny started using coke that much?" asked Harris.

The dead man's partner shrugged.

"He'd toot up before we signed on, like a cup of coffee to get you going. Four, five, maybe six times during the five-hour show. Sometimes more, sometimes less.

"But it was just a phase. Just a phase."

"When did that phase start?" asked Devlin, who knew a great deal about such things.

"Four, five months ago."

"Why?"

Gordon Miller shrugged: "Why not?

"I mean, hey: he could do it, right? It's unbelievable, this life. You go to a party, hang around town. People know who you are. You can get anything you want. *Anything*. How would you handle that?

"Sex? Hell, there's a ton of women. Married women, not just teenyboppers, but older, thirties, forties. I had one broad in her fifties who came up to me . . . They all want to fuck. Like they're missing something and fucking us will give it to them."

He smiled, his grief and wariness forgotten in male comradeship.

"We, ah, we obliged more than one.

"It gets weird, though," he said. He leaned closer to Devlin.

"Like there was this one chick at this mixer we went to for the station, right? Blond, tight little body, tits out here! I wanted to plug her on the spot! She gives me this dazzling smile, says 'Gordy, I just love your show! I met you when you played my eighth-grade graduation dance six years ago!

He shook his head.

"Couldn't handle it," he said.

"How about Johnny?" asked Devlin. "How was he handling it?"

"Johnny made a lot of dreams come true," laughed Gordy. "But we slacked off the sporting last couple years. What the hell, I don't want to blow off my wife and kids by dipping around. Johnny, he wasn't married, but . . . He was getting angry about that scene."

"You mean angry about somebody?"

"No, man. Johnny's somebody would come and go—and come! 'Bout once every month. Plus the others, the groupies. He was bored with it though. Didn't care about that anymore."

"No disgruntled exlovers?" asked Harris.

"A hundred. But nobody special enough or mad enough or crazy enough to . . . Nobody like that."

"What did Johnny care about?" asked Rourke.

"He was worried that he was going bald."

The cops looked at each other.

"Wait a minute!" shouted Gordy. "I'm serious! *That's* serious.

"This is show business, man! You try to make it to the top and getting there ain't all talent! Hell, he had the talent! But . . . he wasn't sure he had the time.

"See, Baltimore is one of the top markets. We spill over into D.C. There's Atlanta, Boston, Chicago, San Francisco, a few big stations blasting the Midwest. They're like Baltimore: all great, all a long way up the heap from cow pasture stations where you read the weather report and announce the hog prices. Man, we are up there in the clouds! Stratosphere city!

"But Baltimore isn't the top of the sky. That's L.A. That's New York. That's heaven. Johnny was so close he could smell it. And nobody ever wanted it more than he did.

"But you got to get a break. Lately, he started worrying he wasn't going to get the break in time to take it.

"Our gig doesn't work if the deejay is a senior citizen," said Gordy. "Johnny heard the young guys racing up behind us. When he looked ahead at the stretch he had left to go, he saw guys who weren't about to step aside. He was afraid he was caught in that squeeze."

"With you," said Devlin.

Gordon shrugged.

"We loved each other like brothers, man. No matter how much shit he gave me on the air. That was just our gig.

"We came to Baltimore eight years ago. My old program manager from St. Paul teamed us up. Convinced me to leave a station where I was safe to work with some hotshot at a station I'd never heard of in *Baltimore!*

"But it worked out. Took a couple years. We had to move over to FM, the city had to crawl out of hard times. But we made it. Had a whole lot of fun doing it, too! Made our mark in the industry.

"We each carried the other further than we could have gone alone. Me, I love it here. I ain't as hungry as I was few years back. I've been fed pretty well."

"And Johnny was still hungry," said Devlin.

"The more he ate," said Gordy, "the more he wanted."

"What did he want?" asked Harris. "More money?"

"Everybody always wants more money," answered Gordy. "Everybody always asks. Our contract was up in six months. He'd have asked for more—we both will—would have, I mean."

"Did he have a solo shot at the big time?" asked Devlin.

"I don't think so," said Gordy. He leaned back in his chair.

But you're nervous about the question, thought Rourke.

"Did Johnny *think* he had a shot at the big time?" the boss cop asked the deejay.

"Yeah, well, . . . He always did."

"More so than lately?"

Gordy shrugged. "He talked about it more."

"Any specifics?" asked Harris.

"You'd have to ask him."

Nobody thought that was a joke.

We'll lose him soon, thought Rourke. He leaned forward, arms on the table.

"How did Johnny get the coke?"

"I don't know," said Gordy.

They all recognized the lie as it lay down on the table between them.

"I mean," said Gordy, "he got it lots of places. Around."

"Same place as you?" asked Harris.

"I'm not going to talk about that stuff," insisted the deejay.

"Could Johnny afford all his coke?" Devlin asked quickly, hoping that shift would keep Gordy from bolting.

"We each get $94,000 a year. Johnny had money."

"What about enemies?" Devlin asked. "You said Johnny had a lot of people who hated him—"

"A lot more who loved him!" interrupted his partner.

"Anyone in particular?" asked Devlin. "Either way?"

Gordy stared at him.

"No," he finally said. Shifted in his seat.

"The other people in the elevator," asked Devlin, "the ones who died with him: you read two of their names and lives in the paper. The third man was named Hershel Bernstein. Worked in the building. Did Johnny know any of them?"

"Not that I know of," answered Gordy.

"Did he know any bad guys?" asked Rourke.

Gordy shifted uncomfortably in his chair.

"What do you mean?" he said. "This is a rough town. Everybody knows somebody bad."

"Sure," said Rourke, "but Johnny met up with one truly evil man. Got any ideas who he could be?"

"No," said Gordy.

That lie joined Gordy's first untruth. The two of them lay wrapped around each other like lovers on the table. They started to smell.

"How about nuts?" asked Harris.

Good, thought Rourke. *Shift Gordy to somewhere safe.*

"You think a nut did that?!"

"Never know," said Harris.

"I imagine you get—"

"Dozens," said Gordy, relaxing. "You wouldn't believe it!"

"Ever have a serious one? Bad threats?" asked Rourke.

"No, not—"

He stopped, his eyes racing backward in time. The two detectives exchanged a glance. Harris poised his pen above the pad.

"Enoch Pruid," whispered Gordy.

"Who the hell is Enoch Pruid?" asked Devlin.

"You tell me," answered Gordy.

"About six years ago, at the old station, we started getting these hate letters from a guy called Enoch Pruid. After the third one, we called the police. This guy said he was going to stab us to death with an ice pick. And something like, 'watch you bleed slowly, slowly, to feed the hungry earth.'"

"What happened?" asked Harris.

"You guys sent some detectives over. One did some research, scared the shit out of us. Seems like there really was an Enoch Pruid. A poet, lived in the 1400s in England. Got locked up in an insane asylum. For stabbing people to death with an ice pick.

"For six weeks, we each had a detective escort us to and from work. They hung out at the station, made sure squad cars cruised by our houses lots. Right after we called the police, the letters stopped."

"Do you remember who handled the case?" asked Harris.

"No, but Terry has a file with the xeroxes of the letters, all that shit. Ask her."

"You said Johnny'd changed lately," said Rourke. "How?"

"I don't know. Maybe it's just my bad memory running out my big mouth, you know? We both were always asking for new things, trying new changes or ideas out. Some worked, some we got to do, some we didn't. I was just rambling."

"How about the coke?" said Harris.

"Look, guys, I want the creeps who did this worse than you did. I loved that man! I really did. But I don't know anything more that can help you. You keep talking 'bout stuff, I keep trying to help you, but man, I think there's some things I should probably talk to my lawyer about, understand?"

The stench of his lies and his nervous sweat filled the room.

"We're just doing our job," said Rourke, one last effort to ease back into Gordy Miller's confidence.

"Look, I just want to go home, okay?"

You're already gone, thought Devlin.

"Sure," said the police lieutenant. No more Mr. Nice Guy. "We understand. And we hope that you do, too."

"What does that mean?"

"We're working a multiple homicide. We appreciate all the help anyone can give us. And it's always better to give us help, to let us help you, than it is to go it alone. It's an ugly, dark, rough world out there, Gordy."

"Yeah," said the deejay.

15

Rourke found Terry sitting behind her desk, staring out the wall-sized office window at the city skyline.

"It can all be a random accident, can't it?" she said before he had a chance to speak. Her eyes didn't move from the glass. He hadn't realized she knew he stood in her doorway.

"What?" he asked.

"Everything," she said.

"Like walking into the right garage at the wrong time?"

"Yeah. Like that. Only maybe it wasn't an accident for Johnny, right?"

"Maybe."

She wouldn't leave the clouds, look at him.

"Maybe nothing is an accident," he said. "Maybe all your choices add up to walking on that sidewalk under the steel beam as it falls off the skyscraper."

She turned, let her brown eyes size him up.

"What are you," she asked, "a cop or a philosopher?"

"What's the difference?"

She thought about it, long and hard.

"You get a regular paycheck," she finally said.

"As long as the city makes its taxes," he said. "Can I talk to you for a minute?"

"I doubt you'll take only a minute." She nodded to a chair in front of her desk.

"You're their producer, right?" he asked as he sat down. She nodded, and he asked, "What does that mean?"

Her smile was wry.

"Didn't used to mean anything," she said. "I made the job up after their show was already a hit.

"Look," she said, "Why don't I tell you what you might need to know, then let you ask questions?"

"Go ahead," said Rourke. "I like to hear you talk."

"I bet you do, Mr. Detective," she said.

"Call me Devlin."

"This is radio, Devlin. Big-time radio. Show business. The emphasis at this station is on those two words: 'show' and 'business.'"

"What about music?" asked the cop.

"That's just the vehicle for what's really important. When I came to this 'hot' station I learned that nobody loved the music *first*. They liked it, they were surrounded by it, they had their jobs because of it, but nobody *loved* it."

"Except you."

"Yeah, well . . . you wouldn't be the first one to say that this isn't my kind of station."

She leaned back in her chair, closed her eyes, and rubbed her temples with her fingers.

"God I'm tired!"

Her eyes opened, locked on Devlin.

"I started out as a deejay. Came here from a station whose music I hated even mo—" She caught herself, smiled. "One whose programming appealed less to my tastes than Eighty-Six-X. I got a chance to do fill-in work here, then the dead-zone show: 2 AM to 5 AM. Replaced a talk show program that nobody listened to. At first they let me program my own music, but—"

"You mean deejays don't pick what they play?" asked Devlin.

"Not at a place like Eighty-Six-X," said Terry. She smiled. "You should remember that."

She's got something, thought Devlin. *And she'll give it to me—in her own time. With her own program.*

"No, deejays don't pick what they play. That's the music director's job. Sometimes with a program director. They control everything but the deejay's jokes—and even those are increasingly a team effort. Hell, that's what I'm all about: a producer."

"Why did you switch from being a deejay?"

"I love being on the air," she said. "But . . . as long as I couldn't pick the music, it wasn't my show."

She shrugged.

"Besides, the show business approach, the 'hot' sound . . . I don't want to hype enthusiasm from my audience like Pavlov tricking a dog."

"If you hate your business so much—"

"Why do I stay around?" She shook her head. "Look at me: babbling on like you're a friend. That's the trouble with deejays: We love to talk."

"Cops love to listen."

They both laughed.

"Don't get me wrong," she said. "I've got a great job. I work at one of the top dozen stations in America. Heady stuff. That gives me a chance to influence the industry, the art. I convinced the station I could make their hottest show hotter, more interesting—background noise development, theme shows. Once I put them in a van for a week and had them broadcast driving around the Beltway. Johnny and Gordy were great! All this real world material! Commuters tuning in to see if they were in the middle of what the city was hearing. Our ratings went through the roof! I've learned so much! I just . . ."

She stared at him.

"I've almost made it to the top, but the mountain isn't like it was supposed to be when I started climbing."

"That happens to a lot of people," said Rourke.

"Yeah," she said, "I suppose so."

"Tell me about Johnny," said the cop.

"Johnny." She shook her head, sighed. "Johnny. That mountain was his problem, too."

"Gordy mentioned something about his ambition."

"Ambition is too weak a word. Call it hunger. That's what made him good. That's what ate him up."

"Is it what killed him?"

"Maybe," she said. "Johnny had more talent for this kind of radio than anyone you'll ever hear," she said. "He had this way of sucking in the audience, bouncing off Gordy. . . . He was number 1 here, and he knew it."

"But he wanted more," said Devlin.

"Johnny'd changed lately," she said. "He'd always been hungry. But in the last couple months . . . he was desperate."

"Weird behavior?"

She watched him, waiting.

"We know about the drugs," said the cop.

"Drugs aren't weird. Not in this world."

"But they are illegal. And a problem."

"But not Johnny's," she said. "They were part of it, but . . . Maybe they were something he was doing because of the desperation."

"Or maybe they led him to it?" asked Devlin.

"Maybe all of the above," she answered. "More. That hunger owned him. And he was going to feed it more."

"How?"

"I don't think Johnny could *completely* tell you what *more* was, because there could never be enough. So he'd take everything he could get."

"Not a healthy attitude," said Rourke.

"Johnny's not a healthy man these days," said Terry.

Her eyes misted and Rourke tried a wild shot.

"You were a lot more than co-workers, weren't you?" he said.

"We were friends," she answered quietly.

"You know what I mean."

She focused on him, whispered, "Nobody knows. Who did you—"

Rourke shrugged. "How I know doesn't matter. But I need to hear your version."

"And we thought we beat the gossips." She shook her head. "Do you have to broadcast it?"

"Believe me," he said, "no one who doesn't need to know will find out from us."

"How about Gordy?"

"That's my question," said Rourke. "Did he know?"

"No! At least . . . No. Johnny and I . . .

"It was one of those office things that we both knew would blow up if it got out. Especially to Gordy. Deejays are paranoid. If Gordy thought I might be favoring Johnny over him—which I never did or would or—

"We just did it, you know?" she said. "We liked each other enough, needed somebody enough, had enough in common. Neither of us were married. It was like we had to get it out of the way. More a relief of frustration than passion, and after a week of absolute secrecy, we ran out of reasons for it to be at all. So we stopped."

"And went on like nothing had happened?" asked Rourke.

"We went on like what had happened—had happened. But it was finished business. Our business. We kept it out of office politics."

"Any regrets or jealousies?"

"Relief," she said. "We both felt relief. That we did it, that we were done with it."

"What about the other people around here?"

"Until you sprung that on me, I didn't think anybody knew. Obviously, I was wrong."

"You said he'd changed lately," said Rourke. "Was that because of you?"

"No, all of that was over a year ago. We'd basically forgotten it."

"Then what was wrong with him? How had he changed?"

She kept her silence for a moment.

"There's nothing I can prove," she said cautiously.

"That's my job," answered Devlin. "What did he do?"

She looked out toward the clouds. Shook her head, then turned her gaze back to the man sitting in front of her.

"He betrayed the music," she said.

"Remember what I said about this being show business?" Terry asked him.

He nodded and she continued.

"Well, the essence of 'show' is pretense, and the essence of 'business' is profit. Put them together without any soul and you've got—"

"Crime," said Rourke.

"Billions of dollars flow through the pipeline every year because of music," said Terry. *"Billions.* We're only a small part of the package. But we're a crucial part.

"Do you remember payola?" she asked.

"From the fifties?" he said. "Deejays getting paid to play a certain record? I thought that died out before the Beatles."

"Nothing ever dies in rock 'n' roll," she told him. "All the old goldies get replayed, and when there's a lot of gold to be made from playing the old songs or the old ways . . .

"But it's now deejays anymore," she told him. Frowned, asked: "How much of this is on the record? I mean, what will I need to swear to in court so everyone will know I—"

"Don't worry about that part yet," he assured her. "When it comes to what might put you in the spotlight, I'll let you know. Right now, I need everything: fact, innuendo, suspicion. Everything.

"And don't worry," he said again. "You're safe with me."

"Sure," she said, repeating her wry smile: "That's what all you boys say.

"So payola." She shook her head, glanced out the window, then turned back to Devlin. "Remember how corruption works—"

"Any way it can."

"That's right," she said. "And nowadays, in radio, it's usually not the deejays. Payola—'play for pay'—isn't even necessarily the nut of the game.

"The game changed after the payola scandals of the fifties. The business cleaned up its act even as rock became a major force in the billion-dollar music river. Add to that the depression that hit the record industry in the early seventies, when baby boomers like us started buying French wine, designer jeans, and diapers instead of Beatles albums. Add to *that* the lamentable fact that the Beatles weren't recording any more albums and the talent level dropped lower than it had been since the fifties. Lot of people quit listening, quit buying. Record companies economized. One place they cut back was their promotion departments.

"Used to be, every record label had its promoters, and there were hundreds of record labels. Come the slump, come the monster conglomerates that gobbled up a lot of the smaller companies, dozens of record labels vanished, as did hundreds of in-house promotion jobs.

"Pity most the music. And those of us who love it. Fewer record companies meant fewer chances for fresh, innovative talent to break through. The less new talent that hit the airwaves, the more everything sounded alike. Turn on the radio, you got skim milk. Which meant fewer people listened and bought, which meant the record companies tried harder to imitate the few big hitmakers, which meant even fewer chances for the innovative artists who might have wooed back audiences and consumers.

"To sell, records must be promoted—or so goes the record companies' theory. Since they cut back their budgets, the slack was taken up by independent promoters.

"The independents started out as middlemen, ended up as czars. They carved vast empires out of what should have been a small gap between record companies and radio stations.

"The independents try to claim responsibility for getting records played on radio stations. The indies carve up America—you take Philly, I'll take Atlanta, Pete gets L.A.—and claim stations. Deejays. The record companies pay them a promotional fee for every record they get played."

"What are we talking about in real world dollars?" asked Devlin.

"I'll give it to you conservatively," she replied.

"An indy might get $2,000 per record he promotes," explained Terry. "He gets that for getting airplay—supposedly. But sometimes he gets it if the record merely makes it to a station's playlist.

"Remember," she said, "Deejays don't pick their own records to play. Hell, with the carts, they don't usually even play *records*: they're tapes, but that's just aesthetic quibbling."

"Sure," said Devlin.

They smiled at each other.

"Which means," she said, "the indies target the music directors. In theory, the program directors oversee the music directors, and the station managers oversee the program directors. Since they're all supposed to understand what's going on at their station, the theory is that so many people can't be corrupted."

"But the theory—" began Devlin.

"The theory is words," said Terry. "Everybody in the industry knows that. I saw an article in the *Wall Street Journal* that estimates corruption through the indies is a $20 million a year scandal.

"The indy goes to whoever can help him. He knows the record company will pay him $2,000 for every record of theirs he gets on a major playlist. An honest indy will not bribe. A good indy will tell you, 'Hey, this song from Amalgram Records won't be too good for your station, but next week, Amalgram will have a great new one from a new group with a lot of talent that's perfect for your audience.' That's what a good, honest indy will do. There are some of those."

"How many?"

"Not enough."

"How about here?"

"Here, we've got three indies competing to claim this market. But before we get to that, let me finish explaining their game.

"They get paid for results. Most stations add new songs to their playlists on Tuesday."

"You mean it's not as they come in, hot from the presses, riding the surge of fresh new talent?" interrupted Devlin.

"Such a cynic," she said.

"The trick is for the indy to get credit for Amalgram's records making the station's playlist—whether he's actually done *anything* or not. That's $2,000 to him. So Tuesday, long distance lines are loaded with indies calling record companies saying, 'Hey, I got you on the air in Atlanta.'"

"Or Baltimore."

"Or anywhere. And if another indy calls in for credit first, then you get zip.

"The indy goes to whoever," continued Terry. "Maybe it's the music director. Maybe its the deejay. The indy says, 'I get $2,000 for this. I pay half of that in taxes, right? So that leaves $1,000. Let's knock off $100 for legitimate expenses—gas, long distance, whatever. Leaves $900. You and me, we can split the $900, your end in cash or . . . or whatever you want: microwaves, tailored suits, tires for your sportscar, . . .'"

"A couple grams of coke," said Devlin.

Silence. He knew he'd scored.

"Sure," she said finally, "Why not? A couple grams of coke. Why not a dozen or so? Just as long as the Amalagram record makes the playlist. Or fuck that, just as long as the indy gets *credit* for getting it on the playlist. Maybe the record would have made it anyway, maybe the indy couldn't have kept it off the playlist if he'd tried. But it's gotten so bad that he gets a 'fee' for every record. New song by Gabriella? Guaranteed smash, right? The record companies still pay the promo fee."

"So where do Johnny Curtis and Eighty-Six-X fit into all this?" asked Devlin. "He didn't pick his own songs, the music director did. And he's got you, a producer. Why should an indy mess with him?"

Terry started to cry.

"You asked about Johnny?" she said; sniffled, stopped her crying. "About how he was? Talented and hot and hungry and . . ."

"He'd started to change in the last few months. Johnny got nasty. His humor always had an edge to it, but it started cutting deep. He didn't care anymore who bled. He'd been highstrung; he became explosive.

"He was pushing to be more: move on, go to New York, L.A. He was good, but there were no slots open in those markets.

"He was pushing us to let him do more, too. I was the producer, in charge of and responsible for everything that went over the air in their show. Our music director, sweet kid, 25, fresh out of computer school who earned her way in here interning . . ."

"*Computer school?*"

Terry shrugged: "Minor in communications. "She's worked out fine—except she has almost no knowledge of music before 1971."

"Jesus."

"A second-generation rocker. She doesn't know its history, but she seems to understand what will sell.

"She's completely honest, but a little naive. She's a team player. She'll never buck the system. She'd no more take a bribe than tell the boss no. The first quality is why we trust her in the job, the second trait keeps her safely in it.

"Johnny . . . Johnny'd been pushing for control in the

music meetings, in deciding what got played when. Some of his arguments were mine: the jocks should have more control over what they do; he's a veteran, knew the music from being alive before there was rock 'n' roll. Since he was on the team, our music director listened to him. Especially since he pushed. Pushed hard."

"And you think he pushed because he was crooked."

She wouldn't look at him; new tears glistened in her eyes.

"Johnny wouldn't have looked at it as being *crooked*. Johnny'd started thinking it was all shit, so why not wise up and grab something for himself?

"If he could get three records a week on the playlist, that would be worth $300,000 a year to some indy. Johnny's cut—in cash or coke or whatever—would top 100 grand."

"Can you think of anybody besides an independent who had reason to kill Johnny? Who stood to profit from his death?"

She laughed.

"He didn't have many real friends. The obvious—"

"Is Gordy," said Rourke. "With Johnny, Gordy was part of a duet—and from what I understand, definitely second fiddle."

"The bounce man," said Terry. "That's what somebody here once called him. Johnny'd bounce all his bits off Gordy, make him the butt of jokes. Johnny was cool, Gordy . . . sometimes Gordy played the fool."

"That can get to be annoying fast."

"This is show business," said Terry. "Gordy might have played the part-time fool, but he had double-billing in one of the biggest acts in the country. As a solo, he'd never have gotten out of the Midwest."

"Still," argued Devlin, "Gordy might think he could make it on his own, maybe even make it bigger. And he might be real tired of being the bounce man. Did he ever complain to you about that?"

"Gordy always complains, but . . . not like that. He knew his star was hitched to Johnny."

"But if Johnny went down in some payola scandal, dragged Gordy with him . . ."

"Be serious: nobody chases white collar crooks. Snatch some lady's pocketbook, all you cops give chase. Smug somebody with pollution or pad the government contract a few million or rig the corporate business so the consumer and the taxpayers get shafted. . . . Nobody chases those crooks."

"Unless they screw up really big or really bad."

"Johnny was too clever to do that."

"Would Gordy kill Johnny to stop him from ditching him?"

"That wouldn't make any sense, would it?" said Terry.

"Murder doesn't always make sense," said the cop.

He waited a moment, then said: "How about you?"

"Me?!" She blinked, flushed. "Johnny was my friend!"

"What I meant was because of you: an exboyfriend who Johnny aced out, a current one who's jealous?"

"There's nobody like that in my past," she said. "Or present. Or foreseeable future.

"Don't you cut anybody any slack?" she asked.

Devlin shrugged his shoulders.

"Who is the indy with hooks into Johnny?" he asked.

She stared at him. Sighed.

"A man named Batelli. Fredrick Batelli. He has an office here, one in Philly."

"How do you know?"

"Know? As in court of law?" She shook her head. "I don't. But of the three indies competing for this area, he's the dirty one. I can smell *that* on him! Lately, Johnny started smelling like Batelli."

"Did he give Johnny coke? Cash? What?"

"Again, I don't know, but I think so. And something more. Johnny used to brag about big deals with smart guys that were going to get him out of Baltimore. He wouldn't say who, but those conversations smelled of Batelli. Once when Johnny gave me some coke—"

She suddenly stopped, realized what she'd just said to a cop.

"Excuse me," he said quickly, "I didn't hear what you said."

"You don't miss a thing," she told him. Smiled warily. "For you—not for the record, but for you—I decided I'm too old for such shit. If I ever wasn't, I only did it for fun. I either paid for it or got it casually from a friend. No paybacks. No playbacks."

"I believe you," he said. And he did.

"What about Batelli?" he asked; quickly added. "And what you confidentially surmise somehow?"

"Johnny got loose and bragged that Batelli was the ultimate source: high quality and no cost. Then he shut up. I

didn't want to hear about such things any more than he wanted
to tell me."

"Where can I find Batelli?"

"In the phone book: Batelli Productions. He's a legitimate
businessman in our profession."

"Sure," said Devlin.

They both shook their heads.

"Are we through?" she sighed.

She slumped in her chair, pale, drawn out. Exhausted.
Her red hair was limp against the chair's back, and she had to
force her hazel eyes to focus on him.

"For now," he said.

When he left, she was staring out her window at the
skyline.

16

Harris pulled the card from the edge of the apartment door.

Rourke used the keys they'd taken from the dead man's
pocket.

Hershel Bernstein lived in a tidy world. The news
magazine on the glass coffee table, the sofa, two easy chairs,
the end tables with their lamps—everything was symmetrical.
One wall held blown-up, framed color photographs: Baltimore's inner harbor, a neighborhood scene of three-step
marble stooped row houses. One picture showed the Orioles
playing the field before a packed Memorial Stadium. Another
photograph showed a pretty woman with short brown hair
laughing as she raced a boy about 10 years old across a green
field. Picnickers in the background were blurred, fuzzy. The
living room's opposite wall held a mythical painting of rural
America: a jovial family strolled through the green farmyard
toward the white picket fence separating the pasture from
their tidy, whitewashed home. In Hershel Bernstein's apartment, sunlight streamed through off-white curtains. The living

rooms colors were tan and yellow, a glint of chrome from the coffee table. The air was stale.

"Not my style," whispered Harris.

"Is anybody home?" Rourke called out. His words carried through the apartment. There was no echo, no response.

The detectives walked softly, spoke in hushed tones. The dining room was small, with a round table and four chairs. The kitchen was clean, with a well-stocked refrigerator and a wall phone with a message slate mounted next to it. The slate was blank.

The apartment's hall ended with four closed doors.

The first closed room was a spotless bathroom.

Behind the second door they found a photographer's darkroom with an enlarger, pans and sinks, shelves of chemicals, cabinets of paper. Three German cameras and several lenses had a cabinet of their own. The sweet smell of celluloid and the tang of developing fluids filled the room.

The third door led to a bright room of white walls. A dozen model airplanes and imaginative spacecraft hung by wires from the white ceiling. A baseball glove rested on a white desk in one corner. Half a dozen model ships sailed the ivory surface of a four-drawer wooden bureau. A pair of new black-and-white hightop sneakers poked out from beneath the bed. A reading lamp and a battered Ray Bradbury science fiction paperback waited on the bedside table.

Twenty-four pictures of a brown-haired, laughing boy covered the wall above his bed.

He had a trim frame and an eager grin. In the pictures, the boy ran in a park, played baseball, carried schoolbooks. One picture showed him staring at a chocolate ice cream cone he held inches from his nose.

In the closet, Devlin found a pair of crisp blue jeans, a black hanger, and an Oriole jacket sized for a teen-ager hanging from one of the three wall hooks. Nothing else.

"Check the drawers," he ordered Harris, nodding toward the bureau.

"Two pullovers, a sweatshirt," said the younger cop moments later.

"Not much of a kid," mumbled Rourke.

The last closed door opened into the master bedroom. The queen-sized bed faced a bureau that supported a television set. There was one chair, a walk-in closet. A framed photograph of the brown-haired woman stood next to the telephone on the nightstand. Her smile was tender.

"Do the drawers," said Rourke as he stepped into the closet.

He found half a dozen men's suits, a rack of shirts, men's shoes, ties, a shelf of sweaters. In the back of the closet, on a wooden hanger, he found a low-cut, electric blue cocktail dress. The closet contained no more women's clothing. As he pawed through the clothes, he heard Harris opening and closing drawers.

"Well?" said Rourke when he'd finished in the closet.

"Lots of men's underwear, socks, handkerchiefs, shit like that. Three of the drawers are empty.

"In that one," he said, pointing to the top drawer closest to the room's entrance, "I found two photograph albums: mostly color shots of the wife and kid, some old black-and-white pictures of people who were probably his folks, some nonsense shots.

"In the one underneath it," said Harris: "Three bras, three pair of panties. One set is black, the other two are pretty, lace. They feel new.

"And in here," said Harris, bending down, then straightening up: "Is this."

Harris held up a short, wispy black nightie.

Rourke found three thick, slick-papered magazines in the nightstand drawer. Two of the magazines were different issues of the same periodical. All three publications were famous for their pictures of naked, beautiful, buxom women between the ages of 18 and 25. The magazines were redeemed in polite circles by the fiction, cartoons, interviews, and news articles scattered among the advertisements for the expensive, brand-named fantasy life.

Rourke held one of the magazines up so Harris could see the cover.

"I have that one," said the younger detective.

Rourke didn't, but he remembered looking through it in the homicide office.

"What do you know," said Harris.

In the bathroom, they found a man's razor, extra blades, one toothbrush, a hairbrush, toothpaste and shaving cream, deodorant, aspirin, two types of cold medicine, mouthwash, an empty prescription antibiotic bottle for Hershel Bernstein, towels and washclothes hanging from racks and stacked in a lined closet.

The only trace of a woman in the bathroom was a bottle of expensive perfume. Rourke picked up the bottle, sprayed the air: a mist of roses and feminine secrets brushed the detectives, then drifted away.

"I don't like this," said Harris as they stood in the living room.

"What happened to them?" asked Harris, nodding toward the photographs of Hershel Bernstein's wife and son. "Where are they?"

17

"That might be him," said Rachel, frowning as she studied the sketch the artist held. "Hard to tell."

"Believe me, dear," said the artist, an anemic man in his late twenties, "I understand *completely*. It's Monday, the sun is barely up, and I'm trying to draw a face you saw for a few seconds from what, fifty feet?"

"You might have his nose too pug," said Rachel. "But the hair is right. It flopped over his ears. And blond or light brown . . ."

"Un-huh," said the artist. "We'll just note that. Unless you want me to do this up in color?"

"Maybe," Detective Perry told him. She stood where she could watch the door without blocking the artist's light. Rachel sat crosslegged on the bed. "We'll let you know."

"Sure," whined the artist. "Maybe when you let me know about a fee."

"Don't worry, Timmy," said Perry. "We'll take care of you."

"Hmph." He pouted.

His pencil slid over the portrait with quick strokes. He sighed.

"Well, as far as I can tell, I'm through," he told the two detectives. He frowned at Rachel.

"Unless, of course," he told her, "you'd like me to sketch you. You have such an *interesting* face."

She smiled: amused but not intrigued.

"There!" cried Timmy. "Just like that!"

"I think not today, Timmy," said Detective Susan Perry.

"Well! Then I better be going. Any objections?"

"Go ahead, Timmy" said Perry. *And remember the breaks we cut you in that drug bust, what will happen if you talk about what you did today.* The artist gathered his materials, struggled into his coat.

Timmy looked back before he left.

"Would you . . ." he started to say, talking to Rachel. He reassessed the situation, turned his remarks to Perry.

"She has such a *marvelous* face! Cheekbones, mouth. Eyes are a touch narrow, but it's a charming flaw. Naturally, I'd need to do something about that nose! Can't have it even that little bit of crooked. Would you mind if I used her? I could work it into other things, or just do an anonymous portrait. Perhaps—"

"I think not, Timmy," said Perry sternly. "You don't want anybody to see her in your work."

"Hmm," he said before he walked out the door. "Pity."

The door closed behind him. Perry walked to the window, watched the anemic man walk to his car.

"Looks like I lost another chance for immortality," said Rachel.

Perry turned, looked at the woman sitting on the bed.

"Had many?" asked the cop.

Rachel shrugged: "Maybe."

Perry sat on the bureau opposite the bed.

Wears too much makeup, thought Rachel as she studied the other woman's face. Rachel suddenly realized she was seeing two women: Susan Perry *and* her own reflection staring at her from the wall mirror rising up behind the woman cop.

Too angular, thought Perry as she met the gaze of the woman pressed against the headboard. Perry frowned: Rachel was focused on something *behind* her. Perry turned her head, found her reflection in the mirror—and behind her own image in the glass, she saw Rachel.

Perry quickly turned her eyes forward once more.

"Looks like it's going to warm up quite a bit," she said.

"Really," said Rachel.

"Yeah."

"Mind if I go for a walk?" asked the cop's charge. Her smile said she already knew the answer.

"Why don't we wait and see," answered the cop.

"I figured."

"Do you want more coffee?" asked Perry. "I can run down to the vending machine."

"No. Thanks."

Neither of them spoke for a minute.

"Do you like being a cop?" Rachel finally asked.

"Sure," said Perry. "The job isn't bad, and—"

She shrugged, as if her point might mean not much.

"Being a cop lets me be as much more than 'just a woman' as I want. If somebody questions that . . . that's their problem."

"I know what you mean," said Rachel.

I think you do, thought Perry.

"How about you?" she asked. "You been a waitress long?"

"Never longer than I have to."

"Do you like it?"

"I like life and being able to live it my way."

"Oh," said Susan. "Good."

"Mostly," said Rachel. "I plan on keeping it that way."

"So do we, Rachel," said Perry, using the other woman's name for the first time. "So do we."

"What happens now?"

"Now we wait."

"I've never been good at that."

"Then you wouldn't make a good cop!" said Perry, and both of them laughed.

"Probably not," said Rachel. She paused a moment; smiled. "Though I couldn't be any worse than some cops I've met."

Devlin tried not to stare at the swollen black eyes that dominated the face of the man sitting on his living room sofa.

"I promise you I won't let you down," said the Duck solemnly.

"I'm sure you won't," lied Devlin.

"We worked out real well last time!" insisted the Duck.

"Forget it, sergeant," said Rourke, anxious to leave the past behind and concentrate on the present.

"When the deputy commissioner called me in, I thought he was was going to fire me." The Duck shook his head. "But then he assigned me to you. I couldn't believe my luck!"

"I know what you mean," said Devlin. "Have you told anybody?"

"No sir! The D.C. said this was secret."

"It is. If anybody asks what you're doing, you're running errands for the D.C. You must never—repeat, never mention that you're working with me, tell anyone what you're doing. Never mention the other detectives or what you see."

"Nobody listens to me anyway," said the Duck.

"Good," said Rourke.

"What are we doing?" asked the Duck.

"The Ward Building murders," said Rourke.

The Duck grinned. This was real police work!

"What do you want me to do first?" he asked.

"There are impounded cars in the department garage. The D.C. has detailed some to us, but I don't want my name or our unit—"

"What is our unit's name?" asked the Duck.

"Ah . . ." Devlin wrinkled his brow; shrugged. "We don't have one. We don't need one."

"Okay."

"Sign the cars out to the D.C.," continued Rourke. "Don't put anything else in the log. If there's any questions—"

"Nobody ever asks me questions," said the Duck. "Not about anything. And if they do, I'm a sergeant, right?"

"Right," said Rourke. He frowned. The Duck wasn't supposed to be clever. "Right."

The Duck smiled.

"If anybody pushes," continued Rourke. "Refer them to the D.C. Just get the cars."

"How many?"

"Three," said Rourke. "We could make do with two, but—"

"I'll get three," said the Duck.

"Bring them here," said Rourke. "Use taxis to shuttle back to headquarters. Have the cab drop you far enough away—"

"So nobody will see me get out," said the police sergeant.

"Right," said Rourke. He felt better about this all the

time. "Right! I'll meet you here this evening. We'll get the cars to the rest of the squad."

"Any particular cars you want?"

"Get the best ones," ordered Rourke. "Nothing too distinctive, no wrecks. And one other thing." He nodded toward the sergeant's uniform. "After you get the cars, change to plain clothes."

"Okay—I mean, yes sir!"

Devlin nodded. This was going too easily, too well.

18

An hour later, Devlin drove Captain Goldstein's family station wagon south from Baltimore on the interstate. Perry rode with him. She stared out the windows at the passing landscape of rolling brown fields and naked trees.

"Harris will be okay with her," she finally said, more to the world than to Devlin. "She doesn't want trouble."

She rearranged the pile of empty styrofoam fast food hamburger boxes on the seat between them.

"What do you think of Rachel?" asked Devlin.

"I shouldn't like her, and I do," was the fast response.

Devlin drove another quarter mile before Perry spoke again.

"I shouldn't trust her," said Perry, "and I don't."

"How is she handling it?" asked Rourke.

"How long are we going to keep her in that motel?"

"I don't know yet," said Devlin.

"Can we keep the rest of the department in the dark?"

"Let's just hope we're being overcautious."

"You counted the dead lately?" she asked.

He flicked the blinker for a righthand turn. The cruiser glided onto the exit ramp following the white arrow on the green metal sign that proclaimed, "Columbia."

For ten miles they drove on a divided highway, open

fields to each side. Giant aluminium electric relay towers linked by sagging black lines marched diagonally across their route. The towers loomed above empty trees. The divided highway became a two-lane paved road; the trees closed in. Signs dictated a speed limit, routes, declared a bike path, warned of children and other livestock. The road curved through low hills. Clusters of buildings appeared at convenient intervals. They passed a sprawling concrete complex of offices; a nicely dressed mother younger than either Perry or Rourke pushed a baby stroller through a parking lot filled with sensible automobiles.

"I always get lost when I come out here," said Perry.

"I never come out here," said Rourke.

One sign told them they'd driven into the city of Columbia; a second said that within that city they'd entered the village of Wilde Lake. They ignored the arrow labeled Recreational Complex, turned right on Thicket Lane into a subdivision called Bryant Woods. Rourke turned onto the road named Open Sky Lane, followed its elliptical path past dozens of tan brick four-plexes with neatly trimmed, dormant lawns, chipped wood paths, and tidy sidewalks. They drove past a house with a rusting red Jeep in its driveway, past the Volkswagen station wagon with a bike rack mounted on the roof, past the house where a beach ball lay next to a puddle of melting snow.

Perry nodded: "There's number 7402."

They parked, left their overcoats in the car. The air smelled damp, cool, blue with a hint of green.

"Supposed to stay warm," said Perry as they walked toward the house.

"Weird winter," said Rourke as he rang the doorbell.

From inside the house came the sound of scampering children's feet, then a firmer step. A pretty woman in short blond hair, bright pastel skirt and sweater opened the door.

Devlin held his badge up.

"Mrs. Maxwell?" he said.

"No," answered the woman. Her lips twitched. "Come in."

The woman led them to a small dining nook where three other women sat around a blond wood table, china cups and saucers before them, a flowered china pot in the table's center. The house smelled of coffee and baked ham.

"Marge," said the woman who'd answered the door, "it's the police."

A woman with short brown hair and a pale face started to rise. She wore a dark blue dress. The older woman seated to her left stayed her with a hand on her arm.

"I'll go with you, Marge," said the older woman.

"No, Mother," answered Marge, gently pressing the older woman's hand, "I'll be okay."

"Me too," said a teenaged girl in blue jeans and blouse. Her lower lip quivered.

"This is my daughter, officers," said Marge. "Jeneene."

"Please?!" begged the girl.

"Do you mind?" Marge's look pleaded more than her words.

"This time it's fine," said Devlin.

Two small boys poked their heads out from behind the stairs.

"Mike! Tommy!" called the woman who'd let them in. "Go back and play in the front room!"

The children ran away, giggling.

"I'm sorry," said Marge as she approached the two police officers, "Let me introduce you. That's my mother, and you met my neighbor Margaret at the door. Those are her boys. They're always . . ."

Her smile froze. She shook her head, looked away. She crossed her arms and hugged herself. Jeneene put her arm around her mother, laid her head on her shoulder.

"It's okay, Mom," she whispered, held back her sniffles.

"Do you want some coffee, or . . ." said Marge.

"No, thank you," said Perry.

"My, I'm . . . I'm sorry the house is in such a state!" Her arm swung wide to indicate the immaculate rooms. "I . . . I didn't even have a black dress."

"That's okay," said Perry.

"Why . . . Why don't we go up to Peter's studio?" said Marge. "That's where he . . . We'll be private up there."

Peter Maxwell's studio was a renovated attic with an A-frame roof and a skylight. Sketches and paintings covered the walls. Devlin recognized Jeneene's features in one drawing taped to the sloping roofs, a wistful, swirling, blue-toned caricature. A framed, color sketch of a young, happy Marge sat on the counter. Her face dominated the sketch, with the lines of her body undefined on the faded paper. The painting implied Marge was nude. She was dressed in a second drawing, and much older. This sketch dangled from the ceiling on two strips of black electrician's tape. In it, she stood in an empty room wearing a smock that hid her body. Her left arm angled across her breasts; that hand cupped her shoulder. Her right arm hung limply at her side, her hand hidden in the folds of the smock. Her expression was blank.

Crumpled sheets of paper spilled onto the studio floor from a garbage can. Boxes and bottles, brushes, pens, pencils, stylus knives sat on sagging shelves. A stack of newspapers leaned against one wall, a pile of magazines made a mountain in a corner. The easel held a blank sheet of paper. The studio smelled of paint and ink, aging newsprint, and dried sweat.

Marge sat in a ragged easy chair; Jeneene perched beside her on the arm. Devlin and Perry pulled two battered chairs close to the wife and daughter.

"We're sorry about Mr. Maxwell," said Devlin.

"Thank you," said the wife.

"Thank you," said the daughter.

"We have to ask you some questions," said Perry.

"We understand," answered Marge.

"First of all," said Devlin, "what did your husband do? Was he an artist?"

"He started out that way," said Marge. "He'd always drawn, even as a little boy. He had these visions, these dreams. Passion. And talent, you can see, he had such talent!"

"Yes," agreed Devlin, making a show of scanning the prints hanging around him. "I can see that."

"Peter didn't finish college," said his wife. "Two years at the Institute for Fine Arts in Baltimore. He sold a few prints, a few paintings, mostly to friends. He had so much talent, but . . .

"We got married in 1964, when we were both 20. We met at the Art Institute. I worked there as a secretary, took a few classes.

"Peter quit school to make money as a graphic artist. After three years, he and two other graphic artists formed their own company. We're far from rich, but we've quit worrying about pennies. I stopped working. The company employs 14 people now. Ten more artists. Peter is vice-president. He spends his time running the business. His art, he does at home."

She paused.

"He was only 41," she said.

"Did he know any of the other victims?" asked Perry.

"I don't think so. You might want to ask Harry Williams."

"Who?" asked Perry as she wrote the name in her notebook.

"Harry was Peter's best friend. He formed the company with Peter. He handles marketing."

"Do you know if your husband had any enemies?" asked Devlin.

"None," said the wife. "Nobody had any reason to hate him."

"Disgruntled employees?" asked Perry. "People he'd fired?"

"No, but you better ask Harry that, too. He knows."

"Mrs. Maxwell," said Devlin, "had your husband acted strangely at all—worried or nervous?"

She frowned; Devlin sensed her annoyance at his question.

"No, he . . . Well, he'd been working extremely hard. Long hours. Sometimes he'd get home around midnight, go in on . . ." She paused, sighed. "Like two days ago. Go in on Saturdays."

"But no mention of trouble."

"No, not at all. I tried to think of that, when . . . After.

"There was nothing wrong with him!" she said. "Except he was tired from working so much. He told me. I was worried about him, he'd withdrawn so . . . tired."

Tears formed in her eyes, ran down her cheeks.

"Even he noticed it," she said. "He had a complete physical. Perfect health. He started working out, running. He'd been quite an athlete in high school. Basketball. Some noons he and Harry played at the Y with some lawyers."

She laughed.

"Peter and Harry used to talk about how a lot of those guys play like it's the NBA Championships," she said. "All the dreams that never could be. That fascinated them."

She shook her head.

"Maybe this is dumb . . ." she began; stopped.

"No," encouraged Perry. "Don't worry about it."

"We got a call yesterday," said the wife, "from our insurance agent. Peter—he never told me, that was the first I knew about it!—he increased our life insurance policy. By a lot. I . . . we get half a million dollars."

The daughter looked at her mother, but said nothing.

"I don't know why he did it!" said the wife. "When we found out . . . My mother wanted me to tell you because . . . because she was afraid you'd find out, then think that I . . ."

"You did the right thing," said Devlin. "When did the insurance agent say Peter had changed his policy?"

"About a month ago."

"And what was his doctor's name? The one who gave him a clean bill of health?"

She told them.

"Had your husband changed at all lately?" Rourke asked again.

"Well," she said. She blushed deeply. Glanced up at her daughter—who returned her glance with a frown.

"Well . . ." said the mother again.

"Jeneene," said Devlin quickly, "this might take longer than we thought. Why don't you show Detective Perry—"

"I'm not leaving," said the daughter firmly. "You can't make me go. I'm not some kid you can trick. I've got a right to hear this."

"Would it be more comfortable for you, Mrs. Maxwell, if we were alone?" said Perry, ignoring the daughter's assertion.

Jeneene tightened her grip on her mother's shoulder.

Marge looked up at her daughter; smiled, patted her hand.

"No," she said, "I don't want my daughter to go away."

"You asked me if Peter had changed," she said. Blushed again. "I couldn't think of any *bad* changes. But good ones . . ."

Her voice trailed off. She smiled, slow and sweet like the girl he'd painted nude years ago.

"Peter . . . had became more amorous lately. I mean, *much* more amorous than he had been in a long time. We were like most couples married almost twenty years. Regular but not . . . but . . . We were . . . good. Real good," she insisted. "But lately, he'd become . . ."

She shook her head, smiled again.

"*Much* more amorous."

"Did, ah . . ." said Devlin. "Did you ask him why?"

"Why would I be so foolish to ask questions?" she said. "I'm 41 too. There's no novelty in me for him anymore. I'm old, not sexy."

"Mom!" pleaded the daughter, "Mom, don't! You're pretty! He loves you, you. . . . Don't talk like that about yourself!"

The mother patted her teenage daughter's hand: *Someday you'll understand.*

"Maybe it was from all his working out," said the wife. "I don't know. I don't care. All that attention, made me feel so . . . worthwhile, so good." She laughed. "And happy!"

"Did you notice anything new or changed about your Dad?" Devlin asked Jeneene.

She shook her head; suddenly frowned, said, "He started reading my *Rolling Stones.*"

"We got her that magazine subscription for her birthday," said her mother. "Peter loved old rock 'n' roll, but the new stuff . . ."

"He brought some new albums," said Jeneene.

"I didn't know that," said her mother, staring at her.

"He said they were for me."

"Well," smiled the Mom. "See?"

"But he'd play them up here," she said, nodding to a battered record player. "And he'd read my *Rolling Stone.*"

"That was probably just so he could talk about them with you," said the mother. An edge entered her words.

"But he never did," said Jeneene. "He pretended he wasn't doing all that."

Mother and daughter stared at each other.

"Jeneene," said Perry, "was there anything else?"

The teenager thought for a full minute. Her face changed to a little girl's again, and she shook her head, looked to the floor.

"Marge," said Devlin, passing her a piece of paper, "this is a standard form. It authorizes us to look around, have the lab team go over your husband's car. We towed it to our garage, but before we release it to you, we want to go over it. Just in case."

"You mean search? The car?"

"And maybe the house," said Devlin. "Though I don't think that part will be necessary."

"What . . . What do you want me to do with it?" asked Marge.

"We'd appreciate it if you'd sign it," said the police lieutenant.

"What if I don't?"

"Certainly," said Rourke, "if you want to talk with your lawyer first . . . We understand and we respect your rights, but it would speed things up to go through other channels."

"You mean you'd get search warrants. Search everything anyway."

"Yes," said Devlin.

"I've got nothing to hide," she said. "*We've* got nothing to hide. Not me or Jeneene or . . . or Peter."

She scrawled her name on the appropriate blank.

"There's one other matter we'd like to clear up," said Devlin. "Does the number 389 mean anything to you? Either of you?"

The girl shook her head.

"What?" asked the widow.

"The number 389," said Devlin. "Perhaps as part of a bigger number."

"I don't understand," said Marge.

"Peter had that number written on a piece of paper folded in his wallet," said Rourke. "The paper was smeared. Much of what was written on it is illegible. The lab is trying, but—"

"Lieutenant, this doesn't make any sense," said Marge.

"It's probably nothing," said Rourke, "but we like to know everything. It could be a safety deposit box number, an address."

"We don't have a safety deposit box," she said. "And . . . Those numbers mean nothing to me. I don't know anything about a slip of paper in my husband's wallet."

"Don't worry about it," said Rourke. His voice was soothing. "This may be one of those obscure details in a person's life that makes no sense. It's probably nothing. We see these things all the time."

"Of course," she said. Her voice was distant, and for the first time haunted by doubt.

"Of course," she said again. Insisted. "It's nothing."

19

There's nothing to worry about, Liam told himself as his elevator dropped to the basement. *You're doing your job.*

And you can do it! he argued to the doubts gnawing at his mind. *These are new days. You can do it!*

The elevator shuddered, stopped. The doors slid open.

The Baltimore police headquarters's basement is part parking garage, part maintenance shops, part storage. Cruisers filled numbered slots along the walls. A dozen civilian vehicles—a maroon van, a brown Jaguar sedan, a black Corvette, less exotic machines—were also parked in that concrete cavern. Liam walked through the civilian cars, his eyes fixed on the green door next to two drink vending machines. A cruiser with its hood yawning open waited in a work bay nearby.

The green door led the Duck into the radio repair unit, where a fellow sergeant presided behind a counter. Two technicians hunched over tables behind the counter, laboring over broken radio units. All through the office were shelves of tubes and wires, electronic equipment. The air smelled of rubber and soldering irons.

"Good afternoon," said Liam as he entered.

The two technicians looked up, fixated on the Duck's black eyes. The sergeant who presided over the garage and the radio repair unit stared, too, as did two uniformed cops he'd been joking with.

The first uniformed cop was Joshua Jones. J.J. for short.

J.J.'s partner was Matt Davis: he'd walked off a movie poster—six-foot-one, ruggedly trim, immaculate uniform, blond hair, classic Nordic features, and perfect teeth.

"Hey, ah . . ." said the sergeant behind the counter, "Yeah. How you doing, Du– . . . Sergeant?"

The two uniformed cops smiled.

The technicians turned back to work, stifling laughter.

"Fine," said the Duck. He heard his voice rise. If only the two beat officers would quit staring! "The deputy commissioner wants me to pick up three impounded cars."

"All at once?" said handsome Matt Davis.

Everyone in the room laughed. Everyone but the Duck. "I'll take them one at a time," he said.

"Best way," said Matt Davis.

Again, everyone but the Duck thought that was hilarious.

The counter sergeant controlled his mirth. He handed the Duck a clipboard. "Which three do you want?"

The Duck chose a Chevy sedan, a Pontiac TransAm, and a Ford compact which, according to the clipboard, had been souped up.

"Why does the D.C. want them?" asked the counter sergeant.

"I don't know," said the Duck. "He didn't tell me."

"Figures," said Matt Davis.

Everyone but the Duck smiled.

The counter sergeant handed the Duck the keys for the Ford.

"I'll be back in about half an hour for the next one," said the Duck.

"Can't wait," said Matt Davis.

Nothing happened with the Ford the Duck ferried to Devlin's.

When Liam picked up the Chevy sedan, he wondered why the two uniformed officers were still hanging around the radio repair office.

Last trip, the TransAm. The Duck noticed that all the men in the radio repair office strolled out to watch him drive it away.

The TransAm was parked nose against a concrete pillar. Liam adjusted the TransAm seat, the mirrors. He turned the ignition key. The TransAm growled to life. He moved his foot from the gas pedal to the brake, shifted the automatic transmission into reverse, turned and looked behind him.

Out the rear window, against the distant wall, he saw his police department comrades watching him over by the vending machines.

The Duck eased off the brake.

The TransAm surged backward.

Twin blasts exploded almost together, echoing through the cavernous garage, drowning out laughter from the four men.

The Duck stomped on the brake. The TransAm squealed to a halt. He whirled, saw nothing but his laughing comrades. Heart racing, he put the car in park, set the emergency brake, and stepped from the vehicle.

Sticky orange fluid spread out from beneath the TransAm's rear tires. Something the size of his wallet lay squashed in the center of the goo. He gingerly picked it up: the can was crushed, burst by the TransAm that had backed over it when it had been full:

Donald Duck orange juice.

The men shuffling by the vending machine pretended not to notice him. Especially Matt Davis.

Run away! cried his practiced heart. *It's just another time! What does it matter!? There's nothing you can do, no difference it makes. Run away! Don't make it worse. Run away!*

"I'm a sergeant," the Duck whispered, so quietly no one heard him. "A Baltimore police sergeant."

He stood as straight as he could, walked as steadily as possible. He carried the crushed Donald Duck orange juice can between his thumb and forefinger.

The four men all watched him. Now *they* were nervous. Liam sensed that. Liked it.

He stopped two steps shy of handsome Matt Davis. The young cop wasn't *worried*: he was dealing with the Duck.

The red-headed giant cop tossed the crushed can to Davis—who caught it easily. Sticky juice trickled down Davis's hand; orange flecks hit his freshly laundered white shirt.

"There's a $25 fine for littering public property," said Sergeant Liam McKinnon, staring straight into Matt Davis's startled blue eyes. "Find out who made this mess, give them a ticket."

"Wha . . . What?!" said Davis.

"I'm a Baltimore police sergeant," said the Duck. "You're an on-duty officer. Littering is a crime. I've given you an order. Let me know who you bust."

He turned, forced his hands not to tremble. He walked proudly to the car; slowly, carefully backed it around. Drove out of the basement, leaving five astonished men in his wake.

Liam felt wonderful.

20

An hour after leaving Columbia, Rourke rang the doorbell on the modest Baltimore townhouse. The Oriental man who opened the door had gray wispy hair and tan skin. He wore a black suit, white shirt, black tie, and an aura of dignified grief.

"I'm looking for the home of Le-Lan Nguyen," said Rourke.

"Le-Lan? Yes."

"I'm Detective Lieutenant Devlin Rourke. This is Detective Susan Perry, and . . ."

"Parlez-vous français?" said the Oriental gentleman.

"Excuse me?" said Rourke, who recognized the phrase from high school.

"S'il vous plaît, je n'aime pas parler anglais. Je ne peux pas bien."

"I'm afraid . . ." began Rourke.

"Manh-Hung!" yelled the gentleman.

He stepped aside, swept his hand toward the house's interior. The two police officers glanced at each other, obeyed his gesture.

"Manh-Hung!" yelled the old man again.

The globe spun as Devlin walked into the man's home; he felt unsure of where his feet stood.

A yard-tall photograph of the Eiffel Tower delicately framed with gold-painted wood dominated the entryway. The cars in the sepia-tinted, black-and-white picture dated from before World War II, the fashions worn by the pedestrians implied the 1930s. The gendarme's uniform was timeless.

In the landscape painting above the mantel, the sea cliffs,

pine trees and white beach implied a distant Eastern shore. A dozen worn snapshots stood watch on the mantel, carefully preserved behind glass. A planter of bamboo stood in one corner. An alcove was scooped out of another wall; in it, lit by electric candles, was a dark wood pedestal for a serene Buddha. Two issues of *Paris Match* sat on the polished cherry wood coffee table.

The rumble of feet descending stairs preceded the entrance of a young Oriental man dressed in gray slacks and a blue shirt. He was handsome, with short black hair and black wire-rimmed glasses. He and the old man exchanged rapid-fire French and Vietnamese. Somewhere upstairs, Devlin heard faint sobbing.

The boy turned to them.

"I am Manh-Hung Nguyen," said the boy. His eyes were bloodshot. "You are police officers?"

"Yes," answered Devlin. The boy glanced at their badges. The old man stared straight ahead.

"Please," said the youth, "be seated."

Devlin glanced down a hallway, saw a calendar hanging on the kitchen wall. The days of the month hung below a sunset photo of men scrambling on sampans tied up to a dock.

"May I offer you tea?" asked Manh-Hung after Rourke and Perry were settled on the couch. Only when they were seated did the old man lower himself into an easy chair. The young man remained standing.

"Thank you, no," said Rourke. Susan shook her head.

"You are here about Le-Lan's murder, right?" said the youth.

"Yes, Le-Lan Nguyen," said Perry.

"She was my sister."

"I'm—We're sorry," said Rourke.

"Neither of you speaks French," said the boy.

"No," said Perry, "we don't."

"My father understands some English, but he prefers always to speak French. Perhaps if one of you spoke Vietnamese. . . . I must act as translator."

"You speak French?" asked Susan.

"Of course."

"And Vietnamese? Your English is terrific?!"

"Thank you. My family came to America when I was

seven. From Saigon. We escaped three days before the city fell. April 27, 1974."

"Are you still in school . . . Mah—Mah—"

"Manh-*Hung*. I will graduate from high school this spring, then go to Boston."

At "Boston," the old man brightened, barked a command.

"To Harvard," said Manh-Hung. "On scholarship."

"That's wonderful!" said Susan. "Congratulations!"

The scholar shrugged.

"Is your mother . . ." said Susan.

"Please, could you not talk to her? Father would tell her what to say anyway."

"We might not need to bother her," said Rourke. "Not if we can find what we need to know from you and your father."

The father spoke another order—this one in Vietnamese.

"You may begin your questions now," said the son.

Rourke and Perry glanced at each other.

"First of all," said Rourke, speaking slowly, "we want to express our condolences. She must have been a wonderful girl."

Manh-Hung spoke to his father in French and received a reply in the same language. So it went during the interview, although occasionally father and son switched from French to Vietnamese.

"We thank you," said Manh-Hung. As he spoke, the father nodded. "My father said that her name, Le-Lan, means Tear of the Orchid."

"That's—" said Susan.

"What does your father do?" asked Rourke. "What is his occupation here in Baltimore?"

"My father is a manager at a small printing plant."

"Has he always done that?"

"In Vietnam, he was vice-president of a manufacturing firm with offices in three Vietnamese cities, Bangkok, and Marseilles."

"Was he in the army? The government?"

"My father prefers not to deal with political matters. He sees them as a source of anguish."

"He's right," said Rourke. "How about the rest of your family? Any political involvement?"

The boy hesitated before answering. "No."

"Not Le-Lan? Not you?"

"My sister was 14 when we fled Vietnam. She had nothing to do with politics."

"How about politics here?"

"No," answered the father. "Rien. Jamais."

Why did you answer for the boy? wondered Devlin.

"You know, Manh-Hung,"said Rourke. "My questions are for you, too. You can translate for your father *and* answer for yourself. I'd appreciate your point of view, your information."

The son stared at the policeman, said nothing.

The father spoke in French.

Manh-Hung answered him, then turned to Rourke:

"My father's answers will cover our family's point of view."

"Where do you go to high school?" asked Rourke.

The boy told him.

The old man frowned.

"Can you tell me—either of you—if Le-Lan had any enemies? Who you think might have killed her or wanted her dead?"

"What do you know of her?" asked her brother after a long discussion with his father. He made the question rhetorical, said:

"Le-Lan was proud, a survivor. A hard worker. She finished high school, went to college in Baltimore. She went to work for that office supply firm, stayed at home, and helped with our family expenses. We pay double mortgage and soon will own this home."

The son smiled.

"My sister took business in college, tried to convince my father that we were losing tax advantages by paying off our house as quickly as possible. But my father does not wish to owe banks. It was a disagreement they had."

"Did they have many?" asked Perry.

"He was her father," said the son. His expression said that answer was sufficient.

"Has your family been having money difficulties?" asked Rourke.

"No," said the son.

"How about Le-Lan?"

"Excuse me?" said the brother, frowning at Rourke's question.

"Her finances," said Rourke. "Was she having trouble?"

The men of the family had a brief discussion.

"No," answered the boy.

"No money troubles? No unusual money habits?"

The father asked the son a question.

"What do you mean, 'unusual money habits'? Why?"

"In a moment," said Rourke. He was tired of the control this family exerted over his interrogation of them. "Was she still contributing her share? Was she spending more than usual? Had she been hoarding money or had money you expected to see—"

"Slower please," asked the son.

He and the father exchanged many sentences in careful French. The father seemed puzzled.

Said the son, "Le-Lan was doing nothing unusual with money."

"What about her having enemies," said Rourke. "Somebody who wanted to see her dead. Perhaps someone who hated the family, hated your father. Anybody who didn't like her, anybody with a violent streak in them? Resentful coworkers? Any boyfriends, current or ex?"

The boy stared at the policemen for a long time. He sighed, turned and spoke with his father.

"We understand you are trying to help," the son told them. "We do not harbor any ill will for any rudeness of your questions."

Rourke glared at the old man whose face was stone.

"My father wants me to emphasize to you that Le-Lan had no enemies. She was a good girl."

"Good girls have enemies too."

"My father says Le-Lan didn't."

But what do you think? wondered Rourke.

"Who does your father think killed her?" he asked.

The family members had a brief exchange.

"My father says America is a violent country. Destiny decided, he says. He says that probably some crazed American on drugs shot all the people in the elevator and that Le-Lan's time on earth in this life ended as it was due."

"And your father says Le-Lan had no enemies?"

The son shrugged.

"Whoever killed Le-Lan did so without knowing her or having any reason other than destiny."

"What do you think, Manh-Hung?" asked Susan.

"My sister is dead."

The unblinking eyes behind his glasses seemed not so young.

"Back to money," said Rourke. "Your sister had $500 in cash hidden on her person. In an envelope."

The boy blinked; quickly told his father.

"What? . . . My father wants to know why."

"So do we. And where it came from. And what it was for."

Again the two family members conversed in rapid French.

"We don't know," the son said simply. "That is the truth."

What isn't? wondered Rourke.

Father said something to son, who in turn asked Rourke, "What more is it you need to know?"

"Who were Le-Lan's friends in the Vietnamese community?"

The son smiled; didn't bother to translate before replying.

"They would tell you nothing."

Rourke believed him.

"American friends?" he asked.

"We are all American," said the young man. "Do you wish to see our citizenship papers?"

"I meant—"

"I know what you meant," said the son. He shook his head. "I'm sorry. I didn't mean to . . ."

"My sister knew the people at work. But none of them were truly her friends, though they all liked her. She had . . . A man at work liked her, gave her a scarf for a Christmas present. We are Buddhist. He never asked her out. He knew she would have told him no."

"Why?" asked Susan.

"She felt he could never understand her."

"Because she was Vietnamese?" asked Rourke.

"Because he did not grow up with death. When Le-Lan was 10, she and her best friend walked home from school through a market square, past a parked bicycle. The bicycle was a bomb. Exploded and blew the arms and head off her friend, knocked Le-Lan to the gutter, and drenched her white dress with her friend's blood. This man could never understand that. Le-Lan felt merging their lives could not work."

After a pause, Devlin asked, "How did he feel about that?"

"He still hoped," said her brother.

"What's his name?"

Manh-Hung told them, said, "But he could not have done this."

"Besides this man, who else can we talk to about her?" asked Susan.

"Perhaps your mother . . ." said Rourke.

"No!" interrupted her son. "She is not so . . . *accepting* of fate as my father. He cries on the inside. She is in no shape to discuss another tragedy with strangers."

"I hope she won't need to," said Rourke evenly.

Those not so young eyes stared back at him.

The father issued a command in French.

"My father wishes to know how else we may be of help to you."

Rourke and Perry looked at each other.

"Tell your father," said Rourke, certain that the old man understood him, "to think hard about how he can help us. We understand his grief, respect his privacy, but we owe Le-Lan all we can do to catch her killer. We all owe her that."

"Yes," said the son.

"Don't you need to translate that?" asked Rourke.

"I can tell him later. Now, if there is nothing else . . ."

Rourke looked at Perry. They stood.

"What's that?" said Rourke as they walked to the door.

He pointed to what looked like a checkerboard on a table in the corner of the living room. The squares were red and black; the pieces round, flat, one group white, one black, with gold-leaf Oriental characters painted on all the tops. Instead of being centered in the board's squares, the pieces sat on the intersections of the lines.

"A Vietnamese chess set," said Manh-Hung. "Similar to Western chess. But our pieces move on the lines. We have cannons, too. The general—the king—must always stay in his fort. And there is a river. On their home side, the soldiers— the pawns—have little power, can only move slowly forward. Once they cross the river, they become more powerful, can move other directions. But they can never go back across the river."

Devlin looked at the boy who would go to Harvard.

"There's one thing you must do for us," said Rourke. He spoke slowly, carefully. "We do not wish to trouble your father. We have some things in the car we think may belong to Le-

Lan, and we wish you to identify them. Will you come with us now please?"

The boy looked back; nodded.

"Manh-Hung!" snapped the father.

Father and son argued briefly in French, a discussion that ended when the boy said, "Mais c'est poli."

Said Rourke: "We can get you out of school to help—if it's not convenient now."

The father glared at the policemen. Spit a few words toward them.

"My father bids you goodbye and thanks you for your efforts to help us."

"He's welcome," said Rourke, returning the old man's glare.

"I'll just grab my jacket," said Manh-Hung.

"Where are these things of my sister's?" asked Manh-Hung. He sat in the front seat of the policemen's car. The woman sat behind him. The cop behind the wheel answered.

"We want you to identify her life," said Rourke.

"Are you trying to be a cryptic Oriental?" said Manh-Hung.

"This is America, Manh-Hung. You're an American. Want me to show you your citizenship papers? You've got responsibilities."

The young man's smooth mask twisted into a face of pain. A tear rolled down his cheek. He shook his head and wiped the tear away.

"We want to get her killer, Manh-Hung," said Susan. "That's all we want to do."

"We want to talk to you without your father keeping his fist wrapped around your words," said Rourke. "We need you to tell us everything you can. That's why you came out, too."

"He'll know," said the son, looking back to the house.

"Yes," said Rourke.

"My father." The son shook his head.

"Do you know what Saigon was? Either of you? That name now without a city? Saigon was a city of dreamers, a city of dreams. Thousands of years as a colony, an empire of a despot or a foreigner or his lackies. So the city became a city of dreamers.

"My father, many like him. Obsessed by France, their

long-gone elegant master. All good things in life are French, and all that is French must be good. Paris is their Mecca. Paris, that sparkling city that closed its doors to us. When we fled, we were forced to emigrate to the last master, America. Richer, but not so elegant.

"My father understands English. He could speak it, but he chooses French. Even in Saigon, in our home, French was spoken. Here, he and his friends smoke French cigarettes, pretend they are sophisticated. But they live in a city of dreams."

"What is it you're trying to hide?" asked Susan. "What is it you're afraid of? What was Le-Lan afraid of?"

"Hah!" Manh-Hung shook his head. "What is there not to be afraid of?

"Life," said Rourke.

"Tell us about Le-Lan," coaxed Susan.

"Le-Lan . . . Chaos shaped her. Fleeing from Vietnam. The refugee camps. She never felt completely safe. Always be ready, she'd tell me. Just in case. Like father, she never trusted banks. They can fail, she'd tell me. Be closed. That $500? If we had to run again, she would need money. That's what I think that $500 was."

"Manh-Hung," said Rourke, "who killed Le-Lan?"

"She was just another one who died."

"What about enemies?" asked Susan.

"They are everywhere."

"Start with Baltimore," said Rourke.

"No," said the boy. "We are emigrants. Nothing ever starts with where we are. Instead, it's where we are from.

"What do you know of what the American press calls the Vietnamese Mafia?"

"Christ," said Susan, "I barely know about the American Mafia."

"Vietnam has a tradition of gangs," said Manh-Hung. "Gangs used by every government to help run the country. Sometimes there was little difference between the gang and the government. You people never understood that *enough*. You always tried to play our game with your rules and definitions, and you always tried to cheat. No wonder you came away from our land so confused and bloody. No wonder you helped us destroy ourselves.

"Not only good people escaped the Communists. Gang-

sters came over too. And there are youth gangs, with names
like Parachutists, Frogmen—macho names for a war most of
them barely remember. Older men, some who were gangsters
before, with the Binh Xuyen, the Hoa Hao—"

"What the hell are they?" Rourke said and Susan asked
the boy to spell the words.

"Originally, paramilitary sects. Sometimes religious.
Sometimes the original group is innocent. But renegades steal
the name. America worked with them, helped make them
strong. Now they are here. To show their gratitude and how
well they learned their lessons.

"Youth gangs are different. They were born in a society
where gangs are woven into the cloth. They are growing up in
the country of Jesse James and Al Capone and TV. The
Godfather."

"Is there a Vietnamese Mafia here in Baltimore?" said
Rourke.

"You . . ." The boy's smile was weak. "*We* Americans,
always looking for a simple answer. There are so few such
answers."

"Try," said Rourke.

"There is a group, a gang . . ."

"And they're tied to your sister?" asked Susan.

"The hell with you!" said Manh-Hung. But he sat still.
Sighed.

"I'm sorry," he said. "My sister is dead and I don't know
how or what to be. I can't be like my father and cry only on the
inside and live in dreams of a magic city of elegant light. I can't
be like an American, cry and beat my breast, and rage
and . . . I'm stuck in between, and I don't know how to act."

"Just be yourself," said Rourke.

"Whoever that is," repeated Manh-Hung.

He cried softly. Devlin passed him his handkerchief. The
boy blew his nose.

"This is the river, you know?" said the son. "My father is
in his house. When I came out to talk to you, I crossed the
river."

"Everybody has to sometime," said Rourke.

"Yes, but they at least know what country they're in. Me,
Le-Lan . . . We only know where we aren't."

"Let me tell you what Le-Lan opposed.

"There are groups of American Vietnamese still fighting

that long lost war. They collect money, have newsletters, make speeches, sometimes buy guns and try to smuggle them to those still trapped in Vietnam who might be willing to fight the Communist regime.

"Some groups pretend to be such organizations, but are only gangs. They demand money from all the Vietnamese citizens to continue the struggle. But the money only feeds the gang. Sometimes the pretense is so transparent no one believes it. But most pay. First, if you do not give money to every crusader who claims to fight the Communists, then they brand you as Communist. Second, these are ruthless men. People are afraid of them."

"Extortion," said Rourke. "Plain and simple."

"Perhaps not plain, perhaps not simple," said Manh-Hung, "but extortion. Even if the crusaders are not gangsters, the pressure to pay is unfair.

"That is not all. Store owners pay the group to avoid robberies. And they rob. In other cities, prostitution. Drugs.

"We are emigrants. No emigrant calls the police. They believe they should avoid the shame, the stigma. America might conclude there are Vietnamese gangsters—"

"But there are!" said Susan.

"Precisely," said the youth. "But if we don't deny it, then people may think we are gangsters because we too are Vietnamese.

"It's not logical," said Manh-Hung. 'My sister said rationality doesn't always matter."

"She's right," said Rourke. "So she fought them."

The brother shrugged.

"She spoke out to our family, our friends. In our small community, such actions qualified as major opposition. She was not the only one, but because she was a woman, people remembered her. She fought to keep father from 'contributing.' She swore they would get no money she earned. He claimed it was family money, and he was the head of the family, so he would decide."

"Did you pay?"

"No," said Manh-Hung. He frowned. "Not yet."

"Do you think these gangsters shot Le-Lan?" asked Rourke.

"No," said the boy. "She was not worth it to them."

"Who are they?" asked Rourke.

"Is this being a fink?" asked the boy.

"It's being smart," said Rourke. "And doing the right thing—which are always the same thing."

"I wonder," said the boy.

"Who are these gangsters?" said Rourke.

"The first one is not the most important," said Manh-Hung, "only the eldest. Perhaps 40. He is half Cambodian. Lower-class. He uses both his Vietnamese name and his Cambodian name. The Vietnamese name he pronounces as if it were French."

"This is not going to be easy," said Susan, flipping over a new page in her notebook.

"That is why they will do well," said Manh-Hung. "Who among you has the patience and the ability to learn the language, the culture of the crimes? How can you beat them?"

"We can start with the names," said Rourke.

"This one, the older one: his Vietnamese name is Pol Bon, only he pronounces it as a first name, Paul. His Cambodian name is Pol-Serang. He was a river pirate, and my father says he was a member of the Bien Xinh in Saigon. He is a big man, cunning but not smart. He claims to have killed many Communists, worked for your CIA."

"You said he's not the most important one," said Rourke. "He sounds bad enough to me."

"He is a brute," said Manh-Hung. "Dangerous, but without brains. He cannot speak English well, so he can't go far in this country. Alone, he would soon meet another brute who was stronger.

"But he has a partner. A boss barely older than me.

"This man is also lower-class. My father says he was born to a man rich with children but poor in imagination. The luckless parent ran out of names. His son was born in the Year of the Pig, so that's what he named him: Pig."

The three of them laughed.

"In Vietnamese, his name is Pham Vam Hoi."

"'Hoi' is pig," said Rourke.

"Right. But he does not use that name.

"He is missing the fourth finger of his right hand, so everyone knows him by his nickname: Tu-Cut. Fourth finger cut off.

"Tu-Cut claims he lost that finger as a Ranger fighting the Viet Cong, but that is such a stupid lie only Americans believe him. He is too young to have been a Ranger. Besides, people remember him from Saigon. He hung around an American navy unit. They taught him many things—including good English. As for his finger . . . Once he got drunk, told someone he lost it in a moped accident in Saigon.

"He is handsome. Girls find him dashing, a romantic rebel."

The young man in the front seat fell silent.

"Did your sister . . ." began Rourke.

"Hah!" snorted Manh-Hung. "She thought him a snake. But I know . . . There have been others, girls raised on rock and roll and magazine pictures who mistake his . . . *charm* for something worth having, who laugh off what is true and real and . . ."

Another cloud passed over the face of the young man already deep in grief.

"Tu-Cut is smart. And greedy. A very dangerous man. With Pol-Serang backing him up, supplying the muscle, the old Bin Xuyen connections, and ways.

"They came over as boat people. There are rumors about how Pol got the boat, how it was run. They drifted here from California, so they have connections out there. They call their group The Southeast Asian Liberation Friendship League.

"But the League is just part of who they are. The real name, the one they call themselves, is Kinh-Ngu."

"Kinh-Ngu?" asked Devlin.

"The Shock."

"Nice name for a gang," said Perry.

"They're not much. As the League, they belong to a lot of other groups. For legitimacy, my sister said. Business groups, charity groups, anyone who will have them. Anyone they can fool.

"They own a bicycle shop. They call everybody, demand money. Give stickers for your window so people know you are not a Communist. We have no such sticker. My two uncles died fighting the Viet Cong, that is sticker enough. I think they steal welfare payments from old people they 'help.' One or two cowboys from our high school supposedly sell their drugs, but I doubt that is much business. They smuggle parcels to Vietnam, but they charge heavily *and* steal most of what is sent, blame the Communists. And of course, there are the games."

"What games?" asked Rourke.

"One, two nights a week, either in their rooms above the bicycle shop or at someone's apartment, they run gambling games. Either Xap Xam or Tu Sac. There is a door fee, and something is always collected 'for the cause.'"

"Of course," said Susan.

"They're not many," said Manh-Hung. "Maybe six men, Sharks."

"How well did Le-Lan know them?"

"She knew who they were, they knew who she was."

"Do you know of anybody else who might have killed Le-Lan?" asked Rourke.

"No," said Manh-Hung, "but give me a name, I find out."

"That's our job," said Rourke.

"Yes," said the brother, "I forgot. This is America, where the law takes care of you."

"Only if you take care of it," said Rourke.

"Ah. Well, no doubt I will learn more of that at Harvard."

"I wish I had wise words for you," said Rourke, "but I don't. Remember Le-Lan at her best, and that she worked hard to give you more of a chance than she got."

"You sound like my father," said the son.

"What does Manh-Hung mean?" Rourke asked.

"It's just a name."

"No it's not," said Rourke, gently. "Your father gave it to you. He'd have never named you Pig."

A shy smile shaped the boy's lips, then they were somber again.

"What does your name mean, Manh-Hung?"

The boy's whisper was bitter, embarrassed. Ashamed.

"Fierce tiger," he mumbled. "Can I go now?"

"Sure," said the cop. "And thanks. Call us if—"

"Yeah," said the kid. "Sure."

Rourke and Susan watched him walk up the sidewalk, enter the house. The door closed.

21

That Monday night, in his dark apartment, on his blue sheets, Devlin and Julia Simmons experienced exquisite sex.

After leaving Nguyen's, he and Perry had gone to the radio station, showed the police sketch to Terry, the receptionist, and Gordy Miller. They all said they didn't recognize the man in the sketch. The detectives cautioned them about disclosing information regarding police interrogations, then left.

Rourke called Julia from a pay phone after leaving the station. He apologized for not having called earlier. She accepted his apologies, warmed. She told him she was fine, busy, tired. Told him all about her problems with her secretary, her boss's latest opinions. She asked Devlin what had been going on in the world; she'd again been too busy to read a newspaper. Not much new, he told her: famine, war, fame, and fortune. Crime and corruption. The evening chill closed around him as he stood at the pay phone. He told her he had a great deal on his mind. Been busy? she asked. Yes, he said. He wanted to talk to her, wanted to see her. Told her so. I'd like to see you, too, she said. Are you busy for dinner? he'd asked. She thought not about her schedule but about her mood. No, she'd answered, she was free. They agreed to meet at their favorite cafe in Little Italy. How will you get there? she asked: Is your car fixed? Don't worry about me, he'd told her. I can make it.

All the men in the restaurant stared when Julia Simmons walked through the door. She ignored them, unbuttoned her Burberry topcoat as she marched toward the rear of the cafe where Devlin sat, his back against the wall.

Julia's chestnut hair swayed below her ears. She had a bold face with a large nose, wide lips, a smooth jaw line that wouldn't vanish under fat as time went by. Her eyes were brown. She carried a bulging briefcase. She wore a brown skirted business suit, a white blouse, and a brown bow tie. She kissed Devlin, then shrugged off the Burberry. Julia's breasts were perfect, her waist was narrow, her hips wide and taut. Clear pantyhose sheathed her sleek, strong legs. She wore expensive brown shoes with a low heel.

"Sorry I'm late," she said as she sat down, clumped her briefcase on the floor, and draped her topcoat over the chair that held his. "The newsletter artist had a fit."

"No problem," he said. "It's been one of those Mondays."

"Me too," she sighed. Her voice was a fine feminine tenor. "I even had to cut Tasha short when she called me."

Tasha was Julia's "little sister." For two years, Julia had volunteered as the troubled 10-year-old's adult companion. Julia saw Tasha at least twice a week, usually more.

Tasha had brought Devlin and Julia together. He'd volunteered to teach a class for parents and children on practical caution in a nation where child kidnappings and murders had reached epidemic proportions. In the cookies and punch reception after his presentation, Devlin was delighted to find that the woman who'd caught his eye was smart, single, and interested in him, too.

"Our Tasha," sighed Julia. "She's discovered rock 'n' roll."

Julia ordered a martini, he had Scotch and water.

She told him about the newsletter she edited, her office, her great boss, her wonderful sister with the two perfect children, the upcoming convention of public relations specialists. He unwound, half-listening.

They ordered dinner. She had fish, he had veal.

As quietly as he could, he described his last two days: the visits to the families, WBBX. He didn't tell her where Rachel was hidden.

"So what's she like?" asked Julia as the waiter placed their salads in front of them.

"Rachel?" replied Devlin, tucking his napkin in his lap. "I haven't had a chance to get to know her."

"Umn," answered Julia. "Will you?"

"I need to use her story," he replied.

"I've always wondered what made women fall off the cliff, become bums and bag ladies like that," said Julia.

"That's . . . that's not what she is."

"Oh," said Julia.

"Don't always look for a label," he told her.

"Umn," she said. She didn't want to discuss that topic again.

They ate dinner. Ordered coffee. Skipped dessert.

"What next?" she said as she stirred her spoon in the delicate cup. She meant Devlin's case.

"I've got some ideas," he said. Smiled straight at her. She smiled back.

They got the check.

They held hands as they left the restaurant. He led her to the Chevy sedan.

"What's this?" she asked.

"Departmental issue," he said. "Just for this case."

"Well," she said, climbing the passenger's door, sliding over the Chevy's seat; he saw a flash of her thigh. "It's closer to what you should have than your clunker."

Her Saab with a sun roof was still parked in a heated, underground garage. She had taxied to dinner.

During the drive to his place, he put his hand on her knee. The crinkly pantyhose teased his flesh. She pressed her hand on top of his.

They parked right outside his building. He found his key, unlocked the hall door with its Apartment for Rent sign. He watched her hips as she walked first up the stairs.

She dropped her overcoat on the living room couch, smiled at him, kicked off her shoes. Yellow light bathed her as it streamed through his bay windows. She strolled back toward his bedroom as he tossed his topcoat and suit jacket on the chair. He followed her, undoing his tie, unclipping his gun-heavy holster from his belt.

The gun went in the bedtable's drawer. He preferred to keep it handy; that made her nervous. As he shut the drawer, he heard the hiss of static when she pulled off her pantyhose. Her skirt lay in a heap at her feet; her white blouse was open. It floated to the floor. She wore white panties, no bra. His shirt was unbuttoned; he dropped it as he kicked off his shoes, unfastened his pants.

"I should really hang these up," she glanced down at her clothes.

"Not now," he said softly.

She walked toward him.

He dropped his pants, pushed off his underwear.

She bent over as she peeled off her panties and her breasts swayed forward, hung down.

Truly, she had magnificent breasts. They were round, looked swollen; so taut they rode out from her chest. Her huge nipples were centrally placed like two blind eyes, brown like their wide aureolas.

The thatch of brown hair between her legs was small, waxed to a proper swimsuit line.

"My socks are still on," whispered Devlin.

"Don't worry," she said; smiled. "I'll take care of that in a few minutes."

They embraced. Kissed. Lowered themselves to the bed.

He lay pressed on top of her; his legs straddled her smooth thigh.

"Why don't you get the light?" she asked.

He reached over and clicked the bed lamp off.

They held each other tightly, eagerly kissed. Devlin ran his right hand up her side, her stomach; cupped her left breast. Her nipple swelled. He kissed her cheek, her neck, her chest. Ran his tongue around her nipple, sucked it between his lips. His hand trailed down her stomach until his fingers brushed her hair line. He cupped her groin; she was wet against his palm.

She kissed his neck, his chest; took him in her hand, stroked him. They rolled on their sides. She gently pushed him over on his back, shifted down on the bed, brushed her hair away from her face. Took him in her hand again, licked him until he was completely wet; took him in her mouth, closed her lips softly but firmly around him. Devlin watched the silhouette of her head move up and down. Her tongue slid all around him, her hand held him tight. . . . He felt terrific. A minute, perhaps two, then she straddled him. Took him deep inside her. Two weeks into their affair, she'd told him it was best for her on top.

He reached up in the darkness, filled his hands with her breasts. They were wonderful. She liked him to caress them.

Once he tried talking with her about their sex life—casually, intellectually. He assured her she was not failing to satisfy him, but hinted they might enjoy some variation. She said, "You don't mean anything perverted, do you?"

Fantasies blew away. He assured her he meant nothing perverted. They never directly discussed sex again.

She moved back and forth on him with a steady rhythm, a dark shape in a dark room. Since he'd turned off the light, neither of them had spoken. Devlin kept his silence through tact. She never replied to anything he said during their lovemaking; indeed, except for quiet panting, she made no noise at all. No requests. No endearments. No words. No whimpers, and certainly no moans. Devlin, normally a vocal lover, became fearful of offending her by saying something wrong during careless passion.

Back and forth, she moved back and forth.

For some reason she always smelled—pleasantly—of orange, and never more so than when they were making love.

She was wet and warm and tight around him. She was incredibly beautiful, desirable. And she truly cared for him.

He cared for her, too. She was smart. Kind. Dependable. Stable. A good person. Beautiful.

A month earlier, cautiously, they'd decided the word *love* definitely somehow applied to their mature, sophisticated, adult relationship.

Back and forth, she moved. Faster.

However, they seldom spoke the word.

He ran his hands along her neck to her face; back to her breasts, squeezed them gently—full and heavy and soft. He rubbed his thumbs on her nipples.

She gripped him tighter with her thighs.

His mind flashed to blood on a concrete floor; Rachel; an electronic voice floating out of radios everywhere; the way a cruiser shudders as it races over Baltimore streets, blue lights pulsating; a war thousands of miles and a decade away; the flat-chested radio producer Terry; Rachel; a black gun barrel; a woman he had known years before who had screamed his name when she came. He exploded.

Julia never had an orgasm until after he had his.

She'd increased her speed, rose up and down on him now, rubbing back and forth. Faster.

He moaned; she leaned back, arched her chest forward; he rubbed her breasts, slid his hands down to grip her shifting hips.

She shuddered.

Once they went to a party, got drunk, stumbled home and made love for what seemed like hours. She told him afterward that he made her eyes roll backward in their sockets. She'd said nothing like that before or since.

He wondered where her eyes were now.

She huddled on his chest for half a minute. He guided her face to his, kissed her. She rose, ground her hips down on him once more. He slid out of her. She unstraddled him, lay beside him.

His socks were still on.

"I missed you," she said after a minute.

"I missed you, too," he told her.

The air was cool on their sweaty bodies. The smell of sex and oranges filled the bedroom. He pulled the sheet and blanket over them.

"Has it been rough for you?" she asked.

"You mean work?"

"Well, no, . . . I meant, you know, without seeing me."

"Of course it's been rough! It's been four nights!"

She kissed him. He felt her smile.

"Good," she said; sighed, settled down beside him. "So now tell me *really* how work has been."

"I've got four murdered people," he told her. "All of them ostensibly innocent citizens, each with secrets haunting them like shadows. The murderer probably came from one of those shadows."

"Which one?"

"I haven't even learned the secrets yet. Could be any one of them."

"We all have secrets," she said.

"Even you?" he asked.

"Not from you, dear," she said. Kissed him lightly.

"What about me?" he said after a silence.

"What about you?" she asked.

"Secrets," he said. "What about my secrets?"

She laughed.

"Either you've told them all to me or I've guessed them."

Both of Julia's alternatives scared Devlin.

"Except," she said, and he waited hopefully, "except for work, of course."

"Of course," he said.

She rolled on her back, settled down comfortably. Beneath the covers, their hands touched lightly.

"Your police rules," she sighed. "I'll be so glad when you're off the street."

"The street is where I live," he told her.

"Yes, Dev," she said, patting his hand. "I know. But that's changed. You're not just my cute detective sergeant anymore. You're a lieutenant. Responsible, respected. Ranked."

She yawned.

"Oh God am I tired!" she said. "There's just so much to do! Everyone knows this is a hot business city, but like my boss says, it's so underestimated."

"What do you think?" he asked.

"You know," she murmured, "you know what they say."

"All that 'they' say doesn't matter," he said.

"Dev," she said, squeezed his hand. "Please, not now."

"You're right," he said.

They lay silently for a minute.

"Lucky," she said. He heard her lick her lips in the darkness.

"Lucky what?" he asked.

"Lucky I've got those skirts and sweater in your closet. They'll go with the jacket I wore today."

She patted his hand.

"Love you," she murmured.

"I love you, too," he said; wondered what difference that made.

He listened to her breath for almost a minute.

"Julia," he said, "I feel like I've wandered into a forest. I hear beasts moving through the trees."

He paused for her to say something.

She snored, softly.

He sighed, rolled onto his right side.

Eventually, he fell asleep.

With his socks on.

22

The beast snapped a branch in the bushes off to the left; the phone rang.

Devlin's hand grabbed the receiver before he was fully awake. He knocked over the bed lamp, heard it *clump* to the floor. Julia stirred beside him in the bed, but she didn't wake.

"Yeah?" hissed Devlin into the phone, his mouth full of dry cotton. His flesh was clammy, the sheets around him sweat-soaked. The bedroom was cold.

"Turn on your radio!" yelled Harris into his ear.

"Wha . . . What?" said Devlin, fully awake.

Julia sighed in her sleep, shifted her legs, and arched her back beneath the covers.

"Turn on your radio! FM, 86!"

"It's—"

"Hurry!" shouted Harris. "I'll hold on!"

Devlin laid the receiver on the table and leapt out of bed, stumbled down the hall to the living room. Darkness still held the city. He clicked on the overhead light. His black digital wristwatch read "Tues 6:21:14 AM." Devlin flipped on the stereo receiver's power switch, spun the dial down from 99.1 to Baltimore's hottest station. Hard charging horns blared from his speakers. Seconds later, he heard a clean-voiced woman shouting her song. He shook the cobwebs from his head, felt the room's winter chill on his naked flesh. He plopped down on his couch, pressed his knees tightly together and hugged his arms across his chest as the woman sang:

I think they got your number,
I think they got your alias, . . .

Gordy Miller's disembodied voice overrode the song's ending:

"Yeah, Baltimore, we're dedicating that one to him, the killer creep out there. You can run, baby, but you can't hide. Not in our town. Not anywhere. You ambushed our man, our brother, and now the cops are going to take you out.

"That's right, a WBBX news exclusive. Our police force has solid clues and leads to the man who gunned down our Johnny Curtis and three other good people this weekend. They got a description. They got a witness. They're building their case. They're going to get the killer. Stay tuned to Eighty-Six-X. We got the inside line and we're going to give it all to you.

Devlin crossed to the stereo, spun the volume control down.

"Shit," he said into the telephone as he stared out his bay window, saw dawn turn the blackness to gray.

"I climbed out of the shower," said Harris. "Had the radio on. All of a sudden, Gordy blurts out this Eighty-Six-X exclusive: 'The cops have a live witness,' he says. 'A great—'"

"Did he say anything about the sketch?"

"No."

"Get him or that Terry on the phone right away," said Rourke. "I don't care what you say, but tell that station no more witness crap."

"Right."

"Tell that asshole Gordy not to even mention us! Tell him he can do all the mourning he wants on the air, but no more about the police or what they know or what they want or what they're doing. His show ends at 10. Meet me at the Ward Building at 9:45."

"I don't know if he'll muzzle for long."

"Do you think many people heard him?" said Rourke.

"Only most of Baltimore," said Harris.

"Shit," said Rourke again. Hung up.

The alarm on his wristwatch beeped.

"Dev?!" called Julia from the bedroom.

"It's okay, honey!" he yelled. "Hang up the phone, would you?"

He turned up the thermostat, heard his radiator's clank.

"What is it, Dev?" said Julia.

She stood at the end of the hall, a blanket off the bed wrapped over her head like a shawl. The wool covered her to midthigh; her bare legs pressed together, her naked toes curled tightly on the cold wooden floor. She shuffled a few steps closer, stopped as soon as she crossed onto the rug.

"What is it?" she asked again.

The blanket fell from her head to her shoulders. Her brown hair was tousled, her eyes sleeping, half open in the morning's soft gray tones.

"You've heard of bad Mondays?" he asked.

She nodded, her eyes opening wider.

"Well this is a terrible Tuesday." He looked out through the windows. *Only five days before the D.C.'s deadline. Two down, five to go.* "And it's barely begun."

"I'm sorry!" she said. He heard concern in her tone.

"Not your fault," he said. He tried to think, couldn't; felt like he was still in the dream forest with the beast.

"Is it an emergency?"

"Yeah," he said. Half-listening.

"Do you have to go?"

"Not that kind of emergency." He shook his head. The morning moved the dream away. "Damn!"

"What can I do?" she asked.

"Noth—Thanks, Julia," he said, noticing her completely for the first time that morning. He smiled. "There's nothing you can do. Have some coffee with me before we go."

"That won't make it better."

"Won't hurt it," he told her.

"What time is it?"

He glanced at his watch:

"Twenty-five to seven."

"It's early!"

"I was going to go check on Rachel."

"Oh," she said.

"Just needed a half hour extra. I'd have kissed you awake after I got ready, made the coffee."

"What about now?" she asked.

"Now?" he said. "Now I don't know. I guess . . . I want to talk to a prosecutor I know, but his mind won't start working for another half hour."

"You still going to try to check on Rachel?"

"I don't know," he said. "That's not the first priority anymore. Not for another couple hours, at least."

"Calling the lawyer is first?"

"Uh . . . Yeah, I guess so. I haven't had time to sort it out, but . . . Yeah, probably."

He glanced vaguely toward the kitchen and the coffeepot; the hallway leading to the shower in the bathroom.

Julia stood only inches from him, the blanket loose about her bare shoulders. She stared up at his face.

"Don't worry about it," he said again, suddenly more aware of her presence. "There's nothing you can do."

"Don't be so sure," she said, smiled.

The blanket fell from her shoulders to the floor as she put her hands on his sides, pressed against him. Must have been the cold that made her nipples so rigid. She kissed his lips. Kissed his neck.

"You'd be surprised what I can do," she said. Tilted her face up to be kissed; was.

"Julia," he said. He put his hands on her shoulders, meant to push her away. She was warm and soft.

Oranges, he thought suddenly.

She pushed her breasts against his chest, her hips against his.

"Julia . . . I . . . We . . ."

"It's not even seven," she said. She kissed his chin, his cheek.

"I . . ."

"Shhhh," she said; whispered: "Don't say anything. You don't have to do a thing."

She laughed: "Unless you want to."

She kissed his neck, his chest. Rubbed her breasts down the front of his body as she knelt. He was already excited when she took him in her hand; stirring before her tongue slid around him; erect before her lips sealed him off from the world. She pressed against his thighs, her body moving up and down as she knelt before him. He wanted to call out her name, tell her things. He slid his hands into her hair, glanced at his watch. Suddenly he wanted her desperately. The beast and the forest disappeared.

23

Devlin heard Terry as he and Harris stalked through WBBX's carpeted corridors.

"You asshole!" she yelled. Her voice boomed out from an office with "Station Manager" painted on its half-closed door. "You can't do this! You can't keep playing this up, carrying on—"

"Of course I can!" the out-of-sight Gordy Miller yelled back at her. "Nobody can stop me! I'm going to ride this all the way!"

No choice now, thought Devlin.

"It's wrong!" Terry said, then Devlin marched into the room. Harris followed, pulled the door shut.

Their entrance surprised the three people in the office. Gordy and Terry stood facing each other in front of an expensive executive desk. The man seated behind the desk was 40, handsome, wore a white shirt and a conservative tie.

"Gordon Miller?" growled Rourke. He didn't break stride, closed on the startled deejay.

"Wha . . . You know I'm . . . Hey!" he yelled as Devlin grabbed the deejay's shoulders, spun him around.

"Grab the wall!" snarled Devlin. He pushed the deejay forward; Gordy had to throw his hands forward, catch himself.

"What do you think you're doing?!" he cried. Devlin's left hand gripped the back of Gordy's neck; the detective jerked the deejay's belt, pulled his hips backward while keeping his upper torso straight.

"What is this?!" hissed Gordy. A trace of fear colored his shock, his anger.

"Officer . . ." said the man behind the desk.

"Devlin . . ." said Terry.

"You're under arrest!" said Devlin.

He kicked the deejay's feet wider apart.

"I didn't kill him!" screamed Gordy.

"My God!" bellowed the station manager. He stood up behind his desk. "What the hell is going on?!"

"No!" whispered Terry. She backed toward the window. "No!"

Devlin roughly patted down the deejay. Gordy's body trembled beneath the cop's hands.

Good, thought Rourke.

"I didn't kill him!" cried Gordy. A sob entered his tone.

"What are you . . ." said the station manager. He hesitated, picked up a telephone. Harris spoke before his finger could punch out a number.

"What do you think you're doing?" The younger detective's voice carried more warning than question in his words.

"Nothing!" said the station manager quickly, hanging up the phone, stepping back from the desk. "Nothing."

Devlin bent Gordy's right hand behind his back, slapped a handcuff on it. He straightened the deejay up, pulled his other hand down, handcuffed it to its mate behind his back, and whirled the deejay around.

"Gordon Miller," he said, "you are under arrest—"

"I didn't kill him!" pleaded Gordy, his face flushed, his mouth twisted. "Please!"

". . . for obstruction of justice, interfering with a police officer in performance of his duty, illegal release of confidential grand jury information."

"Grand jury?" whispered Terry.

"What?!" said Gordy. He blinked.

Devlin leaned until his face was only inches away from Gordy's. The deejay tried to lean away, only to discover that the cop held him by the front of his belt.

"I don't like assholes who broadcast what I'm doing on a murder case all over town!" hissed Devlin.

"I got rights!" screamed Gordy, suddenly understanding. "I got the First Amendment—"

"You got rights, all right!" yelled Devlin, shaking the deejay.

"You have the right to remain silent!" Rourke hissed. "If you should choose to give up that right, anything you say can and may be used against you in a court of law. You have the right to—"

"Please! Please!" yelled the station manager. Devlin stopped speaking. "Please!"

He took a deep breath. So did everyone else.

"Officers," said the station manager. "You can't be serious!"

"The D.A.'s checking whether we can throw your ass in jail, too!" said Rourke.

The station manager paled.

Devlin smiled into the deejay's face:

"You'll love the cellblock, asshole," he said. "You'll really rock 'n roll before you make bail."

"Officers," the station manager said again. "Please, slow down!"

"We don't have time for bullshit," said Harris.

"Okay," said the manager. "But can't we just talk about . . . about all this? Just for a minute."

"One minute!" said Devlin.

"Come on, lieutenant," said Harris. He shrugged. "Cut them a little slack."

Devlin glared at Harris; softened his face, frowned.

"Okay," he said.

"Thank you!" said the station manager to him. He looked to where Harris leaned against the soundproofed door. The manager spoke softer. "And thank you, detective."

Harris shrugged.

"Perhaps," ventured the station manager, "perhaps we should call and have our station lawyer run over here to—"

"Let's go," said Rourke, grabbing the manacled deejay's arm. Gordy winced. "You can send your lawyer downtown to pick him up."

"No lawyer!" shouted the station manager and Devlin stopped his exit motion. "No lawyer. No jail. Let's keep this low profile.

"I understand Gordy mentioned a witness on the air. I haven't listened to the tapes, but—"

"I want copies of those tapes," said Rourke.

"Anything, just . . . just wait a minute. Arresting people, pressing charges . . . We're a news organization, and these murders are big news. The public has a right—"

"He's not a reporter!" snapped Devlin.

"He most certainly is!" said the station manager.

"Could you . . . Would you loosen the handcuffs?" said Gordy.

"Gordon Miller is a police witness," said Devlin. "He did not learn what he 'reported' as a journalist. He's an involved party—witness, *suspect*. . . . He didn't shoot off his mouth to inform the public. He did it to help himself. Build up his damn ratings."

"That's not true!" said Gordy. "I care about . . . Please, won't you take the handcuffs off?"

"You're skating on extremely thin legal ice," said the station manager, his voice suddenly calm.

"Maybe," said Rourke. "Want to find out what happens as we sort it out?"

The station manager blinked.

"My hands," whined Gordy softly. "My hands."

No one spoke for 30 seconds.

"We're running out of time," said Rourke.

"Come on, lieutenant," said Harris. He nodded to the station manager. "He's trying to help."

Ten seconds later, the station manager sighed. Smiled.

"What do you want?" he said.

"We want our job done right," said Rourke.

"What do you *want*?" said the manager again.

"First, no more crap over the air—you play the tragedy for all it's worth. Get your ratings up, make your money. I don't care. But mention what the police are doing or have done and I'll bust the whole station.

"Second, nothing about this to anybody. No leaks to the press and no comment to them if they call. *No* comment. By anybody.

"Third, no bullshit. You think of any we haven't mentioned, you forget it. Keep the lid on your crap, or we'll make you eat it."

The station manager considered Devlin's words.

"You've got a deal," he said.

"Can you control him?" said Devlin, jerking his head toward Gordy Miller.

"He's no fool," said the station manager. "I can vouch for him."

"You are," said Rourke.

"And Terry . . ." began the station manager.

"She's no problem," said Rourke. "She's fine."

He didn't look at her. She stared at the tableau in front of her, her face pale and drawn. Her hands trembled at her sides.

"Please," whispered Gordy, "my hands really hurt!"

Devlin uncuffed Gordy, who moaned, held his hands before his face.

"Hey Gordy!" whispered Devlin. The deejay looked at him. "You're a very lucky citizen. Be a very smart one."

The cops left the office. Didn't speak until they were alone in the elevator.

"Nothing like standing on your dead partner to reach for the top," said Harris. "And telling the world our business as he does it."

"Did he tell the world," said Rourke, "or did he tell one somebody?"

"You really think . . ."

"I think Gordy's an ambitious man," said Rourke.

24

"We need to move her," Rourke told Harris and Perry an hour later as they sat in the motel room next to Rachel's. "Even if Miller hadn't put our shit in the streets: the maids, the desk clerks, too many eyes know about the woman in number 21 with the entourage who look like cops.

"Besides," he said, "we're about out of money."

"Paychecks come tomorrow," said Harris.

"You mean yours isn't already spent?" said Perry, shaking her head.

"We'll get the money," said Rourke. "Right now our problem is where we put her."

The detectives looked at each other.

Rourke sighed.

"Okay," said the lieutenant. "My place. Give her the bedroom. The sofa folds out, we can bunk on it."

"When do we move her?" asked Perry.

"Today." He fished in his pocket, handed her his keys. "You and Harris take her. You stay with her. Gary, go to the Nguyen service this afternoon. I'll be in Columbia at Maxwell's funeral, Goldstein will cover Bernstein's burial."

"His wife and kid still haven't shown up," said Harris. "Who claimed the body?"

"No one. The coroner called a rabbi. The guy's Jewish, should have been buried two days ago, so . . ."

"What about Johnny Curtis's funeral?" asked Perry.

"The captain will cover it, too. He's also arranged for hidden camera surveillance on all four funerals."

"What about the Duck?" asked Perry.

"You know," said Rourke, "he's changed."

"He can't have gotten any smarter," said Perry.

"Maybe not," answered Rourke, "but something's different. We can use him."

"How?" said Harris.

"Babysitting."

"That's crazy!" said Perry. "Our guy is a pro. Two of *us* might not be able to handle him. If he comes after Rachel and only the Duck is there, he'll eat them both."

"We don't have a better choice," said Rourke. He turned to Harris.

"What do you have for me?"

Harris lifted a worn suitcase from the floor, to the motel's unmade bed. He unsnapped the catches.

"There were two suitcases in the trunk of Peter Maxwell's car," he said, lifting this bag's lid. "One was a gym bag: sneakers, shorts, jock. The gym bag sat in plain view on the spare tire. This one was wedged behind a canvas tarp. You wouldn't see it if you opened the trunk—say, to fill it with groceries."

"Like his wife might have done," said Rourke.

"Exactly," said Harris. "Look what's in it."

He lifted out a long wool coat; it's cut was distinctive but old-fashioned, it's cloth a knobby gray and white tweed.

"Maxwell was wearing another coat when he was shot," said Rourke.

"Right," said Harris. "A tan overcoat from J.C. Penney's."

He laid the tweed coat on the bed. Out of the suitcase he lifted first a simple black shirt with snaps, then an old brown corduroy sports jacket, followed by a heavy tan crewneck sweater, a worn pair of green khaki pants, and finally a pair of heavy shoes.

"There's a pair of sneakers in here too," said McKee. "Black hightops. They could be for basketball."

"Why does he have a wardrobe hidden in his car trunk?" asked Perry.

Rourke shook his head.

"I don't know," said the cop in charge. "Yet."

25

"Stay here," Perry whispered.

Her left hand gestured for Harris and Rachel to flatten themselves against the hall wall. Keys dangled from the lock above the knob on the door in front of her. She stood back, turned the knob and pushed the door; her right hand waited inside her coat.

The door swung open.

Perry silently counted to 30. She stepped inside the room, quickly looked both ways: the living room was empty, the hall ran back toward the rear of the apartment.

She moved through Rourke's apartment cautiously, her hand on her gun butt. The back door was secure, the windows locked. There was no fire escape leading to his bedroom windows. The living room's bay windows were higher than the building across the street, so snipers' angles into the apartment were difficult.

"Okay," she said, and Rachel and Harris came inside. Rachel carried her own suitcase; Harris's hands were free—just in case.

"I thought I was the paranoid one," said Rachel.

"That's my profession," explained Perry with a smile.

Rachel let her eyes roam over the home of the man now in charge of her life. She took in the roll-top desk in front of the bay windows, the large black-and-white photograph of a mustang struggling through snow drifts above the couch, the stereo system on the opposite wall with shelves of records and cassettes. She glanced at a bookcase, seven shelves overflowing to a pile of paperbacks on the floor. An unplugged television sat in a corner. She nodded.

"You can tell a lot about somebody from where they live," she said, "how they live."

"What about you?" asked Perry. Her smile was friendly. Rachel shrugged.

"I guess I live here now," she said.

"Make yourself at home," said Perry. "You get the bedroom back there. We share the bathroom. It'll be awkward, but comfortable. And safe."

"That's more than I'm used to," she said.

Rachel wandered back toward the bedroom. Susan Perry followed her as if she had nothing better to do. Harris waited in the living room, stared out the windows. Bored.

In the bedroom, Rachel flipped on the ceiling light. The bed was unmade. She sniffed the air: something.

"You might want to change the sheets," said Perry. "There're probably some clean ones around here somewhere."

"I can make do," said Rachel, but she looked inside the closet.

"Well," she said a moment later. She pulled out the hem of a skirt hanging amid the shirts.

"Does our lieutenant have a secret life?" Rachel asked with a smile.

"Doesn't everybody?" said Perry, her voice picking up the other woman's humor. She moved closer, glanced at the closet, the skirt in Rachel's hand.

"He has a friend," said Perry.

"Ahhh," said Rachel, and they wandered into the bathroom.

Rachel ran her fingers down one leg of inside-out panty hose dangling from the shower curtain rod.

"Good thing he's got a friend," she told Susan. "These aren't Rourke's shade."

They laughed.

A buzzer sounded through the apartment.

"Stay here!" commanded Perry, running to the front room.

Rachel did as she was told, her heart racing. She heard Harris say, "Who is it?" into the intercom, heard a reply she couldn't understand. Heard the front door downstairs open, close. Heavy footsteps on the stairs. She couldn't stand it any longer, moved cautiously to the hall, saw Harris carefully open the door and admit a red-headed giant in a too-short topcoat and suit pants.

Perry noticed Rachel, nodded to the man who struggled valiantly to free himself from his overcoat.

"Rachel," said Perry, "this is Sergeant Liam McKinnon. He's working with us."

The giant turned toward her, a guileless smile on his face.

"What the hell happened to you?!" cried Rachel when she saw his huge black eyes.

The giant blushed.

"I ah . . ." he started, swallowed. "I had an accident."

"You should be more careful," said Rachel.

"Yes," said the giant, strangely serious and appreciative of her offhand advice, "I should."

"I got to get going," said Harris, suddenly anxious to leave.

Perry glared at the junior detective.

"Fine," she said. "Do you think you've got enough time to make it to the funeral?"

"Oh sure," he said. "Plenty of time."

He nodded his farewells, scurried out of the apartment.

Perry walked to the bay window, watched him exit the building, climb into the sedan, and speed away in the warming afternoon.

Her head ached, her eyelids drooped. She looked at the Duck: he outranked her, and Rachel would know that. Mustn't let Rachel get nervous, sense anything was not what it should be.

Should she do it? No one had tailed them, the street still seemed clear and safe. What were the odds?

Favorable, she decided, completely favorable. And if she didn't get some rest soon . . .

"Sergeant McKinnon?" she said. "as the lieutenant told you, we're to keep Rachel safe. Some guy might be gunning for her, but he doesn't know she's here. We're staying locked up tight in here, no one in or out, only us using the phone. Somebody has to be on guard, make sure nobody gets in. As long as she stays away from the windows, everything should be okay. I was up all night. Would you mind if I took a short nap in the bedroom? Anything happens, I'll hear it and be on my feet fast."

"Sure," answered the giant. "That's fine with me."

"Thanks," said Perry. She double-checked the lock on the door, smiled wanly at Rachel as she walked back to the bedroom.

"Have a good nap," said Rachel.

"Take care," said Perry.

Everything will be fine, the woman detective told herself. *Just fine.*

"Well," said Rachel, looking at the red-haired giant. "What next?"

26

The cemetery was neat and clean that Tuesday afternoon. The brown grass would soon turn bright green. There'd be flowers on the low hills, and leaves would fill the trees that bordered these acres of the dead. The coffin waited beside an open grave. Three workmen who'd tried to be invisible during the brief ceremony now stood next to that polished box, waiting for the mourners to climb into the cars parked a short walk from the hole. Most of the mourners had reached their vehicles: car doors opened, slammed shut. Engines started. A few cars pulled away. Half a dozen people circled the widow and daughter as they stood by the black limousine parked behind the hearse. The widow shook hands, accepted hugs from women who dabbed their cheeks with tissues. The daughter stood beside her, in a trance.

Devlin waited until only Mrs. Maxwell's mother, the neighbor, and her husband encircled them.

"Excuse me, ma'am," he said, stepping into the circle of critical eyes. "Could I see you a moment?"

"I'll be fine," she told her mother, who'd grabbed her hand. The widow smiled reassuringly toward her daughter, let the policeman lead her away.

"I'm sorry to trouble you now," Devlin told her.

"There's no trouble you could bring me worse than what I have," she said; shook her head, smiled her encouragement.

"I've got some things I want you to look at," he told her. He led her to his car. As they walked, he noticed a short man in a soiled raincoat standing vigil ten feet from the coffin. The gravediggers hesitated to resume their work with this stranger watching.

The widow caught Devlin's glance.

"That's Harry," she said. "Peter's partner."

Devlin and the widow reached his car. The policeman turned his back to the crowd so no one could see him take a sketch from his pocket.

"Do you know if your husband knew anyone who looked like this man?"

The widow stared at the portrait.

"Is that him? Is that who . . ."

"We don't know who shot your husband, Mrs. Maxwell. This is just a drawing of a man who might be involved. Or who might not."

"It's not a very good drawing," she said. "When you're an artist's wife, you become quite a critic. But . . .

"No," she said, "he doesn't look like anyone I've ever seen."

"Thank you," said Devlin. "Please don't mention to anyone that I've shown you this."

"Okay," she said.

"Would you take a look in the back seat of my car?" he asked.

She did.

"Do you recognize any of those clothes?"

The widow frowned.

"That can't be . . . The pants and shoes, shirt . . . Maybe the shirt is the one Peter used to wear to paint in.

"But that coat! When we met at the institute, he had a coat like that. He loved it! Wore it all the time. I haven't seen it in years, not since he formed the company. How did you . . ."

"It was in the trunk of your car," he said.

"Why?"

She didn't know; hadn't known.

"With those other clothes?" she asked.

Devlin nodded.

"I don't understand," she said.

"They were just there," he said.

"But why?"

The daughter's voice came from behind Devlin:

"Mom?" the detective turned. The girl stood a few feet away, her face pale, her lips trembling. "Can we go now?"

The widow looked at the cop—who nodded.

"Please call me," she said, "If there's anything . . ."

"Sure," he said. Watched as she led the daughter away. They drove off in the mortician's limousine.

Harry still gazed at the coffin.

"Mr. Williams?" said Devlin.

"You're the cop, right?" said Harry without turning away from the grave.

"Yes."

"You know how long I knew Pete? Twenty-three years. Longer than his wife. We were closer than brothers. Twenty-three years. That's what they're waiting to bury. You ever bury twenty-three years of your life?"

"No sir," lied Rourke. "May I talk to you?"

Harry sniffled, blew his nose in a handkerchief, and wiped his cheeks.

"Give me a second, will you?" he mumbled.

They walked toward Rourke's car. Harry's tears dried by the time they reached the policeman's car. The afternoon was crisp. The two men thrust their hands in their overcoats, shrugged against the cold. They heard the shovels of dirt hit the coffin.

"Do you know anyone who wanted Peter Maxwell dead?" asked Rourke.

"No." Harry's voice was weak.

"Was your firm having any trouble?"

"Just routine stuff," said Harry. "Nothing every business doesn't have?"

"You're sure?"

"Sure as I can be on a day when I don't give a damn about business."

Rourke wanted to tell him he couldn't wait for a more agreeable day, but echoes of earth hitting the coffin tempered the policeman's impatience.

"Have you ever seen this man before?" He handed Harry the sketch.

"No," said Harry after memorizing the image. "But if I ever see him, you'll hear about it. One way or the other."

"We need to talk to this person if we're going to find out who killed your friend," said Rourke. "*Talk* to him."

"You mean he didn't do it?"

"We don't know who did it," said the cop. "And please keep all this confidential."

"Sure."

"Does the number 389 mean anything to you?"

"No."

"Those clothes on my back seat? Have you ever seen them?"

Harry glanced in the back seat; looked away, looked back again. His eyes met the detective's, then flicked away. Looked beyond the gravediggers.

"Shit," said Harry.

"Harry," said Rourke, his voice sharp and hard. "You have answers I need. Don't make me pry them out of you."

"You got to understand," said Harry.

"Something was wrong in Peter Maxwell's life," said Rourke. "You know what it was."

"You got to understand," repeated Harry.

"You've got to help me."

"How old are you?" asked Harry suddenly, catching Devlin by surprise.

"Midthirties," answered Rourke, warily.

"Yeah, well wait until you're in your early forties," said Harry. "Like Pete. Like me. Maybe then you'll understand.

"Pete had too many damn dreams."

"How can that happen?"

"You can outlive your dreams. You can wake up one morning, because you ran out of time, or because you chose other dreams, or because they weren't ever real. . . .

"And maybe all those dreams start to fool you. Maybe you get so tangled you don't know what's tangle and what's true, what you really want to do. Hell, what you're doing."

"Could we try this in real words and facts?" said the cop.

Harry shook his head.

"Older I get," he said, "the less I understand facts."

"Try telling me about the clothes," said Rourke.

"They're Pete's. I accidentally caught—*saw* him wearing that coat and pants. Boots. Like the old days."

"When you were in college."

"Yeah."

"Where was he going in them?"

"He was going back," said Harry.

"I don't get it."

"Sure you do," said Harry. "Sure you do."

The detective blinked.

"It started five, six months ago," said Harry. "I'd felt it coming for a couple years. Here he was, Peter Maxwell, successful vice-president of a solid business. Married to a great woman, great kid, healthy, great life behind him, great life ahead. Great.

"But then the dreams and the ghosts started eating at him.

"Some midlife thing," said Harry, shrugging. "Me, I never had many dreams or much talent. No wife. Never had too many illusions—or dreams.

"Somehow, Pete and I started drinking at a new bar. . . ."

"Where?" asked Rourke.

"Fitzgerald's, down by the Inner Harbor. All lawyers and bankers and fancy women kind of bar. A meat rack."

"Did he go there often?"

"For a while. Then he found someplace new."

"Where?"

"The Red Moon. Up by the Art Institute. I went there with him once. Not my kind of bar either."

"Why?"

"Too young."

"Was Peter a drinker?"

"He didn't go to bars to drink," said Harry. "He went for the people, the . . . the pulse. What might be there."

"What was there?"

"Look," said Harry, "you're not going to tell. . . . None of this has anything to do with his murder."

"We'll see."

"I don't want Marge to find out."

"If she doesn't have to, she doesn't have to."

"Lately he'd been talking about a girl. Laura somebody."

"He was having an affair."

Harry shook his head.

"I don't think so," he said. "Not like that. He was a good man. He hated cheating husbands, didn't want to be that kind of man."

"Then what was this Laura to him?"

"I don't know. We only talked about her a couple times. She came up in conversation like a bird from nowhere. He told me she was just somebody he'd met. I pushed him around about what he was doing, that kind of stuff. He shut up, told me never mind."

"Why the extra clothes?"

"You got me. Maybe they let him be somebody else."

"Do you know if he ever used another name?"

Harry shook his head.

"You know any of these Red Moon people?"

"We never hung out with them," said Harry. Devlin heard some anger. "Pete probably knew we wouldn't all fit. They were . . . I don't know, I got bad vibrations when he talked about them."

"Like they were bad customers? Dangerous?"

"Like maybe Pete didn't know who they were and thought he did. Like he was deluding hiself. Or they were tricking him."

"About what? How?"

"I don't know."

"Were they dangerous?"

"Anybody can be dangerous. I don't even know who these people were."

"Can you guess?"

"You know all I know."

At least all you'll tell me now, thought Rourke.

"So what are you going to do?" asked Harry.

"Police business," said Rourke.

27

"So tell me about your accident," Rachel said to Sergeant Liam McKinnon as they sat at Rourke's kitchen table.

"I got run over by my own car," he said. Swallowed. Watched her closely.

She raised a steaming coffee mug to her lips, took a sip. He followed suit.

"Yeah," she said, "that happens."

"It does?" he asked.

"Sure," she said. Then laughed.

"Try not to make a habit of it, okay?" she said.

"Okay."

"Those eyes must hurt."

"No. But my sunglasses got broken. I need a new pair of mirrors."

"Why do you wear mirror sunglasses?"

"Because no one can see where I'm looking."

"So?" said Rachel.

"So . . . Cops are supposed to look like you can't see where they're looking. Aren't they?"

"Cops should be able to see what they need to look at. Mirrors annoy people. That doesn't make you a better cop."

She paused for another sip of coffee; thought a moment, shrugged, and said:

"I knew a guy who wore mirrors over his eyes to hide and make people think he was cool."

"Was he?" asked the big cop.

"I didn't think so," she said.

"For any kind of glasses, it's the quality of the lens that counts, not whether they're cool."

"Okay," he said.

He shifted uncomfortably in his chair.

"Do you mind if I take off my jacket?" he said.

"Take off your tie, if you want," she told him. "I hate dress codes."

"Thank you," he said seriously. He stood, draped the suit jacket over his kitchen chair.

"Holy shit!" she said, staring at his metal-heavy shoulder holster. "I don't know everything about cops, and I don't know much about guns, but why are you carrying such a huge pistol?"

"They let me," he said. Nervously sat down, folded his huge hands in front of him on the table. "Isn't it okay?"

"It must be okay, but why?"

"It's a .44 Magnum, the most powerful handgun in the world."

"So?"

"So . . ." he paused. Frowned.

"What do other Baltimore cops carry?" she asked. She didn't care about guns, but this giant interested her; charmed her. Besides, he stood between her and death.

"They carry .38s."

"Well, that's a cannon. Can you hit anything with it?"

"I practice all the time," he said. "Mostly I practice drawing. For plainclothes duty, like today, I practice hours drawing it from my shoulder holster."

"And then what?"

"Then . . ." He shrugged, confessed softly: "Then I . . . When I practice at the range . . . It kicks so much, is so heavy, I . . . I miss the targets a lot.

"But it is the world's most powerful handgun," he said.

"Lot of good that does you if you can't use it."

"I'm not too bad with the .38," he said shyly.

"Then why don't you carry it?"

"In the movies, Clint Eastwood carries one like this. He's a great cop and—"

"This isn't the movies. And you're not Clint Eastwood."

"No," he said, "I guess I'm not."

"What do I call you?" she asked suddenly. "You call me

Rachel. Notice how nobody introduced me as Miss Dylan? Or Ms.? I guess I don't rate a title."

"Sure you do!" he said. "I'll call you—"

She laughed.

"You call me Rachel!" she ordered. "I don't care about the name. The respect that goes with it . . . Well, I might deserve it, but if I don't get it, there's not much I can do. Not with you guys."

"I'll tell the others."

"Don't bother," she said. "Let them figure life out on their own."

"Yeah," he said.

"So what should I call you? Sergeant?"

"My name is Liam."

"Is that what your friends call you?"

"I . . . I don't have a lot of friends." His voice turned glum. "Just a dog."

"What does he call you?" she asked.

"Dogs can't talk!" he snapped. Then he noticed the smile on her face, the twinkle in her eyes. He laughed, let her laugh with him.

"They, ah . . . Nobody calls me by my name."

"Why?"

"I don't know. Nobody calls me anything. If they speak to me, they end up calling me sergeant.

"They've got another name for me," he said. "But I don't know why."

"What is it?" she asked gently.

"The Duck," he said. "Duck. They think I don't know, but I do. I'm not deaf."

"No," she said. "And I don't think you're any kind of duck either."

He blushed.

"I'm not so sure about that," he muttered.

"I haven't heard a quack so far," she told him.

He thought for a moment. Smiled.

"So," she said, "what shall I call you?"

His smile broadened.

"Call me the Duck."

They both laughed.

"People are going to think that's really weird," he said.

"The hell with them," she told him.

He blinked.

"The hell with them," she said again. "If they laugh at you for being yourself, then the hell with them."

"Yeah!" he cried. "The hell with them!"

"That's not going to be so easy," he added a moment later.

"No," she said. "It isn't."

"Sometimes life is so hard!" His sincerity kept his observation from being a whining complaint.

"That's life," she told him. She shook her head, spoke more to herself than to him.

"Sometimes . . . sometimes life is incredibly awful. Terrible things happen. To you. To others. There's no reason for some of it. It's unfair and it hurts more than you imagine. You can't bear it, but you don't die. You keep going. The terrible doesn't change, doesn't get any less terrible. But you go on. You find out that much of it is up to you. So you do what you can. You suffer the terrible, rejoice in the good, survive the rest. Whatever else . . . the hell with it."

She suddenly focused on the Duck, who stared at her with rapt attention. She blushed, shook her head.

"Philosophy 101, right?" she said. Avoided his gaze. "The world according to Rachel Dylan."

"I never went to college," he told her.

"My time there was brief," she said. "Brief but bloody."

"But you know so much!"

"Not so much."

"You knew about sunglasses and mirrors and being cool. You knew about guns and you're not a police officer. You probably don't even like guns. You know about names and . . . other things."

"See? Already you've run out of what I know, and you haven't even run out of fingers on one hand."

"I can count without using my fingers!" he said, hurt.

"It's a joke, Liam," she said. Stared straight at him. "A joke. I'm not laughing at you. If it's a joke on anyone, it's a joke on me."

"I believe you," he said.

"That's more than some of your colleagues do."

"They expect you to lie."

"Most people do."

"I expect you to tell the truth. To me, anyway."

"Why?"

He shrugged.

"I don't know," he said. "Sometimes Sam, my dog, likes people, sometimes he doesn't—before they do anything. I get feelings like that, too. I got one with you. I like you. I trust you."

She shook her head.

"Not many people . . . Certainly no cops! . . . Thanks.

"But you've got to be careful, Duck. Those kinds of feelings can turn out to be the biggest trap door you'll ever step on. Sometimes, you give it all to someone and he turns out to be the absolute worst person you could have given anything to.

"Happens to everybody," she said. "No matter who they are or how smart they are."

"You're no trap door," he said.

"We'll see," she said. Smiled. "We'll see."

He stared at her, confidence and sincerity radiating from his blue eyes.

"I'll do my best," she finally said. "For you."

"That's good enough," he said.

Rachel watched the second hand slowly sweep round a cheap clock on Devlin's counter.

"Would you . . ." he began; halted, began again: "Would you do me a favor?"

I can probably beat him to the front door, she thought, gathering her feet beneath her chair. *He won't shoot me. Not for that. Not this one.* She was suddenly frightfully aware of how much larger and more powerful he was than she.

"What?" she asked, barely finding the strength to get the word out. She tried to act casual, unafraid. *Don't give him fear. Don't give him that encouragement.* Tears burned in her eyes. They wouldn't fall, but they were there.

Pepper shaker on the table, she thought. *Scoop it up as I bolt, get the cap off as I head for the door.*

"Teach me things," he said.

"What . . . what do you mean?"

"You're so smart, you know so much. . . . Nobody ever taught me anything, explained anything to me. Would you . . . teach me?"

"About what?" she said as her heart slammed against her ribs.

"Like you have. About sunglasses and people and how not to be dumb."

"That's all?"

"Is there more?!" he said. "Isn't that enough?"

"You mean . . . talk with you? About life? What goes on around you? Around us?"

"Yes!" he frowned. "What did you think I meant?"

She sighed. Fear flowed from her like water, and she suddenly realized she needed to urinate.

"Oh, Duck! You're one in a million."

"Lucky for the million," he said.

They laughed.

"See?" she said. "You don't need me! You already know how to laugh, and that's half the wisdom of the world."

"What's the other half?" he asked.

"Knowing how to handle when you cry."

"It's probably not as simple as it sounds."

"It's not."

"This is probably against departmental policies," he said, "becoming friends with a witness. We are friends—aren't we?"

"Yeah." She smiled wryly. "Sure."

"It's probably against policy," he repeated.

"Most likely," she said.

He paused for a moment; smiled.

"The hell with them," he said.

They both laughed.

"But one thing," he said.

"What?" her stomach tightened again.

"What can I do for you?" he asked.

She shook her head.

"Duck, you're guarding me, protecting my life."

"That's my job."

"You are one in a million, aren't you?"

He beamed.

"You want to do something for me?" she asked and he nodded eagerly, happy as a puppy. "Tell you what: I teach you about life, you teach me about Baltimore and about being a cop."

"Why?"

"Learning about Baltimore is why I came here," she said. "Learning about being a cop . . ." She shrugged. "It's an unexpected and unwelcome chance I got dealt, but it would be dumb to pass it up.

"Remember that," she said.

"Yes ma'am!"

"Call me Rachel."

"Yes Rachel!"

"Hey, Duck?"

"Yes, Rachel?"

"Want another cup of Rourke's lousy instant coffee?"

"Sure," said the Duck. "Why not?"

28

"I thought you should see that right away," Captain Goldstein told Rourke. The older man nodded to the file folder on the kitchen table.

"Yeah," answered Rourke.

"So," said Ruth Goldstein as she bustled into the kitchen, "you and my goldbricking husband going to sit around here all day, or you going to do some real work like the city is paying you for?"

"Well . . ." began Devlin.

"I know, I know," interrupted Ruth. "Just practicing. Getting in shape. For retirement. Hah!"

She shook her head, then peered over the tops of the glasses that had slipped down her nose.

"Are they empty?" she said, directing her comments toward the two mugs beside the file folder.

"I'm fine, thanks, Ruth," said Devlin.

"Me too," her husband smiled.

"You," said the wife, "you should have another cup. Wake up now, the sooner the better."

"I'm fine, dear."

"Hmph." She shook her head. Pushed her glasses up her nose, then jabbed that same forefinger toward Devlin.

"Before you let him send you out of here, come say goodbye."

"Yes ma'am!" said Rourke. He saluted her.

"Underneath all that sweet *goyishe* charm and innocence, you always were the most sarcastic one."

She left the kitchen.

"How's she doing?" Dev asked when her footsteps faded into the depths of the house.

"With what?"

"With everything. Being sick. You retiring."

"Oh, well, with *everything*!" answered the older man, exaggerating his tone and expanding his gestures.

Captain Goldstein's workday patter took its tone from Baltimore's big city streets; like most American cities in the 1980s, Baltimore's street tone was black and hot-radio hip. Devlin marveled that when Captain Goldstein saw his wife, his hardboiled street tongue instantly reverted into the ethnic rhythm of his roots.

"Well, with everything she's mad all the time."

"Mad?!"

"Ruth wakes up mad," explained her husband. "It's what gets her going, keeps her going. Now . . ."

He shrugged.

"She looks good," said Devlin. "She's lost a little weight."

"She's always been so tiny next to me. Back in high school, I was afraid I'd crush her. Like a bird. Once, I mumbled something about being worried she was afraid I was too big— Not like *that*! We didn't even dare *think* too much about things like that! I mean . . . We were just kids, and kids then . . ."

"Kids now, too," said Devlin.

"You think?"

"I think."

"Yeah, so do I. But now, they don't stay kids as long. We were kids such a long time, Dev! Even after I came on the force, rolled my first body, had my first citizen smile and then sucker-punch me. . . . It took me so long to quit being a kid!"

"Not so long."

"Seems like it. Seems like I just got here."

"And now you're going to retire."

"Yeah," said the captain of homicide. "Yeah."

"Second thoughts?" asked his subordinate. Asked his friend.

"Second? Hell, I'm still fighting with the first!

"But Ruth . . ." He shook his head. "She's here all alone, all day. Worries about me, even though I mostly sit in the office. Hell, I'm a cop. I don't need to look for trouble. I carry the badge and gun, I got the eyes: trouble won't leave me alone."

"Ruth worries?"

"All the time. The doctors say she needs to have as little stress as possible. Her worrying about me is something I can change."

"What does Ruth say?"

"About what?"

"About you retiring."

"She grumbles, complains, but you know: it's good for her."

"So you told me. What about for you?"

"Ruth is the best thing in the world for me," pronounced Goldstein, "and that's that."

Rourke smile, nodded.

"I envy you," said the detective to his boss.

"For what?"

"For having something that basic."

"You'll get there," said the captain. "You'll get there."

"What was it you were saying about when you two were in high school and—"

"Oh yeah," said Goldstein. "Back when all this beef was muscle, sitting in the Dodge parked in front of her dad's row house, worried I'd squeeze her too hard. Crush her like a bear. She laughed, told me I was a bear, all right: her Teddy bear. Somehow, her calling me Teddy in private became public."

"But your first name is Edward," said Rourke. "Ted and Teddy are natural nicknames for—"

"Whoever heard of a Jew called Teddy?!" said the man of those names. "Ed, Eddy, but *Teddy*?! When my Mom first heard it, she told me that's what the Irish called their kids."

"So maybe you're a little Irish," said Rourke. "Everybody is."

"Then it evens out," said the man with many names, "because everybody is a little Jewish."

They laughed.

"I hear you two laughing!" yelled Ruth from somewhere inside the house. "My husband calls you up on the telephone, tells you to come over and work, and what do you do? You end up kibbitzing like a couple of yentas!"

Devlin and Teddy smiled to each other—quietly.

"What are we going to do about Bernstein?" the captain said. "His funeral? Me, the rabbi, the mortician, the receptionist from his office—who came because nobody else was going to. And that was it. Not even enough people to carry his coffin, let alone sit shiva. Nobody disliked him, she told me. But nobody cared about him."

"Sounds like a great place to work," said Devlin.

"Like any other," said Ted. "But him . . . So quiet he might as well have not been there, she said."

"He isn't there now."

"But his family. No sign of them. You figure the wife had him bumped off, took a powder with the kid for Florida and some blond charter boat stud she met on the sly?"

"That's a possibility, given the evidence," said Rourke.

He shook his head, continued.

"You know we don't even know her first name? Or the boy's name? When Perry's off the bodyguard shift, I'm going to have her dig up their marriage certificate, a birth certificate for the boy, anything so we can backtrack the wife, find some of her kin."

"If they weren't married in Baltimore, if the kid wasn't born here—"

"Yeah," said Rourke. "I know. Saturday afternoon, I'd have said Hershel Bernstein was the easy one, the victim most likely to be acquitted of everything except bad luck. Now, he's turning out to be just as big of a question mark as the others."

"We got another problem," said Goldstein. "This morning I got a call from Greg Sonfeld, the mayor's boy. One of his friendly, 'just touching bases' bullshit bluffs. Glad to see you Sunday, he told me. And by the way, what are you doing at the D.C.'s office?"

"What did you tell him?" asked Rourke.

"Administrative and logistical shuffling. Then he asked about you. So I told him you were part of that. He fished some more, didn't get anything."

"Good," said Rourke.

"Not so good," said the captain. "Then he called the D.C.

More pointed questions, official questions. The D.C. held his mud about the investigation, but he changed the party line."

"That shit! If he betrayed us . . ."

"What did you expect? We didn't get the worst. The D.C. told him he didn't know exactly what we were doing, promised to investigate our activities fully and report officially to the mayor. Did a nice job of covering himself and cutting out Sonfeld."

"When does the D.C. report?"

"Sunday, when our week ends."

"So . . ."

"So we still got our shot, but he's set us up. If we screw up, he'll feed us to Sonfeld to save his own ass."

"Screw up *what*?! We're just trying to do our job!"

"Now that you got rank, you'll find that there's doing your job right and there's screwing up, and that they're sometimes the same thing as far as the department is concerned."

"Tell me again why I wanted to be a lieutenant?"

"Beats me," said Goldstein. "How are you guys holding out?"

"So far, still standing."

"What are you going to do about this?" asked the captain, tapping the file folder that lay between them on the kitchen table.

"Wish I knew," answered the detective.

29

The telephone buzzed twice in Devlin's ear.

"Narcotics, Sergeant Wilder."

"How you doing, Hank?"

"Dev! How the hell are you?"

"Fine. I got someone for you."

"Yeah? For what?"

"Aren't you curious who?"

"I'm curious who after you tell me for what. Then I'll know if I want you to tell me who."

"Could be a midlevel coke connection guy."

"Could be anybody then, right? So what's the big deal?"

"Could be more."

"So. Okay. Who?"

"Guy named Fredrick Batelli."

"Never heard of him. How do you spell that?" Devlin told him.

"So? What am I supposed to do now?"

"Some work and some favors."

"Yeah, well, work I got. To spare. To give away. Favors I don't give out so easy. For who are these favors?"

"Me. Sort of."

"Don't bullshit me, Dev. You want something? Fine, ask for it. Odds are you got it. But don't bullshit me."

"Good day for you so far, Hank?"

"Fuckin' Tuesdays. Ass end of Mondays. So what does this Batelli tell his neighbors about his life?"

"Says he's in the music business. He's really in the money business."

"And you think some of it is South American snow?"

"Somehow, but he could be more. Like a family man."

"Hey, don't you read the official departmental reports? We don't have family men in Baltimore."

"That's a relief."

"So what do you want me to do with this Batelli guy?"

"I want you to put him in front of your telescope. *Your* telescope, my man. Not the squad's."

"Getting high and mighty, are we Dev? No more team player now that you got your bars?"

"Cut the shit on me, Hank. I want this quiet."

"Well . . . What you want and what you get—"

"What is this, Hank? You forgetting who you're talking to?"

Neither of them spoke for several seconds. Finally the narcotics detective sighed.

"Shit, Dev. Don't mind me. I been on this serious narc gig too long. The fuckin' razor's edge of crime."

"I been there," said Dev. "Boy, have I been there."

"You work narcotics, Dev?"

"Not exactly."

"Not exactly is your life story, Rourke. Nobody *exactly* ever understands what the hell you're doing."

They both laughed.

"Okay," said Hank, "give it to me straight and simple, 'cause I'm just a fuckin' sergeant too long on streets where everybody's in another dimension."

"Look Batelli over real good, but real quiet. He's in the phone book. I doubt you'll see any of your business in the open. If you do, when I'm through with him you can have him for the grinder."

"Now that sounds like fun. I could use a good laugh."

"Don't misunderstand, Hank. Batelli is no street corner runner or bartender making some extra bucks. He's big-time business."

"What has that meant since the first Colombian skipped on a million bail and left twice that much behind in cars and cash?"

"Be nostalgic," said Rourke. "And be careful."

"I suppose you want this yesterday."

"The day before."

"Where do I call you?"

"Ah . . . I'll call you."

Hank laughed.

"I been there!" he said. "Give me until late tomorrow."

Devlin hung up the pay phone and walked back to the car.

"Will he do it?" asked Harris when Devlin slid into the passenger's seat.

"And right," said Rourke.

"Where to?"

Devlin picked the manila file folder off the car seat.

"Something else to take care of," he told Harris.

"Always," replied the younger detective as he pulled the Chevy away from the sidewalk. "Always."

30

Devlin heard the cocking *click* of a revolver.

"It's me!" he yelled as he quickly backed away from his apartment door, his keys dangling in the lock.

"Who me?!" bellowed a man's angry voice from inside the apartment.

"Me Rourke!" he yelled. "I live here!"

"If you live here," yelled the voice, "then you'll know who it is in here."

"I know!" hissed Devlin. "I . . ."

Oh shit! thought Rourke. *What the hell is it?!*

A floor board creaked inside the apartment.

"McKinnon!" yelled Rourke. "Liam . . ."

"Okay," said the voice, suddenly light and easy.

"Sergeant?" said Rourke, still standing away from the door.

"Yes sir?"

"Would you uncock your revolver?"

"Sure."

Devlin heard the *snick* of metal.

"I'll let you in, too," called out the Duck.

"That would be nice," said Devlin.

"How you doin', sir?" asked the Duck as he let Devlin enter his apartment. The Duck's .44 Magnum dangled from his right hand.

Devlin glanced toward the back of the apartment. A rumpled, just-awakened Susan Perry, gun in hand, stood next to Rachel.

"My fault," said Devlin after a moment. "I should have called and let you know I was coming."

"That's okay," said the Duck. "We all make mistakes."

Rourke stared at him.

Perry stared at him.

Rachel smiled, spoke to Devlin.

"You ought to be more careful," she said. Nodded to the Duck. "I thought he was going to blow down the door with that cannon."

"You and me both," said Rourke.

"Let me get my shoes on," said Perry, retreating to the bedroom.

"Now *that* could have been an example of when we use signal 13 calls," the Duck said to Rachel. "That's why we carry that radio."

Devlin walked toward the open roll-top desk in his bay window. He tossed the file folder on it, took off his topcoat.

"What's this?" he asked. "A police academy extension program?"

The Duck laughed.

"Not exactly," said Rachel.

"That's good," said Rourke, the edge still in his voice, "because you'd have a little trouble with the application."

"What do you mean?" said Rachel. Her neck tingled.

Susan walked into the room.

"Detective Perry," said the lieutenant, letting everybody know his words were not a suggestion, "you could use some coffee. Why don't you and Sergeant McKinnon go have some in the kitchen?"

Let's cut through the bullshit, thought Rachel.

"Not a bad idea," Rachel said, her words free of sincerity. "There's a can of coke in the fridge. I think I'll join them."

"I think you'll stay here with me," said Rourke.

Perry jerked her head. The Duck smiled encouragingly at Rachel as Perry led him into the kitchen. Perry closed the door.

"You always in such a great mood when you come home from work?" asked Rachel.

She flopped down to the couch, put her feet on the coffee table.

"Do you always delude yourself with this tough act?" said Rourke. He sat in the desk chair, his voice calm while his eyes chewed her image.

So, thought Rachel. *Something new. Something that's made him mad. Something . . .*

Her eyes flicked to the desk. To the file he'd brought with him. She blinked, then looked back at him.

"What's that?" she asked.

"It's why you'll never get admitted to the police academy."

She frowned, uncertain.

"And why you probably already know a lot of what they'd teach you there," he added.

Rachel waited, forced him to make the first moves, and bought herself time to think.

"We ran a check on everybody involved in the Ward Building shooting," said Rourke. "Punched all the names into all the computers we could find. And guess what was there?"

Rachel didn't answer.

"At the murder scene, the only known person with a criminal record," continued Devlin, "was you."

So that's it, she thought. She kept her face calm.

"What about the killer?" she asked. "What about his record?"

"Rachel Sara Dylan," said Rourke.

He opened the file folder but seldom glanced at the computer sheets it contained as he lectured her.

"Born March 9, 1946. Barton, North Dakota."

"Small town," she said. Evenly. Casually informative. "Still is. Good place to grow up. Better place to leave."

"Smalltown girl," he continued. "Father's occupation shown as retail store manager. . . ."

"J.C. Penney's. A dollar earned is a dollar earned, he always said."

"No occupation for mother."

"Tell that to any mother and she'll laugh you to death."

"Arrested, 1968, Chicago. Assault, public disorder, riot charges."

"Arrested *August* of 1968," she corrected. "Democratic convention. Arrested three times that week, actually. Twice they didn't bother to book us."

"And once they took you to the bench. They gave you a fine for disorderly, other charges dismissed."

"That's not all they gave me," she said. She brushed her hair back from her forehead. Devlin squinted, saw the scar.

"You must have seen news photos," she continued. "Maybe TV clips. This is my souvenir from peacefully working within the system by exercising my First Amendment rights in Lincoln Park. A mounted policeman charged us, club swinging. I almost made it to the trees. I can still smell the tear gas, hear the screams, the bullhorns and the sirens, the horses' hooves thundering up behind me. When they picked me up, threw me in the paddy wagon, they decided I had been arrested for assault. The judge figured that mass of bloody bandages on my head was sentence enough. In that chaos, who cared about one scared kid from North Dakota who got her head clubbed in by a cop?"

"Says here you were a college student."

"Full scholarship, University of Chicago. Great school. They wanted to find a bunch of us bright, smalltown kids, mix us in with all the urban overachievers for *balance*."

She shrugged.

"Not a bad idea," she said.

"You only finished one year," he said, guessing. "Never more than a freshman, right?"

"Why?"

"Come on! You remember. It was the times."

"And you got busted."

"Politics," she said.

"Second arrest," he countered. "San Francisco, 1969. Shoplifting."

"One pint of milk, a package of bologna. First-time heist from a convenience store in the Haight. I was starving—not hungry, starving. Those papers should read, 'charges dropped.'"

"They do."

"The owner was a nice old lady who'd been hassled by us hippie kids too much. And by too many of the creeps who took over the street scene 10 seconds after it flowered. She came to the station house to process the paper, saw me in handcuffs, sitting at a cop's desk and trying not to cry, offered to let me work it off. I worked for her until too many real crooks forced the store to close."

"Two arrests," said Devlin. "Politics and survival."

"That's right," she said, evenly. Her heart beat harder. She wanted to lick her lips; didn't want him to notice.

"The record is blank for a few years," said Devlin.

"I wish that were true," she whispered.

"1972," said the cop. "Los Angeles. Busted. Possession of heroin."

"Days of hell," she mouthed, seemed to be reciting a

lesson rather than talking with Rourke. "Days of pain. Days of sorrow."

"A couple bags—" began Rourke, but she interrupted.

"My first smack score." She shook her head. "Seems like when I commit a crime, I get busted first time out. I'd only snorted it twice before. Never a needle. I was . . . I was looking for peace, some rest. Couldn't find safety. There was no sanity. I was settling for escape. Wrong, but it was the last link on a bad chain."

"Remanded to a drug rehab program."

"Got lucky, got a smart counselor who sent me to a shrink with a social conscience who helped me figure out a few things."

"What about your folks?"

"Dead by then," she said. "Dad just after the Chicago convention. Liver cancer. It ate him up three weeks after he found out. He died ashamed of me and not caring to hear any more of my side. My mother . . . Six months later she died because he wasn't there. Last time I went to that damn small town was for her funeral."

"Brothers and sisters?"

Rachel shook her head.

Rourke gave her a moment to recoup before he spoke.

"After California . . . nothing until now."

"Well," she said, her wry smile returning, "I wouldn't put it that way."

"What were you doing in the Ward Building garage, Rachel?"

"Witnessing a murder."

"Why were you there?"

"What difference does it make? What business is it of yours?"

"Everything about you is my business!" he snapped.

"Or really, Mr. Cop?"

"Really."

"You *cops!*" She spit the word. Surprised by her own anger, she still charged ahead with it. "You're all so—"

"We're trying to do our job," countered Devlin.

"Oh really!" she said, sitting straight up. Tears burned at the back of her eyes. Her heart raced.

"Really," said Devlin. *What's going on?*

"Let me tell you about you cops and doing your job! It's all just power for you. Self-righteous power. You're sitting there, high and mighty and clean to the world. Upright and acceptable. Doing your *job* for society. You want to know about your job? I'll tell you about your job!"

She was on her feet, yelling. In the kitchen, Perry and the Duck sat at the table, tried not to look at each other as they listened.

"You're sitting there judging me. For some smack. Soul eater, that smack, right? One of the baddest bads, and I did it, so that's my score, right?

"I know the smack was evil, but it was the last link in an ugly chain you cops helped build."

"Chicago—" he began. She interrupted.

"Chicago was baptismal blood and wasn't near as bad as . . .

"You want to know why I flirted with smack? What made me block out all my school smarts and street smarts and . . . What *pain* . . .

"You're so tough, you're so important. You say everything about me is your business, huh? Well, you really want to know?"

"Rachel . . ."

"You want to know, I'll tell you. You know why I was strung out and beat down and . . .

"Lots of things," she said. "Things you couldn't understand."

"Don't be so sure," he said. Even in her rage, she heard a gentleness in his words. But she didn't care; couldn't care. Not then.

"Back then, I was raped. Twice. And one time it was a cop."

"Oh, Rachel, I—"

"One of you *cops*. New Mexico state trooper. I was hitchhiking at the edge of the desert and he had gun and a badge that said he could hurt anybody he wanted to. There I was, gypsy on the road. He was king of the road, so he . . .

"He even took my $43. Said that now I could a figure a way to earn more. Left me in the desert. Drove off in his big police car."

"Rachel, I need to protect you! I want to! But I've got to know everything! The truth!"

"The *truth*! You don't want to know, you can't—"

"Yes I can. Yes I do. Trust me."

"*Trust you?!*" She shook her head. "Why the hell . . . Who the hell."

"I'm—"

"You're a *man*, and a cop. And such a straight arrow you could never understand or care or—"

"Try me."

"Oh you'd love that, wouldn't you, *lieutenant*."

Rourke stared back at her, with concern, not anger.

"What else, Rachel? You're not telling me everything."

Tears flowed down her cheeks.

"That's enough," she sobbed. "That's enough."

"No it isn't," he told her.

She felt the weight of him pressing on her even though they weren't touching. She wanted to push it off; she wanted to embrace it. She wanted it over.

"Rachel . . ."

"Please!"

"We have to . . . *I* have to . . ."

"What is enough?" she sobbed. "Haven't I had enough? I thought . . . So I did, so I . . ."

"What do you want to know? The name of the man who reached down and cupped my heart with his hand and held it and took everything I had to give and then just walked away, not even a goodbye note? Emptied the cookie jar and left me flat? You want to know his name?!

"Or . . . or do you want to know her name."

"Whose?" he asked gently.

She surprised him.

"My little girl's," she said. Sobbed openly.

"Oh Katie! Katie! What they did to you!

"So it was just a stupid, rip-off love affair, right?" she said, staring at him through her tears. "That's what they all are, and big deal, right? After the blood is dry, big deal. You survive. Everybody does. Anybody can.

"But . . . but suddenly you're pregnant and you remember how good you felt when you had love to give. It turned out to be the biggest shit in the world who you gave it to. But never mind: when you were giving it, you did something. . . . wonderful. Something special. You made a chance for there to be someone worth the love. Someone to be with forever. Someone to pass on to the world. Something good after all those years. . . .

"So no more abortions. The hell with how hard it will be and what will people who don't care about you say. You can do it. The two of you. And she's born *perfect*! Wonderful. At six months, you can already see she's smart.

"Working two jobs, making it happen, sharing babysitting, the hell with anything else but her and she loves you, trusts you.

"Then she's sick. Real sick. So you call on the world, call *society*, ask them for what they say they provide.

"But you forgot: you and Katie aren't part of society. You live at an address on the wrong side of town. So the ambulance . . . An hour, and you call five, ten times and they keep telling you to calm down, it's on the way.

"But it's not there, so you run to a neighbor. You get to the hospital where it takes 10 minutes to get anybody to listen, another 20 to get a doctor. He lifts your life out of your hands and goes behind swinging doors.

"Two hours later he and nurses and other doctors come back. Too late, they say. If only you'd brought her in just a little sooner. You tell them about the ambulance that didn't come and they tell you about a breakdown in the system. You tell them about screaming in the emergency room for someone to listen to you. They send you home.

"Only you don't have a home, just a place with an empty crib and toys and little pajamas with feet and . . ."

She hugged herself, rocked back and forth. Snapped her head up. Tears streamed down her cheeks.

"You people who say 'trust me.' We'll come when you call. We'll help you when you need it. We're on your side, those cops charging you in the park aren't real. Neither is the ambulance that won't come."

She slumped down to the couch; spent, finished.

"Rachel," he said softly. "I wish I could erase the pain from your past."

She hadn't expected that from him.

"But I can't," said Rourke, "Now we've got four murders and I have to know where I stand."

"No more time for me, huh?" she said.

"This is your time. What were you doing in that garage?" Her voice was flat, steady. She sniffled.

"A friend was going to meet me there, sell me some joints."

She swallowed. She was being led, felt it, wanted to get there as quickly and painlessly as possible. Survive.

"Marijuana," she added.

"I know what a joint is. Why were you buying some?"

"Because I wanted to get high." she said, surprised at his stupid question.

"I like grass, coke if it's offered. . . . I don't do smack, no pills either, no more psychedelics."

"What was the guy's name?" he asked her.

"You don't need to know his name," she said. "He's just a guy, a harmless, undependable wimp who was doing me a favor and didn't show up."

"When we picked you up at the hotel, you were wearing a coat. Your jacket was still at the Empire. What happened?"

"I figured the deal would take five minutes. Nick would never know I was gone if I left my jacket.

"When that guy shot at me, I ran for the quickest corner—which was the opposite direction from the cafe. Four blocks later I saw a thrift store, bought the coat with the money for the joints. I hid in the library until dark, caught a bus back to the hotel. Saw cops parked out front. I didn't care who they were there for, I didn't want to be seen. First thing you do when you move into a place is check the ins and outs. I climbed the fire escape, then . . ."

She focused on him for the first time since her outburst. Her eyes were round and large, like a fawn's.

"Rachel . . ." He leaned forward, elbows on his knees, hands open and pleading in front of him. She didn't shy away. "You must understand my position.

"I'm building a homicide case. A man shot four people, probably killed Nick, tried twice to kill you. I've got to catch him, and then after I do that, I've got to see that he stays caught, that I've got a good case for a prosecutor. A solid case that will convince a jury to lock him up forever."

She nodded.

"And that will make you safe," he added.

She nodded again.

"Right now, the best tool I got to nail this guy is you. Because of that," he said, nodding to the file folder, "we're shaky.

"Let me put it to you the way a defense lawyer could use it.

"The prosecution's main witness has a record as a crook and drug user, was at the scene of the crime to make a drug buy. She has no fixed address, no consistent means of support."

"What are you telling me?" she said.

"Rachel, the record you make in life haunts you forever. When you least expect it and are most vulnerable, up it pops."

"You're lecturing me like my high school guidance counselor," she said.

"Who sometimes was right."

"So?"

"So I need to be sure you're not a junkie."

"What?! After you guys sitting on me for all these days? . . . Supposed to be street-wise cops, and you can't be sure that . . . I thought you needed to trust me."

"I do."

"Then trust me."

"Sometimes it's not that simple. Or easy."

"What are you leading up to?" Rachel asked. Her eyes were slits.

"We can't take you to a hospital," he said. "Or bring a doctor to you, run specimens into the lab. You're not supposed to exist. The only way I can figure to built it into the record so we can use it if we need to . . . is to have Susan check you out."

"What do you mean, 'check me out'?"

"Needle marks."

"Tracks?!" she yelled. She wore a long-sleeved blue sweater. "My arms are—"

"Not just your arms."

Neither of them spoke for a minute.

"Oh God!" she whispered at last. "You keep me locked up, pry all through my life, and now you won't even leave me . . ."

She glared at him.

"You bastard."

They had no more to say to each other.

"Sergeant McKinnon!" yelled Rourke.

The big man bustled into the living room, smiled at the two people who sat glaring at each other.

"Yeah?" said the Duck. "How you guys doing?"

"Keep Rachel company for a minute," said Rourke. "I need to talk to Detective Perry."

"Sure," said the Duck. He frowned, turned to his new friend who sat on the couch.

"Is everything okay?"

She didn't answer.

The bedroom was close and quiet, cooler than the rest of the apartment. The shades were drawn. The yellow overhead light cast ominous shadows on the walls. Susan swallowed.

"Rachel, I . . . I want you to know, . . . I don't like this."

"Just part of your job, right?" The reply was hard, cold as the night beyond the curtained window.

"Yes," said Perry.

"Far be it from me to stand in the way of someone doing her duty," hissed Rachel.

First the sweater peeled over her head. The material muffled a sniffle. She kicked off her shoes, stood one-footed while she pulled off each sock. She stared at Susan. Swallowed. Sniffled. Rachel's wet eyes broke contact with Susan, focused to the world far beyond the policewoman's shoulder. Rachel unbuttoned her shirt, hesitated, then quickly dropped it to the floor. She wore no bra. Rachel's brown nipples puckered with the cold and she felt the first wave of shame. She sniffled, and Susan tried to ignore the tightness in her throat: *Do the job*. Rachel unsnapped her jeans, pushed them to the floor. She moved quickly to her panties, hooked her thumbs in their waistband, peeled them down over her legs. As she bent over, Susan heard her whimper, stifle a sob. Rachel stood upright.

"Is this all right?" She tried to tough-talk the words, but they came out as a plea.

Susan nodded.

"Could you . . ." said the cop.

Without waiting for her to finish, Rachel extended her arms, showed Susan first their bottoms, then their tops. The policewoman scrutinized Rachel's legs, the inside of her thighs, the tops of her feet, the sides of her hips, along the sides of her rib cage, every place Rachel could have injected a hypodermic needle. Rachel shivered. Goosebumps covered her flesh.

But no track marks. Anywhere.

"Okay," whispered Susan.

Rachel quickly stepped back, her arms crossing against her chest, her eyes wide and wet.

"It's okay, it's over!" said Susan.

Rachel trembled.

"It's so cold!" she sobbed.

Susan grabbed a blanket off the bed, started toward Rachel.

Who backed up, bumped into the bureau.

"It's okay!" said Susan. "I won't hurt you. I won't touch you."

The naked woman let Susan wrap the blanket around her. Tears streamed down Rachel's cheeks.

"It's okay," said Susan, backing up. The light burned cold. She felt like she had to vomit. Her hand groped behind her, found the doorknob. "I'll leave you alone now."

Rachel watched her leave.

From behind the closed door Susan heard a long, wounded wail.

"You can knock off, Sergeant," Rourke told the Duck as they stood in the living room. They kept their eyes averted from the hall, from the closed bedroom door. "Perry and I will spend the night."

"Yes sir," said the Duck. "I . . ."

He stopped.

"Say whatever's on your mind," ordered Rourke.

"I like Rachel," he said. "She's a good person."

"Yeah, I like her too," answered Rourke.

"I don't . . . I don't like us making her unhappy. Sir."

Rourke smiled.

"Was that a criticism of command, sergeant?"

"I don't know. Sir."

"Call me Devlin."

"My name is Liam."

"I remember."

The Duck finally smiled.

"Well, Liam, I don't like making her unhappy either."

"That makes me feel better."

"You're not . . . Liam, I like you, but . . . She is a witness. She's also a woman. And smart, funny, too. Great smile. But she's police business, not personal business. And a woman like her . . . A man like you . . . She could be . . ."

"What could she be, Devlin?"

Rourke sighed.

"Dangerous," he said. "She could be dangerous."

"Only for a man like me?"

"Well, I, ah . . ." Devlin laughed. "No, Liam, I think she could pretty dangerous for any man."

"But not for me." The Duck shook his head. "I think you're afraid I might get a crush on her."

"That, ah . . . That . . ."

"That won't happen." The Duck shrugged. "She's a friend of mine. I don't feel that other stuff for her. Though I know how somebody could."

Rourke smiled. "Go home. Get some sleep. But before you do, I want you to do me a favor."

"Anything!"

The bedroom door opened, closed. Perry stood in the hall a moment, stared at her feet. She looked up, saw Devlin and the Duck, joined them.

"She's clean," she said, her lips tight. "I wish I felt the same."

The woman detective turned away from her superior, walked back to the bathroom. Shut the door. Devlin heard her turn on the bathtub.

"Ah, sergeant . . ." said Rourke.

"Liam."

"Liam," he said, "here's what I want you to do."

Devlin told him.

"When you get it," said Devlin, "bring it back here. Get a receipt, but hell, we'll all probably be bankrupt long before the department thinks about reimbursing the small shit."

"I don't understand," said the Duck.

Devlin explained the department's budget plan for the Ward murders' investigation.

"You guys are paying out of your own pockets for everything?" asked the Duck.

"That's right."

"How come you haven't asked me for money?" he said, obviously hurt. "I'm on the team, aren't I?"

"I . . ."

"You're either on the bus or off the bus," said the Duck.

"Who taught you that?" said Devlin, remembering.

"Never mind," he said an instant later, "I can guess."

"Well?" demanded the Duck.

"Liam," said Rourke, clasping the big man's shoulder, "you are most definitely on the bus."

"Great!"

"So can you kick in a little for gas?" asked Devlin.

"Tonight I've only got the sixty bucks in my pocket—"

"Hold on to it," interrupted Rourke, "don't waste—"

". . . but tomorrow, after the bank opens, I can get us about $274,000."

Devlin blinked.

"What did you say?" he asked the Duck.

"I said I can get us about $274,000."

"Two hundred and seventy-four thousand dollars?!"

"Probably more. They keep paying interest. We can get a mortgage on my house, too. It doesn't have one now. Plus sell my stocks and bonds."

"Liam, that's a . . . that's *more* than a quarter of a million dollars. And you've got it sitting in the bank?!"

"It's not safe to keep it around the house. Even a policeman's house."

"Where did you get a quarter of a million dollars?!"

"My folks died," said the civil servant. "My father . . ." Liam shrugged.

"Oh," said Devlin.

"I don't need it," he said. "It's kind of a headache."

"I bet."

"Tomorrow I'll get some cash to pass out to the team, okay?"

"Sure—but keep track of how much, and who gets what!"

"Of course! Will $5,000 be enough to start?"

"I, ah, . . . $5,000 should be just fine."

"Good." Liam smiled. "I've got some other good ideas too!"

"Don't go overboard on good ideas!" cautioned Rourke. "Take it easy. And everything—*anything*—having to do with the case, make sure you have my approval first."

"Sure! After all, you're the bus driver."

Liam left, his size 12 feet pounded down the stairs. The treet door opened, closed.

Devlin glanced around his apartment. He heard Perry splash in the tub, spoke quietly to himself.

"I'm the bus driver." He shook his head.

31

The story ran on page 4 of Wednesday's Baltimore Star:

Police Say No New Leads
in Ward Building Murders

by
Gary Ebbenhouse

A spokesman for the police department said yesterday that despite rumors, the police have no new leads in the four murders that took place Saturday in the parking garage of the Ward Building.

"We have a fully competent team of homicide investigators working the case," said the spokesman. "And we will keep the public responsibly advised of all progress."

The spokesman would not identify the investigators, saying, "That's police business," and refused all further comment, including refusing to answer questions regarding rumors that the police have a witness to the slayings.

The witness rumor started Monday morning, and was broadcast over Baltimore radio station WBBX, FM86. An announcer for that station, Johnny Curtis, was one of the murder victims.

A spokesman for WBBX refused to comment on questions regarding the murders and the rumor and referred reporters to the police department. The station also refused to provide reporters with any tapes of the station's programming since the murders.

Meanwhile, the mayor's office yesterday issued a "routine" press release that said, "The city administration is confident that currently the police department is doing all within its power to solve this weekend's terrible crimes."

Special Mayoral Assistant Greg Sonfeld said the press release was designed to "express our support of the department and reassure the citizens that we are all working diligently to serve justice."

The killer showed no emotion as he read the newspaper story. The paper lay neatly folded next to the plate of bacon and sunny-side-up eggs on the coffee shop's table. He read the story two more times while the egg yolks congealed into two withered yellow eyes.

He ate them. And the bacon, the two slices of whole wheat toast—the only thing healthy about this greasy hotel breakfast. He drank a second cup of coffee.

"Everything all right, sir?" said the cashier as he paid.

"Yes," lied the killer, "everything is fine."

When he was safe in his hotel room, the door solidly locked and chained, the killer's face twisted in anger.

Rumors, the paper said. Rumors. They didn't spring spontaneously to life, and the way they were killed was not through formal, cover-your-ass "No comments" in the newspaper.

A witness.

There could only be one, the scared rabbit. She was supposed to be dead.

What had the other newspaper said? He reached under the bed, pulled out his briefcase, spun the combination lock, and pushed the antitheft catches in their proper sequence. The newspaper story on the explosion at the London Hotel was tucked inside a memo book with the stories about the Ward Building murders. The story didn't name the explosion's victim.

So maybe there was no victim.

He couldn't assume she was dead and that he was safe. Rachel Dylan had to be dead *for certain*.

He felt foolish: twice he'd missed.

Waste no time on recriminations. Move on.

He dialed the private work number; the client answered on the second ring.

"Yes?" said the client.

"Remember me?" said the killer.

The client hesitated, finally said, "It's been a long time since I've heard from you. A very long time."

"There may have been some further unexpected developments," said the killer.

"So it seems. You can't forget our deadline."

"I didn't plan on encountering my current problem."

"And it is your problem! I expect you to solve it so our business can be finished!"

"Don't lecture me." The killer's voice grew cold. "My work will be complete."

"How soon?"

"Soon enough."

"And what am I supposed to do?"

"Just don't make any mistakes," said the killer.

"Other than hiring you?"

The killer paused, said, "There are a number of ways our association can end."

"Not if you want to keep your reputation intact and our contract viable," said the voice on the other end of the phone.

"Careful," said the killer, sarcasm dripping from his words, "you might scare me."

He hung up before his client could reply.

32

Even instant coffee makes a morning smell good, thought Rourke that Wednesday morning as he sat at his kitchen table. The rumor story in the newspaper troubled him, but there was nothing he could do.

From the living room couch came the sound of Perry

mumbling in her sleep. They'd split the night shift; he slept first.

The bedroom door opened, closed, followed by the same sounds from the bathroom door: Rachel.

Rourke was on his feet with the first door sound, carrying the package the Duck had brought the night before. He was in and out of the bedroom before Rachel returned.

Long night, thought Rachel as she shuffled back to the bedroom. Part of her wished it would never have ended, that she wouldn't have to leave this alien room and face the people who controlled her universe.

Do what you must, she thought to herself. Shook her head. How like her mother, who'd lived on homilies. Long ago, Rachel left home and her mother's homespun view of life, yet her own path seemed blazed by one aphorism after another.

You're either on the bus or off the bus, she thought. If only it were half that simple.

She was wondering whether to make the bed when she realized something had changed in the room. The curtains were still drawn, the shades down, the two pillows seemed to be in the same place she'd left them. Her jeans still hung on the chair. Her personal possessions on the bureau . . .

A yellow rose in a white bud vase. On the bureau where it hadn't been before she went to the bathroom. She took the card from the small envelope.

"Sorry."

No signature, but she knew.

The rose smelled wonderful. She looked around the room, tried to feel cynical, but couldn't stop a smile from curling her lips.

By the time she had dressed, straightened the room, Harris had arrived. The younger detective and Rourke stood in the living room, while Susan made up the sofa bed.

". . . so you'll have the day shift here with McKinnon," Rourke was telling Harris when Rachel walked out of the bedroom. "I'll be back late this afternoon, pick you up for tonight."

Rourke turned, saw Rachel staring at them from the hallway. He nodded to her.

"There's water for coffee boiling in the kitchen, and Harris brought donuts," he said.

"Okay," she said. Nodded back. Went into the kitchen.

"How's it going?" Harris whispered. "How's she doing?"

"Fine," said Rourke.

Susan glared at him, stalked into the kitchen.

"What's with her?" asked Harris.

"Nothing," said Rourke.

The downstairs door buzzed. Rourke answered, heard McKinnon's cheerful voice; buzzed him in.

"It's going to be a great day!" said McKinnon as he bustled inside. "Like spring!"

"You'll be stuck inside for most of it," said Rourke. "You're here with Harris."

"Fine. If I could leave for a couple hours this afternoon, I can get the money from the bank."

"What money?" asked Harris.

"Our financial problems are over," said Rourke. "The sergeant here is in charge of disbursing funds from now on. Be straight with the money, and give him receipts."

Susan and Rachel walked into the living room, steaming cups in hand.

"Huh?" said Harris.

"Great to be working with you, Gary," said the big man.

"Ah, sure . . . ah . . ."

"What's the matter?" asked the sergeant.

"Nothing!" said Harris. "I just . . . I couldn't remember . . ."

"You don't know my name," said Liam McKinnon.

"Well, . . . I mean, you're a sergeant, and—"

"Why don't you call me what everybody else does?"

"What . . . What's that?"

"Duck," said Liam with a smile. "Call me the Duck."

The big man smiled, crossed the room to say hello to Rachel and a stunned Susan Perry. Harris edged next to Rourke.

"What did I miss yesterday?" he whispered.

33

"What was your relationship to the deceased?" Rourke asked the man wearing horn-rimmed glasses, a properly knotted tie, crisp white shirt, and conservative gray suit.

"I was Mr. Bernstein's supervising manager," he answered.

Every strand of the horseshoe of hair around his bald dome lay properly in place. He faced Rourke from behind his executive's desk. This Ward Building office had glass walls: one of them overlooked the street, the others formed a box within a larger box on the fourteenth floor. In the larger box, piped music floated through the grid of electric lights hung above a maze of plastic partitioned cubicles. As he'd walked through the maze, Rourke heard a steady *click click click* of chirping computer keyboards. This white collar factory maze smelled of electronics and pine-scented air freshener.

"And what were his duties?"

"He was a bookkeeper for Dix Beverages. We still use that name, although we merged into a diversified service provider. Real estate. Credit management. Nursing homes. Bernstein worked on the first Dix Beverage accounts. Always had. He'd been with us nine years."

"Did he set company policy, control large sums of money, anything like that?"

"You mean did his job entail any duties that would have provided someone a profit for killing him?"

"I couldn't have put it better myself, Mr. Bell."

"No, Bernstein was a mere functionary. Loyal, of course, and trusted, but with only a functionary's responsibilities."

"Uh-huh," said Rourke. "What was he like?"

"Dependable, though with little initiative."

"Yet he was working on Saturday," said Rourke.

"We've been experimenting with flex-time here at Dix

Beverage, lieutenant. Bernstein worked a varied schedule, interfacing his minimum hours requirement with necessary tasks. Last week he chose not to work most of Tuesday, so he needed to work Saturday."

"His mistake."

"So it seems."

"What were his chances for promotion?"

"He was on-line within the system. There was no advancement sequence from his position."

"That might have dampened his initiative."

"Some people are born to serve in a particular slot," said Mr. Bell. "Obviously, Bernstein was one of those people."

"What was he like *personally*?" said Rourke.

"I haven't the faintest idea."

"But you were his manager."

"Only for the last three years. Before that promotion I worked on the financial side. This administrative position is a routine step on the executive track."

"Moving up?"

"You disapprove?"

"Curiosity, Mr. Bell, that's all. Cops are curious."

"So I see."

"Can I look at his workplace?"

"That would be unproductive."

"If necessary, I can get a court order."

"You misunderstand me. Of course you may see where he worked. However, since he doesn't work there anymore . . . On Monday, we cleaned out his cubicle, reassigned his zone. We found nothing of interest. We saved the picture of his family on his desk, the photos from the walls of his cubicle, and will return them to his next of kin. When they call."

"Why didn't you check with us before disturbing his desk?"

"Company policy is to move forward." Bell shrugged.

"And all he had in his desk . . ."

"He had nothing personal. The company provided him with all his pens, pencils, et-cetera."

"Did he have any close friends in the company?" asked Rourke.

"Kept to himself. Didn't join the bowling team or other activities for employees of his level, never attended the picnics. I imagine he spent his spare time with his family. Family is important to them."

"Excuse me?" said Rourke. "Them?"

"Well . . . He was a Jew."

"Uh-huh."

"And family . . ." Bell turned up his hand, a worldly gesture. "Family is important to the Jewish people."

"Family is important to lots of people."

"Of course it is," said Bell, not understanding the change in Rourke's tone. "I've always admired that in them. And, naturally, he was a fine bookkeeper."

Devlin closed his eyes. Nothing good would come out of nailing Bell on his anti-Semitism. The investigation would suffer.

But I might like it, thought Rourke.

"About his family," he said, "can you tell me their names?"

"Why, no." Bell gestured to the computer terminal beside his desk. "Actually, no one seems to know their names, not even our computer. I hoped you could tell me."

Bell frowned.

"There's no trouble, is there?" he said. "The company is sensitive to . . . There'll be no further problems here, will there?"

"Trouble, Mr. Bell?" said Rourke. "One of your accountants is murdered in the building. I'd say that was trouble. And you supervised him for three years, yet can't answer basic questions about him.

"But," he said, "I'm sure that you won't need to worry about explaining such troubles to this big-hearted company."

Rourke smiled, left.

34

"I'll be right back," Paul McKee called out to his only two fellow detectives in the homicide office as he walked out the door.

"Yeah, sure, knock yourself out," said Detective Smith, a 44-year-old slab of pale beef in a green polyester suit. He resumed his conversation with his partner, Detective Cooper, who was a year older, black, just as poor a dresser, and almost as lazy.

"Anyway," said Smith, "this guy goes to the doctor, has a full physical 'cause he's feeling funky and he's looking for a cure."

"Maybe we should send Captain Goldstein to see that doctor," whispered Cooper.

The two men laughed.

"Be careful," said Smith, "this place might be bugged."

With exaggerated caution, Cooper pulled open the center drawer of his metal desk. Baltimore homicide detectives share desks, possession rotating with each shift.

"The only bugs in here can't talk!" said Cooper.

He and his partner thought that was hilarious; so hilarious, they ignored the phone for its first two rings.

"Hey man!" Cooper finally said. "You going to answer the phone?"

"Nah," said Smith, "what do they think this is? The fire department?"

Cooper joined him in laughter, but nodded toward the phone.

"All right, all right," said Smith, his hand reaching for the receiver, "But don't forget where we were."

He picked up the telephone without stopping his conversation with Smith.

"Guy goes to a doctor because he's feeling funky— Hello, homicide."

"I was wondering if you could help me," said a man's voice.

"What's your problem, Mac?"

"Well, I'm supposed to be meeting with one of the detectives working on the murders in the Ward Building," said the man.

"Yeah? It's not my case."

"So I'm across the street from where we were supposed to meet, and I realized neither of us knows what the other one looks like, and I've also forgotten his name, so . . ."

"What do you want me to do about it?" said Smith.

"He said he was the youngest guy working the case," said the man on the phone. "Do you know who that would be?"

"'Minute," said Smith. He turned to his partner. "Hey, who's that kid working the Ward stuff? Harris something, right?"

"Yeah, Gary Harris. Why?"

"Gary Harris," Smith said into the telephone.

"That's right," said the man. "Gary Harris. What does he look like?"

"Hey," Smith again called out to his partner, "how would you describe Harris?"

"Pale," said Cooper, his smile looking like ivory against his ebony skin.

The two detectives laughed.

"Detective Harris is a white guy," Smith told the man on the phone. "Kid, under 30. Kind of brown hair, about six feet. He ain't skinny and he ain't fat."

"Are you a detective too?"

"Yeah? Why did you ask?"

"Your description. . . . Thank you."

"No problem, buddy," Smith said as the phone clicked.

"Anyway," he told Cooper, "the doctor says to this guy, 'I got some bad news and some worse news.'

"'What's the bad news?' asks the guy.

"'You've got 24 hours to live,' says the doctor.

"'Hell, if that's the bad news, what's the worse news?'

"'I should have told you yesterday,' says the doc."

McKee walked back into the squad room as they laughed.

"Anything happen?" he asked two of the six men he hated.

"Nothing important," said Smith. Then he told the joke about the fat woman and the dwarf.

In a Mall at the edge of the city, the killer shook his head at the bank of pay phones. Why couldn't a cop that dumb have been working the case?

How smart is Gary Harris? thought the killer.

35

The English words on the black-ink-on-white-posterboard sign in the dirty, second floor window above the bicycle repair shop read: The Southeast Asian Liberation Friendship League. A vertical row of black, Oriental characters ran down the sign's left side.

The neighborhood was a mixture of Spanish, black, and American Indian, with a spattering of Orientals: The corner grocery store was run by a Korean family who'd just saved enough money to sponsor a cousin to emigrate, begin another corner store on another marginal block. The Korean store broke even only because the family worked 15-hour days, seven days a week, behind bulletproof Plexiglas walls.

"Not exactly the kind of place where I'd expect to find the saviors of the Eastern world," Perry told Rourke as they gazed up at the window from the sidewalk.

"Or Al Capone's successors," said Rourke.

The noon sun was warm; they'd left their topcoats in the car. Rourke led the way through the door next to the bicycle shop; dust, rat poison, dead cockroaches littered the narrow stairs they climbed. Perry knocked on the second floor landing's door.

"Yeah!" called a booming voice from behind the wood. "Who there?"

"Police," said Rourke.

They heard a drawer slide inside the room, quickly stepped out of line with the door.

"Police who?"

"Baltimore police," said Perry.

"What you want?" called the voice.

"We want in," yelled Rourke. "Now!"

The two cops heard a mumbled conference. Footsteps. The lock turning. The door opened enough to show a man's brown face.

"You police?" he said.

The two detectives showed him their I.D.s.

"Oh, sure. Come in."

The man who opened the door was Rourke's height, but weighed more than 200 pounds, most of it distributed on the chest and stomach under his white knit sweater. He wore black pants and work boots. Rourke put the man's age at 40, give or take a few hard years: his brown eyes were cloudy. His black hair was cut military short, and his face was like the moon: round, cratered, a cast of yellow.

Rourke walked straight into the room. Perry stayed next to the door, her back against the wall, her vision encompassing the room as well as the man who'd let them in.

The office was makeshift: mismatched three-drawer metal file cabinets against one wall, boxes stacked in one corner, a hand-cranked mimeograph machine in another, half a dozen empty wooden chairs, and a wooden desk with an ancient snake-necked lamp next to a black dial telephone. The desk was strewn with styrofoam hamburger boxes, napkins, soft drink cups, and French fries scattered beside a ketchup puddle on the cardboard back of a yellow legal pad. The room smelled of ink and fast food.

The man sitting behind the desk tilted back in the creaky chair, crossed his shining black loafers on the desk top. He was young and handsome, lean like a mongoose, with black hair razor-cut over his ears and a thin black mustache. His cheekbones were high, his brown flesh smooth. His black eyes twinkled. He wore a navy sports jacket, powder blue shirt, and dark pants. The teeth in his smile were white, and sharp.

"What can we do for you officers?" he said in an accent-free voice.

"We're looking for Pham Vam Hoi," said Rourke.

"I'm him," said the mongoose.

Also known as Tu-Cut, thought Rourke. The man kept his hands crossed behind his head; Rourke couldn't see his maimed hand.

"I expected someone much older," said Rourke. He made himself comfortable in one of the chairs. Perry and the moon-faced man kept their feet.

"Why?" asked the mongoose.

"President of the Southeast Asian Liberation Friendship League," said Rourke. "That sounds like a title for a wise old man."

"I'm 26," said Tu-Cut. He smiled. "I know we all look alike to you. I'll take your mistake as a compliment."

"What does the League do?" asked Devlin.

"Why do the police want to know?" replied Tu-Cut. "Have we broken any laws?"

"I'm curious," said Rourke. "What do you do?"

"We are a nonprofit organization. Primarily educational. We have some self-help programs, refugee assistance programs. Cultural projects. We do whatever we can to help our cause."

Tu-Cut answered Rourke's question before he could ask it.

"Our cause is the defeat of the Communist hordes who stole our homeland, the foe that many of your brave countrymen died fighting. In the meantime . . ." He shrugged. "We do what we can to help our people here and their relatives trapped under the oppressors' thumb."

"So you're fighting a war."

"All mankind is fighting a war, officer . . ."

"Lieutenant Rourke."

"Ah, a lieutenant of the police. Indeed, we are honored. You must forgive Pol Bon's inhospitable delay in admitting you. This is a rough neighborhood. Crime is everywhere. We are cautious."

"Good policy."

"You haven't told me why you're here, Lieutenant Rourke."

"Le-Lan Nguyen."

"Lovely girl."

"Dead."

"America turned out to be a different promised land than she expected."

"You knew her."

"I try to know all the members of the Vietnamese community. Laotian and Cambodian, too. I also know many Koreans. Chinese, Japanese. Filipinos."

He smiled.

"And Italians. Blacks. Hispanics."

"A man for all people."

He shrugged.

"I have my calling."

"How well did you know Le-Lan?"

"We were more than acquaintances."

"And a lot less than friends."

"We did not see eye to eye on certain matters. She had a misimpression of our work. The League is traditional American politics. We are anti-Communist.

"I know nothing about her murder. I wish you luck in catching the killer."

"How many guys like you two work for the League?"

"Unfortunately, the League can only pay a few of us our expenses. Our people can afford so little. A dollar bill here, five dollars there. No one gets a salary from the League. Ask our lawyer."

"But how many . . . volunteers like you are there?"

"The number varies."

"Say half a dozen?"

"You said that number, not me."

"How do you live?"

"We all have jobs," said Tu-Cut. "I own the bicycle repair shop downstairs. Some of my League comrades work for me."

He shrugged. "Baltimore has a harsh economy. We do what we can."

"How much money do you collect for the League?"

"That amount varies, too."

"What happens to it?"

"All funds we collect go straight to the League. We have our expenses. . . . You know. Overhead."

"How much?"

"We are a new organization, still growing, still organizing."

"All your papers are in order," said Rourke.

"We have a lawyer. An American lawyer. I'll give you his name and number. He handles such things for us."

"Do you or the League have any guns?"

"We are a peaceful organization."

"Do you have any guns?"

"We comply with all firearms laws."

"Do you have any guns?"

"Do you have a warrant that says I must answer such questions?"

"We're on a murder investigation," said Rourke. "You do want to cooperate, don't you?"

"As the law says."

"Who do you think killed Le-Lan?"

"Some psycho. Some fool. Some petty American criminal."

"Worked out well for you, didn't it? One of your critics gets killed. I bet contributions to your League increased. People learning from what happens to your opposition."

"Those are ghoulish thoughts, lieutenant. I was a soldier in Saigon. I have seen and thought enough ghoulish thoughts in my day. I will not indulge in them now."

"You know what a shakedown is, Tu-Cut?" said Rourke, suddenly addressing him by his street name. "Extortion? Blackmail?"

Tu-Cut's eyes narrowed. Slowly, deliberately, he placed his hands palm down on the desk, as though the sight of his amputated fourth finger would impress Rourke. "Are you here making charges?"

"I'm investigating a murder, Tu-Cut," said Rourke.

He glanced around the room. A fold-out magazine photograph of a naked blond woman hung in the hall leading back into the apartment behind Tu-Cut. The fold-out was from one of the magazines Hershel Bernstein kept in his bedside drawer.

"Why does the League call itself Kinh-Ngu?" asked Rourke.

"I beg your pardon?" said the man who led the gang.

"You know," said Rourke, "Kinh-Ngu."

Tu-Cut stared back, refused to reply.

"The Shock," said Rourke. "You know what that means."

"I speak my native tongue," said Tu-Cut.

"You also speak English," said Rourke, "and you're in America now. On my turf. No matter what name you use or what you claim to be—a crusader, a charity, a political group, a soldier, an innocent man. Hell, an animal, like, say . . . a pig."

Tu-Cut's face paled, as did his hands that suddenly pressed down on the desk. Behind Rourke, Pol Bon growled, but the expirate glanced at Perry's ready face—saw beneath, and stood still.

Tu-Cut swung his feet off the desk, leaned across it.

"What reason is there for us to continue this discussion?!"

Rourke smiled, shook his head. Stood and looked down at the mustachioed mongoose face; the mangled hand pressed on the desktop. Rourke slid a business card into the phone's dial.

"If you learn anything about Le-Lan's death," said the cop, "you call me. Otherwise, our next meeting won't be so pleasant."

Tu-Cut ignored the card, kept his eyes on Rourke.

"It's been a pleasure learning about you and your gan—" Rourke chopped the word short: "You and the League. I hope we didn't interrupt your lunch."

"Don't worry, lieutenant," said Tu-Cut. "Nothing spoils my appetite."

"What do you think?" asked Perry as they sat parked down the street from the bicycle shop. A minute after they settled in the car, Pol Bon bustled out the side door and into the shop.

"I think we've got trouble," said Rourke. "Right here in harbor city.

"Those are bad hombres. Tu-Cut is as sly a piece of shit as I've met. I think Le-Lan's father is smart to worry about them. *The Shock*."

Rourke shook his head.

"We need to slam them before they get any bigger. They're going to get bigger, whether or not they drop this 'League' scam. That's just part of their program, one face of many. America's branch of the Mafia started as an extortion gang preying on their fellow Italian immigrants in New Orleans, New York."

"But did they do the butcher job in the Ward Building?" asked Perry. "Were they gunning for Le-Lan? Gang's aren't notorious for their neatness."

"Maybe," said Rourke, "but there had to be more in it for them than just quieting a not-so-vocal critic."

He thought for a moment.

"I'm going to have Goldstein pull everything he can on them from Immigration, State, the Pentagon, and all those types. On them and on the Nguyens. Maybe we got a grudge killing here, something that started back in Saigon."

"You mean maybe the boy lied," said Perry.

"Maybe he doesn't know what the truth is," answered Rourke.

The lieutenant in charge of the case shook his head.

"I wish I believed we'd get enough before Sunday," he said.

"On the Le-Lan angle," said Perry as she put the car in gear, "or on everybody?"

"Yes," said Rourke.

36

"I thought you'd be by sooner," said Terry Cassidy. She nodded to three cassettes on her desk. "The tapes of Tuesday's show."

"Thanks," said Rourke. "I appreciate it."

"I wasn't aware we had any choice," she said, her voice cooler than the air outside her windows.

"Emotionally Yours," Bob Dylan's latest romantic ballad, echoed into her open door from the ceiling speakers piping in her station's program.

He's no relation to Rachel, thought Rourke, remembering that the singer had changed his name.

Terry's face was grim, set tight; her sleek form tense as she stared at the cop in front of her.

Rourke glanced at the door: "Mind if I close that?"

She shrugged. He closed the door.

"I appreciate all your help," he said, after he sat down again. "Getting me the tapes. Keeping Gordy under control."

"You play rough, don't you, lieutenant?"

"Murder is rough work."

She shook her head, sighed, and her body relaxed. Her eyes softened; this woman who loved her position and disliked her job stared at Rourke, said, "Do you like it?"

"Being a cop? Being all things necessary to any situation? Yeah, I do."

"But what about the boring stuff, the paper shuffling?"

"I thought you were going to ask me how I could stand the blood and violence and action," he said.

"No, I understand that," she said.

"Really?"

"Sure. Why?"

"Well . . ." He shrugged. "I have some friends, especially some women. . . . They have a hard time with that stuff."

"I didn't say I liked it," said Terry. "The blood, hurting people, finding hurt people . . ."

"Nobody sane likes that," said Rourke.

"But I understand the allure. It's like no-nonsense music. The story may not be pretty, but there's purity, a basic reality."

"Well. . . . poetry it isn't."

She laughed.

"But how about the other stuff? The paperwork?"

"That I hate."

"But don't lieutenants do most of that?"

"Yeah," he said; paused, frowned.

"But," he continued, "like a friend of mine keeps telling me, the promotion means prestige.. Recognition. More chances to do more things, more clout. More money. It's safer."

"And you're on the upwardly mobile track."

"What?" asked Rourke.

"The . . . the success track? Did I say something wrong?"

"No," he told her. "I just heard someone else describe himself like that.

"Didn't like him," added Rourke.

The room was comfortable. Rourke didn't want to leave.

"Ah . . . . You like it any better at the station?"

"It's the same place," she said, "the same song, the same music. My job is in flux, but . . . They'll let me stay, if I want."

"Do you want?"

"Yes and no," she answered.

"I know what you mean," he said, laughed.

"What about Gordy?" he asked.

"The surviving half?" She shrugged. "He'll dance in the limelight as long as he can. Hope he gets noticed and appreciated for who he is. He's still dazed by Johnny's death. He'll survive.

"Can I ask how the case is going?" she said.

"Can't tell you," he said.

"I figured that," she said. "I wasn't sure, but . . ." She smiled.

So did he.

They looked out the window.

"Almost spring," he said.

"Yes."

"Do you remember when you were young and—"

"Neither of us is over the hill," he interrupted, and she laughed.

"Yes, but neither of us is a kid either."

"Thank God."

"But . . . don't you sometimes wish you could have that certainty again, that sense of freshness?"

"Not if I had to give up all I worked so hard to learn."

"I don't want to go back!" she insisted.

"Some people do," he said, thinking of what Harry Williams said about his friend Peter Maxwell.

"Then they're lost.

"But just to take off," she said, "go forward. Turn on the radio and ride the highway."

She shook her head.

"Sound like a song, don't I?" she said.

"Not a bad song."

"No," she said, "not a bad song."

She nodded her head to the door he'd closed.

"They don't play enough good ones around here," she said.

"I have to go," he answered. His abruptness startled both of them.

"Sure," she said. "I understand. Back to work."

"Yeah," he agreed lamely. "Back to work."

"See you around," she said. "Good luck."

37

The killer sat on the bed, flipping through the Baltimore phone book.

E, F, G, H. H-a, H-a-n, H-a-r-, Harris.

Harris, G.

There were 15.

Harris, Gary.

There were 11.

He frowned. Picked up the telephone receiver, punched 9, got a dial tone, dialed 411.

"Directory assistance. What city please?"

"Baltimore."

"Yes?"

"Do you have an unpublished listing for a Gary Harris or a G. Harris?"

Silence for 10 seconds, then:

"No, sir, we do not."

"Thank you." He hung up.

What if he lives in the suburbs? He could live anywhere within 30, maybe 40 miles of Baltimore. Why couldn't he have had an uncommon name?

The killer shook his head. He knew where he wanted to end up, but he wasn't sure how to get there.

Yet.

38

An hour after he left the radio station, Rourke breathed the stale air of Hershel Bernstein's home. A fine layer of dust had settled on the glass coffee table; otherwise, the apartment hadn't changed. Rourke stared at the pictures on the wall, the smiling faces of a woman and a little boy who were nowhere to be found.

The phone rang.

He picked up the receiver on the end table.

"Hello?" he said.

"It's me," said Susan Perry. "The Bernsteins have no paper. No driver's license for her, no marriage certificate, no divorce record, nothing in the civil files, no school records for him, no birth certificate for the boy, no voter registration for her, no synagogue has heard of them, no traffic citations, and no more ideas. Got any?"

"Depends on my next call."

They hung up. Devlin looked at his watch: 2:33. He dialed the number.

"Narcotics, Wilder."

"It's Devlin."

"I don't know about Batelli dealing soda," said Wilder, "but he's a shady. No arrest record, but I checked with a couple crime commissions, some cops I know in New York, Philly, a guy in Los Angeles. Batelli keeps cropping up in wiretaps, and he's got ties to the Chicken Man."

"Who got car-bombed in Philly," said Rourke.

"That's the one. Nothing you could take into court, but they were friends, and their friends were friends."

"Almost like family."

"Almost exactly like family. Batelli was a silent and invisible partner in a porno production company. . . ."

"And the Mob dominates porno," said Rourke.

"Especially that company. Batelli got out of porno, went into some music business—that's what he runs out of his office here. Has an office in Philly, too. Belongs to the Better Business League.

"He has a Mutt and Jeff team who work for him. One of them has a record because of some strong-arm union stuff. The other guy came out of Miami, where he's known as a pal, not a player."

"But he could be."

"In Miami? Hell, anybody could be."

"Anything here you got on him or his people?"

"Nope. But if you've got anything . . ."

"I was hoping to get something from you."

"Sorry, Dev. All I can confirm is that you still got a good nose for shit."

Rourke walked through the deserted apartment one more time before he left. He flipped through the photo album from the bedroom drawer. Hundreds of pictures of the wife, the son. Hundreds of backdrops. They must have grown weary of seeing Bernstein aim his camera at them, but their faces never showed it.

"You have to be somewhere besides in here," he said to a picture of mother and son laughing toward the camera as they came out of a shopping mall.

When he left, he took the photo album with him.

39

Poor Devlin! thought Julia as she drove toward his apartment. We'll both be so glad when he quits chasing killers, settles down into his lieutenancy.

She smiled; couldn't help thinking he'd look cute in a uniform with the little gold bars on his shoulders.

He might not need to wear his uniform every day. Not

that she minded, but he'd look so handsome in a proper Brooks Brothers suit. A nice gray, or a blue pinstripe.

Not that he was a bad dresser now. Just a little too . . . limited. Two suits, two sports jackets that were acceptable, one ancient one she hated. He looked . . . *extreme* enough without having his clothes cut him out from the crowd.

When Devlin had put in a year as a lieutenant, acquired some marketable experience on his resume, he could move over to a decent-paying corporate slot with a promising future. J.B. would help, she was sure of that. A recommendation from J.B. Zuckerman, director of the Better Business League, packed a lot of weight. And maybe her brother-in-law could find a slot for Devlin at his company.

She wanted Devlin to be so happy! He was such a wonderful man! If only . . .

That edge, she thought, that damn edge he runs along, that he draws through everyday life. A vision of a straight razor being pulled across a white piece of paper flashed through her mind. Paper, yet as the razor slid through it, blood beaded up, turned the cut into a crimson line.

If only he could stay away from that edge, let it be, he'd be so much happier! she thought. He had to get off the streets to do that. She could help him. She would help him! Give him a good home. Pull him back from that edge.

Julia glanced at her watch. She could pick up her skirt at Devlin's, get it to the cleaners, get back to work, and grind out the newsletter before the executive committee dinner at six. Tasha's birthday was coming up, and Julia still wasn't positive the gift she'd chosen was perfect. Maybe she could meet Devlin after dinner. She smiled.

There was Devlin's old Camaro, parked against the curb, dead to the world. Why would anyone want such an impractical machine?

She nosed her Saab into the space in front of his car.

Who had rented the apartment downstairs from him? she wondered as she walked to the building, noticed the landlord's sign was gone. She used her key, let herself in.

Her mind was on a million things as she trudged up the stairs: What to wear to work tomorrow? What about switching printers at work? What was the correct approach for agenda items of the Young Professional Women's group? What should she wear to her sister's tomorrow night, what should Devlin wear? Should she go for her MBA?

She fiddled with the apartment door lock: her key always gave her trouble. Finally, the lock turned, she pushed the door open, looked up . . .

And saw a man glaring at her over the sights of his gun.

40

"Understand me," Frederick Batelli told Devlin and Perry as they sat in Batelli's plush office with its plaques on the wall, "I'm a businessman. What I do, I do for profit.

"You come here unannounced. No warrant, no reason. I pay my parking tickets. So do my boys. We want no trouble from the law. If we got any, well, the music business is good to me. I can buy lawyers."

"Must make you feel very secure, Mr. Batelli," said Perry.

"That's me: very secure.

"You tell me you're investigating Johnny Curtis's murder. More power to you. I deal with maybe a dozen jocks his size up and down the East Coast, and he was one of the best."

"How do you mean, 'deal with'?" asked Rourke.

"You two wouldn't be here if you didn't know my business. I'm an independent promoter. He was a deejay. We worked together."

"Made money together," suggested Rourke.

"His station played songs I represented, so sure, I made money. I marketed the hell out of those songs."

"And how did you do that?" asked Perry.

"All on top of the table," answered Batelli, a heavyset, handsome, middle-aged businessman in a three-piece blue suit.

"That's not what our information says," said Rourke.

"Then you've bought a bill of goods," countered Batelli. "One you'll never sell to any jury."

He leaned forward.

"I'm a busy man," he said. "Yesterday was a big day for me. Without Johnny Curtis or his lousy station, I made four grand. For being fast with the phone. How much did you two make?"

Without waiting for an answer, he waved his hand.

"You're thinking maybe I had Johnny in my pocket. So let's pretend I did—which I didn't, but let's pretend. Let's pretend that the schmuck could deliver, could get me something I wanted—like maybe an extra record of mine on the air every couple weeks.

"Why would I want to kill him?

"One, he'd be making me money, and money is what it's about.

"Two, it would be my game. He could play it my way or walk. So I lose him, big deal. There's always another Johnny.

"So where's my profit in his hit? You gotta remember: you want to understand a deal, figure the profit.

"Johnny being hit made you two come here and waste my time. My time is money. Any way you figure, him getting dead costs me."

"What if Johnny got an attack of conscience?" said Rourke. "What if he wanted to turn you in, talk about being in your pocket?"

"Man, he couldn't find a cop who'd care. And it would be his word against mine. Only thing he could accomplish by playing the rat would be to ruin his life. He rats, he gives himself the fall. That guy wanted to go nowhere but up."

"So if you didn't kill him," said Rourke, "who did?"

"How the hell should I know? Who does he do good, dead?"

"Nice guy," said Susan as they walked to their car.

"Swell guy," said Devlin. "Mobbed up to his $50 haircut. He had Johnny Curtis in his pocket, gave him coke and promises of bigger things—which would have only led to more profit for Batelli."

"So did he or his boys whack Baltimore's favorite deejay?" asked Perry.

"Like the man says," replied Rourke. "Figure the profit."

Rourke frowned.

"I wonder if Johnny really was profitable?" he said. "Coke

is one bad habit, maybe he had more. Maybe he was short on
cash to support his vices. And maybe he was into Batelli or one
of his buddies for big bucks and wasn't likely to pay."

"It's a theory," said Susan.

"Great," replied Rourke, "just what we need, another
theory. I'll have Harris chase down Johnny's cash and assets,
just in case.

"Right now," he said, "drop me at home. I want to see
what's happening there."

41

The killer got a haircut. Any police description of him no
doubt included medium to long hair, so he had the vapid woman
in the walk-in salon chop his hair brutally short. The
shearing revealed a high forehead and encroaching skin at his
temples. He brushed the hair flat. He'd dye it black. He had
various black mustaches in his briefcase to replace the natural
growth he'd shaved off after his visit to Nick.

After his haircut, he drove by police headquarters.

Damn! he thought.

The cop shop had at least two entrances: the glass front
doors and an open-mouthed garage on the right side of the
building. The garage emptied into a controlled access street
running alongside headquarters. Cars could exit two ways.

Finding Gary Harris could be difficult; not losing him
might be harder still. The killer could only watch one entrance
to police headquarters at a time, and Harris might use either at
random.

Damn you, Rachel Dylan! thought the killer. *Why do you
have to die so hard?*

42

The first thing Devlin noticed when Perry dropped him at his building was the "Apartment for Rent" sign was gone.

Wonder who my new neighbor is? he thought.

The second thing he noticed was the dog.

The dog had short black hair with rusty colorations, a stubby tail, a huge head, and a powerful, wide-chested body. He lay sprawled on the front stoop, soaking up the sun. He raised his head, watched Devlin walk up the sidewalk. When Devlin reached the steps, the dog dropped his head back to his paws. But his eyes never left Rourke.

"Easy boy," said Devlin. "I don't bite."

The dog wagged his stump of a tail.

And wouldn't move. Devlin had to step over him, expose his groin to a strange animal. He pushed the intercom button.

"Who is it?" The Duck's voice over the intercom.

"Devlin."

The door buzzed, and Devlin slid inside, careful to block the entrance so the dog couldn't follow.

The dog watched Devlin enter, then stretched out to catch the last rays of the day.

"I had to shove some mutt out of the way to get in," Devlin told the Duck when he opened the apartment door.

"That's Sam!" said the Duck as Devlin walked into his home. "My dog."

"What the hell is . . ."

Then Devlin saw Julia glaring at him, her feet planted firmly on the living room floor. Rachel sat on the couch, smiling. Gary Harris, shamefaced and nervous, shuffled by the hall.

Devlin's eyes swung back to Julia.

"What the hell are you doing here?" he said.

"You gave me a key!" she snapped. "Didn't you expect me to use it?!"

"We had a little misunderstanding, lieutenant," said Harris.

"Misunderstanding!" yelled Julia as the Duck said: "Everybody's fine!"

Rachel said nothing.

"Do you know what they did to me?!" yelled Julia.

"Look," yelled Harris, "I didn't—"

"Hey!" said the Duck, "nothing bad—"

"*Hold it!*" bellowed Devlin. The room fell silent.

"This is my house," he said in a quiet but firm voice. "My home. I'm in command. I say who talks when."

No one challenged him.

"Now," he said, nodding to Julia. 'Why are you here?"

"I thought I was welcome!" she snapped. "I drop by to pick up some laundry and leave you a note. I end up almost getting shot, being held prisoner, not even allowed to make a phone call, and manhandled!"

"Manhandled?" he asked.

"I had her take off her coat, raise her suit jacket so I could be sure she wasn't packing," said Harris. He blushed with the memory.

"And he went through my purse!"

"I ran upstairs as soon as I heard the door open up here," the Duck said quickly.

"Where were you?" asked Rourke.

"The second floor apartment. Setting up my cot."

"Setting up . . . In a minute," said Rourke, staying the Duck with his hand. "Harris?"

"We heard her on the stairs," said the youngest detective on the squad. "Heard her keys in the lock—though from the trouble she had, I thought maybe they were skeletons or some kind of pick. I zeroed her as she walked through the door. I'd have made her assume the position, but she convinced me she might be your girl, so . . ."

"So you made me . . ." Julia started to say, but Harris talked over her interruption.

". . . so I only made her drop her coat, lift her jacket. Give me her purse. I didn't want to let her go or make any calls until you cleared everything up. I didn't want to radio you, let the whole department hear you were up to something, no matter how cryptic."

"I called the dispatcher," said the Duck. "You weren't still at the last number you phoned in."

"Would you give Julia and me some privacy?" said Rourke.

Rachel looked at Harris and the Duck. All three trooped into the kitchen, shutting the door behind them.

"Now," said Rourke, "honey . . ."

"Quite an arrangement you've got here!" she snapped. "We can't live together because your apartment is too small and in you move . . . that blond!"

Devlin blinked.

"What are you . . ."

"They held a gun on me!"

"That's their job. They did right."

"But to *me*!!"

Not hysterical, he decided. *But she's way overloaded.*

"Look, Julia, you walked into something innocently. Nobody's blaming you. . . ."

"Blaming me?! For what?! I'm the one who—"

"Who walked through the door. And you're lucky. Nothing bad happened. You met Rachel, know what happened when she walked—"

"Rachel! Hah! I'm nothing like her!"

"That's right," said Rourke. "Nobody is trying to kill you."

She blinked; the fire dimmed in her eyes.

"You could have at least told me!" she whispered.

"I've been too busy."

She shook her head, not buying that.

"Couldn't you . . . stash her someplace else?!"

"No," said Rourke. "Look. I don't have time and I don't need to justify my duty to you."

"Nobody's asking you to."

Now her eyes glistened, wet.

"We're in the middle of something—"

"You're damn right we are!" she said. Her voice quavered. "You gave her a rose!"

"What?"

"A rose. I saw it in the bedroom. I went in to get my skirt. The card has your handwriting. You gave her a rose!"

"Forget it," said Devlin. "That's business."

"Julia," he said, putting his hands on her shoulders; she flinched, but he kept his grip. "This is an incredibly complex case. Don't blur issues. For five days I've been running on adrenaline and instincts. I'm tired, sore from that bomb, got a long night ahead of me."

"Do you still love me?"

"Of course," he said.

The pit of his stomach fell away.

"Nothing's changed between us," he said.

"Except her."

"Rachel?"

"Who'd you think I meant?"

"Julia, there's nothing with me and Rachel."

"Devlin, they had a gun, a big one—"

"Just like mine," he interrupted.

". . . and he pointed it right at my forehead and . . ."

She slid into his arms. Sobbed.

"Oh Devlin!" she cried against his chest. "I'll be so glad when you're through with all this awful gun stuff!"

He patted her back.

"How long you been here?" he asked.

She leaned away from him.

"I don't know," she said. "About an hour. Never get that newsletter done. Have to go to that dinner tonight and . . ."

She shook her head.

"Look at me," she said, an embarrassed smile curling her lips. "Cop's girl, career woman. Acting like a spoiled child. "I'm sorry," she said.

"It's okay," he told her.

She closed her eyes, tilted her head back. They kissed.

"What did you do while you were waiting?"

"Sat around. Talked a little."

"What do you think of Rachel?"

"Oh," said Julia, vaguely, "she's not like I expected."

"What did you two talk about?"

Julia shrugged her shoulders, gave him the *Don't-bother-to-ask-me-because-I-won't-tell-you* look.

Wonder what went on with them? thought Devlin.

"I have to go," Julia told him. She looked up, sincerely asked, "May I?"

"Sure! Of course!" he said. "But you can't . . ."

"Don't worry. I won't tell anyone."

The kitchen door opened. Rachel tiptoed into the room.

"Sorry," said Rachel. "I have to go to the bathroom."

"It's all right," said Julia. "I was about to leave."

As Rachel watched, waiting, Julia put her arm around Devlin's neck. Kissed him deeply.

"Don't forget," she said. "Tomorrow night we're having dinner at my sister's."

"I'm not sure . . ." He looked at her. "I'll try my best to make it."

"You don't worry about that," she said. Grinned. Glanced sideways at Rachel, who stood watching them, her face impassive.

"Stay out of trouble tonight," Julia told him.

"Don't worry," said Rourke. "I've got my hands full already."

"So I see," said Julia.

Then she left.

Rourke sighed deeply.

"She forgot her laundry," said Rachel.

He turned, looked at her; couldn't help it, grinned.

"You want to go remind her?" he asked.

They laughed.

"Okay," Rourke told the Duck five minutes later as they sat at the kitchen table. "What have you done?"

"Well," answered the Duck, "I started thinking."

Devlin nodded encouragingly.

"What we need to do is protect Rachel, right?"

"And find the murderer."

"Well yeah, but protect her.

"I saw the vacant apartment sign, figured what the hell: Sam and I could move in. That way we'd be close. We don't need much furniture. We never use half the stuff in the house. This way, I can be close 24 hours a day, maybe free a full shift off of you others.

"Besides," he said, "I can afford it. And . . . I'd rather be here, doing something, instead of waiting around home. I waited for too many years already.

"It's okay, isn't it?"

Rourke sighed.

"You really like that dog, don't you?"

"He's my family now. Even legally."

"Legally? What do— Never mind: I don't want to know."

"Can we stay?"

"Sure," said Rourke. "It's not a bad idea—if you're comfortable."

"Don't worry about Sam and me," said the Duck. "We're fine. Besides, this way he gets a chance to know who I work with. He likes you guys. Rachel, you."

"How can you tell?" said Rourke, amused.

"If he didn't, he'd have ripped your leg off." The Duck frowned. "Or peed on your foot. Sometimes he gets confused."

"After all," said the Duck, shrugging, smiling at himself, "he's a Duck's dog."

43

Three names eliminated, thought the killer, *eight to go*.

A horn honked in the night outside his hotel room. He dialed the next number on his list.

One ring. Two. Three, and a male voice answered: "Hello?"

"Hi, I'm wondering if you can help me?"

"I don't know. Who is this?"

"My name is Bob Samuel," lied the killer.

"I don't know you, do I?" said the man.

"No," laughed the killer, "not really. I'm from Boston, and I'm trying to track down my best friend's best friend."

"Did you look in the mirror?"

They both laughed.

So far, so good.

"No, his old best friend. His name is Gary Harris."

"So's mine."

"I know, but there are so many Gary Harris's in Baltimore."

Come on! the killer urged silently: *This is the perfect time for you to volunteer something about yourself, asshole!*

"Tell me about it," said this Gary Harris. "I'm always the one people get wrong."

"Really?"

"Yeah."

"Well," said the killer, "the only thing I know about the right Gary Harris is what he does for a living."

Do it! thought the killer. *Tell me you're a cop and let me say then you're the wrong guy and hang up!*

"What's he do?" said the Gary Harris on the phone.

"He's a policeman."

"Well, said Harris, Gary, "it's your lucky night."

Shit! thought the killer. *What lie will let me off the hook without alerting this cop?*

"Because," said Gary Harris, "I'm not the one you want, but I know who is."

The world reeled; the killer felt as though a cool breeze blew across his brow.

"Really?!" he said.

"Sure. You ain't the first to get it wrong. Most of the others were women, though."

"Yeah, that sounds like my friend's buddy."

"Nice guy. 'Bout the third wrong number, I called around until I found him. You talk to the old geezer Gary Harris who used to be a railroad engineer?"

"No," said the killer, "I didn't get to him yet."

"You're lucky. He'll talk your ear off before you get what you want."

"Really."

"Yeah."

"What about . . ."

"The cop, yeah. He's the one who lives on Elmwood."

The killer scanned the list: *Harris, Gary. 1229 Elmwood.* He read the address to the man on the phone.

"Yeah, that's him."

"I guess this is my lucky night," said the killer.

44

Fitzgerald's looked like a slick magazine ad come to life; was one of half a dozen chic fern bars not far from Baltimore's Inner Harbor. Devlin felt foreign that Wednesday night when he walked in wearing the topcoat from Peter Maxwell's trunk.

Customers sat on delicately carved wooden chairs at two of Fitzgerald's water-worn plank tables. The first group was an overweight couple in sweaters who whispered seriously over their draft beers. At a table ten feet away, two middle-aged men talked baseball and taxes, their suit jackets draped over the backs of their chairs.

The bar was long, high-gloss wood with a brass rail, padded stools, and three customers. The mirror ran the length of the bar, guarded by rows of bottles and flanked by framed reproductions of old newspapers' front pages. The headlines screamed about Dillinger, World War I, Prohibition, and other ancient history. The bartender wore red suspenders over his broad shoulders, a bow tie, and a beard.

One of his charges sitting at the bar wore a suit and tie. That man's companion shed his suit jacket. His shirt was white, his tie paisley. His cufflinks and left hand had a glint of gold. He combed his hair in a foppish wave; its gray nicely offset his swarthy tan.

A juke box played in the corner. Down that way, at the far end of the bar, sat a lone woman. Her black hair was sprayed into a style 20 years old. She looked a hard 30. Her face was pretty, but puffy, heavily made up. She wore creamy brown lipstick, a white blouse that strained across her bra. She had too much belly beneath her tight gold slacks. A cheap fur jacket draped the stool beside her, and a tall glass sat before her on the bar; she stroked the glass with manicured short fingernails, an office woman's hand. She propped her left elbow next to the glass, held her cigarette high so the smoke drifted to the ceiling through the collection of beer steins hanging from the open wooden beams.

Devlin walked to her end of the bar, sat two stools away. Through her cigarette smoke he saw her watching him from the corners of her eyes.

"What are you having, my man?" the bartender asked Devlin.

"Draft," said Rourke.

"We got—"

"Whatever's light."

"You got it," said the bartender, winking as he shot a finger at Devlin.

The woman inhaled deeply on her cigarette.

Wonder if she's recognized Maxwell's coat? thought Devlin.

The restless man in the white shirt and paisley tie wandered into their corner. He stared at the play sheet in the juke box, dropped a quarter in the machine, and punched a few buttons.

The juke box whirred. The Penguins serenaded the bar with "Earth Angel."

"You can thank me for that," the man in the paisley tie told the bartender, the woman, and Rourke.

"Mind if I bum a cigarette?" he said, looking at the woman. "I'm trying to quit."

"Here," she said, passing him one and taking one for herself. "Funny cure."

"If I have to bum 'em, I don't smoke so many," he said.

"Cheaper, too." Her words were amused.

"Not really," he said. "Because now I have to buy you a drink."

The bartender answered the man's beckon. The man looked at Rourke, pointed to his beer—just in case they were together. Rourke shook his head. The man shrugged—and smiled. He turned his attention to the woman, who ordered vodka with water-back. He asked for a brand-name Scotch, neat.

"Are you trying to quit drinking, too?" she asked him as he pulled a crisp $20 from a wallet obviously full of them.

He dropped the $20 on the bar, picked up her matches, and lit their cigarettes.

"What do you think I am?" he asked her. "Crazy?"
They laughed.

Gary Harris walked in the bar carrying his police radio;
stood at the door scanning the faces.

"Yes sir!" said the bartender, doing the one-of-the-guys
strut to meet Harris further up the bar. "What do you need?
Something to warm the night?"

"No thanks," said Harris. "But I have some questions."

"Shoot," said the bartender, casually leaning on the bar.

"Have you worked here long?"

"Since hell thawed out," said the bartender.

Harris politely smiled.

"Don't mind the jokes," said the bartender. "Got to keep
laughing to stay ahead of the shit—but I don't need to tell you
about that."

"No," said Harris, "you don't. If you've been here that
long, you might be able to help me."

"Pleasure."

"Do you remember ever seeing this guy in here?"

Harris handed the bartender a picture of Peter Maxwell.
The bartender studied it carefully.

"No," he finally said. "But I see a hundred guys in here on
a busy night. Lot of them like him, give or take a few years."

"How about anybody who looks like this?" he said,
passing him the killer's sketch.

"Nope. He looks . . . We're mostly a coat and tie crowd,
you know? I'd notice an army jacket."

"Got a couple names for you then," said Harris.

"Bet I've been called all of them!"

Again, Harris smiled at the man's humor.

"How about Peter Maxwell?"

"Nope. Know a few Peters, but none of them look like
either of the guys in the picture. Don't know any Maxwells."

"How about a Laura. Good-looking, in her early
twenties?"

"Hey! Fitzgerald's is legendary for its good-looking girls!"

Their conversation carried throughout the bar. All the
customers listened closely, tried to be invisible.

"But Laura doesn't ring a bell," said the bartender.

"What's this about?" he asked the cop.

"Just routine," said Harris. He nodded farewell, left.

"Come back soon!" the bartender called to Harris's exit.

The bartender shook his head. He lifted a hose spigot from the chrome holder, squirted coke into a glass. Walked down to Rourke's end of the bar. He looked at the closed door, shook his head, and blithely told his waiting audience:

"I hate cops."

The woman and her new companion laughed. Devlin smiled.

"Hey, Lewis," said the man in the paisley tie: "What did he want?"

"Some poor sons of bitches who are probably late on their alimony payments," grumbled the bartender.

"Ain't that the truth," said the customer, taking a deep drag on his begged cigarette.

"You divorced?" asked the woman.

"Honey," he said, "that's a long, long story."

"Did you know the guy?" asked Devlin.

"Nah," said the bartender, shaking his head. "He showed me some pictures that didn't light up the old memory banks, but hey! They're a little crowded and seen a lot of booze."

The man and the woman chuckled.

"What else did he want?" asked Devlin.

"Some chick named Laura! Can you imagine that? How the hell does he expect to find somebody in Baltimore when all he knows is her name is Laura and she's pretty!"

"And maybe she's been in a couple bars," added Devlin.

"Yeah!" said the bartender, shaking his head.

"I knew a Laura once," said the woman. Smiling.

"Yeah?" said the man who'd bought her a drink, his eyes looking beyond her to the guy two stools down.

"Who was she?" asked Devlin.

"A good friend," said the woman. Laughed. "In high school.

"Long ago and far away," she added. She stared straight ahead, looked off into nowhere.

"She was naughty," she finally announced.

"Oh yeah?" said the man who wanted to quit smoking. "She sounds interesting. Tell me more."

"Well," she said, and Devlin stepped off his stool. He dropped a $5 bill on the bar.

"Be right back," he said.

The idea hit him as he walked back from the bathroom. He retraced his steps to the wall between the doors marked

"Men" and "Women" and the pay phone that hung there. He pulled out a notebook, flipped through its pages until he came to the number he'd copied in large red numerals from the paper hidden in Peter Maxwell's wallet: 389.

That sequence of numbers didn't match up with the pay phone.

"Got another phone?" he asked the bartender when he returned to his stool. "The one back there is on the fritz."

"Sure," said the bartender. He lifted a receiver off its wall mount, handed it to Devlin. The touchtone buttons were in the handle, and the seven digits printed on the label didn't contain the 389 sequence either.

Harris was outside waiting in the car. Devlin tapped out Harris's home phone number, feigned interest in the no-answer rings.

"Guess she isn't home," said the bartender as Devlin handed him the phone, scooped up his change while leaving a generous tip.

"Guess not," he said, walking to the door. "Thanks for everything."

"Any time," said the bartender.

The door closed after Devlin.

"Hey, Lewis," said the man now definitely with the woman: "Who was that guy?"

The bartender shrugged:

"Beats the hell out of me."

"So?" said Harris as Rourke climbed into the car parked two blocks from Fitzgerald's.

"So the answers you got were true, even if they weren't straight," answered Rourke.

"Yeah, I figured."

"The way Maxwell's friend talked, this wasn't his place anyway."

"Don't mean to insult a lieutenant or anything," said Harris, "but you look ridiculous in that coat. It's two sizes too big."

"Even without this coat, I'd have felt ridiculous in that bar. You know who was in there?"

"I didn't recognize anybody," said Harris, worried he'd overlooked something.

"Husbands, that's who." Devlin shook his head. "Dads."

"I know what you mean," said Harris. "I hope when I'm 35 I'm not stuck in there,"

"I'm 35," said Rourke.

"Yeah," said Harris, starting the car, anticipating his orders, "but you're no husband. You get to go to the Red Moon."

45

Street lights illuminated grim and empty sidewalks as Harris drove the car across a bridge. The buildings were dark, sagging townhouses, locked storefronts. The street lights shimmered on the ghostly pale stucco of the Art Deco Circle Theater. The movie marquee advertised a Truffaut festival, but there was no movie that night.

"Drop me there," said Devlin, pointing to a spot half a block before the nightclub with a glowing red neon globe hanging above its door. "And give me more time."

"It'll take a few minute to find a place to park," said Harris, eying the jammed street. Most of the parked cars were at least six years old.

The Red Moon was a narrow building. A faded black-and-white poster decorated the entrance and advertised the movie *Stop Making Sense* by Baltimore boy David Byrne.

Red saturated the nightclub: it's walls and ceilings glowed crimson in the blue and red neon lights; a scarlet cigarette haze floated above the rose-hued faces of the crowd.

Devlin wedged himself into the pack of customers at the bar. The small round tables on the wall behind him were full, as were the ones against the back wall. Open stairs led to a rear landing, where half a dozen patrons played dinging pinball and electronic games.

The bartender had wire glasses, long hair, and a harried expression on his lean face.

"You want a beer?" he shouted to Devlin above the din. "It's dollar night."

"Sure," answered Rourke.

"How about a coke?!" yelled a girl in blue jeans and a black turtleneck sweater.

"Draft or can?" asked the bartender.

"Ah . . . Doesn't matter."

The bartender filled both their orders at once, slopped beer from the heavy glass mug he set in front of Devlin, then darted to customers waving at the other end of the bar. Devlin took a drink, then looked around Peter Maxwell's secret hideaway.

The body heat from the crowd combined with the scarlet cigarette fog gave the Red Moon an oppressive atmosphere and, for Rourke, a sense of the surreal. Eras from his history jumbled together all around him. Juke box consoles from the fifties mounted on the bar offered a potpourri of Rourke's musical heritage: "Heartbreak Hotel" by Elvis Presley (1956), the Classic's IV's "Spooky" (1968), "96 Tears" by Question Mark and the Mysterians (1966), half a dozen hits from the mid-sixties by Motown's Supremes, Bruce Springsteen's "Badlands" (1978), and from 1985, "Dancing in the Dark." Rourke recognized a dozen of the eighties New Wave songs listed, assumed many of the titles he didn't know were also contemporary, the kinds of songs WBBX only played if they were already a hit—or had the helping hand of someone like Batelli. As he turned to look at his fellow patrons of the night, the juke box switched from the Jam's current hit, "The Bitterest Pill" to the Rolling Stones' 1966 "Mother's Little Helper:"

Of the Red Moon's hundred or so customers, Rourke doubted more than a dozen were older than 30. An equal number might have been younger than 18, false I.D.s in their pockets and fear of discovery competing with rebel thrills in their hearts. The crowd's style was deliberate extremes. One either moved in a languid, blasé stupor, sat passively at a table staring out at nothing, or marched through the bar with an exaggerated air of intense dedication, attacked conversation with highly animated gestures and a tone that implied terrible importance.

Most of the men wore blue jeans or green khaki pants, boots, sneakers, sports jackets over T-shirts. Black T-shirts were the favorite, although Rourke saw a few neon prints and rock concert souvenir shirts. In this crimson darkness, a dozen men and half that many women wore sunglasses. Most everyone had shed their outside coats. Rourke kept Peter Maxwell's coat on, though no one needed any kind of a coat inside the Red Moon. Only one other man wore his wrap: a hulking gorilla with greasy black hair, who wore a fifties black motorcycle jacket resplendent with silver zippers.

The men who stood out in the crowd would have been ignored on any average American street: three men in their midtwenties, their ties stuffed in the handkerchief pockets of their sports jackets.

The women seemed more extreme than the men to Rourke, though only a few of them had the days' shaved heads, purple- or orange-dyed hair, spiked Mohawks. A woman with cropped dyed blond hair, a leopard print skirt, and chubby thighs covered by black mesh stockings gave a cigarette to a lean woman with waistlength black hair, sticky white makeup, blood red lipstick. Many of the women wore blue jeans, men's shirts, bulky sweaters. Rourke saw no women without make-up.

The crowd behind him parted to let one of the bar's three black customers glide through, a handsome smiler with Rastafarian dreadlocks and an arm full of record albums. A short woman with curly red hair excitedly met him. They kissed each other's cheeks; she led him to her table. The path they cleared through the crowd showed Rourke three of the tables against the wall.

Two lean, pale young men sat at the first table, their eyes shyly downcast, each with one foot still in the closet as they nervously tested their hidden personae in public.

Through the shifting crowd, Rourke glimpsed the trio at the second table. The person he saw best was a man of about 50 with thin silver hair hanging over his ears, a weathered face, and a body long past its tone beneath a frayed brown sweater. The man caught Rourke's gaze, stared back with sorrowful eyes, as he continued talking to the much younger couple: ". . . let alone Kerouac."

Rourke had a clear view of the woman at the third table. Like the man with the silver hair, like Rourke, she was older than most of the people with whom she shared this night. She was perhaps 30. Her strawberry hair was tangled. She wore a black blouse and a haggard look Rourke knew too well: she was a nudge away from suicide or homicide; without that nudge, she'd sit at that table forever.

Rachel could fold into here, thought Rourke.

"Want another?" asked the bartender.

Rourke glanced at his empty mug.

"Hey, it's dollar night," said the bartender. He blinked, frowned.

"Do you know me?" asked Rourke quickly.

"No," said the bartender haltingly, "though . . . something about you. . . . You look familiar. Were you here another time?"

Rourke laughed.

"I'll have another beer," he said. "It's dollar night."

Rourke glanced in the mirror behind the bar: Harris, standing at the door. Their gaze met. Rourke shook his head. Harris went to the far end of the bar, faded into the shadows. Few people noticed him.

"Will you watch my beer while I go the can?" Rourke asked the bartender.

"Hey, I'll try, but—"

"I'll save your place," said the lean, good-looking man sitting next to Rourke who wrote rock reviews for the local hip weekly paper and studied to be a professional horse player.

"Thanks," said Rourke.

The bartender pointed to the second floor landing where the pinball wizards played.

"Pay phone up there, too?" asked Rourke.

"If someone hasn't ripped it off again," answered the bartender.

Rourke wasn't sure of the gender of the sweatered person huddled over the pay phone opposite the bathroom doors. He went through the door marked "Men?," entered a green-walled closet with a sink and a toilet stall with a basketball-sized hole kicked through its wall. The walls were so covered with black ink graffiti that most of the scribblings were illegible. On the door inside the stall, Rourke made out the phrase, "If I didn't have me, there'd be nobody." The slogan on the toilet seat read, "Knee Deep in Shit Again."

When he left the bathroom five minutes later, no one
stood at the pay phone. He glanced at the dial. The number
printed beneath the plastic read, "555-3897."

"Three, eight, nine," he said.

The phone rang.

Rourke answered it: "Hello?"

A woman's voice asked for Mary.

"Who is she?"

"Like, you know."

"Guess she's not here."

"Okay. Tell her I called, okay?"

"Okay," he said. Hung up.

Rourke edged his way through the crowd. He had to
weave around a drunk, six-foot-four bearded beanpole wearing
earphones connected to a belt-clipped tape recorder, slide
between two women. He'd settled on his stool, picked up his
beer, when he heard her yell above the music:

"Excuse me!"

She touched him lightly on his shoulder; he whirled fast,
scared her.

She was a pretty 19, with brown hair neatly combed to
her shoulders. Her makeup was conservative, and she had a
fine though not outstanding figure. She wore two sweaters, a
pale white crewneck beneath a black cardigan vest, and blue
jeans. Her eyes were wet.

"Where . . ." She swallowed. "Where did you get that
coat?"

"Hello, Laura," said Rourke in his friendliest voice.

"How do you know who I am?"

The rock reviewer watched the two of them closely. From
the shadows of the bar, so did Harris.

"We have to talk about that," Rourke told Laura.

The juke box blared "Heartbreak Hotel."

"Who are you?" she yelled over the music.

"I can't hear you," Rourke lied. He pointed to the area by
the door. "It's quieter over there. Come on."

He stood up, took his beer, and casually motioned for her
to lead the way. She glanced over her shoulder. Rourke
followed her gaze. There were half a dozen tables against the
back wall. He couldn't tell who she looked to: the two men
sitting with their backs against the wall, staring impassively at
nothing or the group of whispering college girls. Laura turned
and walked where Devlin directed.

They found a quiet space by the door amid the Red Moon's cacophony. She glared at him.

"I don't know who you are," she hissed. "But I want to know how you know my name. And how you got that coat!"

Her lips twitched again.

"My name is Devlin Rourke," he said. He flashed his badge and I.D. so only she could see them. "I'm a police detective."

Her eyes closed. She bit her lip.

"Peter!" she said softly, about to cry. "He . . . He . . ."

"Let's get out of here," said Rourke.

"But . . . the people I'm with . . . My coat. It's cold."

"We won't go far," he said. "I'm parked up the block. And here. . . ."

He draped Maxwell's coat around her shoulders, shrugged to resettle his sports jacket. She pulled Maxwell's coat closed. A tear ran down her cheek.

"Your friends will watch your coat, won't they?"

"How do I know if I can trust you?"

"Smart girl. You saw the badge and the I.D. with my picture. If you have any doubts, go to the pay phone, call the police, ask about me. Ask for a cruiser of uniformed officers to come check me out."

She shook her head.

"I'm already in enough trouble," she said.

"Then we really do need to talk."

She nodded. Walked out of the bar.

They'd gone half a block, Rourke had just spotted the car where Harris parked it when he heard the man yell behind them.

"Hey!"

Rourke whirled—stepping backward as he did so he was ahead of the girl to his left, keeping her at the edge of his vision while he watched the two men coming after them. One hurried faster than the other. Neither wore coats.

Behind them, Harris stepped out of the Red Moon.

"I've had it with your bullshit, bitch!" yelled the first man as he stormed up to them.

"Larry! Please!" said Laura.

Larry was one of the two men who'd sat against the bar's far wall. His black boots made him three inches taller than Rourke. Larry had brown, curly Semitic hair, pale skin. He wore a black shirt, blue jeans. His thick lips were pressed tight in anger.

"You fuckin' walk out on me with another one of your businessman good-timers and—"

"Please, Larry!" begged Laura.

"I don't think we've been introduced," said Rourke. His voice was even, steady. His hands waited by his sides.

Larry paced closer to Rourke and Laura, a jittery, raging gait. Larry's friend slowed to a walk, stopped 20 feet away, unaware of Harris quietly coming up behind him.

Rourke saw Larry's eyes flick over what looked like an older, leaner, and smaller man. Larry hissed:

"You keep your fucking face shut or you'll end up with more trouble than you've ever seen!"

"Stupid play, Larry," said Rourke.

"Really?" said Larry, a new light shining in his eyes. He smiled, stepped to within arm's length of the asshole bothering him. "Well let me explain why . . ."

Larry had practiced the move alone in his bedroom. He'd never used it. After his, "let me explain why" cue, he'd quickly cock his right hand up by his face: maybe he was going to hit the asshole, maybe he was going to wipe his brow. Didn't matter what the asshole thought because he'd fall for the fake. Quick as a wink, Larry'd throw a hard jab with his left hand, which would catch the asshole unawares and smash him in the stomach, knock the wind out of him, and double him over. Larry would smash his right fist down on the asshole's neck, and he'd collapse at Larry's feet.

But that night Larry's plan fell apart. When Larry cocked his right fist, the asshole stepped *back*; when Larry threw his left jab, it brushed past the asshole.

Who knocked Larry's left arm further off target and smashed his right fist into Larry's left kidney.

Larry gasped. The night went white. Laura's face reeled in front of him. A vice grabbed his left wrist, jerked his arm in a hammerlock, then whirled him around, smashed him face first against a boarded-up door. His feet got kicked out from under him, and he fell to his knees. Hard metal bit his left wrist. The man grabbed his right hand, bent that behind his back too, snapped metal around that wrist, and Larry couldn't move his hands. He was jerked to his feet, and the asshole hissed in his ear:

"I told you it was a stupid play, Larry! I'm a cop! Now don't move a fucking inch!"

Harsh hands patted down every inch of his body.

Behind them, Larry's companion saw the blur of the fight begin; saw his friend thrown into a doorway by the man who'd seemed too old to be tough. Larry's friend bolted to help his buddy.

But someone tripped him, and he crashed to the sidewalk. He rolled over—froze when he saw the man with the police radio in one hand and a revolver pointed straight at him in the other.

"Get up slow!" said the cop, "Then lean over and grab that car!"

"Oh shit," moaned Larry's friend. "Oh shit!"

He heard the cop who tripped him call for a squad car over the radio. Down the street, he heard the other cop reading Larry his rights, knew that he'd be next for that speech. And softly, in the winter wind, he heard Laura sobbing.

46

"Oh God, this is so terrible!" sobbed Laura as she sat in the front seat of the idling Chevy. She stared at the mist on the windshield, remembered when her Dad taught her to write on the fogged glass of the big red Dodge.

But the Dodge was long gone. Behind the Chevy's steering wheel sat a cop who'd wrapped her in a murdered man's coat. In the back seat sat the other cop. Her father would be home in Annapolis tonight, watching television, calloused hands resting on the frayed arms of his easy chair. He'd watch the 11 o'clock news; suddenly hear his daughter's name and that she was some tragic criminal. He'd grab his chest, fall forward. Dead before the weather report.

"It's all my fault," she sobbed.

"What's all your fault, Laura?" asked Devlin, gently.

She gestured out to the night, shook her head.

"This!" she cried.

"We just want to talk to you, Laura," said the one in the back seat.

"About . . . Peter?"

"Yes," said Rourke.

"What will happen to Larry?" she asked. "And . . . Mark?"

"Did they know Peter Maxwell, too?"

"Larry met him a half dozen times. Mark never knew Peter."

"Did Larry and Peter get along?" asked Harris.

Laura shook her head. The tears were over. For now.

"Larry didn't like Peter. Was jealous of him. Of me."

"Larry's excitable, isn't he?" said Harris.

Laura turned slowly. Looked at Rourke, at Harris.

"Larry . . . You have to understand him," she said. "Everybody at school . . ."

"The Art Institute?"

She nodded.

"Everybody knows Larry is talented," she continued, "but he's an artist, and artists—"

"Artists are people, Laura," said Devlin. "Did Larry ever have a run-in with Peter Maxwell?"

She shook her head. "Larry chose to respect my rights with Peter."

Larry knew Peter Maxwell could beat the shit out of him, thought Rourke.

"What exactly were your 'rights' with Peter Maxwell?" asked Rourke. "I don't understand."

"We didn't either," she said. Smiled. "Peter and I . . ."

"How did you meet?" asked Rourke.

"In the Moon. I was carrying an artist's portfolio, and he asked if I drew. We talked about spatial relations, light, paint. He was so sweet, sincere."

"When was this?" asked Harris.

"A couple weeks before Christmas break," she said.

"Did you see him much after that?" asked Rourke.

"When I got back from break."

"How often?"

"Four, five times a week. After my classes, sometimes at night, in the Moon. Sometimes he'd take me to dinner."

"How long had you been lovers?" said Rourke.

"We . . . how did you . . ."

"Don't worry about it," said Harris, backing up his boss's bluff.

"Lovers. . . . Love is such an *imperfect* term," said Laura.

In the back seat, Harris rolled his eyes.

"I mean," she said, "we weren't lovers in the sense we loved each other. We did nothing that detracted from his loving his wife. We really didn't!"

"Uh-huh," said Rourke. "What did you do?"

"Sometimes we shared each other," she said. "He never spent the night."

"How did you feel about that?" asked Rourke.

She mistook his question for personal or perhaps philosophic concern. "Sharing is the best thing you can do," she said.

"Didn't you mind sharing Peter with his wife?" asked Harris.

"But . . . we . . . That was the way it was," she said. "Like . . . a poem with irregular rhymes that leads to a deeper truth."

"What?" said Harris.

"Never mind," said Rourke. "How did Larry feel about your affair with Peter?"

"He didn't know we slept together," she said; revised her wishful thinking: "He didn't understand. It . . . Larry and I . . .

"Sex is no big deal," she said. "Is it?"

"Did his wife know?" asked Harris.

"Of course not!" she insisted.

"Where were you two headed?" asked Rourke.

"Headed?"

"In your affair. Where were you going, what was your future?"

"Future? We . . . The moment, the now was so precious, we didn't . . . The future takes care of itself."

In the back seat, Harris sighed audibly.

"He told you he was married?" asked Rourke.

"Of course! We were completely honest with each other."

"What did you do?" asked Harris.

"Talked. About everything: art, the way the world worked, his student days at the Institute, my father . . .

"Sometimes he talked to me like I was his daughter or his wife—or as if we had been lovers once long ago. Sometimes he talked to me like I wasn't even there."

"Did he ever talk about changing his life?" asked Rourke. "Leaving his wife? Leaving his business? Anything like that?"

"He loved his wife—he really did. And his daughter. He said she was smart, but he had trouble talking to her. She wants to be an accountant or something.

"I told him not to worry," said Laura: "You know kids: at that age, kids want to be all different things."

She's not much younger than you, thought Rourke.

"What was troubling him?" he said. "His business?"

"He was proud of it!" she said. "I mean, who wouldn't be? They were the best graphics art company in the city.

"He used to . . . He kept saying he didn't have the touch anymore."

"The touch?" asked Rourke.

"For painting, drawing, art. And that bothered him, but there was something more."

"What did he think of Larry?" asked Rourke.

"Peter didn't like him. Said Larry always talked about going somewhere, doing something, but he never did anything. Didn't have the guts to jump into the business, didn't have the guts to chase the art.

"He was wrong, of course," said Laura quickly. "It's just that Larry is so sensitive, so . . .

"Peter was a more practical man," she said.

"Did he ever talk about having any enemies?" asked Rourke.

"Who could hate Peter?" She shook her head. A fresh tear rolled from her eye. "When Larry showed me the newspaper story . . ."

"Larry showed you?" asked Rourke.

"On Sunday," she said. "He was so shocked. Sympathetic. He's so sensitive."

"I'll bet," said Harris.

"His wife . . . She doesn't know about me, does she? About Peter and me? There was nothing wrong, but I don't think a wife would understand."

"You'd be surprised," said Rourke, "but no, she may not know. And maybe won't need to."

"Thank God!" said Laura. "I never want to hurt her or their daughter. Or anybody! How can you go through life hurting people?"

"It's easy," said Rourke. "Who killed Peter?"

"I can't understand him dying like that!" she said. "Nobody would want to hurt him. So I figure it was just a mistake of destiny."

Devlin wanted to hold his head.

Forget it, he thought. *She's just a kid.*

"What . . . What will happen to Larry."

"Depends," said Rourke, though he had few doubts.

Later that night, after Rourke and Harris had questioned her friends without learning anything pertinent, they sent two scared young men home, charges of assault and disturbing the peace dropped.

"What about me?" asked Laura.

"Nothing," Rourke told her.

"Will this . . . this be in the papers?"

"No," he told her. "This is a confidential investigation."

She closed her eyes and leaned against the window. Her breath fogged the glass.

"We'll drive you back to the Red Moon," said Rourke. "Wait until you get your coat, then take you home."

"No thanks," she said. "I'd rather . . . I'll get home alone."

"Whatever," said Rourke.

"Can I . . . can I keep Peter's coat?"

"Sorry," said Rourke. "It doesn't belong to you."

"Yeah," she said, "I know. I just wondered. Thought I'd ask."

She shook her head.

"Peter always told me to try, you know?" she said.

Rourke and Harris sat outside Harris's rented bungalow, the Chevy's engine running.

"So much for Peter Maxwell's secret life," said Rourke.

"What about Laura?" asked Harris.

"I forgot anybody could be that young," said Rourke.

"Do you think Maxwell would have ever upped his ante?"

"As in leaving his family? I doubt it. If he was smart, somewhere deep inside him, he knew he was just going through a phase, some sort of—"

"Validation," said Harris.

Rourke looked at him.

"I watch the sincere talk shows," said Harris.

"Shit," said Rourke.

"Do you think Maxwell's wife knew? Or suspected?"

"She suspects now," said Rourke. "No matter how this turns out, she'll always suspect something. But if she knew before, she's a great liar, with a cool enough head to be deadly."

"Tomorrow," continued Rourke, "get the phone records for these people—the wife, Laura, Larry. Maybe one of them has a psycho friend from out of town we can spot."

"Have to be a psycho friend," said Harris. "None of them have the bucks to afford a pro, even if they could find one."

"You'd be surprised how cheap some people work," said Rourke. "And we should check with Larry's hometown cops and high school guidance counselor. Maybe his juvenile record got wiped clean by a court. Maybe he's wild enough to kill on his own. A .22 could be a teenager's rabbit pistol."

"What did you think of the Red Moon?"

Rourke shook his head.

"I think it's one of those places we all should have been. And left. Great place to visit. It would be hell getting stuck here."

"We keep finding maybes," said Harris. "The idea was to lock onto a certain enough trail—"

"Before we ran out of time," said Rourke.

"Yeah. Maybe not catch the killer but at least lock on to his trail before we had to surface. What if this Sunday comes and we got nothing but more maybes?"

"Damned if I know," said Rourke.

"Damned if you don't," Harris told him.

Rourke watched until Harris was inside his house and the lights came on. The lieutenant drove home.

Neither policeman noticed the man huddled down in the front seat of a car parked across the street from Harris's house.

Finally, thought the killer, who'd feared Harris would never come home—though why anybody would want to call that dump a home was beyond him. Dumb cops, working all hours for a salary that didn't let them live much better than the average ghetto crook.

The killer had been waiting for four hours, almost froze to death in his parked car. He hadn't run the engine to keep warm, hadn't want to attract attention.

He glanced at his watch: 1:17. The lights went off across the street.

In for the night, thought the killer. The killer was 20 minutes from his bed. If he got back here at 6:30, he could find a place to roost, be there when Harris left for work.

Tomorrow, the killer thought. *Tomorrow*.

Thursday morning Rourke woke with the gut feeling that he controlled nothing, knew little, and had lost his way.

So much for your personal life, whispered his mind. *Now tell me about the Ward murders*.

"Wish I could," mumbled Rourke. He rolled to his back on the sofa bed; sniffed the air: coffee, *real* coffee. Rachel led the revolt, the Duck provided the cash, and Perry had purchased a coffee maker, a grinder, and several pounds of beans.

Susan walked into the front room just as Rourke sat up, scratched his stomach beneath the blue sweatshirt. His gray sweatpants didn't match the blue police issue top, but they'd been the only sleepwear he could find in the hall closet. He licked his dry lips, yawned to rid his mouth of cotton.

"I'm not cut out for nights on the town, anymore," he said.

"Don't complain about getting old," said Perry. "Not to me."

"Who said anything about getting old," he muttered.

"I'll get the paper," said Susan.

"Then I'll wait on my shower."

He swung his feet off the bed, picked up his unholstered gun from the table close to his pillow. His shoulder holster hung from the desk chair. Rourke shoved the gun in the holster; the rig dangled from his hand as he shuffled to the bathroom to brush his teeth, shave. Susan left the apartment to get the paper off the stoop. Rourke kept the bathroom door open, ran the water slowly, quietly, so he could concentrate on the building noises.

He'd just lathered his face when he heard a knock. He stepped into the hall, holstered gun in hand, his eyes locked on the apartment door.

"It's me," he heard Susan say.

She opened the door slowly, stepped inside, shut it.

"Okay," he said. "Do you mind sticking around until I get cleaned up?"

"I'll catch up on the news," she said, waving the paper.

Forty minutes later, Susan had left and Rourke sat at the kitchen table with a cup of coffee and the *Star's* comic pages to catch up on Spiderman. He heard the bedroom door open.

Rachel stood in the kitchen doorway. She wore her blue sweatshirt and Rourke's missing blue sweatpants. Her eyes were full of sleep.

"Good morning, dear," she said, giving Rourke a momentary start. "Did the children get off to school all right?"

"Yeah," he said, grinning. "Sarah is over her cold, and little Ben wants his fingerpainting on the wall for parents' day."

"Little Ben," said Rachel, shaking her head. "What a character."

She crossed to the refrigerator, opened it as she said, "Do you know if the kids left us any donuts?"

"I didn't even think to look," he said. Quickly explained: "Sarah insisted on making their lunches today."

"That Sarah," said Rachel. She pulled a box of donuts out of the refrigerator, flashed him a triumphant smile. "She's so good."

She set the donut box on the kitchen table.

"Ben ate all the chocolate ones right away," explained Devlin as Rachel poured herself a cup of coffee.

"That Ben!" she said, sitting opposite Devlin. "How are we going to teach him to share without spoiling his wonderful spirit?"

"It's a rough one, all right." He handed her the cream. Opened the donut box, chose cinnamon.

"I'm sorry I slept in this morning, dear," said Rachel.

"That's okay, honey." They grinned. "You've had a hard week."

"And it's only Thursday. How did you sleep, Dev?"

"Not good. Not bad, but not good. I couldn't seem to slide into any dreams. Maybe that's what kept me tossing and turning."

"Too much liquor?"

"Too much too much," he said. "And not enough."

"So," she said, picking up a plain donut, "figured out who my nightmare is and how you're going to catch him?"

Rourke shook his head.

"Think you will?" she asked.

"Rachel . . ." He shook his head again, smiled. "Remember I told you you could trust me? That I wouldn't lie to you? That we had a pact?"

"Well," she said, shrugged. "I don't remember it being worded quite that way but . . . I know what you mean."

"Most of police work is eliminating, patiently taking what's left and figuring out how it fits into what happened. Going from there to the person you need to lock up. For us, working covertly so no crooked cop can see us, working with a deadline . . . different game.

"We've got no score so far. Lots of maybes, lots of sordid little secrets, but no solid answers."

"Where does that leave me?" asked Rachel.

"Alive, for one thing," he said.

"And free?"

"Freedom is important to you, isn't it?" he asked.

"Hey! I'm an American, aren't I?"

They laughed, stopped and focused on each other. Looked away, took a long drink of coffee.

"Rachel, I know this hasn't been pleasant, but—"

"It could have been worse," she interrupted. "It could have been a lot worse."

"I've tried to run it the best way it could go," he said. "Everything I did was—"

"Yeah, I know: nothing personal."

"Of course it was personal. I don't want you to die."

"Losing a witness is bad for your record, right?" she said.

"That, too," he said.

And suddenly they were both embarrassed.

"It's been okay," she said. "Once you get to know you guys, you couldn't ask for better babysitters. Or bodyguards.

"Or friends," she said softly.

"Outlaw to cop," he said.

"Yes," she said. "Outlaw to cop. Person to person."

They lost words. He stood, poured them both another cup of coffee. Sat down across from her, took the cream she handed him.

"That outlaw to cop . . ." she said. "I'm not bad. But I don't react just because of what the politicians write into laws. I blow grass, try coke, did the heroin, all of which I don't expect you to understand."

"You'd be surprised."

She looked at him.

He looked back. Sighed deeply.

"I understand about the drugs."

"Well, as a cop, you've no doubt seen enough."

"I've done enough," he said.

Her eyes widened, her jaw dropped.

"You?!"

"Me."

"But . . ."

"My badge sits over a heart just as human as yours."

"When . . . How . . ." She shook her head. "I don't even know how to ask the questions!"

"Maybe I wouldn't answer them." He shook his head. "But maybe I would. Maybe this isn't the smartest thing to do, tell you—"

"Think of it as fair," she said.

"Fair?!"

"You know most of my secrets," she said. "All I know about you is what I've seen. You at work, where you live, your books and records, how you treat people and how they respond to you. I shot my mouth at you because I was angry and hurt and—"

"Rachel, that was—"

"I'm not sorry. I don't want you to be sorry you tell me anything either. I'm a great secret keeper. I'm a great *secret*."

"Is *that* who you are!" said Rourke, mockingly.

"Maybe," she said. "Who are you?"

Devlin felt dread, but more than that, he felt relief. He smiled, said:

"Once upon a time, I forgot who I was.

"About 1978, 1979. I was working the wild side, and I discovered cocaine. Not as something to bust, but . . . I liked it."

"You!"

"Me. Devlin Rourke. Cop.

"Back in 1980, I led this schizophrenic existence. I was a hotshot homicide investigator, hard arm of the law. And I spent my 'personal' life toking up illegal grass, snorting soda. I told myself I was engaging in an American's right to dissent, but in truth, all that was a justification I used to blind myself. A rationalization.

"I'd given my *word* to society that I'd be straight, swore an oath and took their money. I did that because it let me be a cop, and I love that job. If I've got a destiny, that's it. Not selfishly busting the law, giving bucks to bad guys.

"There was also the simple truth that I'd put myself in jeopardy, out where somebody could drop a rope on me and jerk it.

"What I eventually realized was that if I got jerked, pulled out of what I can do best, then everybody suffered. Then maybe Cooper and Smith . . ."

"Who are they?" she asked.

"Two dildo detectives," he told her. "If I'm not out there on the line, then those two dildos will be handling more homicides. They'll screw up a thousand ways from today, let killers walk. And sure as hell, one of those killers will kill again.

"So there was that.

"And then . . . Somebody jerked the rope."

"Who?! What?!"

"Long story," he said. "For another—"

"I know, I know: another time."

"Anyway, I beat them. And I quit coke. Neither was easy." She laughed.

"But," he said. "But."

Their cups were empty.

"You're not who people expect you to be," she told him after they'd said nothing for at least a minute.

"I know. And that's not always easy."

"I know," she said.

"You, ah . . ." she swallowed, started again. "You know . . . I won't tell anybody any of that stuff."

"I know," he said.

Someone knocked on the apartment door.

Devlin blinked, fought the urge to yell, *Go away!*

"Who is it?!" he yelled, sharper than necessary.

Rachel looked away.

Rourke remembered, stood, and put his hand on his gun.

"It's me!" came back Harris's muffled voice.

"Just a minute," called Devlin.

Devlin stood off to the side when he unlocked the door. It opened slowly.

"How you doin', boss?" asked Harris.

"Fine," said Rourke, though his voice didn't sound like it.

"The Duck heard me on the stoop," explained Harris, "let me in so I didn't need to buzz. He'll be up in a minute."

"How's traffic?" asked Rourke.

"Medium," said Harris. "No problem. Good morning, Rachel."

"Hi, Gary," she said from the kitchen doorway. She ran her hand through her rumpled hair. "There's coffee."

"Not yet," said Harris, anxiously looking toward the back of the apartment. "I, ah . . ."

"It's free," said Rachel. "My shower can wait."

"Thanks." Harris hurried down the hall.

"So what's the plan?" asked Rachel.

"I wish there were more to it," said Rourke. "Harris and I will tear Bernstein's apartment apart. Maybe we missed something the first time. Then we'll chase down another dozen alleys. Perry has this shift off. Her mother's coming to town."

"Poor Susan," said Rachel. "Her mother sounds like a piece of work."

"Well," said Devlin, "she's no day at the beach."

"Are you going to leave now?" she asked him.

"Soon as Harris is ready and the Duck gets here."

"Will you be gone long?" she asked. Her eyes sought his. He looked back.

"I don't know," he said. "If we get a lucky break. But it's been a while since I've relaxed. I'd like to come home. Hang out."

"Sounds great," she said.

"Yeah."

The toilet flushed.

"Damn," he said. "I . . . I've got to go out to dinner tonight. I don't think I can get out of it."

"That's okay," she said.

"Where's dinner?" she asked. "With Julia?"

"Her sister's."

"Ah, the in-laws," she said.

"Give me a break!" he snapped.

They both chuckled, looked at something else besides each other.

Water ran in the bathroom sink.

"She seems like a nice kid," Rachel said.

"Who?" asked Rourke.

"Julia."

"Oh. Yeah."

"Wholesome."

Rourke didn't answer.

"She's no dummy, either," said Rachel. "We, ah, we talked a little yesterday."

"What about?" asked Rourke.

"Oh, you know," said Rachel. "Things."

You won't tell me either! he thought.

"What's wrong?" asked Rachel.

The bathroom door opened. Harris walked toward them.

"Nothing," said Rourke. "Just this damn case."

"You'll be fine," she said. "You'll do okay."

They heard the sound of heavy human feet on the stairs: the Duck.

Followed by the scamper of four paws: Sam.

"I'll see you tonight," said Rachel.

"I might be late," Rourke told her.

"I'll wait up," she said. Smiled.

Harris walked up to his boss, said, "I'm ready!" just as the Duck knocked loudly on the door.

"Great day, isn't it?" he said after they let him and Sam in.

"Well," said Rachel, "so far."

47

W*hat's going on here?* thought the killer as he sat in his car half a block from the apartment building to which he'd followed Harris. *Some sort of car pool?*

He scanned the bay windows of the three-story, converted townhouse with binoculars: nothing.

Twenty minutes later, the sun flashed off the glass front door as it opened: Harris, with some cop-hard older guy. They glanced at the sky, took off their overcoats. Harris's companion looked unhappy as they walked to their car. They both looked tired.

Stick with Harris?

Yes.

The killer let another car get between them before he slid into traffic, locked on their trail.

Come on, cops: lead me to that Rachel Dylan.

48

Should I use the knife? thought Devlin.

He sat on Hershel Bernstein's glass coffee table, staring at the sofa cushions on the floor. With his Swiss Army knife, he'd already unscrewed every light fixture, every outlet plate in the living room. Pried apart every picture frame. He could cut open the cushions, make sure nothing had been hidden inside them, or he could figure that his eye was right and no one had tampered with the cushions' factory seam.

There had to be something! he thought. *Somewhere there had to be something.*

He heard a *thump* from the boy's bedroom where Harris labored.

Devlin wiped sweat off his forehead. They'd been working for an hour. The living room looked bombed, the bathroom was a shambles. They'd checked inside the toilet's float ball, then had a hell of a time putting the toilet back together so the water wouldn't run.

Knifing the cushions would make a worse mess. He leaned back on the coffee table, looked again at the red-covered photo album. He lifted it around to his lap, slowly turned the pages.

Hundreds of pictures of two people now lost somewhere in the world. A mother, a son. Together with the white collar factory where he worked and this apartment, these pictures showed the sum of Hershel Bernstein's life.

The mother at a shopping mall.

The kid playing baseball.

Mother and son quarreling about something as she tried to get him into a car somewhere in the city.

Scenes of a large picnic, though the creep at Dix Beverages said Bernstein never went on company picnics. The wife and kid laughing on a checkered blanket. The wife standing next to cars in the parking lot. The mother and son racing up a grassy hill. Same clothes, same day. *Is that Druid Park?* Here's the mother in winter, bundled up against the snow.

What's Rachel doing right now? he wondered as he flipped through pictures of the woman Bernstein loved.

God, I don't want to go to that dinner! he thought. Julia's sister and brother-in-law were wonderful. Smart. The two kids were fairy-tale children, just like Bernstein's son. And they seemed—

Devlin froze.

Blinked.

Quickly flipped back through the photo album's pages.

"That's it," Harris said as he walked into the living room. "The boy's room is done. Do you—"

"Wait!" yelled Devlin as he scanned the photo, looking for . . .

Found it: the picnic sequence, the wife standing in the parking lot. In the background a woman was looking at her, her mouth open, maybe speaking; the woman was closing a car door—her car, not the registered Bernstein vehicle. Rourke saw her license plate.

"Get the magnifying glass in his darkroom!" yelled Rourke.

"Maryland plate," said Rourke a minute later as he moved the glass above the photo. Rourke squinted, peered through the magnifying glass—and read the license plate.

"Got it," said Harris, writing the number in his notebook.

"Yeah," said Rourke. "I think so. I think so."

49

The killer waited 15 minutes, then left his car parked in the bus stop. He walked across the street, risked running into the two cops coming out of the high-rise apartment building.

Is this where you've got her? he thought.

The glass case in the lobby listed all the tenants. Within seconds, he found Bernstein, H.

So that's why you're here.

They wouldn't stash a witness in a victim's building. He walked to a deli at the corner, bought coffee. He sat where he could see the building doors and the cops' car. He could make it to his car in time to catch them as they drove away.

Where will you go next?

Wait a minute! he thought. That's the wrong question. Not where will you go, he thought, but where have you *been*? Usually, cops check in at headquarters before they pound the pavement. Yet Harris had picked up the other cop, and started work immediately. Why weren't they following standard operating procedures?

"So will there be anything else, dear?" asked the elderly waitress. "Some more coffee?"

"Thank you, no," said the killer. "I think I've got all I need."

50

"Yes?" said the woman from the photograph as she kept them standing on the front porch. "How can I help you?"

"We're police officers," said Rourke. He and Harris held their I.D.s and shields toward her.

"Oh my God!" she said, clutching her chest, "my husband, what's happened to—"

"Nothing's happened to him, ma'am," Rourke reassured her.

"Is he here?" asked Harris.

"Why no," she said. "He's at work."

"Does he own a 1983 Ford station wagon, license plate number Maryland 973-413?"

"Why, we own a Ford station wagon, but I don't know the license plate number. The car's in the garage if you care to—"

"That probably won't be necessary, ma'am," said Rourke.

"What is this about?" she asked.

"We're looking for Mrs. Hershel Bernstein and her son," said Rourke. "And we're hoping you can help us."

"I don't know anybody named Hershel Bernstein," she said. "Or his family."

The two policemen looked at each other. The older one reached inside a photo album he was carrying, handed her a picture.

"Isn't that you in the background of this photograph?"

"Why yes," she said, "it is!"

"And you say you don't know Mrs. Bernstein?"

"That's right."

"She's the other woman in the photograph. Perhaps you better look again."

The woman did. Glared at Rourke.

"Officer," she said, "I don't know what you're trying to pull here, but that woman is not named Bernstein."

"Excuse me?" said the younger cop.

"Well, I should think so!"

"Ma'am," said the other cop, "do you know the woman in the picture with you?"

"Of course."

"Who is she?" asked Rourke.

"Why that's Alice," said the woman. "Alice Pittard."

"Alice," said Rourke. "Does she have a son?"

"Jimmy," said the woman.

"Is this him?" said Rourke, opening the photo album and showing her a picture of a laughing boy about to catch a baseball.

"Why, yes, yes it is. But that was taken last year. My, how he's grown!"

She looked at them, frowned and said:

"What is this all about?"

51

The black-gloved hands lowered the binoculars. The shades were pulled on the first floor of the townhouse where Harris had picked up the other cop, half open on the second floor. The third floor windows were too high up to offer the killer a good view.

He'd been parked at the corner for 20 minutes. He glanced in the rearview mirror: the glued-on mustache looked natural. His close-cropped, dyed black hair changed the image he'd had last week.

Wonder if women will like this haircut?

A red-breasted robin hopped across the hood of his car, scouting for spring in the city.

Be patient, the killer told himself. *Be thorough*.

He unbuttoned his coat—just in case. Besides, the day was warm. He got out of the car.

Without appearing to, he kept his eyes on the apartment

building as he walked toward it. From time to time he glanced at a scrap of paper, as if it showed an address.

He reached the sidewalk leading to the building, glanced at the paper in his gloved hand, then walked to the glass door.

Locked!

He turned the knob again. Nothing.

Three mailboxes on the wall: the bottom one said Gage, the name tape for the second one was missing, the third one said Rourke. Neither of the names meant anything to him.

He had lock picks in the vest he wore under the buckskin coat. It would be easier to get a crowbar, stroll to the door, force it . . .

And then what? he thought. He rattled the knob again.

"The apartment's been rented," said a deep bass voice behind him.

The killer started to turn, heard a bestial growl.

Slowly, he thought. *Easy.*

A red-headed giant towered over the killer. The dog must have weighed 60 pounds. Half that weight seemed to be in the dog's bared teeth.

"Easy, boy," said the killer.

"It's okay, Sam," said the giant.

"Nice Sam," said the killer.

Sam growled, low and husky in his throat.

"He doesn't like you for some reason," said the giant.

"Yeah, well . . . Sorry."

"It's not your fault," said the giant. Frowned. "Probably."

"What was that you said?"

"I said it's probably not—"

"No, before. About the apartment."

"It's rented."

"Oh," said the killer. "Damn!"

"It's a good place."

"Looks like it," said the killer.

The two men stared at each other, each trying to think of something to say.

"Well," said the killer.

"Well," said the giant.

"I guess you must be Gage or Rourke," said the killer.

"No," said the giant.

He was puzzled, suspicious, and the killer sensed that.

"Well," said the killer, "if it's rented, no use sticking around here."

"Probably not," said the giant.

"See you around," said the killer. He smiled, edged past the dog, and strolled down the sidewalk toward the corner.

Sam growled.

"Easy boy," said the Duck, patting his friend who'd desperately needed to step outside for a minute. Meeting the stranger triggered massive guilt in the Duck for leaving Rachel alone. His words were as much for himself as his dog. "It's okay. He's gone now."

52

"How kinky do you think this is?" Harris asked Rourke as they sat outside an ordinary house in an ordinary Baltimore neighborhood.

"This is the United States of America. The eighties," answered Rourke. "How kinky do you think it could be?"

"Shit," said Harris.

Their radios crackled:

"Unit 17 in position," said two borrowed vice detectives parked in the alley behind the ordinary house.

"Hold 17," Rourke said into the radio.

"Do you think we need seal them off like this?" asked Harris.

"Better safe than sorry," answered Rourke.

"Do you figure she's a bigamist?"

"I figure she's a victim," said Rourke.

"I don't understand."

"We better get started," said Rourke, climbing out of the car. He led Harris up the sidewalk that bisected an ordinary lawn.

Harris rang the doorbell.

"Yes?" said the woman who answered the door—the same woman in Bernstein's photo collection.

"Mrs. Pittard?"

"That's right," she said. Her eyes moved from one man to the next: they were salesmen or missionaries of some sort.

"We're police officers, Mrs. Pittard," said Rourke. They showed her their badges, I.D.s. "May we come in?"

She nodded.

The living room was cheery, bright, and tastefully decorated.

"Would you like to sit down?" she said, nodding to the sofa.

They did. She sat in the chair across from them. The oldest detective put a red photo album on her brown wood coffee table.

"Is your husband home, Mrs. Pittard?" asked Rourke.

"He's at work."

"And where is that?" asked Harris.

"An appliance store downtown," she said.

"Do you know why we're here?" asked Rourke.

"No. I'm scared."

"Of what?" asked Harris.

"The police never bring good news. My son, Jimmy, is—"

"Where is he?" asked Harris.

"At school. Isn't he?"

"As far as we know," said Rourke. "Will he be home soon?"

"Not for an hour. He . . . What's going on?!"

"Mrs. Pittard," said Rourke, "do you know Hershel Bernstein?"

She frowned.

"No," she said, "the name isn't familiar."

"He worked as an accountant for Dix Beverages," said Harris.

"I've never heard of Dix Beverages."

The two policemen looked at each other.

"You realize we can check on all this?" said Rourke, though he hadn't the faintest idea what such a check would entail.

But for Alice Pittard, "check" meant the omniscient police could find out anything she lied about.

"You can check all you like," she said, anger creeping into

her tone, "but you won't find anything. I don't know any Herzel Bernstein."

"Hershel," corrected Harris.

"Whoever! I don't know any Bernsteins at all."

"How about this man?" asked Rourke, handing her a copy of Bernstein's employee identification card, with its photo of a shy accountant used to standing on the other end of the camera.

"I don't know this man," she said. "And I don't like this! I'm going to call my husband right now. And maybe an attorney."

"I think it's a good idea to call your husband," said Rourke. If you want an attorney, fine. But you'll probably want to keep this private."

"Keep what?!" she cried out.

Rourke shook his head, said:

"It's a long story."

"I don't understand," said Alice Pittard. She sat beside her husband on the sofa. The red photo album lay on their coffee table.

"This . . ." she said, "this Hershel Bernstein—we don't know him—but . . . He has pictures of me, of Jimmy. Some of them three years old. And you say he has more all over his apartment? That—"

She shuddered. Her husband patted her knee.

"And he was one of the people murdered in the Ward Building last Saturday?" said the husband. His tone held less panic than his wife's, but no less concern. "He is dead, isn't he?"

"Yes," said Rourke. "You don't need to worry about him."

"But why?!" cried the wife. "Why? Why me, why Jimmy?"

"I don't know why *you*," said Rourke. "I don't think it was personal."

"Not personal!" she yelled. "It's my—"

"It's your image," said Rourke. "That's what he stole. Try to understand: that has nothing to do with you."

"You're wrong," she insisted. "You're wrong."

"You're a victim," said Rourke. "An innocent victim of someone's obsession. He made you the family he didn't have.

"Maybe once you were out shopping, picking Jimmy up.

He saw you, thought, what a great woman, cute kid. Maybe that's when he took his first picture. Maybe he followed you home, maybe not. Maybe he saw you again somewhere else.

"One picture, one encounter. Then another. Then watching the house, following you. I should have noticed: the pictures were always taken in someplace public. He stayed in the distance, telephoto lenses. Watching. Clicking pictures. He built a life around you."

"A life for what?" interrupted the husband. "Voyeurism. What next? What would he have done if—"

"Probably nothing," said Rourke. "Touching your reality would destroy his fantasy that he wasn't alone."

"And people believed him?" asked the husband.

"Why not? In a big institution like his company, people work as strangers. In a city, how well do you know your neighbors? People believed what he told them because they didn't care enough to think otherwise."

"Awful!" said the wife. "What right did he have to . . . borrow my life, Jimmy's life?!"

She shook her head and a tear rolled from her eye.

"And so sad," she said.

"How . . . elaborate was his game?" asked the husband. "What kinds of . . . pictures, things, did he have in his apartment?"

"All perfectly innocent," said Rourke. No need to mention the boy's clothing, the negligee.

"I . . . I can't stop shaking!" said Alice Pittard.

"It's okay, dear," said her husband. "It's over. He's dead."

"But I didn't even know what was happening! I was being . . . Over and over, and I didn't even know! How can I ever feel safe . . . private. . . . How can I ever feel normal again?"

No one answered her.

"Just for the record," said Rourke, "where were you last Saturday?"

The husband blinked. "I wish I'd been in the Ward Building garage. Shooting sickos."

"Is that where you were?" asked Harris.

Mr. Pittard glared. Didn't answer.

"We're doing our job, sir," said Rourke.

"There was an after-Christmas closeout sale at the store," said the man who Hershel Bernstein wished he'd been. "I spent all day demonstrating washing machines. My wife was there, too, serving coffee. You can check."

After they left, Harris called the store manager, who confirmed the man's claim.

The husband walked the police to the door.

"Don't worry," Rourke assured him. "We'll keep you informed, let you know if there's anything else."

The husband shook his head: "Maybe we're better off ignorant."

53

What the hell as I doing here? thought Devlin as he gazed past the lace curtains, through the clean glass of the second floor bedroom window, over the tree-lined street into the black, star-dotted night. This room was cozy, warm; the night crisp, cold.

What the hell am I doing here?

Ostensibly, he'd come to this child's room for his and Julia's coats, which lay on the 11-year-old girl's pink bedspread.

What the hell am I doing here?

The evening had been charming.

He'd surprised Julia in her office that was crammed with memos, stacks of newsletters, piles of trade magazines. Calendars and posters from the Design Institute, a print from a museum in Cincinnati, a display of classic print ads and mock-ups of her organization's publications covered all her walls except her window to the world. Her eyes left her paper buried desk, found him standing in the door.

"You're early!" she said, patting her hair. She smiled, sensed something wrong, though who could know what. "You look tired."

"I am."

"Did you sleep well last night?"

"Not particularly."

"That's because you've been sleeping alone," she said. Laughed.

"Must be," he said. Smiled.

"Ah . . ." She glanced at her watch. "We'll hit the rush hour traffic, but since it's a long drive . . ."

"Might as well get started," he said.

"Sure," she told him. "If we're early we can play with the girls. Have an extra drink."

"I could use a drink," he said.

They met a white-haired man in a three-piece blue pinstripe suit as they walked through the bustling reception area. Devlin felt the man's bright blue eyes measure Julia from head to toe.

"You remember Mr. Zuckerman, don't you Devlin?" said Julia.

Those blue eyes flicked over him.

"Yes," said Devlin.

"How are you?" said Zuckerman. His handshake was ambivalent.

"Leaving early, Julia?" he asked.

"Is that okay?" she replied.

"Of course, dear," he said. Smiled as he patted her shoulder. "Of course."

"I'll be in early tomorrow, J.B.," she said.

"Fine," he said. "Nice to see you again, officer."

"Isn't he sweet?" whispered Julia as her boss walked away.

"Sure," answered Devlin.

They drove for 45 minutes to a Delaware community popular with commuters to Baltimore and Philadelphia. Trains stopped here, and the interstate highways were close.

Unlike Peter Maxwell's engineered Columbia, this had been a quaint town that evolved into an expensive American village. Families begun in Columbia moved here. The houses were barnlike, with acres of lawn. The sedans in the driveways were often owned by the Company. The mailman dropped checks from New York banks through front door slots, checks signed by oil conglomerates, chemical multinationals, diversified industrial giants. Dads left home before dawn, returned home after dark. Moms sometimes worked, too; ran decorating stores, day care centers, curio shops, had "careers of their own."

For most, this community was a reward, and they'd live in

it or its like until they retired. For some, there would be other neighborhoods, far more exclusive, far more expensive. Only a few citizens of this community would fall across the tracks to the old part of town, wind-blown streets where fathers didn't ride the commuter train unless they drove it, where clapboard homes hid fathers whom hard times had robbed of work and chained to sofas.

Julia's sister greeted them with hugs at the door. Julia often praised her sister's lithe form and beautiful hair, though Devlin couldn't understand why Julia considered her older sister's nervously thin body and limp brown hair superior to her own lushness.

Julia crossed her sister's threshold and inhaled the sweet smell of paradise. Her nieces scampered downstairs squealing her name with delight. They hugged her; shyly hugged Devlin, too.

Devlin knew he made Julia's sister nervous. Perhaps she suffered from the unease policemen engender. She trembled as her arms fell away from their embrace and brushed the gun on his hip. Once, he'd heard her say they didn't allow toy guns in their house. And here, in her home, was a man with a *real* gun clipped to his hip! Most likely, he made her nervous because he might be the man her beloved sister would marry. Gun or no, *that* was an awesome consideration.

Beloved of each other the sisters were. Julia had followed her sister to the same university, to the same sorority. Devlin wondered if Julia chose Baltimore for her career before or after her brother-in-law had accepted a transfer there.

The three of them went into the living room. The two sisters had a martini before six, laughing at the sin of it all. Devlin knocked back two Scotches, saw the sisters exchange a glance. The husband came home early, too. Had a drink with them before he went upstairs to spend quality time with his children. Devlin liked the husband, a modest man with a quick sense of humor and a fine mind. He came downstairs in time to greet the other couple: a man who, like him, had just moved up a level in the company pyramid; his wife, who talked about the two-week, "and-spouses" retreat the company had sponsored at a nearby Ivy League college where families were educated about the way the Company approached the world.

Somehow Julia's sister had found time after her shift in the

antique store she co-owned to cook a Beef Wellington feast.
Merry conversation flowed around the perfectly set dinner
table. Halfway through the meal, the man sitting across from
Devlin allowed as how "cop shows" were his favorite television
fare—they didn't get out to movies as much as they used to
these days.

"I don't watch much television," said Devlin, suddenly
glad he hadn't had any more to drink.

The man blinked.

"You know," said his wife, "I don't think we in the public
properly appreciate the police."

"That's okay," said Devlin, "we don't appreciate you
either."

The wife blinked.

Julia smiled at Devlin from across the table.

And Devlin suddenly felt ashamed and embarrassed.

"What, ah, what are you working on now, Dev?" asked
Julia's brother-in-law.

"I'm on a special assignment under the deputy chief," said
Rourke. "A study on the response to street crime."

"Sounds fascinating," said the brother-in-law's co-worker.
"And damn important."

"I think it's just terrible," said his wife. "Sometimes I don't
feel like I'm safe anywhere."

"You're not," said Rourke.

Nobody liked his blunt answer.

"You used to work homicide, didn't you?" asked the other
male guest after an awkward silence.

"Yes," answered Rourke.

"Too bad you quit. We could use you now. That Ward
basement murder nonsense. You're not working that, are
you?"

"I'm not in homicide anymore."

"That's right," said the man. "But I was thinking, maybe
you got a piece of it somehow."

"Such investigations are tightly held," said Rourke,
sharpening both his hearing and his wits.

"Do you have any idea who's working on the case?" asked
the man again. Julia's sister frowned at his persistent curiosity.

"No," said Rourke.

"So how are they doing?" asked the man. His voice took
on a conspiratorial tone and a TV accent. "Got any ideas what
went down?"

"Four people were shot," said Rourke. "You might know more about it than me."

Everyone laughed.

"Are you ready for dessert?" asked the hostess.

"And coffee," said Julia. She looked at Devlin. "For everybody."

Over homemade banana cream pie and coffee, the host told a funny story gracefully lampooning himself. Conversation drifted to the benefits of marriage, how lucky they all were to be living as they did. What could be done to make the world better. From there to a dozen light topics. Five of the six people relaxed; Devlin appeared to.

Julia's so happy, thought Devlin. *Haven't made her real happy lately.*

Have to do better about that. Somehow.

The sister laughed. She caught Devlin looking at her, smiled a warm greeting.

She's perfect in her way, thought Devlin. *Could be a portrait in a magazine, an inspirational TV show.*

Damn it! he thought. *What is this with you tonight?*

He shook his head, but no answers came.

Just an irresistible desire to leave, get out, get away. Get home.

After explaining that he had an early shift, sharing in the regrets, he went upstairs to get their coats, feeling guilty, feeling the fool. He walked through the oldest girl's doorway, didn't turn on the light. The shadowed forms of china dolls watched him from the bureau. He walked through the darkness, gazed past the lace curtains, through the clean glass of the second floor bedroom window, over the tree-lined street into the black, star-dotted night. This room was cozy, warm; the night crisp, cold.

What the hell am I doing here? he told himself.

"Devlin?" called Julia from the bottom of the stairs. "Are you ready?"

He turned from the window, glanced around the room. Went downstairs without comment.

"What's wrong?" Julia asked him as the car hummed over the dark interstate highway, the lights of Baltimore sliding closer.

"What do you mean?" he asked her.

"At dinner. All night."

"I don't know," he said, not bothering to deny it.

"Do you want to talk about it?" she asked.

"I don't know if I can," he answered.

They drove a dozen miles before he spoke again. The car was silent. They'd played the radio on the way out, the station that broadcast from the Ward Building, but Rourke had turned the radio off. He didn't want to turn it on again, worried about finding a station that wouldn't annoy either of them.

"It's just work," he said, his eyes looking up to the rearview mirror, locking on the black ribbon trailing into the blacker void behind him. "It must be just work."

She didn't answer.

They drove home through the night.

54

Devlin and Rachel sat in his bedroom.

The hour was late.

There was nowhere else for them to go.

Susan Perry dozed fitfully on the living room sofabed, her gun on the nightstand.

"Still cold out?" Rachel asked Devlin.

She sat on the bed, up by the pillows. She wore a blue crewneck sweater, black jeans. Her hair was soft, fresh, golden in the light of the deco bedtable lamp. Rachel bent her legs so her chin rested on her knees. Her feet were bare.

"Yes," said Devlin, "but you can feel spring in the air. Tomorrow should be wonderful."

Devlin sat cowboy-style on a kitchen chair he'd carried into his bedroom, his legs grasping the chair back as he leaned over it, his chin resting on his crossed arms. He'd put the chair at the foot of the bed, faced Rachel across its length.

"Did you have fun at the in-laws?" she asked.

He laughed.

"That bad?" she asked.

"Not bad," he told her, "but I felt so kattywhompus."

"Katty-*who*?" she laughed.

"Kattywhompus. Crooked, off-course."

"Well, you have lost your home to me," she told him.

"That's not a problem," he said, shaking his head. Both of them realized how quickly and sincerely his answer came.

"I feel so out of place," he told her. "Since the Ward Building massacre. I'm used to walking through strangers' lives, but with these four people—Bernstein and Johnny Curtis, Le-Lan and Peter Maxwell—

"None of them were who they were."

"Huh?" she said.

"They weren't who they were. They walked through the world with one face, but that face was a mask. Their true face was secret. Johnny Curtis was an independent deejay who sold his soul trying to gain glory. Peter Maxwell was living as a father and family man while sneaking back to his youth. Le-Lan was living free here in America, yet she secretly carried tribute for the horrors of her past. And poor Hershel Bernstein: he lived in a stolen fantasy.

"They lived behind masks. The masks were a burden, false protection against the world, and a pitiful legacy. They died trapped with their masks on a cold Saturday afternoon in an underground garage."

"It can always end just like that," Rachel told him. "For anybody. It's all just a shot away.

"One in the head," she said. Then, after a pause, a shrug: "Or like junkies, one in the arm.

"But what about you?" she asked. "Why so kattywhompus?"

"I don't know, Rachel.

"I was with good people, solid people. Honest, sincere. They're the kind of people I try to protect. They live straight, don't hurt anybody, try to do the best they can in life."

"Don't you?" she asked.

"Not like that. I've lived too long on the edge. Gives me a peculiar perspective. I know it's all just a shot away. So do they. They gamble that it won't come. I expect it.

"Remember how I told you when I was doing drugs how I forgot who I was?"

She nodded.

"Well, maybe I've done that again, gotten off course. I'm wearing a mask, too. All of a sudden, I feel—"

"Kattywhompus," she smiled.

He nodded.

"What does Julia say about all this?" she asked.

The question embarrassed him.

"Julia. . . ." He shook his head. "I haven't . . . She . . . She's a good woman."

"Yes," said Rachel. "She seems to be."

"She . . . she's not used to the edge. Hasn't had any time on it, so she doesn't understand. That's not her fault."

"No," said Rachel, "nor does that make her any less a person than you or me."

"That's right!" said Devlin.

"Just different," said Rachel.

"That's right," said Devlin again.

"I understand," said Rachel, and he knew she did.

"This is my town," he said. "I love Baltimore. I'm no world traveler, but I've been around—America, Europe. This gritty harbor city isn't paradise, but it's what I got. It's in my blood. The edge is here for me to run along. I got a job to do, a place to do it."

He shook his head.

"What about you, Rachel?" he suddenly asked.

"What about me?"

"Come on," he said. "You've told me about your past. All of that was rough. But now what? Are you just a gypsy?"

"What's wrong with that?" she asked, tension creeping into her tone. She straightened until she sat with her back against the wall.

"Where you going, gypsy?"

"Where I want. That's what America is all about, right? The westward migration, the—"

"The idea is to get someplace," he told her. "Where are you going?"

"Not like Peter Maxwell," she said. "No place I've been."

"Where you going?"

"If I weren't a woman, I'd be—"

"Still a drifter."

"Yeah! But *acceptable*. If I'd have been a man, you wouldn't be questioning me. . . ."

"There's so much out there to see!" she said, shifting

arguments abruptly. "You've never seen the sun set into the ocean at Mazatlan, the sun rise over the red desert in New Mexico. You know Baltimore, well, there's a hundred cities I've seen and a million more I haven't, and each one is different. I'll take all that with me to that killing shot. I've got so much more to see I—"

"Bullshit," whispered Rourke.

"Sure, there's a lot of world out there. More than you could learn in a hundred lifetimes. And everybody should always keep looking, keep learning. But that's not what you're doing on the road.

"You're wearing a mask, Rachel. You're pretending to look, you've got the mask of a searcher. But what are you searching for?"

She didn't answer him.

"You know," he told her. "Deep inside you, you know. But you've been kicked around so much, so hard, you don't want to admit what you want anymore, because not getting it has cost you so much pain and heartache. You're afraid."

"Of what?" she said bitterly. "I've been betrayed, beaten, hungry, raped, ripped off, lost a child, been shot at and bombed. If that's your world, I'll take a mask on the road. That shot hasn't hit yet, and as soon as I get free I'm gone, so—"

He shook his head, interrupted her.

"You'll never get free your way.

"You're running. From ghosts. From things you didn't settle where you've been. You try to leave the ghosts behind you, keep moving. But they're always in your shadow. That hometown you say you hate, the pain. That man. Your little girl. You've got to turn around someday. Take off your mask. Face them. Maybe go back somewhere and bury them. Or you won't be free, you'll just be moving."

They didn't speak, didn't look at each other. The night outside the bedroom window seemed empty and dark.

"Are you always so rough when you're kattywhompus?" she finally said. Her voice was tired, resigned.

"So what do you want, Rachel? What do you think you're doing? Why are you searching? What's all this freedom for?"

She didn't answer him for a minute, but he waited, and she knew he'd wait until she answered.

"I want to be true," she finally said softly. "Real. Worthwhile. And happy."

"And your mask traps you on the road."

She said nothing.

"Come on, Rachel," he whispered. "You can do it."

"Do what?"

He shrugged.

"Get off that road."

"And get shot?"

"Devlin shook his head:

"You can buy a bullet anywhere.

"Maybe . . ." He swallowed, suddenly nervous. "Maybe you should start by taking a good look around, really seeing."

He paused for a moment.

"Maybe I should do that, too," he said.

They stared at each other until their eyes ached.

"I'm tired," whispered Rachel. "So tired."

"Me too," he answered.

A dog barked in the alley. Devlin's mind shifted as much as it could. The dog didn't bark again, and Sam downstairs was silent.

"It's late," said Devlin.

"Yes," she agreed.

"I guess . . . I guess I better let you go to sleep."

She looked at him. Dozens of questions shimmered in her eyes.

"I guess so," she whispered.

He stood. Awkwardly. Walked to the door.

"Good night," he said.

"Good night," she said.

The bedroom door closed behind him, she heard his first fading footstep, whispered, "Devlin."

Then said no more.

In the hall, he glanced over his shoulder, heard nothing. He waited for the door to move. It didn't, and he sighed, shook his head and hated time.

55

Tomorrow, thought the killer as he drove back to his hotel. *Tomorrow it will be over.*

At least Rachel Dylan will be done.

He slowed as he neared an intersection where the traffic light had just turned from green to orange. He saw no other cars on the dark streets, but he stopped for the signal anyway.

Don't want to pick up a traffic ticket now, he thought.

Tomorrow brought him tremendous risk. Rachel Dylan might not be in that third floor apartment.

He was sure she wasn't in the ground floor apartment. He'd called the Gage listed at that St. Paul Street address in the phone book, gotten a tired man who'd told the "telephone pollster" he worked at a downtown department store. The killer believed him.

The killer wasn't sure about the second floor apartment. That was probably where the red-headed giant with the dog lived—the man who seemed to work at home. Rachel Dylan could be in that apartment, the giant could be a cop, but what he'd found out about the third floor apartment made him doubt it.

Rourke, the mailbox had said. On a hunch, the killer had called the police department again.

"Could you connect me to Detective Rourke?" he'd asked the switchboard.

"We have a Lieutenant Rourke," had been the reply.

"Maybe that' him. Which unit does he work?"

"He's on special detail. I'll transfer you to the deputy chief's office."

"Could you just give me that number instead? I'll call directly because I need to make a pit stop now."

That crudity disrupted the switchboard operator's caution. She gave him the number. He didn't write it down.

Something definitely was in that townhouse apartment building. Harris and the other cop seemed to be pulling shift duty from there.

His plan was simple and historically proven: blitzkreig.

The outside door would be forced, quickly and quietly. He could make his way to the second floor without being heard.

Twenty seconds.

He'd place a radio-detonated bomb on the second floor door.

Twenty seconds to stick the bomb on the door, ten seconds to climb the stairs, another twenty seconds to stick another bomb on the third floor apartment door.

Small bombs, just enough explosion to blow the doors in and stun the people inside.

Fifty seconds in target zone until then, he thought. Rounded his estimate up to an even minute.

Blow the top apartment door first.

Then, as he raced through the blown third floor door, he'd blow the second floor apartment door beneath him.

He'd charge into Rourke's apartment, blast anybody he'd see.

If Rachel Dylan weren't there, he'd race down to the second floor apartment. The red-headed giant and his dog would be shell-shocked from their bomb. He'd finish them off, check for Rachel.

Either way, he'd flee out a back door, down the back steps, into the alley he'd scouted that night.

Damn that alley dog who'd barked!

He'd emerge on a different street, walk to his car, drive away. By then, the neighborhood would be pouring into the streets, drawn by the twin explosions. He could fade into the chaos.

Start to finish, he estimated the blitzkreig would take three minutes. And then the Rachel Dylan problem would finally be solved.

If she were there.

If she weren't, if there were only nontarget personnel in the two apartments . . .

The cost of doing business.

He'd wait until the morning shift was established. The night shift would probably leave before 10 AM. After he saw

hem go, he'd drive his car to the block around back, park it,
stroll around the corner, down to the apartment building. The
street would be empty.

Tomorrow.

56

"So what are we going to do today?" asked the Duck Friday
morning.

The four cops and one witness sat in Rourke's living room.
Sam lay curled by the door. The morning sun lit the room with
promises of a great day and a fine future. Devlin opened a bay
window that had been shut since Thanksgiving. The fresh air
smelled of growth, of life; birds sang in the trees along St. Paul
Street.

It was 8:47.

Devlin sighed.

"We've only got 48 hours," he said. He looked at his
troops. Susan Perry had bags under her eyes. Gary Harris was
pale. What Rourke had seen in the mirror that morning had
looked 10 years older than the image he'd seen the week
before. "And we're running ragged.

"Our operating theory has been that only one of the four
victims was the target, that the others were witnesses killed
because they were in the wrong place at the wrong time. What
Rachel saw, what happened to her, the bomb at the London
Hotel, Nick from the diner—All support our assumption of a
professional killer.

"We've also assumed that our guy might be a cop, or at
least have a wire into the department, which is why we've
worked outside.

"We've been all over the four victims. Each had a dark
side, but so far we've found no tracks from their dark sides to
the Ward Building garage. We've got lots of data, leads,
theories, but no direct trail of blood.

"Anybody have any suggestions?"

No one spoke.

"I was afraid of that," said Rourke.

"You think the shooter is still out there?" asked Perry.

"Of course he's still out there," answered Rourke. "We haven't caught him."

"I mean—"

"You mean," interrupted Rourke, "still out there as in standing across the street, sniper rifle in his hand, waiting to pick off Rachel."

"I don't know about that. Part of me says yes, he's just around the corner. Part of me hopes Baltimore is a distant memory for him. What bothers me is the *feeling* that somehow we've missed something that's been right in front of us all along."

"What do you want to do?" asked Harris.

"You mean besides sleep?"

Everybody laughed.

"Look," said Rourke, "we've been assuming the targeted victim had a conscious link to the person who hired the gunman, right? That the victim would recognize the motive for his murder. But suppose the target was totally unaware that he was in jeopardy?"

"Like how?" asked Harris.

"Like suppose Peter Maxwell's daughter had a boyfriend who wanted to marry her and knew that the father would object? Like that teenager who paid his buddy to kill his mother because his mother wouldn't let him stay up past nine and watch TV."

"If it's a boyfriend to that daughter, then that shoots your pro killer idea," said Susan. "I doubt she'd know anybody who could find a pro killer, let alone afford one."

"Don't get locked on *why not*," said Rourke. "Look for *why*. For what could be. The daughter was just a hypothetical example. Maybe the mother had a shadow suitor, like Hershel Bernstein, and maybe the guy knew he had to get rid of Peter Maxwell before he could try to turn his fantasy into fact."

"If we hunt that far afield—" began Harris.

"Then who knows what we'll find?" said Rourke.

"The point is, we've got not much. And we need it all."

"So what do we do?" ask the Duck.

"We tried to find the killer through examining his victims. Let's try two new tracks.

"Let's look at the living. Who cares about them and how? Who's profited by one of those deaths? Who filled Bernstein's slot in that data factory? What didn't happen because one of those people died? Johnny Curtis made his station hot. Maybe one of the station's competitors decided they didn't care how they upped their ratings and revenues.

"Maybe," he said. "Maybe, maybe, maybe."

"That's a lot of . . ."

"You're damn right," said Rourke, interrupting Harris. "But they're one way we've got to go."

"What's the other?" asked Perry.

"The killer," said Rourke. "We've kept the spotlight off him so he wouldn't find out we were looking. Let's shine a little more light his way—not enough to tip our hand, but maybe enough to show us something about this guy. Let's sound the drums."

"We know cops in other towns. I'm tied into the feds, have lines into Philly, New York, D.C. Susan, you worked that case where the guy killed his wife in Pittsburgh and his mother-in-law here. You must know a few cops there."

"Texas, too," said Perry. "And I dated a deputy for the Dade County Sheriff's Department, so I can tie into Miami, South Florida."

"Land of the quick or the dead," said Rourke. "How about the rest of you?"

"I don't know anybody but Baltimore policemen," said the Duck. His face was flushed.

"Don't feel bad, Duck," said Harris. "The best I can do is a Maryland trooper who let me badge my way of a speeding ticket."

"I know small-time crooks from coast to coast," said Rachel, smiling. She wore the same blue, crewneck sweater and black jeans as the night before.

They all laughed.

"We'll skip you on this detail," said Rourke. He looked her in the eye for the first time that morning. She looked back. They both flushed, smiled nervously.

"And you, too, Gary. Maryland troopers are too close to home."

"Susan, Captain Goldstein and I will work our phones. They should be safe."

"I don't know," said Perry, "my mother's there."

They all laughed.

"I may have to shoot her to get at it," said the woman detective. "Why is it that she insists on visiting me, then spends all her time on the phone long distance to her friends she left at home?"

"Mothers are the biggest mysteries of all," said Rachel. "Sometimes they do the most irrational, aggressive, stubborn—"

"M is for *meshugge*," said Susan with a smile.

"For us," interrupted Rourke, "m is for murder."

"What happens if we've got nothing to give the DC Sunday morning?" asked Harris.

"His first inclination will be to cover us up," said Perry. "If he thinks he can't get away with that, he'll shoot us and toss our corpses to that shark Sonfeld."

"What about the *case*?" asked Harris.

"I'll figure something," said Rourke, hoping he was right. He looked at his watch: 9:14.

"Okay," he said, "if we get started now—"

"What about me?" asked Rachel.

"Ah . . ." Rourke swallowed. "I, ah . . . We still need you for the case. And I've got this feeling about the killer still being somewhere, so—"

"I wasn't asking to go away forever," she said quietly. Looked straight at him. "But I've been cooped up here almost a week."

"Look at it outside!" she said, gesturing toward the window, toward the street lined with parked cars, toward the world.

"It's gorgeous! All I want is . . . It's spring! Can't I *see* some of it before it's all gone?"

"But you're safe in here!" insisted Rourke. "I know it's frustrating, but I—we don't want anything to happen to you."

"Things happen no matter where you are," she said quietly. "No matter who you're with. They happen. To me. To you. To everyone."

Rourke and Rachel had locked their gazes on each other. He broke away; found Susan staring at him, a puzzled look on her face.

"You think the killer believes I'm dead," said Rachel. "Even if he's out there, it's a big city. It's not like he's lurking outside my front door. All I want is a little fresh air. Just for a couple hours. I'll be all right. I'll be safe."

She stared at the police lieutenant, at his troops; at him.

"I won't bolt," she said.

She paused, then said:

"You believe me, don't you? And you understand?"

The breeze through the open window cooled Rourke's brow, enticed his skin, his bones.

He glanced at Perry, who nodded once—quick and certain.

The risk factor, what was the risk factor?

He couldn't know. Logic seemed to say *not much.*

But he had this feeling. . . .

The breeze brushed him again. He felt the pull of spring, knew what it meant to be cooped up, what it could do to a person.

"Okay," said Rourke with a sigh. "I understand. Out you can go, but—"

Rachel's smile lit the room; her cry of delight woke Sam, who raised his head from his paws to see what all the fuss was about.

"*But,*" said Rourke, "not alone."

Her smile twitched, her eyes filled with questions.

"I . . . We've got to chase the case. The Duck goes with you everywhere, or you don't go."

"Okay," she said. She smiled at Liam. "Want to come outside and play?"

"Sure," he said, "Dad said it was Okay."

They all laughed.

Rourke glanced at his watch: 10:02.

"Let's get rolling."

"I'll go to Captain Goldstein's, work his phone with him. Susan, you and Gary start from scratch again."

Those two detectives groaned.

"Start with Peter Maxwell," said their commander. "Maybe Laura's father figured out Maxwell was the creep seeing his daughter."

"This is going to piss a lot of people off," said Harris.

"You're lucky," said Rourke. "Later today, the captain and I will tackle the Nguyens."

"That ought to be fun," said Perry.

"When you're done with the Maxwell angle," Rourke told her, "go over to Dix Beverage. Shake the shit out of that place."

"What happened to low-key?" she asked, smiling.

"Somebody needs to shake that profit prison." He smiled, joked: "Maybe you should take your mother."

"*Oy!* What she would do to that place!"

"Yeah," said Rourke, "Let her daughter do it instead."

"What about Johnny Curtis?" asked Harris.

A sudden ambivalence seized Rourke. If he delegated that, he wouldn't visit the station. See anybody.

What the hell is going on with you? he thought.

Do what you should, he decided.

"I'll take care of that," he said. "I have a special fondness for Gordy Miller."

He turned to Rachel. Smiled.

"You ready for your adventure?"

"Ten seconds!" she said, racing back to the bedroom.

She actually took twice that long; ran back to the living room carrying her leather jacket and sneakers. She sat on the couch, hurriedly put on her shoes as the others prepared to go.

"Sergeant," said Rourke.

The Duck drew himself up to his full height. He buttoned his suit coat across his ample girth. His gaze to Rourke was steady, confident, sure.

"Yes sir!" he said, humor in his tone, a smile on his lips.

"You're in charge. The two of you have until 5 PM. Stick to public places, keep a low profile. Do you have your radio?"

"Yes sir!"

He patted the unfamiliar bulge on his left hip beneath his suit coat where the radio hung in its department-issued belt strap. In the days when he'd foolishly carried the .44 Magnum in a shoulder holster, there'd been no room under his suitcoat for the radio. In these new enlightened times, his regulation .38 rode on his right hip, the radio on his left, which left his hands empty and free.

"Close and frequent contact. Radio me your location. Don't mention you're guarding anyone, or Rachel or—"

"I understand," said the Duck, and Devlin knew he did.

"Every 50 minutes," said Rourke. "And every time you

eave the car. Don't miss any check-ins. Watch your back. I don't expect anything, but . . . Don't relax."

"No sir!"

"Just . . . Do your job, sergeant."

"Yes sir!"

"I'm ready!" said Rachel, standing, slipping into her jacket.

The Duck held up his hand, addressed Rourke:

"Do you mind if Sam stays in your apartment?" asked the Duck. "He likes it here. I've taken him outside already, so he should be fine until we come back. I'll clean up any mess—"

"Sure," said Rourke. "Sam's fine here."

"Hear that boy?" called the Duck.

Sam trotted over to his master. The big man bent over, patted his sides vigorously.

"You're going to be just fine, aren't you? I don't have to worry about you. You're all okay."

The Duck straightened up, shook his finger at the dog.

"Now you be good. I'll see you tonight."

Sam rubbed his head against the Duck's leg.

Rourke glanced at his watch: 10:21.

"All set?" he asked the people who stood with him in his living room.

They nodded *yes.*

Rourke's eyes met Rachel's. Her face was flushed, excited. Happy. For a moment he forgot his worries.

"Have fun," he told her, almost whispering it.

She nodded.

Over Rachel's shoulder, Rourke saw the puzzled look return to Susan Perry's face.

"And be careful," he said; forgot about the others, said: "For me."

"I will," said Rachel. "For you."

Rourke put his hand on the doorknob.

57

What the hell now? thought the killer in his car parked in the alley. He ducked behind the dashboard as Rachel Dylan emerged from the townhouse, surrounded by a crowd who had to be cops.

The killer wore his black gloves and a tan raincoat over his utility vest. Bombs, radio dentonation equipment, a lock-busting tool, blast goggles and earplugs, and ammunition filled the vest pockets. His .22 pistol was holstered on his belt, and a 12-gauge, sawed-off Remington 1100 pump shotgun with a pistol grip was tucked into a sleeve sewn inside his topcoat. The five-shot, 22-inch weapon was perfect for close-quarters blitzkreig. At ten feet, the shotgun blasted a two-foot wide circle of #4 buckshot through anything in its way—closet doors, sofas, a dazed witness, or a disoriented cop.

But there were four cops: Harris and the hard guy who had to be Rourke, plus a woman and the giant he'd met before—they had to be cops, too.

The dog was nowhere in sight.

They laughed and joked as they walked to their cars: Harris and the woman cop in one, Rourke in another. The big cop led Rachel Dylan to a third car; she turned to the others, waved goodbye.

She wore a leather jacket, didn't carry a purse.

What kind of woman is she? the killer wondered.

Dead.

Then and there, he could have popped her with the .22 pistol. He could make the shot, but he couldn't escape.

The four cops would recognize the .22's *crack*. Before she hit the ground, they'd spot him and return fire. The alley trapped him like a shooting lane. One cop might miss, but not four.

I've waited this long, I can wait a little longer.

264

They could be moving her to a new safe house, taking her to the airport. Following the convoy was tricky, but possible. He'd have to improvise, maybe wait until she went to ground again.

But she was in his sights.

58

"This is the best day!" said the Duck as he drove through the city, spring flowing through the open car windows, his friend smiling beside him in the front seat.

Rachel leaned back, closed her eyes, and let the wind blow through her hair.

"If it isn't," she said, "it'll do."

"What do you want to do?" he asked her. "If you want to go shopping, there's downtown or malls, markets—"

"Let's just *go*," she said. "Keep moving for a while. Stay outside."

She rolled her head to the left on the back of the seat, stared at the smiling giant beside her.

"Show me your town," she said.

So he did.

Neighborhoods of flat rowhouses with marble stoops. Downtown's bustle. The Lexington Market and Johns Hopkins University. Little Italy and Locust Point. Industrial Cambden to swank Charles Place. This man who'd spent all his adult years cruising the city now showed them to a friend. For years he'd overheard conversations that never included him, absorbed more than he realized. Now knowledge flowed from him with an ease he wouldn't have believed possible two weeks earlier:

This was Billie Holliday's old neighborhood. . . .Shock trauma medicine started at that hospital. . . . That hole-in-the-wall bakery has the best pastries in the city. (No thanks, she didn't want one.) *. . . That restaurant has more than*

1,000 pieces of original art scattered through its two floors, including Picassos, a Rembrandt."

"Maybe we'll go there for dinner sometime," Rachel told him.

"Can we?" he asked.

"Sure, if it's all right with Devlin."

"Will you ask him?"

"Of course," she said. "Of course."

He beamed at her, turned left on Cuba Street, cruised through a pocket of quaint homes in the midst of warehouses, factories, and railroad tracks.

"You like books, don't you?" he said eagerly.

"Yes, I love to read."

He blushed.

"I've never been good at it," he said. "Don't do it much."

"We'll have to change that."

"You'll . . . I mean, I know how to read, but . . . You'll help me learn about books?"

"Sure," she said. "That's our bargain, right?"

"Right!"

"If you love books, you should love Baltimore!" he told her. "Lots of writers came through here. That Mencken guy. Edgar Allan Poe and Hammett somebody."

"Dashiell Hammett," she told him.

He repeated the name twice to himself.

"I got it," he said. "I'll remember."

He laughed.

"All those writers, and I never met any of them. They never wrote about me."

"Don't feel bad," she said. "Just because nobody writes about you doesn't mean you're not a great story."

"Really?"

"Really."

"Did anybody ever write about you?" he asked.

"Almost," she said. The Duck saw memories flow in her eyes. "But men owned most of the typewriters."

"Now you can get one," he said guilelessly.

She blushed, smiled, said: "Yeah, I guess I can."

They didn't speak for several blocks. He glanced in the car's rearview mirror. Traffic in this neighborhood was light, only a couple other cars moving on the street.

"Come on," he said, "I've got something special to show you."

They rolled over secondary highways, through city streets, climbed a steep road to a park where the trees were green with buds.

"Federal Hill," the Duck told her. "Where we were going to defend against the British. You'll be able to see the Francis Scott Key Bridge, the island with Fort McHenry."

They reached the top of the hill, a field of brown grass and trees. A couple holding hands strolled along the sidewalk. A mother pushed a baby carriage. A carload of Japanese tourists was parked next to a litter barrel; they were taking pictures of each other. A sign at the entrance of a curved road looping away from the main path read, "Emergency and Service Vehicles Only."

"Maybe I shouldn't do this," he said as he turned into the looping road, "but we qualify."

He drove 30 yards, parked. Radioed Rourke their location. They left the car, walked half a dozen steps to the edge of the earth.

"Isn't it great!?" he said.

The blue sky arched above them, the city spread out at their feet, a crescent of black, brown, and green squares, with diamond glints of glass, dots of red roofs, giant gray factories, and huge white oil tanks. The topography rose from distant suburban townhouses to skyscrapers bordering the glistening gray harbor that sprawled toward Chesapeake Bay. They could see freighters floating on the water, the masts of the docked U.S.F. *Constellation*, the navy's first ship, preserved as a museum in the Inner Harbor.

"You're right, Liam," she told him. "This is spectacular."

"I come here a lot," he said. "Stand up here, think."

"What about?"

"Everything," he said. "Why I'm here, what I'm doing. All these years," he grinned, shook his head. "Until this case, working with Lieutenant Rourke and you, the others, I've always felt like a duck out of water."

They laughed.

"Now," he said, "now I feel like I've made it, like I finally belong."

"You did that yourself, Liam."

"Well . . ."

Her voice was firm, positive:

"That's one lesson you need to learn right now. Believe right now.

"You changed your life. You made the decision. You took the actions. Everything else is just opportunity. You got lucky, but the luck would have been wasted if you hadn't made the right choices."

"That's the way it is with most of what's important," she told him. "Took me a long time to believe it, but it's true. You can't count on anybody or anything other than yourself when something must be done."

"You can count on friends," he told her.

"You should be able to," she said. "If they're really friends. If they don't dodge what they should because the world gives them an easy out. Most people choose to fold rather than fight and maybe fail."

"Not you," he said.

She shook her head.

"I've folded more than I like," she said.

"Everybody has," he said. "I spent my life ignorant and confused. But I won't do that no more. And neither will you."

"You've got a lot of faith in a drifter you barely know," she told him.

"Sure," he said. "I've got faith in you."

"That's a hell of a burden to give to somebody, Duck."

"Nah," he shook his head. "You can handle it."

They stared at the city, at the sea.

"Look at the Aquarium," she said, pointing to the jumble of cubes and colored glass in the Inner Harbor. "Stands out, doesn't it?"

"You ever been there?" he asked.

"Tried to, but the lines were too long."

The sunlight bouncing off the harbor made the Duck squint. He put on his new, nonmirrored sunglasses.

"Doesn't look crowded now," he said. "Want to go? It won't take long, and it might be our last chance before the lines get bad."

"Sure," she said, smiling at him. "Why not?"

"It's a good day to learn about fish," he said.

They laughed as they walked back to the car.

* * *

What the hell is this? thought the killer. He sat in his car parked next to the jabbering Japanese tourists. *The official police tour of Baltimore?*

Damn the Japanese tourists, the lovers, the mom and her kid! Too many witnesses for a clean kill. They were so spread out he might not be able to get them all. Then he'd have the Rachel Dylan problem all over again. Maybe worse.

Rachel and the cop walked back to the car, started back out on their journey. He waited until they were out of the restricted drive, down the road, then eased his car into gear to follow them. The Japanese tourists waved.

"Sayonara!" he heard one of them call; the others laughed.

"Hiroshima!" he hissed back.

They went into another world.

Rachel and the Duck rode up the outdoor escalator to the Aquarium's second-story glass ticket booth. There was no line, though three empty school buses waited on the Inner Harbor's quay leading to the Aquarium. The killer lagged behind, wary of being spotted.

They passed through a turnstile, under blue and green neon tubing, walked along mirrored walls and glass columns of bubbling blue water into a sunless, damp world. The carpeted path led them along a kidney-shaped, empty dolphin pool, where water lapped against concrete walls. In the black void above their heads hung the bleached skeleton of a whale.

The clamor of children and tourists greeted them as they trooped up the inclined path. Glass-cased exhibits lined the walls: aquariums, terrariums—glowing worlds in a dark cavern. Hidden loudspeakers piped in the cries of gulls, barking seals, and the echoes of whale songs.

"Look, look!" cried a child as he ran up the ramp, past Rachel and the Duck. "Way up there in that glass cage! That's a shark!"

The killer heard the boy's shout, stopped beside three giant photographs of fish eyes. He couldn't see his target but knew she was up ahead. Waiting for him.

A woman's voice floated above the squeals of school-children:

"One of the ironies of nature is that the blue whale, the largest creature ever to inhabit the earth, feeds on animals which are very small. Most whales eat small crustaceans, mollusks, and fish. The exception is the sperm whale, which sometimes feeds on sharks and even the giant squid."

Dumb kids! thought the killer: *Can't they read for themselves?*

The Aquarium was clammy. The killer's black gloves unbuttoned his tan overcoat. He'd shed his cumbersome utility vest in the car. Snug in its inside sleeve, the shotgun was a reassuring weight.

A mother held her son close, directed his eyes to a spiney creature nestled in a water-filled glass box:

"See?" she said. "Sea anemone. They trick the fish into coming close, then sting them and stun them, then suck them into their mouths."

Up the incline they walked: the children, the tourists, the killer, Rachel, and the Duck.

A little girl in a red cardigan sweater, T-shirt, and blue cords haltingly read the panel beneath the glass container, while the eight-legged creature in question, green and black and undulant, crawled along the sand floor of its cage:

"The . . . terrible reputation . . . of the octopus . . . is unearned. The octopus . . . is really a shy, intelligent creature that . . . seldom preys on anything bigger . . . than a crab . . . or lobster. . . . The octopus is . . . actually . . . quite reasonable, . . . except toward its prey."

"Mary!" yelled her best friend Elizabeth. "Come on!"

Mary scampered away from the octopus, up the ramp, deeper into the darkness.

Up. The ramp led past five frightening panels entitled "Creatures of the Abyss," deep sea fish with needle teeth half as long as their body, indigo eyes, sickly pale flesh, and totally black, gaping mouths. Panels to the side of the path lectured on hiding, camouflage, migration, long-distance drifters.

"Now this is the most amazing thing in the world I know," a woman in her forties told her mother as they stood before a backlit color map of the world that delineated climatic regions, not countries. Both women wore polyester pantsuits; the mother's was pink, the daughter's aquamarine. The daughter pointed to the map, continued:

"All the eels in the world swim from wherever they are to the Sargasso Sea—that's what they call the Bermuda Triangle—to spawn."

"Seems like an awful long way to go for not very much," said the old woman.

"Mom, what do they know: they're just fish."

Beyond them, the Duck paused by a panel photograph of three stark fish with luminous eyes.

"Glad I got good sunglasses," he told Rachel.

She laughed.

They walked on, followed the ramp past the simulated sea cliff home for dozens of excited puffins, murres, and razorbills, aquatic birds from Iceland, who roam the sea ten months out of twelve, stopping only to breed. The museum shop by the main entrance sold puffin stuffed dolls. Rachel told the Duck she didn't want one.

Baltimore's Aquarium is a jumble of geometric shapes, cubes and boxes stacked on each other like a child's blocks. The top block has a sloping triangle glass roof: the Rain Forest.

The sign on the narrow door of the spiral staircase leading to the rain forest solarium noted the humidity would be 75 percent, the temperature 85°, the climate of a South American jungle.

"I never wanted to live in a jungle," said the Duck as they left the cool dark world below, climbed the stairs into the tropics. He squinted at the bright sunlight streaming through the glass roof, filtering through the leaves of the palm, banana, chocolate, papaya, and coffee trees. The thick air was sickly sweet with orchids. His shoulder brushed a bamboo thicket, and he heard a parrot *caw*, the trickle of a stream. He squinted toward the parrot sound, saw a flash of orange plumage.

Something neither child nor tourist moved in the trees ahead.

The Duck's right hand swung up to his stomach, toward his gun holstered beneath his suit coat. He hesitated, blinked, and the thing shook the brush again. Rachel tried to walk on, but the Duck reached in front of her with his left hand, stopped her forward motion; gently pushed her aside as he walked deeper into the jungle.

"*Who-who whew, who-who whew,*" called the jungle bird. Maybe it was a sun conure, a blue crowned mot mot. Duck didn't know and didn't care. His eyes tried to burn away the foliage around the bend.

One step.

Two.

Three, and he reached the curve in the trail. Right hand ready by his belt buckle, he turned the bend.

Stopped.

Stared.

Shook his head, grinned.

"Come here," he called to Rachel, who'd waited trembling at the trail's head.

"Look," he said, pointing to a branch swaying with alien weight.

A tan, monkey-faced, two-toed sloth dangled upside down from the branch. Its black eyes saw them, blinked.

"Bet I'd have been in trouble if I'd shot him," the Duck told her.

"Better in trouble than dead in the jungle," she said.

They looked at each other, forced smiles.

"Come on," she said, "let's get out of this place."

They moved quickly through the brush, found the exit stairs, walked back down into darkness.

The carpeted ramp zigzagged down, a switchback through the hollow core of a half-million-gallon sea tank. The walls that aren't glass are purple. Black silhouettes of sharks adorn the purple walls: the great white shark, tiger shark, sand shark, nurse shark, thresher and hammerhead and bull sharks, all wooden and harmless.

The real monsters swim inside the tank. Duck and Rachel leaned against the blue steel railing, eyes fixed on the glass wall. Blue light colored the core behind them. Sunlight filtered down into the tank water. White sand made the floor; the far wall was a mirror. The orchestra of excited schoolchildren seemed to be a surface sound; the dominant sound was eerie, silent and deep. Small fish darted nervously beyond the glass. A manta ray flapped its wings, blinked its eyes, its rope tail trailing behind as it disappeared around the corner.

And suddenly he was there: six feet long, seven feet, more; silent, strong, lateral fins motionless as he glided past them, the eye on their side open, unblinking. Jagged teeth hung down from his top jaw; his long snout pulled his half ton of insatiable hunger through the water. Rachel and the Duck looked up in the tank, saw his dorsal fin cutting the white surface of the water; saw it from *below*—not from the safe surface or earth where they could safely walk, but from *below*, in his world.

"Come on, let's hurry," whispered Rachel.

"Okay," said the Duck, though he wouldn't have minded lingering, watching those death legends glide by.

Perfect light, thought the killer. *Good enough to see, dark enough to not be seen.*

The three of them were alone on the zigzag ramp.

Timing, he thought. *Timing!*

He quickly walked down the ramp, overcoat unbuttoned, his gloved hands at his side.

Rachel and the Duck turned the switchback corner and started down the next ramp. Rachel led. They faced the man walking down the ramp above them and to their left. He was ten feet away, closing the gap between them: Just another tourist, a white man in a tan overcoat with short hair, who seemed as anxious to be free of this dark place as they were. He walked down the ramp so fast it seemed difficult for him not to run. But he didn't put his hands on the rail to steady himself.

Six feet separated them.

The Duck glanced up.

He's as nervous as the man who wanted to rent the apartment, but without a mustache, thought the Duck. *Wears black gloves, too.* He looked down the ramp to where a boy stood, uncertain of which way to go.

The Duck heard the footsteps of the man pass by them. Stop.

Suddenly, the Duck knew something was terribly wrong.

He whirled. His mind registered the *whirr* of cloth as the killer jerked the shotgun from inside his coat. The Duck saw the blur of *weapon* swinging through the air. The killer had intended to blast Rachel first, the cop second, but when the cop turned, he had to shift targets in mid-motion. That change gave the Duck his chance.

His massive hand grabbed the swinging weapon. Metal smacked flesh: Metal stopped, the shotgun barrel halted at a harmless angle.

Get it! thought the Duck: he jerked with all his might.

Don't lose it! thought the killer: he tightened his right hand's hold on the grip, grabbed the short barrel with his left hand.

The Duck's 245 pounds of flesh, bone, muscle, and grit

once momentarily stopped a rolling cruiser. That effort was nothing compared to the strength he summoned now.

The killer felt his arms almost wrenched from their sockets as some primal force jerked the shotgun he wouldn't release. His body slammed into the blue steel railing. He flipped over it, spinning as the Duck pulled with all his might.

The killer squeezed the trigger.

The shotgun blast twisted the gun from their hands, sent it spinning to the ramp below.

A load of #4 buckshot pulverized a basketball-sized crater deep in the glass wall above them.

The water inside that tank shook.

Wire sensors imbedded in the glass reported a tremor and possible weakness to the Aquarium's central computer. Water-tight doors slid shut on each end of that section. A red light flashed on the monitoring board in the Aquarium basement.

The board's attendant was in the bathroom.

Rachel jumped at the shotgun's roar. She ducked; saw the Duck stagger and a man in a tan overcoat fly past him as though by magic.

A thousand cracks mushroomed like an instant cobweb from the shotgunned crater; that glass wall creaked and groaned. The water beyond it rocked in waves. Small fish darted about in trapped panic. A tiger shark glided to and fro.

The killer crashed on the ramp at Rachel's feet. His shoulder and hip crunched into the carpet, but he kept his wind, rolled, and stood, faced her.

Recognition lit her face the instant before he smashed his fist into her stomach.

The Duck regained his balance, charged, and slammed his huge hands into the man's back, propelled the killer down the ramp into a face-flat sprawl.

White fire burned through Rachel's windpipe. Her mind novaed. The lower half of her body fell away. She slumped to the floor, both hands clasped around her middle; fought for breath. Her mind cleared. Through her desperate gasps for oxygen, she watched two men battle for her life.

Like some big men, the Duck had never been in a fight. Even as a child, his size had intimidated everyone. Besides, all the schoolyard bullies steered clear of the kid whose father was a policeman.

His father's provisions for his career combined with the

department's assessment of his abilities kept the Duck from normal police work in which he'd have experienced violent situations. Only once in his carefully orchestrated career had the Duck ever been involved in an aggressive situation, and that had been four years earlier, the first time he'd worked with Devlin Rourke.

This Friday, in the Aquarium's dark world, he alone faced a seasoned killer. He knew that before his foe slammed down on the ramp.

But this was his job: he didn't know how to do it, but do it he would.

The glass wall creaked and groaned.

Suddenly, a seven-year-old boy stood between the Duck and the killer. The shotgun blast had terrified him. He ran the direction he'd been facing: up the ramp. Halfway to nowhere, he froze. A man in a tan raincoat flew past him, sprawled on his face, rolled over, and grabbed at his hip.

The killer screamed as he drew his .22 pistol.

Head lowered, arms outstretched, the giant cop exploded toward him, a gorilla sprung off a coiled spring.

The killer fired:

Once.

Twice.

Three times.

In the basement control room, the attendant strolled back from the bathroom. By now, three red lights flashed on the control panel. He saw them when he was ten feet away; dove for the button that rang alarm bells throughout the Aquarium, shrill clangings amid the screams of children and tourists who'd heard a shotgun blast.

The killer's bullets slammed into a hand-sized grouping above the Duck's heart.

Above the bulletproof vest he wore under his shirt, as required by Baltimore police regulations.

The bullets hit him like jabs from a Hell's Angel's pool cue. He knew they were bullets, saw the gun in the killer's hand. The bullets didn't slow the Duck. Four steps, a dive, and he'd be on top of the killer, smothering him with his bulk, the only thing he could think of to do.

Then he saw the boy.

In the line of fire.

The Duck scooped the boy up, whirled him high through

the air as the killer fired twice more: one shot smashed into the vest over Duck's kidney; the other missed him completely splattered against the blue railing.

Rachel drew her first painless breath.

The glass wall behind her squealed so loudly she heard it above the alarm bells, the panicked cries from people fleeing out the Aquarium's emergency exits.

The boy felt himself flying. The giant man swung him so high his legs cleared the railing on the ramp above where the men fought. The giant let go. The boy dropped to the carpet. He ran up the ramp.

The killer fired again as the Duck lifted the boy through the air. He aimed for the cop's head, a sure kill.

But the cop's arms were swinging the boy, and they blocked his head and face. The killer's bullet tore through the Duck's massive right bicep, had only enough remaining force to dent his cheek, tear the skin.

Bring him down! thought the killer. He hadn't counted how many rounds he'd fired, but he knew he had to halt the cop, neutralize him before he drew his weapon.

The killer aimed carefully; fired.

The bullet slammed into the Duck's right thigh just as he released the boy.

The Duck screamed, his leg buckled.

The killer fired again, before the Duck could twist to face him.

That bullet slammed into the Duck's back. His unprotected back: Baltimore issues its policemen bulletproof vests that guard only their front. A policeman is supposed to face the attack.

The slug punched between two ribs, missed the spine, cut through the top of the Duck's left lung. He gurgled, twisted as he fell to his knees.

Cops practice drawing their weapons for hours until it becomes second nature: on police ranges, at home in front of their closet door mirrors.

The Duck had practiced for hours. For his whole career.

Now, on his knees, as alarm bells rang and the glass wall above him groaned, as he faced a prone killer zeroing him with a pistol, the Duck reached for his weapon.

His right hand at the end of his wounded arm had enough

strength left. Easily enough. That trained hand jerked up under his suit coat, to his left armpit.

Only the cumbersome, nonregulation .44 Magnum wasn't there; the shoulder holster wasn't there.

The Duck hadn't had time to practice being enlightened, so his right hand instinctively slapped his left side, while his regulation .38 rode secure on his right hip, where it belonged.

Slumped against the rail, Rachel saw the Duck slapping his empty armpit, saw the puzzled look on his face. Understood.

And she saw the killer.

Again over a gunsight.

Only this time, she wasn't his target.

The killer aimed. Pulled the trigger.

The bullet slammed into the Duck's groin.

He moaned, fell backward.

"No!" screamed Rachel. She dived forward.

The killer fired his last two rounds. Both bullets tore through the Duck's groin, his stomach. One slug shattered his aorta, the other ripped a hole in his right lung.

Rachel flung her body on top of her friend.

The killer fumbled in his pocket for an ammunition clip.

The glass wall above them exploded.

Twenty-five thousand gallons of sea water, small fish, half a dozen octopus, thousands of plankton, assorted plants, two moray eels, five wheelbarrows of white sand, and a seven-foot tiger shark blew out of that shattered world.

The tidal wave slammed down on Rachel, the Duck, and the killer, washed over them before it rushed to emergency drains in the basement.

Rachel raised her head, gasped. She wiped seaweed and water from her face, blinked her eyes clear.

Saw the killer.

He'd been rolled over on his back by the tidal wave, washed further down the ramp. He was coughing, sputtering, his hands waving as he sought equilibrium, groped for his lost pistol and ammunition clip. He struggled to his knees, shook his head. Looked up.

Saw Rachel sprawled across the immobile cop.

Rachel pushed aside the Duck's soggy suit coat, found his .38, still snapped snug in his holster. She fumbled with the safety strap, jerked on the gun butt.

The killer somersaulted down the ramp, bounded to his feet, ran two steps. He hit the emergency door handle with all his strength, flew through the exit, and was gone before she freed the gun from its holster.

The Duck groaned.

Rachel spun off him.

A terrible sucking noise came from the ramp above her, something heavy up there banged against the rail and ramp, shook the floor where she knelt beside the Duck. She glanced up, saw the tiger shark flopping on the ramp, its white stomach bouncing off the carpet, its neck gills frantically opening and closing as it drowned. That fearsome mouth yawned and chewed the air futilely.

The Duck groaned again.

Like her, he was drenched, smelled of brine and the ocean. His eyes blinked furiously. She wiped the water from them, and they opened, gazed up at her.

"Rach'l!" he gasped, tried to yell. "The man, apar'ment, same one, he—"

"Hush," she said, her eyes frantically searching the dark core of the ring tank. She heard screams below her, frantic shouts.

"Doctor!" she yelled. "Get a doctor!"

No answer sounded in the echoing chaos.

"Rachel," he said, his voice clearer.

"It's okay," she said. "Everything will be okay."

"The man—"

"Hush, baby. He's gone. You're safe."

The sea water had washed him clean. Now a thin stream of red ran from his nose, his right cheek looked like he'd been kissed with scarlet lipstick. He couldn't move his right arm; it lay palm up on the ramp. The coat sleeve on that arm grew sticky, its stain darkened. And his crotch. . . . A massive crimson flower blossomed between his legs. Red tendrils ran down the damp ramp.

"The radio," he said, his voice remarkably calm. "Showed you how. Use the—"

Before he said "radio" again, she was frantically searching for it under his coat. Its leather harness was empty. Somehow, somewhere during the fight, during the flood, it disappeared. She peered all around their ramp, below them, above to the flopping shark.

"I can see it!" she said. "It washed downhill. I'll go . . ."

"No," he said, his left hand plucking at her sleeve. "Don't go. Don't leave me alone. Won't make any difference."

He closed his eyes, winced.

When he opened them, he saw her face, slick with the salt water of the sea, of her tears.

"Don't cry," he said. He had enough strength left to reach up, brush her cheek.

He smiled again, tapped the damp ramp where he lay. "Duck finally in the water," he said.

"Oh God!"

"Did my job, didn't I?"

She nodded, knew he saw her but that wasn't enough.

"Yes!" she yelled. "Yes! You did your job, Duck! You did the best job in the world!"

"I'm a cop," he said.

She sobbed.

"Ge' clear," he said. "Call lieutenant. Radio."

He feebly gestured with his left hand.

"Wach' out. Protect 'self. Take gun. Run."

"Oh, Liam! I'm sorry! I'm so sorry!"

"Sorry," he said, frowned. Lucid again. "What are you sorry for?"

"I made you . . . Your gun wasn't where . . ."

"You're my teacher," he said. "You taught me good. You taught me right."

She sobbed; yelled for a doctor again. Got no reply.

"You're my friend," whispered the Duck.

"Yes! Yes!"

"Sam have puppies?" he asked. Blinked.

Rachel sobbed.

"Funny," he said.

"What, Liam?" she said. She pressed his left hand against her cheek. His face was pale. "What's funny?"

Then he died.

She heard herself scream; heard the echo. She sobbed, her head hanging low.

Suddenly she grew cold. She laid his hand on his chest. Reached out, closed his eyes. Held her hand pressed against his damp, forehead.

His .38 lay on his stomach, and on the ramp beside his pocket lay his money clip thick with bills, pocket change. His nail clipper.

She grabbed the money clip, stuffed it in her jacket's flap pocket. Grabbed the pistol. Stood. Looked around:

The shattered world of the Aquarium.

The drowned shark.

Sergeant Liam McKinnon, dead at her feet.

Then she turned and ran down the ramp, through the same door as the killer. Disappeared into bright sunlight.

59

"What's wrong, *boychik*?" Mrs. Goldstein asked Devlin as they sat in her kitchen late Friday morning.

Devlin's silent police radio lay on the table between them, tuned to detectives-only communication channel. A grandfather clock ticked in the living room.

"A beautiful day," said his captain's wife, "and you got black clouds in your face. So what's wrong?"

"Nothing," he told her; forced a smile.

"*Bupkes!* You're in my kitchen. That means no *bupkes* allowed. What's wrong?"

"You've been a cop's wife long enough to know most of the answer," he said.

"Wives don't always get the answers they need."

"Well, no matter. You're lucky: soon he'll retire and—"

"Retire! Don't call that luck!"

Devlin frowned.

"But you worry about him getting hurt, hate his job—"

"Who says I hate his job?" she asked him.

"Ah. . . . He does."

"Hah! What does he know?"

"You said—"

"Listen to me, Mr. Hotshot Detective: I married a *man*. And he's the best damn cop in the country, you better believe it!"

"I do," said Devlin.

"My Teddy saves the world," she announced. "Every damn day. What other wife is so lucky to be married to such a man?"

"But . . ." He hesitated, plunged ahead into a topic he feared to discuss. "Your heart—"

"Hah! My heart! What do you know about my heart?!"

"I know the doctors say it's sick," said Devlin. "They say a big shock, too much stress, not enough good care, and you could die."

"So? That happens to your heart, you'll die, too."

"Come on," he said. "Be realistic."

"Realistic? Hah! You want to know about my heart? It's a bum muscle. It's supposed to beat without a skip. It doesn't. But it's gotten me this far, so how much can I complain? My heart is not just a muscle. It's where I live, and it overflows with my Teddy.

"He's the best damn police captain in the world. I'm lucky he loves me. I'm not the easiest woman."

"I don't know about that," said Rourke, smiling.

"That's right," she said. "You don't know."

He kept smiling as he checked his watch. Glanced at his radio. The hour he'd spent at WBBX netted him nothing. Gordy had called in sick. Devlin had been all business when he'd talked with Terry. So had she. Then he drove to Captain Goldstein's. The captain was at headquarters, making sure a wall of official paper masked his secret task force. The Duck and Rachel were at the Aquarium, with a check-in due in five minutes.

"You cops are like his family," she said. "Taking care of you and making sure you do your jobs is part of how he saves the world every day. He loves doing that."

"In case you haven't realized it yet, *boychik*, you are what you love. The more you work at what you love, the more of it you get. The more of it you get, the better off you are.

"So," she said; nodded her head emphatically.

"So?" he asked.

"So *feh* on retirement!"

"But it will relieve the stress on your heart if—"

"Are you crazy? Do you have *borsch* for brains, and is it stopping up your ears so you can't hear?

"My heart is full of Teddy, and Teddy's heart beats good because he's the best cop in the world. If he loses that, then he loses part of himself. That happens, part of my heart gets cut out, too. So, how good for me is it to have part of my heart cut out?"

They stared at each other for a minute.

Devlin blinked.

"Have you . . ." he said, frowned. "Have you talked like this to your husband? Told him?"

"Hah! He's my husband. He knows."

"Don't be so sure," he said.

"Well," she said, thrusting her chin, "he *should* know."

"Maybe he should," said Devlin. "But sometimes you miss something about someone you love because they're so close."

"Hmmph," she said. "So what am I supposed to do?"

"Help him. If you love him, you help him. It won't be easy, because he thinks he's doing the best thing. But you love each other, and if anybody can get him to see the true score, it's you."

She smiled in spite of herself.

"I do have a way with him," she admitted. "But—"

"No buts! You love him, you've got to do what's right." He paused. "And not let your pride set all rules."

"Hmmph!"

"Yeah: hmmph."

"So what about you, *boychik*? Who helps you?"

"I don't need any help—I mean, not now."

"Hah!"

He glanced at his watch again.

"Got a date?" she asked.

"No," he said, "but—"

"Teddy said he'd be back from headquarters in an hour. He'll call if anything is happening. You don't expect any news anyway, right? Besides, I know you're not nervous about that."

"What am I nervous about?"

"A woman."

"Which one?" he said before he could think.

"Now that's a good question," she said.

"No," he said, "it's not a woman."

"It's always a woman," she said. "Boys like you, it's always ultimately a woman."

"What's this, 'boys like me'? I've got a girlfriend—"

"Boys like you always got a girlfriend. But no wife,

boychik. You got no wife. Don't give me that lone wolf crap: wolves mate for life. And you got nobody. Why?"

"Your husband took the last good woman."

"Hah! Would I have been trouble for you in my day!" she said.

They laughed.

"So why no wife?" she said.

No way off this hook, he thought.

"Maybe . . ." He'd never thought of it this way before: "Maybe I've never found anybody who really wanted to walk with me *and* who really could—*and* who I wanted to walk beside."

"Where would you go?" she asked.

"Wherever," he said.

"Look hard, *boychik*," she told him. "And look true. Look at yourself. Sometimes you hold *yourself* so close you can't see who you are and what you're doing. Like my Teddy and this retirement.

"Remember, *boychik:* what you got is *now*, and if you're not looking in the right places, doing the right things . . ."

She shrugged.

The phone rang.

The lab technicians had clamped floodlights on the upper beams and railings inside the ring tank. Their glow made the blue mist shimmer.

Captain Goldstein, Rourke, and Ken Urtz stood on the ramp where the Duck died. A blood-soaked white sheet covered the Duck's body. The damp air stank from the dead shark on the ramp above them. Urtz held a plastic bag containing the sawed-off shotgun in one hand; his other hand held the plastic-bagged .22. Another evidence technician yelled up from a ramp two levels below that he'd found an ammunition clip for the pistol; other technicians probed the mist with flashlights.

'Where's the sergeant's gun?" asked Captain Goldstein.

"Don't know yet," answered Rourke. His voice was flat, distant. "Could have washed down below."

"Do you think he got off any shots?" asked Goldstein.

"The kid the Duck saved didn't see him draw," said Rourke. "But he fled before it was over."

"What about Rachel?" asked Goldstein.

"I don't know," said Rourke.

"There's no reason for the guy to have snatched her," he told Rourke. "He wants her dead."

"She didn't stick around, didn't call in," said Rourke. "I'm betting she didn't go back to my place."

"What's she doing then?" asked Goldstein.

"I don't know," Rourke said. "Nothing adds up."

"You think she's alive?" said Goldstein.

"Yes," said Rourke. "I don't know why, but . . . She's alive. I can feel it."

He nodded to where the morgue attendants were laying a stretcher next to the blood-soaked sheet.

"And however it played out, he kept her alive."

"Not your fault," said Goldstein. "Whatever you're thinking, Rourke, it's not your fault. Nobody could have planned for this."

Rourke said nothing. His expression didn't change.

As the morgue attendants lifted the heavy stretcher, Harris joined his bosses. The detectives moved to let the stretcher pass.

Harris's face was wet, his eyes bloodshot. He opened his fist and showed them three loops of black elastic band. Each policeman slid one over the badge they'd pinned to their suit coats.

"Where's Perry?" asked Rourke.

Harris nervously looked at the captain before he answered.

"She's in the cruiser." He paused. "She radioed some other officer, and he brought . . . She's reloading her gun. Hot loads."

"She gets the first shift at my place," said Rourke. "In case Rachel checks in. I want one of us who knows Rachel there at all times. Give Perry another partner."

"Her mood . . . Probably good idea to keep her off the streets and out of that guy's sights," said Harris.

"It's not Susan I'm worried about," said Rourke. "I don't want her killing him. At least, not before he tells me what the hell this is all about.

"Harris," said Rourke, "find that artist. I want sketches of Rachel. Get them to the print shop. I want three thousand of them, plus three thousand of our killer sketches. Every cop gets one. Get them out on the wire. State police, FBI, all the cities around us.

"Captain, I want—"

"You got it," said Goldstein. "Whatever. That's from the commissioner. He hasn't said so yet, but believe me, he will."

"I want every available cop on the streets," said Rourke. "With those pictures."

"Guys who are off duty are already pouring in," said Goldstein. "Sick guys. They heard. Everybody wants in on this."

"Every motel, every hotel, boardinghouse, the airports, bus stations, taxi cabs—"

"Like a blanket, son," said Goldstein, "we'll cover this town like a blanket."

"The papers," said Rourke. "The TV stations. I want the killer's sketch given to them. Not Rachel's, but his."

"If the killer is a cop," said Harris, "we're—"

"I want every fucking badge in town after him!" yelled Rourke. His words echoed through the darkness and mist. "No more bullshit!"

"What about Rachel?" asked Harris. "If she's spotted—"

"Either one," said Rourke. "They find either one, get me there."

"This is mine," he said. "They're both mine."

Rourke turned . . .

And saw the deputy commissioner walking up the ramp. The passing stretcher briefly wedged the D.C. against the rail. Blood-stained sheets brushed his pants.

"Men," said the D.C. "Terrible, this is terrible."

With a nod, he cut Rourke away from the others. They walked up the ramp, toward the dead shark. The fish stench turned Rourke's stomach.

"Look, lieutenant," said the D.C., "however this turns out, . . . I want you to know I'm sorry. For this, for sticking you with"—the D.C. nodded toward the departing stretcher—"with that sergeant. If I hadn't done that—"

"You gave me the best man on the force," said Rourke. He turned, started to walk away.

"Lieutenant!" yelled the D.C. Rourke stopped, faced him.

"You know what your deadline is?!" yelled the D.C. "When you nail that son of a bitch!"

* * *

Saturday drizzled: an early morning fog turned into rain by late afternoon. Baltimore policeman Matt Davis's face glistened as he stood in line at a McDonald's. He wore a blue nylon jacket over his white uniform shirt and black-banded badge. He'd left his police hat in his car, didn't care that his blond head got soaked. The jacket covered his gun belt. Nothing about him said *cop*. A pretty brunette woman who loved him stood by his side; nervous, scared: since yesterday, Matt had seemed trapped in a wasteland she couldn't cross. He'd lost his smiles, his jokes, his cocky walk. An icy silence wrapped itself around him. When she tried to talk about it, he said, "I put orange juice bombs under his tires."

The biker who swaggered into the restaurant was big, strong, and certain that he was the cleverest creature on earth. Rainwater dripped from his greasy hair, trickled through his matted beard. He saw a friend standing toward the front of the service line, swaggered over, and cut ahead of all the squares.

Matt's girlfriend held his arm tight. He seemed not to notice the rude biker. She silently prayed for the line to move faster.

"What's happening?!" the friend asked the biker, who replied with a crude joke. They laughed.

"Did you hear about that cop?" asked the friend as they moved a step closer to ordering their hamburgers.

"Cops mean shit to me," sneered the biker.

His friend thought that was hilarious. Matt's girlfriend felt his arm flinch.

"But the one who got shot in the Aquarium," said the biker's friend: "Did you hear about him?"

"Shot in the Aquarium?" said the biker. Shook his head. "Who got him? A guppy? Stupid cop."

Matt Davis exploded through the line, grabbed the biker, and threw him face first against the far wall before his girlfriend registered Matt had shaken her grip.

The biker growled, turned to fight some fool, and found himself faced with a screaming madman.

Behind the counter, the manager dialed the 911 police emergency number.

Any punches the biker landed made no difference. Matt's whirlwind fists hit him a dozen times—body, face, kidney shots. Matt grabbed the biker when he started to fall, slammed his back against the wall, then threw him across the restaurant.

Half the customers fled as soon as they saw the fight; half

stayed to watch. None of them were stupid enough to get in the way. Matt's girlfriend shrank into a corner, horror paling her face.

The biker bounced off the far wall. Matt tore into him with half a dozen body jabs. When the bearded man slumped to his knees, Matt knocked him flat on the tile floor with a hard right hook.

The patrol car responding to the manager's summons squealed to a halt outside the glass front, blue lights spinning as two officers raced inside the McDonalds.

"Don't you ever say that!" yelled Matt.

He straddled the biker, lifted the man up by his greasy shirt as he yelled at him.

"Don't you ever say that! Don't you ever call him stupid! Don't you ever, ever say that!"

One cop pulled Matt away from the dazed man. As he did, Matt's jacket came open, exposing his white police shirt and badge.

"Shit," said the other cop as he bent to help the biker.

When the sergeant arrived on the scene fifteen minutes later a second squad car was parked in front of the restaurant. A small crowd huddled under the awning. Matt sat on the curb, oblivious to the rain as tears ran down his cheeks. One of his fellow policemen stood behind him. The biker's friend had vanished, not wishing to deal with anyone wearing a badge. The biker sat inside the restaurant, dabbing at his swollen face with a towel. His nose had stopped bleeding, but not his split lip. He held his ribs with his other hand, had difficulty sitting straight and breathing comfortably. A policeman stood nearby.

The sergeant talked to the first officers on the scene, to the manager, to two citizens who'd volunteered as witnesses. The sergeant talked to the girlfriend, remembered a story he'd heard told around headquarters. He had the policeman guarding the biker clear the room. When the restaurant was empty except for himself and the biker, he crossed the tiles, sat in the swivel chair across from the battered and bruised man. The sergeant smiled.

"This is going to be the only informal, friendly, off-the-record chat," he told the biker, who stared at him with sullen, blackening eyes. "So pay close attention."

"My men checked your injuries. If you're half as tough as you think you are, they won't bother you after tomorrow."

The biker blinked: this wasn't what he'd expected.

"You're in Baltimore, son," said the sergeant. "But you're not from here. My men ran a check on you. There are 14 outstanding tickets on your car, three on your motorcycle, and you've got a couple speeding violations on your sheet. Buck knife in a case on your belt. And you're a big son of a bitch. You look like trouble about to happen. Probable cause is written all over you. A cop would have to assume you were dangerous.

"What happened here is you fucked up. Shot your mouth off at the wrong time in the wrong place. But maybe you're thinking you're the injured party. Maybe you want something done about that. Press charges, lawsuit, whatever shit you can come up with.

"If that's what you want, fine. Those are your rights. You got more, and if you want to make this formal, I'll read them to you. After we do that, we'll take your complaint. We'll act on it in due course as provided for by law. We'll take a good look at you through the law, too. So will our friends on your hometown force. So will the state cops. Feds, DEA. We'll look long, we'll look hard. We won't forget about our job, no matter how long we need to look.

"But this is Baltimore. You might not want that. You might want to take my business card I'll lay here on the table. That card won't get you anything but a good word when you need it. I'm betting you're going to need it. It's no get-out-of-jail-free card, but . . ."

The sergeant shrugged.

"Your parking tickets. Did you know they could get waived? Just like they could suddenly get ruled unduly delinquent and turned over to the tow truck boys.

"But it's all up to you. You can ask to talk to me formally, and I'll take out my notebook, start taking officical steps. Or you can say fuck it, I stepped in my own shit. Walk out of here to clean your boots and never look back.

"I don't have a lot of time. We're looking for a cop killer, we're looking for his friends. Or any of his fans. All the boys want to talk to those sons of bitches. Want to talk to them real bad.

"Right now, I'm on my coffee break. I'm going to go behind the counter, pour myself a cup. Walk back here. If you're still around, I'll figure you want to tell me about a problem you got. If you're gone, I'll figure all your problems just walked out the door."

The sergeant smiled, did as he said, stood at the coffee urn with his back to the biker. Slowly poured himself a cup of coffee. When he turned around, he stood in an empty restaurant.

Outside, in the rain, a cop sat on the gutter and cried.

Devlin spent Sunday staring at the phone in his apartment. Rachel didn't call. Julia did, but he made her hang up immediately. She'd heard what happened, came to the apartment. Put her arms around him, hugged him, and cried for the big man she barely knew. Devlin patted her shoulder, told her there was nothing she could do. Made her go home. He'd spent Saturday directing teams of detectives who shook down everyone involved with the case. No question was out of bounds, no innocence unchallenged. Nothing new shook loose. From midnight Saturday until three in the morning, he and Susan cruised Baltimore's streets, found nothing. Devlin woke at dawn, went to the living room, and relieved Harris, who'd been staring at the phone during the darkness. Rourke spent three hours Sunday morning cruising the streets with Perry. She dropped him off at his apartment, picked up Harris, and took him home for a brief nap. Perry picked up another detective, cruised the city as Harris slept, and Rourke stared at the phone that didn't ring.

Nothing I can do, thought Rourke as Sunday's light faded into night. *Nothing I can do.*

60

They began arriving before dawn on that beautiful spring Monday nine days after the Ward Building massacre.

Forty Maryland troopers, with their own color guard.

A squad car from New York City, two detectives, three uniformed officers.

Two squad cars from Philadelphia, two from Pittsburgh,

half a dozen from Washington, D.C., one from Roanoke, two from Richmond. Four Virginia state police cars. The Annapolis police chief came with two of his men in a brand new cruiser. Military police drove a Jeep up from the Pentagon. Departments from Maryland, Virginia, Pennsylvania, West Virginia, and Ohio sent cruisers, cops. Three New Jersey trooper cruisers coincidentally rendezvoused with two New York state police cars on the turnpike, and together, in perfect formation, all five vehicles headed south to Baltimore.

Somebody killed a cop.

Cops came to bury their own.

Two Texas Rangers flew in from Austin. A Cook County deputy sheriff who'd been vacationing in Florida gave up his specially packaged airfare, rerouted to Baltimore-Washington International Airport. He didn't know that six cops from Florida rode the plane with him until they landed and all of them converged on an airport cop in the lounge.

San Francisco's sheriff came. So did a Montana highway patrolman who the week before was shot at by a PCP-crazed 15-year-old. All three bullets had missed; the patrolman overpowered his assailant, locked him up, and had been shaking ever since.

Feds came: Drug Enforcment Agency, Federal Bureau of Investigation, Secret Service, Treasury Department, National Park Police. Congress's Capitol Hill Police Force and the Supreme Court's police force each sent cruisers.

Someone murdered an on-duty cop.

None of the out-of-town cops knew the Duck. They all knew his badge.

The Baltimore police force was everywhere. On-duty cops patroled the regular beats. A special contingent worked traffic detail. Motorcycle policemen waited at dozens of intersections, cruisers herded the processional. Off-duty cops drove every vehicle the department could spare, carrying out-of-town cops in them.

By 10 AM, the funeral home overflowed with policemen in dress uniform, brass and shoes shining. By 10:30, cops lined both sides of the sidewalks. Men and women, black and white, Hispanic, Oriental. Cops in cheap polyester, cops in custom-cut three-piece suits. A dozen undercover cops came; they wore sunglasses, kept their collars turned up for the TV cameras and newspaper photographers.

The mayor came.

So did the lieutenant governor.

So did a deputy attorney general.

At eleven, led by the Baltimore Police Department's color guard, pallbearers carried the Duck's casket outside. A line of 300 police cars, three abreast, stretched behind the hearse.

The Duck's squad carried his coffin: Captain Goldstein, Devlin, Susan, Gary, and two rookies chosen by lot from the last class to graduate from the Academy. They all wore blue dress uniforms, black bands on their badges. Sam trotted behind them, a long leash tied to the black box; he didn't bark, didn't balk at the crowd. The pallbearers slid the coffin in the hearse, climbed in Baltimore police cruisers parked behind that long black carriage. Sam rode in the middle cruiser, on the front seat between the captain and Devlin.

In front of the hearse, three motorcycle patrolmen kicked their steeds to life as the cops, the newsmen, the dignitaries, and the curious scrambled to their vehicles. Hundreds of engines ground on.

Captain Goldstein radioed a command.

All the Baltimore police cars turned on their headlights. Their blue emergency lights spun round. Behind them, all the police cars followed suit. Flashing red and blue lights stretched down the street as far as the eye could see.

The motorcycle escort raced their engines; blew their sirens once.

The parade rolled forward, slow and silent through the heart of Baltimore. Flags hung at half-mast. Traffic patrols closed intersections. The Ward Building's black mirror walls reflected the pulsating yellow, red, and blue river. Clerks, shoppers, office workers, schoolchildren, and tourists stared at that long flashing line.

Their route led past Baltimore Fire Company No. 14. When the motorcycle escort was three blocks away, the fire doors rolled open. The engine company marched out in formation, blue shirts, black pants, freshly shined shoes. They formed two lines at the edge of the driveway, parallel to the parade's path, stood at ease, their hands clasped behind their backs. Eyes forward. The company commander slowly drove the main hook and ladder unit his men had been polishing since midnight to the curb. As the motorcycle escort rolled by, he called his men to attention. When the hearse passed in front of them, the commander reached up, pulled on the cord and rang the bell:

Rang it once for the policeman on his way back to the earth.

Rang it a second time for the firemen and policemen who'd preceded him.

Rang it the third time for us.

The cemetery at the edge of Baltimore was green and lush with spring. Policemen wearing white gloves directed the cars to parking spots. The force reassembled beside the open grave. Led by the color guard, pallbearers carried the coffin to the hole, eased it onto the support straps. Devlin held Sam's leash.

An officer turned on the waiting microphone. By custom, the police commissioner or Captain Goldstein should have spoken. Neither of them had challenged Devlin's claim to that task.

Devlin looked terrible: pale, drawn, shadows under his eyes. He stood before the mircophone for more than a minute. The crowd waited silently. A bird chirped in the trees a hundred feet away.

"His name was Liam McKinnon," said Devlin.

His amplified voice echoed over stone crosses and Stars of David deeply etched in marble slabs; over cement markers with only a name.

"We called him the Duck."

Devlin had to step away from the microphone, grit his teeth. He leaned back.

"He was a good cop. He died doing his job, doing it bravely, with dignity. Doing it right. We'll miss him."

Devlin stepped back into the ranks. Glared straight ahead.

Captain Goldstein nodded to the commander of the color and the funeral director.

"Company, attention!" yelled the police commissioner.

Every cop snapped to.

A seven-man honor guard, rifles at port arms, marched to the grave's edge. Their squad leader barked the orders:

"Ready, aim, . . . *fire!*"

They did.

"*Fire!*"

They did.

"*Fire!*"

They did.

Sam barked once.

A bugler blew taps.

The coffin sank into the ground.

After a moment, the commissioner turned and walked to his car. The pallbearers stood their ground. The other officers walked to their cars and drove away. As the last of the mourner's cars started to drive away, the color guard marched to their vehicle, followed by the funeral director.

When the slamming of car doors was over and the roar of departing engines had subsided to a fading purr, Devlin walked to the edge of the open grave. Sam came with him.

Devlin looked down into man's last black hole. Sunshine twinkled off the coffin's polished wood. Behind him, a bird sang.

"See you, Duck," he said. Walked to his car.

The others followed him.

As they drove away, Sam looked back.

61

Sunshine burned Rachel's eyes as she ran down the Aquarium's fire escape. Alarm bells and screams filled the crisp air.

Where are you, you bastard?!

She ran to the front of the building, her eyes searching across the Inner Harbor, along the quay, toward downtown.

Children and tourists, teachers, uniformed Aquarium employees swarmed around her like panicked fish. She realized she held the Duck's pistol, thrust it into her waistband inside her jacket—but kept her hand close to the gun butt.

Where are you?!

Think: he didn't find you accidentally, he followed you. If he followed you . . .

Sirens screaming, klaxons blaring, a fire truck raced past her toward the Aquarium. A police car followed in its wake.

The parking lot.

She dodged a boy crying for his mother, ran through the curiosity seekers streaming toward the Aquarium.

Too late.

The green Ford sedan rolled toward the parking lot entrance. Rachel dodged behind a man wearing earphones connected to a small tape recorder on his belt. He lumbered ahead of her, oblivious to the woman hiding in his shadow.

Rachel peered around her shield in time to glimpse the driver as the Ford pulled away.

Him!

She blinked, squinted. Memorized the license plate.

More sirens converged on the Aquarium.

This time, she thought, *this time it's just me.*

The parking lot attendant loaned her a phone book.

"What's going on at the Aquarium?" he asked, his eyes ignoring the curiously soaked woman in front of him for the distant fire trucks, police cars, and milling crowd.

"I don't know," she said.

The building was within walking distance.

"Thanks," she said, handing him the book.

"Yeah, sure," he said, while he watched the flashing lights and cursed the bad luck that kept anything interesting from happening to him.

Woody Fadiman scratched his head, fumbled with the key to his apartment, wondered if the paint flecking off the door contained chemicals that might kill him. He sniffled: might be a cold. He'd stuffed newspaper in all the window gaps and plaster cracks, took 1,000 milligrams of vitamin C a day, and the cold virus got him anyway.

Dangerous world, he thought as he opened his door, stepped inside—

Saw her sitting on his iron cot.

"Hello, Woody," said Rachel.

"Wha . . . wha . . . !"

"Come in and shut the door."

Woody did as he was told.

"How did you . . ."

"I told the manager I was your sister."

"Oh," said Woody. "She lives in . . . in Akron, I think."

"You never showed up, Woody."

"Where?"

"In the garage. We had an appointment. Remember?"

"I meant to talk to you about that!" said Woody. He started
to pace and wave his hands. "I really did. It's not my fault."

"It never is."

"What happened was very complicated. It was cold,
right?"

"Right, Woody."

"And I meant to get to that garage—by the diner, right?—
That was a real cold day, see, and—"

"Forget about the garage deal, Woody."

". . . and I was across town, on this very important
. . . Forget about the deal?"

"It doesn't matter any more."

"Well, I had the grass, but . . ." He shrugged. "You
know."

"Yeah, I know. Do you know what's been going on?"

"You mean with Banana Anna who runs the laundromat
and her old man getting . . . Why are you here?"

"I'm staying with you for a few days."

"Oh." He slowly turned his head around his apartment:
one room with an iron frame bed, a hot plate, a bathtub that
leaked, pipes that clanged. At night, mice played in the hall.
"Ah. . . ."

"I can pay five dollars a night."

"Sure! Plenty of room! Not too bad a place for—"

He frowned.

"Why can't you stay at your place?"

"Landlord problems."

"Gotcha covered," said Woody, winking. "What about
your job?"

"I'm doing something else now. I'll sleep on the floor. I
found your extra blankets and an old sleeping bag."

"Sure. Great."

"You might need to do some errands for me."

"Hey, Rachel, I mean, we know the same people and I
like you a lot. Friendship is great and all that, but—"

"I can pay you."

". . . so you know I'll do anything I can to help you."

"Mostly you can keep your mouth shut."

"You know me!"

"Yes, I do, Woody. If anybody knows I'm here, you lose five dollars a night. Maybe more. Plus, I'll be real mad at you."

"You saying I'm a rat? I ain't no rat! Ain't nobody ever said Woody Fadiman was a rat. I've never—"

"You talk a lot, Woody. Don't mention anything about me. If anybody mentions my name, don't say anything."

"I'm not stupid."

"You like to talk, Woody."

"Don't play tough with me."

She glared at him. He broke in 10 seconds, looked away.

"Okay," he said. Shuffled his feet. "Okay."

"Have you eaten today?" she asked.

"Uh . . . Yeah, I think so. I'm not hungry, though."

"Got any weed?"

"Look, I told you I was sorry I missed—"

"I've got cash."

"I've got a couple joints on me."

She pulled a five-dollar bill from her jacket, turned it round in her fingers. Dropped it on the bed.

"Fair?" she said.

"Oh, sure! I'd lay 'em on you free, but—"

"Yeah, Woody, I know. But the world isn't free."

"That's right!" he said, scurrying over to snatch the bill from the bed, put two crudely rolled cigarettes in its place. "That's what I always say."

"What are your plans, Woody?"

"Me? I . . . I don't know. Going to hang out."

"I want to be alone."

"Hey, no problem: I'm a busy man."

"Do you have a radio? TV?"

"What would I want those for?"

"Keep in touch with the world."

"Why?"

"Never mind. Go get something to eat, okay? Come back when it's dark. Bring me a burger, some milk. There's nothing but frost in your refrigerator."

"No problem, Rachel, but I don't—"

"Dinner's on me." She lifted two more fives out of her pocket; soon she'd need to use the Duck's larger bills. "Bring me the change."

"Sure!" said Woody. He grabbed those bills, too, tucked them inside his tattered coat.

"You know," he said as he moved toward the door, "it'll be fun having a woman around."

"Don't get any ideas, Woody."

"That's not my style," he said softly; looked at her.

"Sorry," she said.

He shrugged: "For what?"

"For forgetting."

Woody wandered to the door, his mind riding a fifteen-dollar dream. He stopped, frowned. Turned back to his guest. "I'll see you—"

"When it gets dark, Woody."

"Right. When it gets dark. With your dinner."

Then he left her alone.

Rachel fell into smoke.

She'd cried for an hour after Woody left—gut-wrenching sobs that curled her into a fetal position on his hard bed, wet her face until she ran out of tears. A thousand memories invaded her mind: the Duck, Devlin, the shark flopping on the ramp. An empty Nebraska highway. The bomb blast at the London Hotel and the ambulance that never came for a baby who wouldn't stop crying. The face of the murderer who'd tried to kill her, three times, who'd killed as innocent a man as she'd ever meet, a man who'd cared for her and gave her his life.

So much is owed, she thought.

And nobody else can square the ledger.

Devlin was a good man. He'd tried, and failed. She could call him now, tell him what she'd learned at the Motor Vehicle Registry, but what good would that do? Even if his bureaucracy didn't get in his way, his *law* would. Law: men with badges that let them do what they wanted and not have to pay. The law meant lawyers, and lawyers laid off debts so they never got paid. The killer could get the best lawyers. If Devlin managed to succeed where he'd repeatedly failed, then the lawyers would take over. Then nothing would happen. Then the debts would mount up instead of being paid off.

I can't carry any more.

This time she wouldn't run. She wouldn't fold or do what was convenient. So much was owed—by her, to her. She'd collect, she'd pay off. Maybe her life was one grand equation adding up to this play. Didn't matter. That's where she was now.

Rachel scratched a match against the metal bed frame, fired up a joint. Used it all. She lay back on the bed, burned out and filled with her own smoke. She felt herself falling back into the haze, falling toward one clear and certain moment.

62

Four hours after the Aquarium battle, the killer sat on the bed in his new hotel room.

Shaking.

A line of blood trickled down his shaved head.

What the hell was happening?!

Once in the garage. Again with the bomb. Third time in the Aquarium.

What the hell has gone wrong?!

The killer was his own religion. Good and evil, right and wrong, God, karma . . . He'd long ago rejected such superstitions. Political ideology meant nothing to him. Personal expediency was his only ethic, the only standard by which he measured life. Anything that furthered his goals was good. He was the ultimately rational man. He controlled himself. He did not fail.

What's gone wrong with me?!

Rachel Dylan.

Who was she?

He'd missed her three times. Once he could understand. Even twice. But three times!

He shuddered.

The blood trickled toward his right ear, tickled him.

He was a practical businessman. He should cut his losses, leave this market. An unpredictably hostile environment had arisen. The hell with the client!

But this wasn't a client matter anymore. This business was personal.

This wasn't about the risk factor of leaving a live witness. He could adjust to that danger.

If he didn't get her, then it was because he couldn't. He'd failed. If he'd failed against Rachel Dylan, then he was losing his touch. His center was coming unwound. She'd haunt him. Each day, he'd come apart a little more. Slowly, certainly, the ghostly consequence of his failure would gnaw at him. He'd get sloppy, make mistakes. And inevitably, the world would come crashing in on him.

Either he'd get Rachel Dylan, or she'd have gotten him.

He walked to the mirror. Suddenly realized his shaved head was bleeding. He pulled a handkerchief from his pocket, dabbed the blood away. He'd bought clippers, razors, everything he'd needed at the first shopping mall he'd passed on the way from the Aquarium to the airport. Taking the time to make his purchases and braving discovery as he shaved his head in the most remote men's room at Baltimore-Washington International Airport had taxed his nerve. He'd shaken so much that he'd cut his head, but the styptic pencil had stopped the bleeding until now.

Had thinking about Rachel started it bleeding again?

Absurd! he thought.

Then he trembled: he'd seldom thought the absurd before.

Something else! Think of something else!

So this is what you'll look like bald. He cupped his hand over his mouth. The dark brown Fu Manchu mustache in his briefcase would draw eyes from his face. No one would link the mustachioed bald man with any description the police had.

He ran his hand over his freshly shaved head. He'd come to Baltimore with long hair. Cut it short because she'd seen him. Shaved it off because she'd seen him again.

She's whittling me down.

The man in the mirror blinked. A new trickle of blood appeared on his head.

She drew first blood. Three times I tried, and she drew first blood.

But he'd covered his tracks.

His favorite pistol was lost, his shotgun was lost, his back and ribs ached from his fight with the giant cop. The city would be hunting him. He was well hidden, invisible with his new image, but he'd have to lay low for a few days, wait until the streets cooled down. Then . . .

Then he'd start hunting her again.

He ran his trembling hand over his shaved head, smeared blood across his skull and palm.

If I don't get her, next time she'll take me down to the bone.

63

Here we go, thought Rachel, that Monday as she pushed her way through the glass doors like gangbusters.

"Good morning!" she called out to the startled woman behind the counter. "Sorry I'm late."

"Wha— Excuse me?" said the counter clerk.

"I got lost getting here," said Rachel, still moving. She marched behind the counter, her shoes clicking on the floor. She wore a dark brown suit picked out Saturday by Woody, who oddly had exquisite taste. Her shoes were uncomfortable, but he'd assured her they went better with the suit than any others he'd seen in her size. Rachel pushed open the swinging door in the counter, strode into the work area. She plunked down the worn Salvation Army store briefcase on a table beneath a wall poster reading: Rent the Best—And Pay Less!

"What— Who are you?" said the clerk.

"Excuse me?" said Rachel, frowning.

"What can I do for you?" said the clerk, regaining her composure.

"Well," said Rachel with a conspiratorial smile, "if you're lucky, you won't have to do much, right?"

"Look, I don't understand, and—"

"You really don't know, do you?" Rachel showed surprise.

"No." The clerk shook her head and was about to get angry.

"Christy Macy," said Rachel, sticking out her hand—which the clerk automatically took. After they shook hands, Rachel pushed the clear-lensed glasses Woody bought her at a discount drugstore back up her nose. "Central Audit Tracking Team. Didn't you get the review notification memo either?"

"Oh shit!" said the clerk. "Nobody ever tells me anything!"

"I know the feeling," said Rachel. "Don't worry. It's a fast buzz-through. I'm mainly checking your turnaround logging procedures, your M–71s, inventory sheets, and system operations."

If only the jargon hasn't changed since last year's two-month job in Memphis! thought Rachel.

"Wouldn't you know it?" moaned the clerk. "Typical Monday morning."

"Don't worry," said Rachel, winking at the clerk. "I worked a counter in Memphis, and I know just how you feel."

"Really? Memphis?"

"Yes," said Rachel.

"Do you know a Mark Ashford who—"

"Does he still manage the airport outlet?" asked Rachel.

"Yes! I've never met him, but over the phone . . ."

"Sounds like a sexy Southern gentleman, right?"

The clerk laughed.

"That's him!"

"Well," said Rachel, telling the truth, "Southern he may be, gentleman he is not. He's the kind who always rubs against you in the hall, and you'd be amazed how often his arm 'accidentally' brushes across your breasts.

"And," said Rachel, "the only thing sexy about him is his voice. Besides, he's got a wife and three kids."

"No!" sighed the clerk.

"Yes," said Rachel, "so if he starts in with that *'bout time to ramble on* spiel of his—"

"I've heard that!"

"You'll hear it again. He's been in Memphis for 10 years, and he'll be there another 10, if the company doesn't transfer him."

"Next time he calls, I'll tell him hello for you."

"Please!" said Rachel. "Don't even tell him you saw me."

"Never mind," said the clerk, "I got the picture."

"Great," said Rachel.

"How do you want to start?"

When Rachel checked the license plate from the killer's car at the Motor Vehicle Bureau, she'd discovered the car belonged to this rental company. She'd checked the phone book and with Woody's help decided this office was the most remote of the company's branches. Woody knew she was running a scam, but he didn't know what.

Rachel made an elaborate show of looking over her shoulders.

"Are we alone?" she asked.

"My manager is due in at noon, but he'll probably be late. We don't get much business here, and—"

"Look," said Rachel, "I've been staying with relatives. They picked me up at the airport. I'm due in Philly tomorrow, and I've got more of Baltimore to do. So . . ."

She looked around again; the clerk looked with her. Rachel suppressed a smile.

"Tell you what," said Rachel, "I'll play with the computer, run a printout or two to stick in my file, check some of your records so I can say I did, then get out of your hair. I figure you're 100 percent anyway, right?"

"Oh, right!"

"Good. Then we might as well get it over with."

"Would you like a cup of coffee?" asked the clerk.

"Love one," said Rachel. "My relatives aren't well stocked."

"The pot over there is fresh," said the clerk. "I'll bring you one."

Rachel moved behind the glowing computer terminal. The keyboard looked the same, and if she could just remember . . .

"Shame you weren't here earlier," said the clerk from across the room as she poured coffee into two cups. "You missed something."

"Really?" said Rachel automatically. Her fingers hesitated above the keyboard, then typed in a brief command. "What?"

"Cop funeral," said the clerk. "Drove right by here. Must have been a thousand cars, whirling lights and everything."

Rachel closed her eyes, pushed a command key. When she opened them, the screen showed her what she'd asked for.

"Thanks," she whispered; louder said, "I saw part of it."

"Quite a sight, wasn't it?" asked the clerk as she put a steaming cup on the counter next to the machine.

"Yes," said Rachel, "it was."

He'd turned in his car at BWI Airport.

Rachel stared at the flashing screen. She felt like she would throw up.

He'd turned in his car at the airport.

Too late.

"Are you okay?" said the clerk.

Rachel blinked, shook her head.

"Yes," she lied, "I'm fine. Just tired."

"Do you want another cup of coffee?"

Rachel didn't, but that would get the clerk out from behind her back, where she watched her every move.

"Yes, thanks."

The clerk took Rachel's empty cup across the room.

"I'll have to make some more," she said.

"Thanks. Fine."

He can't have left town!

Rachel closed her eyes again; willed it not to be so.

"Excuse me," said Rachel, "do you know our staff at BWI?"

"Sure. Today there's only one girl out there."

"I bet nobody's told her about me either," said Rachel. "You check out great. Could you call her, tell her I'm on my way?"

"Sure. Anything else?"

"What do we have for wheels on the lot?"

The killer had checked his car in an hour after the Aquarium battle. The airport rent-a-car clerk Rachel talked to wasn't the one who helped him, but the clerk went overboard to help "Christy Macy."

He's covering his tracks, decided Rachel. Since she'd willed him not to leave Baltimore, there was no other reason he'd have checked his car. Doing that relieved him of a machine whose description the police might have and led anyone on his trail to the airport.

But, insisted Rachel, he's in Baltimore.

She knew enough about running and hiding to analyze his play. He'd need another car. He wouldn't rent one from the same company—or if he did, not at the airport. She made a printout of all cars rented since the Aquarium battle, with the name, home address, and local phone number of each customer.

But what if the killer rented from another company?

BWI had three rent-a-car companies. There were at least three more in the city. She had to gamble he'd stay with a big company and play every chance she had.

At the airport, "her" company's chief competitor had the neighboring stand, one also worked by a lone woman clerk. A partition separated the two firms' outposts. Business was slow that time of day. Rachel dispatched the clerk from "her" firm on time-consuming chores. Rachel worked the stand herself, processed customers, and pretended to audit the computer system. As she feigned interest in the flashing computer screen, Rachel befriended the woman clerk for the competition. Within half an hour, Rachel had steered their conversation to the differences in company computer and bookkeeping processes. Rachel waited, her kidneys crying out for relief. Inevitably, between flight arrivals, the moment came when her "competition" needed to go to the bathroom. As fellow workers in the trenches often do, Rachel volunteered to watch the woman's stand.

When the bathroom door swung shut on the departing clerk, Rachel scurried behind her computer, punched in the proper command,—then stood there, stomach churning while the computer printed out records for all customers since the Aquarium shooting. Rachel stuffed the printout into her briefcase, cleared the woman's computer, and returned to her own machine 10 seconds before the bathroom door swung open and the clerk returned.

"Any problems?" she'd asked.

"No," said Rachel.

"How you coming with your stuff?" asked the competitor just as Rachel's co-worker returned.

"I think I've done all I can here," answered Rachel. She smiled sweetly at the two women. "You've both been great!"

She ran up Woody's telephone bill calling directory assistance operators in the hometowns of men who'd rented cars from either firm.

He'd better be as cautious as I think he is, thought Rachel, *or I don't stand a chance of catching him*.

The car she'd seen had been rented by a Dallas man, but the Dallas operator had no one by that name at the address shown in the rental company records. Rachel assumed the killer followed the same pattern with his second rental car. If she turned up a phony name, she might turn up the killer.

She got one on the thirty-fourth call from the rival firm's list, a light blue Ford registered to Bruce Barlow, St. Louis. The St. Louis operator showed no Barlow at the address on her printout; indeed, showed no Bruce Barlow in the city.

Got you.

64

*T*his is where it all began, thought Devlin as he stood on the concrete floor of the Ward Building garage Tuesday, the morning after the Duck's funeral. *This is where the answer must be*.

After the funeral, he burned a tank of gas cruising Baltimore, watching the city work its way through another Monday, slide into evening, doze off into night. But he found no sign of Rachel or the killer. Devlin went to sleep at 2 AM, woke with first light. Now he stood in the dank garage, the scent of spring touching even this cavern steeped in fuel and exhaust fumes. The morning rush hour was over, the building's workers were upstairs in the offices of a radio station, a data factory, a graphics firm, an office supply business.

No trace of the carnage remained. No bodies made islands in a red lake on the garage floor. No stain marred the concrete. No shell cases glistened in the faint electric light, no police lines traced where in one wink of a cosmic eye, dozens of lives were forever altered.

He looked terrible. The silver steel elevator doors 20 feet away reflected his blurred image. He'd shaved and showered, but half-moon shadows cupped his bloodshot eyes and his face was gray. He wore a sports coat but hadn't had the energy for a tie.

That red lake swallowed me.

"Great day, isn't it?" called out a man's voice behind him.

Devlin whirled: the squat building superintendent walked to him from the shadows and rows of parked cars. The superintendent's gray cloth windbreaker was zipped to his neck. His hands in his pockets jangled coins.

Devlin said nothing.

The superintendent looked up at the detective, then followed the cop's gaze to that lake that wasn't there on the floor.

"Is that what brought you here today?"

Devlin shrugged.

The super frowned; thought about it, then slowly smiled.

"Wait a minute," he said. "I got it!"

"What?" asked Devlin.

"I know why you're really here."

"Why?" asked Devlin.

"The car!"

Devlin wrinkled his brow.

"You know," said the super, "my old Mustang that got shot up. I remember you saying it was a nice car. Got it all fixed up again—all except the rear window. One little star dent in that glass, but everything else: cherry shape. And seein' as how it's you, I'll make you a good price."

"No," said Devlin, "that's not why I'm here."

"You sure?"

"Yes."

"Damn! It's a good car. You really should get a look at it somewhere where the light is good before you make a decision. But, I guess I was wrong, made a mistake. I—"

White fire exploded in Devlin; he reeled from the blast. As the fire burned away the darkness, he grabbed the super by the jacket.

"What did you say!?" screamed Devlin.

"Wha– Wa– Who—. . . !"

Control flowed back through Devlin's veins. He released the superintendent, held his hands up to calm the sputtering man.

"I just . . . the car . . . I'm sorry. Don't—"

"Take it easy!" commanded Devlin. "What did you say?!"

"Wha– . . . ? I said I was sorry, made a mistake."

"Yes! But not about the car! About that!" cried Devlin: he pointed to where the lake of blood had been. "You made a mistake about that!"

"I don't understand!" wailed the short man, who wished someone would rescue him from this crazed cop.

Memories flooded through Devlin: Four bodies on the cement floor, dressed snugly for winter's last bitter day: Tu-Cut saying how "we all look alike to you people"; the superintendent, grimly doing his duty and identifying bodies, walking toward the lake of blood and suddenly blurting—

"What did you say?!" Devlin asked again. His eyes focused back in time. "You walked to the edge of the blood, looked and said . . . 'I made a mistake'—No! That you were wrong—no, it was . . .

"'Not her!'" cried Devlin. "That's what you said: You looked at Le-Lan lying there and before you had a chance to think you said, 'Not her!'

"And then you said . . . you thought it was . . . somebody else! Who did you think it was?!"

"You mean dead?" asked the superintendent.

"Yes! Who did you think Le-Lan was?!"

"Well, for a second, I got her mixed up with Thel Chang."

"Who's Thel Chang!?"

"She works upstairs in that investment firm that's been in the papers," explained the super, eager to be back on familiar ground. "Gorgeous Oriental gal, and hell, that other one lying there dead, all wrapped up in that scarf and this light, anybody could make that same mis—"

"Holy shit," whispered the superintendent.

For the first time in four days, Devlin smiled.

65

Rachel sat in Woody's apartment, talking on the telephone to the manager of the Regis Motor Inn, the twenty-seventh such businessman she'd called that morning.

"Excuse me," she said, "I know you're busy, but this is long distance and it won't take but a minute. We're calling from United Credit Search."

Rachel shifted on Woody's bed. She didn't glance at the name and address written on the yellow legal pad. She'd asked about that name 26 times, more than enough to memorize it.

"We're tracking a skip who's burned a bunch of credit bureau clients," said Rachel. "He hops around, uses phony names."

"Un-huh."

"We think he's in Baltimore."

"How much has he stuck people for?"

"So far, twelve grand, with phony charges still popping up."

"Son of a bitch—excuse me!"

"That's okay, I hate these deadbeats, too."

"How's a man supposed to make an honest living when he gets a hundred screw jobs a day? And skips aren't the worst! Let me tell you about the workmen who—"

"If it's a problem we can help you with," interrupted Rachel, "just contact us through the credit bureau."

"Right, I forgot: this is long distance. How can I help?"

"We think he's using the name Bruce Barlow, with a St. Louis home address, driving a brown Chevy Citation rental car."

"Hold on a second, I'll check the book."

Rachel rubbed the bridge of her nose while she waited: *So tired*.

One minute.

Two.

This is long distance, Rachel thought. Didn't the man have any respect for her scam?

"Don't know if we can help you or not," said the manager, coming back on the line, "but we might have him."

"You do!?"

"Maybe. Our Bruce Barlow is a white guy as bald as an egg and has one of them droopy mustaches. That him?"

"Bald?!"

"Yeah."

"Oh."

Could be. In the garage, his hair was long. Cut short in the Aquarium. Maybe he's always been bald, been wearing wigs.

"He's sick," said the manager. "Terrible cold. Hasn't left the motel for a couple days. He pays one of the maids to bring him lunch and dinner. If he's your man, he's going nowhere."

"Have you seen him?"

"Hell, no! I don't want his cold."

As if he were reading the question forming in her mind, the manager said, "He's given us a cash deposit for five days. Said something about his credit cards being botched up."

"I understand," she said. "Look, he's not a total match. I don't want to get gears grinding before we're sure. Don't want to cause any problems for anybody who's innocent. Or for you."

She sensed the manager suddenly realize his long-distance conversation might have unpleasant consequences.

"Hey, look," said the manager, "I don't want to cause any trouble or—"

"Or get burned," said Rachel.

"He's clear with us."

"For now," she said. "By the way, if he's legitimate, you don't want to worry him about our discussion."

"No way! I don't want to get sued!"

"You've done nothing that's wrong, but—"

"But that doesn't stop lawyers!"

"You're right. So the best way to handle this is not to let the guy wonder if anybody's noticed him. Your clerk—"

"He won't bat an eye, I'll be sure of that!"

"Great. Let us do the rest. We'll send our local rep out to get a look at him. Your Bruce Barlow won't even know he's been checked out. If there's a problem, we'll make sure it won't reflect in any way on you or the motel."

"Thanks."

"Just doing our job. What room is he in?"

"Two hundred. Second floor corner, overlooks the parking lot and the office. He requested it."

"Thanks a lot."

"Hope I helped."

66

Thel Chang wore a red dress and was pretty in a hard-used fashion. She stood five-foot-four in black high heels. She didn't cut her hair until she was 26, had been famous on the campus of Maryland's Towson State University for the ebony mane that hung below her tight hips. There wasn't a man who saw that hair, her petite form, and her smiling, pretty face who didn't feel a flame in his heart.

She still lit fires in men's hearts, though she no longer caused universal ignition when she walked down the street. After a nasty romance swept away the last of her innocent expectations, she'd stood before the bathroom mirror one tearful midnight and with her sewing scissors chopped her hair short against her skull. She still dreamed about great chunks of black hair falling slowly to a white-tiled bathroom floor. Of course, her hair grew back, but she never let it hang free again. That morning she wore it cropped full around her face; she was wondering whether it was time for a trim.

The years changed more than her hair. Her hips were tight, though more padded. Time and too many cigarettes paled her olive complexion, puffed out the smooth lines of her cheekbones and jaw. Instead of radiating sweetness, her wary-eyed expression said *show me*.

She wore crimson lipstick, and her long fingernails were painted scarlet.

When Baltimore Detective Paul McKee, two FBI agents, a lawyer from the attorney general's office, and Devlin Rourke walked through her office door Thel was wondering where to go for lunch; whether to go at all, given the belly she'd been growing from too many martinis.

She'd met McKee and the FBI agents before. The lawyer looked like a wire-rimmed glasses wimp, and Devlin looked like just another badge.

The sign on her office door on the seventeenth floor of the Ward Building read, "The Blake Fund."

"Hello, gentlemen," she said, her voice as pleasant and calm as she could make it. "I didn't expect to see any of you here today."

"Are we alone?" asked McKee; he'd flirted with her for weeks.

Her desk faced the hall door, with the wall of windows at her back. Closed doors waited on each side of the room. The sign on the door to her left read, "Jackson Blake." The sign on the door to her right read, "Ross Martin."

Her eyes flicked to the Ross Martin door. When she looked forward again, Devlin, the lawyer, and McKee had reached her desk. The two FBI agents stood by the exit.

"Well, yes, we're alone," she said. "Mr. Martin—he's at one of your offices, isn't he?"

"We know," said Devlin. He sat in the chair in front of her desk. The lawyer and McKee flanked him. "I sent for him."

Thel pulled a cigarette from the pack on her desk; picked up her lighter and struck the flame. The lighter wobbled.

"We don't have much time," said Devlin. He introduced himself, said, "Do you remember the murders in this building's garage ten days ago?"

She nodded; her expression was puzzled, worried. She took a jerky drag from her cigarette.

He pulled out an 8-by-11-inch black and white photo from a file and dropped it on her desk:

Le-Lan Nguyen, dead in a lake of blood.

"This was supposed to be you," said Devlin.

"The garage is poorly lit. She wore a heavy coat with a scarf around her neck, bundled up high that hid most of her face. She had black hair—Oriental black, like yours. Skin color and eyes like yours. The killer only had a second in which to aim and shoot.

"She was supposed to be you. The others were just witnesses."

Thel Chang closed her eyes, swayed. Devlin thought she might faint. She pushed away from her desk, walked to the wall of windows. She crossed her arms over her crimson dress, smoke from her cigarette rising to the ceiling. She stared out at the city. No sound came to her through the glass.

"You're supposed to be dead," said Devlin. "And you will be, too, if you don't let us help you. If you don't help us."

"That son of a bitch," she hissed.

No one spoke for almost a minute.

"We've figured out most of it," said Devlin. "That your boss Blake turned his investment company into a scam, that's he's raked off millions and has skipped where we can't find him.

"What we can't figure is why he wants you killed, whether he's hired somebody to do it or whether he's trying himself, and he's just got us fooled into thinking he's a pro.

Thel didn't turn from the glass as he continued.

"We figure you know something that would nail him or help us find him. You may not know what you know, but he wants to keep you from talking."

She said nothing.

"That's the merciful theory of your life," said Devlin. "The other theory says you're part of the scam, and Blake is cutting you out to cover his ass and grab your share. Whether your co-worker Ross Martin was in on the scheme with you two, we don't know.

"But Ross Martin doesn't matter for now. You do. One way or another, you're in this. You're supposed to be dead, and without us, that's where you're headed.

"Help us, you save yourself. If you don't . . ." Devlin shrugged. "You might as well go through that window right now."

"Miss Chang," interrupted the assistant attorney general, "I want to emphasize that Detective Rourke is in no way making any kind of threat. I'd also like to advise you of your rights. You are a suspect in several felonies. You have the right to an attorney, you—"

"I know my rights," she said, not turning from the glass. "I don't like lawyers."

The officials of law and order looked at each other,

JUST A SHOT AWAY

wondered if that statement qualified as an informed waiver of
the right to counsel.

"Miss Chang," said the prosecutor, "if you should at any
time change your mind—"

She nodded, took a deep drag on her cigarette. Stared out
the window.

The prosecutor looked at his colleagues; shrugged.

"That son of a bitch," she said; didn't turn around.

Devlin raised his hand; kept his partners quiet.

Thel looked at the cigarette smoldering between her
fingers. The ember glowed against her flesh. She dropped the
cigarette, ground it into the carpet. Looked back out the
window.

"Thirty-six years," she said, staring out at the horizon
from Baltimore's most impressive skyscraper. "And this is
where it's over."

She finally turned toward the four men, but spoke to
Devlin.

"I used to have this really great hair, you know?"

Devlin nodded.

She was crying; rather, tears rolled down her face.

"You guys," she said, shook her head. "You think you
know so much. You're so stupid. So slow and so stupid."

"Tell us," said Devlin.

"You don't even know how much money we got, do you?
Hell, I don't even know, and I did it. Helped do it."

The prosecutor coughed nervously.

"Hah!" she shook her head, smiled; walked around her
chair and then slouched down in it. She put her black high
heeled feet up on her desk, leaned back in her chair shaking
her head, tears rolling down her cheek while her voice was
curiously gay. Her red dress slid up to her thighs, but the men
didn't look. Her words held their attention tighter than any
magnet ever kissed steel.

"You don't know anything," she said. "All you know is
shadows. You don't even know where Jack Blake is or what to
do about that."

"Tell us," said Rourke. "We'll know what to do."

"Too late," she said. "Too late."

She rolled her head from side to side like a drunk.

"We can protect you," said Rourke. "He won't be able to
kill you if—"

"Hah!" she said again. "Blake never killed anybody and he sure as shit won't now."

She smiled at the puzzled glances the men gave each other.

"You want Blake?" she said. "You want him? He's right here."

"Where?" said McKee, who'd spent weeks searching for the man.

"Here," she said. "In this building."

Rourke began to shake.

"You get it now?" Thel asked Rourke. "You seeing the light? Blake never tried to kill me. He didn't hire it done.

"It's Ross!" she said, jerking a finger toward the closed door bearing that name. "Ross Martin!

"The son of a bitch.

"Blake was too naive to be smart like Ross and me. Ross. . . . He's so smart and so slick, and he's goin' t' get us what's good after all these years, our last break, our last chance to be big time, too.

"You want to know where Blake is? He wanted what I'd been giving Ross. He wanted it bad. I called him at midnight. Told him to meet me in our new office so we could *break it in.* He raced over. I told him to use the garage elevator. Keep it a secret from Ross Martin and everybody so we wouldn't jeopardize the company's reputation and his great name. Oh, how he loved hearing all that!

"The garage wasn't finished. We'd moved in, but the building's grand opening was a week away. I surprised Blake, was waiting down there. He couldn't take his eyes off me. He parked his car, ran to me. Even during the day that garage is dark. At night . . .

"Blake reached for me, bent to kiss me. Martin came out from behind the pillar with the lead pipe and—

"And he made me hit him too. So we'd be in it together. Seal our love in blood. So we could trust each other. We lifted steel plates off the part of the floor that wasn't finished, dug a hole in muck, even carried away the extra dirt in plastic trash bags. Covered him up, put the wood forms in place. The next day they poured the concrete.

"You want to know where Blake is? He's under the garage."

67

The Regis Motel looked like the motel where Devlin hid Rachel the night of the Ward Building massacre. Indeed, the Regis looked like a thousand other American motels: two stories, a parking lot facing the double deck of rooms, office on the first floor. An orange neon "No / Vacancy" sign atop a brown steel pole. The motel walls were white stucco; the railings, steel landing, window trim, and doors were a creamy tan; the flat roof was black tar with aluminum gutters.

The motel was a hundred yards from the Beltway on a service road. On a concrete plaza across the road from the motel were a gas station and a convenience store. A glass telephone booth stood next to the road at the entrance to the plaza.

Rachel parked the rental car next to the phone booth, used binoculars to scan the motel. She wore her leather jacket, sweater and jeans, sneakers. The purse bought to go with her suit lay beside her on the seat. Inside the purse were a notebook with directions to the motel and its phone number, a pen, and the Duck's .38.

The binoculars showed her little of interest. Sometimes a faded lime green curtain swayed in one of the room's windows. A maid emerged from a room on the first floor, pushed a cleaning cart to a closet, then disappeared into the office.

Wonder if she's brought him lunch?

Rachel glanced at her watch: 1:27.

Probably.

Wonder if he's even there?

She scanned the parking lot, found a vehicle answering the rental car's description. She couldn't read the license plate, wasn't sure if she'd trust that anyway. Woody had switched the license plate from her car with one from a clunker abandoned

315

behind his apartment building. If the killer was paranoid
enough to hide out, he might have switched his plates, too.

The far corner room on the second floor was his.

*He can see the parking lot from his window, see where his
car is parked and whether there's anyone close by.*

The binoculars pulled the room window and door close to
her. The curtain moved. Just a flutter, enough so someone
could check, be sure nothing dangerous had entered his
environment.

Rachel's heart raced. Her mouth went dry.

So you are there!

Her eyes hadn't seen who moved the curtain, but her
heart was certain who was inside that room.

Her bladder screamed for attention.

There were restrooms alongside the convenience store. It
was unlikely she'd miss anything while she visited them. She
hid her car in behind a mountain of old tires, and walked to the
building.

The idea grabbed her as she walked back to her car.

The phone booth: alone, empty by the side of the road.

No more waiting.

She walked to the booth, didn't close the folding glass
doors. Dialed the motel. Asked for Mr. Bruce Barlow's room.
There was a pause, a whirr.

Then the phone rang.

The killer was dressed in shirt and slacks, stretched out on
his bed watching a rerun of "Leave It to Beaver" on television.

The phone rang.

He jerked; his stomach fell away.

The phone rang again.

No one should be calling me!

The phone rang again.

Who knows I'm here?

He whirled off the bed, grabbed the Browning 9mm
automatic pistol that had been resting beside him.

The phone rang again.

What the hell do you want?!

On the television, Ward Cleaver smiled benevolently.

The telephone rang.

The killer stood to the side of the windows, peered
around the edge of the lime green curtains.

The telephone rang.

No one stood outside his door. No strange cars sat in the parking lot. He couldn't see below the walkway to the office. Cars buzzed by on the secondary road, but he saw no police cruisers, poised to roar in for the bust.

The telephone rang.

His naked scalp prickled with electricity. He ran his hand over his bald dome, expected to find it wet with sweat but found only stubble.

The telephone rang.

His palms were wet; the gun belt felt slick.

The telephone rang.

He grabbed it, held it to his ear.

Nothing.

Not even heavy breathing.

Like listening to a vacuum.

Ten seconds, twenty, a minute, a minute and a half.

The killer said nothing.

Neither did the person on the other end of the telephone.

Come on, damn it! the killer cursed silently. *Say something!*

The person hung up.

The dial tone buzzed in the killer's ear. He depressed the hang-up button, released it, dialed zero. The phone buzzed twice.

"Front desk."

"This is Mr. Barlow."

"How are you doing? The maid said you seemed better today."

"I am, thank you. I was sleeping and the telephone rang, but I only grabbed it in time to hear the person hang up. Did you call me?"

"No sir, that call came from outside."

"Outside? Are you sure?"

"Sure!"

"Who was it?"

"I don't now, sir. They asked for you, but didn't give their name or leave a message."

"Man or woman?"

"To tell you the truth, sir, I was so busy, the voice was so husky . . . I'm not sure. Is anything wrong?"

"No," insisted the killer, "I just wasn't expecting any calls."

"Should I hold your calls?"

"No, put them through. And take detailed messages if I'm not here. Okay?"

"Sure. Anything else?"

"No. Thank you."

The killer hung up.

That wasn't a wrong number.

No one could know I'm here.

Someone does.

Someone out there, in the world. He put his suitcase on the bed, opened it, considered his hardware. All that equipment. What did he have that would help him now?

He took out two spare clips for the 14-shot 9mm Browning and chose a small .25 caliber automatic, double-checking to be sure it was fully loaded and chambered. The .25 went into an ankle holster, which he strapped on. He closed the suitcase, made sure he had money, other necessities. The Browning's hammer was on half-cock; he thumbed the manual safety off. He thrust the Browning in a shoulder holster, put on a safari-style windbreaker, and dropped his spare clips in the jacket pockets. Checked himself in the mirror.

His bald image still startled him.

Somebody wants to talk to me.

And he was an obliging fellow.

68

The man behind the mirror acted like he ruled the world with nothing to fear.

How much of that is pose? wondered Devlin.

The man behind the mirror sat on a metal folding chair pulled up to a table covered with ledgers, legal pads, and files. The room he sat in was small, lit by bright lights dangling high above his head. There were no ordinary windows in the room, only one door and the two-way mirror, beyond which stood Devlin.

The man in the room knew the mirror was a window, yet he seemed untroubled by that or the fact that he sat in an interrogation room of the Maryland state's attorney.

Ross Martin.

He wore a brown, three-piece tailored suit; Italian, handmade loafers. His wristwatch was gold. He was handsome: square-jawed, high-cheekboned, with deep-set brown eyes and hair trimmed to accentuate his high forehead and balding, patrician dome. His shoulders and chest were broad, his stomach trim from squash. He wore no rings on his manicured fingers. Sunlamps at his health club kept his tan rich, and his dentist made sure his teeth were always white.

The man seemed to be reading an account book. Devlin watched him turn a page.

Does that ledger tally up his dead? thought Devlin.

His boss, Jackson Blake.

The four people in the Ward Building garage.

The fat man from the diner.

The Duck.

The woman who had the heart attack in the London Hotel.

And what about Rachel?

The gunman's description didn't fit Ross Martin.

But they're all your dead, thought Devlin.

Devlin and his team took a search warrant with them when they went to collect Thel Chang. Devlin searched Ross Martin's office, sat in his padded leather desk chair, and stared at the walls with their plaques, mementos, and framed, autographed photos of a successful entrepreneur who worked in the shadow of a famous financial genius. One photo showed him accepting an award for charitable work by a Baltimore businessman; in the background of that photo, Devlin recognized Julia's boss, J.B. Zuckerman, and mayoral assistant Greg Sonfeld, as well as several prominent politicians and churchmen.

How long did you plan this? wondered Devlin as he watched the man behind the mirror turn another page. *How many moves, how many secret strands of a web no one else knew was there?*

According to the FBI's auditor, seven to twelve million dollars had vanished in a kite scheme run through the Blake Fund. Investors' money was used as collateral for loans from banks, which in turn was used for more collateral for even greater loans—a process repeated many times. The auditor found bank officers who'd approved loans to the Blake Fund later getting personal loans from the fund. Minor investments along the way provided a skeleton of legitimacy. These investments—a shopping mall construction program, a resort development package—were a long way from becoming profitable ventures. A handful of investors had recently pulled out, taking their profits from the remaining capital of the Blake Fund. Other investors—banks and individuals—waited in often willful ignorance for the fund to pay off.

"It's all one big happy family," the auditor told Devlin. "The banks, the investors, the Blake Fund. Businessmen cutting sharp deals among themselves—usually with other people's money—pension funds, old ladies' life savings. Everybody profits—on paper. Some of the bankers got dazzled by flashy presentations and Blake's reputation. Some made sure that they profited on the side. All of them ignored common sense or bent good rules. When the illusion collapses, what will happen will be a travesty."

All the pieces hadn't been fit together on that day. The auditor told Devlin that from the way the books were constructed, and from the assistance Ross Martin had been giving them, Jackson Blake looked guilty of hundreds of counts of fraud. In the last few days, indications began to appear that Thel Chang was not merely an innocent employee.

"About a week ago, Ross Martin seemed to start dragging his feet," the auditor told Devlin as they watched him from behind the mirror. "Until now, he's been concerned and shocked, helpful. Angry at Blake. Now he gets amnesia, hesitates."

"He is stalling," said Devlin. "He wasn't supposed to need to, but there were some glitches."

"What's he waiting for?" asked the auditor, who knew nothing of the last visit his colleagues made to Thel Chang.

"One more murder." Devlin shook his head. "Or maybe two."

"I don't understand," said the auditor.

Perry and Harris entered the observation room.

"Lieutenant," said Perry, "we talked to the building superintendent. The Chang woman's story is possible."

"Do you want us to get a warrant, go after Blake's body?" asked Harris.

"Blake's body?!" said the auditor.

"No," said Rourke, "not unless we must. Rooting around in the foundation of a building requires a ton of permissions."

"Something else," said Perry.

"What?" said Rourke.

"A woman pretending to be a company inspector for a rental car company bluffed her way past some clerks, messed around a downtown office and the airport booth, checked out a car. The woman fit Rachel's description. The clerks made a positive I.D. off the sketch."

"When did she get the car?" asked Devlin.

"Yesterday," said Perry.

"All she took was a car?" he asked.

"They don't know for sure. She went into their computer."

The three detectives stared at each other.

"To build her credibility?" asked Rourke. "Cover her tracks? Or was she looking for something?"

"What do you think?" said Susan.

"Put out a bulletin on the car," he ordered.

"Already done," answered Susan.

"But surveillance only: Don't stop that car unless there's trouble. I don't want to spook her. Find her, radio me."

"Will someone—" began the auditor.

Devlin cut him off:

"Tell me about Ross Martin," the cop asked him. "You've been auditing this mess with him for weeks. What's he like?"

The auditor walked to the glass wall that separated him from the man in the other room. The equation fell into place.

"Suddenly I see a spider," said the auditor. "All through this he's been cool as can be—oh, he gives a great show, all concern, surprised, helpful. . . . Everything an innocent man should be, he seems. But when you realize . . . When you look again . . . He's a spider. Never liked him. Now . . .

"He's ruined thousands of people," said the auditor. "Do you realize that? When the Blake Fund crashes, a dozen banks, savings and loans . . . Can you lock him up?"

"Right now I'm not worried about him," said Rourke.

"But he's at the center!" said the auditor. "I heard what you said. If Blake is dead, then Martin must be at the center!"

"I'm worried about who Martin has turned loose," said Rourke.

He stared at the glass wall.

No time left. No other way.

He felt nauseous from his own bile.

If I'm wrong and I blow it, then all the blood is my blame. The blood that's been spilled, the blood that's yet to flow. If I'm right and pull it off, that monster behind the mirror ends up eating a part of me.

But not everything.

He asked the auditor to leave, waited until he was gone.

"Susan," said Rourke, "stand outside this room. No one gets inside the observation room, no matter what. Harris, you come with me, guard the door to the interrogation room the same way."

"What are you going to do?" asked Harris. He wasn't sure he wanted to know.

Susan's eyes burned bright; she had no questions.

"Never mind," said Rourke. "But remember: the man behind that mirror has blood dripping from his fingers. Half a dozen murders. If he comes out of either door without me, he's an escaping felon. He'll have to take my gun away from me to get out of there. That means he's armed, dangerous, and desperate. Don't hesitate."

"What do you mean, 'Don't hesitate?'" said Harris.

"He means—" said Susan, but Rourke interrupted her.

"Do what you must," said Rourke, "but don't let him get away."

"Is that what you're going to do?" asked Harris.

"Come on!" said Susan. "Let's go!"

"Just do what's right," Rourke told the young detective.

Ross Martin looked up from the ledger book as the door to this mirrored room opened.

The man who entered had black hair with hints of silver, worry lines on his face, awful pallor. His hands were thrust deep in his pants pockets. He used his heel to shut the door.

"If you're looking for the auditor," said Martin, "he stepped away for a moment."

Rourke shook his head. He walked past the seated man to

the mirror. The reflecting glass showed his haggard image, and over his shoulder, Ross Martin, sitting at a table piled high with ledgers.

"Can I help you?" said Martin.

"I'm a cop."

"Oh."

"I'm a good cop," Rourke told the mirror.

"I've been impressed by the caliber of the police officers I've met during all this," said Martin.

"Yes," said Rourke, "I bet you have."

Martin stared at Rourke impatiently.

"I've been looking for you," Rourke said, a chill entering his voice. "Now that I've found you, I don't much care."

In the mirror, Rourke watched Martin coil inside himself.

"We've got Thel," said Rourke, still talking to the mirror.

Martin's lips twitched. Rourke saw him start to say something, think better of it.

"But I don't want to talk to you about that," said Rourke.

"About what?" said Martin. "Thel? What do you mean, you've 'got' her? I don't understand."

Rourke turned, stared at Martin.

"You're a bold son of a bitch, aren't you?" said Rourke. "And smart. God, you're smart!"

"Can't you make up your mind whether to insult me or compliment me?"

"Maybe you can get a shrink to say you're crazy," said Rourke. "Maybe a court will buy that, but I don't. You're too successful to be crazy. You're a man who believes that what he wants is what he should get.

"Thel told us everything."

"Everything?" asked Martin. "I don't understand."

"You won't cop to a bluff, right? Hit you with a pile of evidence no jury would overlook and you'll still play the cool and clean role. Outraged, maybe. Shocked."

"Detective . . . Detective Whoever You Are, if—"

"I'm your doom, asshole!"

"I don't need to stay and be insulted by a rambling madman," said Martin. He started to rise.

"*Sit down!*" screamed Rourke, lunging forward. "If you walk out that door, a cop will blow your ass away!"

Martin hesitated, his hips poised an inch above the chair.

"You know what that's like?!" hissed Rourke. "Walk out a

door expecting to go somewhere and somebody blows you away?"

Martin lowered himself down to the chair.

"Look," said Martin, "I really don't know what you're talking about!"

"We know it all," said Rourke.

Martin licked his lips.

"So does Thel," said Rourke. "She knows she was supposed to die. Why you gave her a list of errands last Saturday, complete with a timetable. Nice setup. She's upstairs now, with her lawyer, telling a stenographer how you two buried Blake in concrete but kept him alive on paper, shuffled around his credit cards and signatures on loans, airline vouchers, motels. Made him into your scapegoat.

"But I don't want to talk to you about that," said Rourke, shaking his head.

"Detective, if you're arresting me, you've already gone too far without advising me of my rights and letting me have my attorney here. You—"

"You're great at this, aren't you?" asked Rourke, taking his hand out of his pants pocket and sweeping it over the ledgers piled on the table. "You're great at all this paper, all the rules and the dodges and the procedures. You're a whizz. But we'll nail you anyway."

Rourke ran his hand along the back of his neck.

"We've got capital punishment in Maryland," said the cop. "For certain murders of the first degree—for the actual triggerman, not his accomplices. But on a paid hit, both the triggerman and the contractor are on the execution line.

"It's been a long time since Maryland executed anybody, but there's still that room 'cross town with a chair and a bucket underneath it where cyanide pellets hit the acid.

"I can't make up my mind about capital punishment," said Rourke. "What do you think of it?"

For over a minute, Martin wouldn't reply. Finally, he licked his lips, said, "I've never given the topic any thought."

"Really?" said Rourke. He shook his head, paced the room as he continued.

"On the one hand, it makes society no better than the murderer we kill. We say no one has the right to take a human life. We make some confusing exceptions for that like war, when we can slaughter millions and send millions more off to do it and die. Capital punishment has never been proven or disproven as a deterrent to crime."

Martin didn't speak.

"The worst thing about executions is that once society throws the switch, there's no saying *sorry* if we've made a mistake, and God knows society makes millions of mistakes.

"On the other hand," said Rourke, facing Martin, "capital punishment works—not as revenge, which solves nothing, though it makes some people feel better. Capital punishment is more a case of singular prevention rather than a universal cure. It prevents one killer from ever harming anybody again—a prison guard, another prisoner, a contract hit he buys from inside the joint, somebody when he escapes, whoever: the dead can't kill."

Rourke shook his head. Stared straight at the man sitting in front of him. Martin's brow was damp with sweat.

"Can't make up my mind," said Rourke. "But I know one thing: if you believe in capital punishment, you have to be willing to throw the switch yourself."

"What do you want?!" hissed Martin.

"I don't want to talk to you about what you've done," said Rourke. "I don't want to talk about murdering Blake, hiring out the botched hit on Thel, the people that died because of that."

"I refuse to talk to you!" said Martin. "I've done nothing wrong. You're keeping me prisoner, you're not giving me any of my rights. I won't say a word about anything until I see my lawyer and then you'll be sorry: you don't ever want to play games with me!"

"Yeah," said Rourke, "I figured that."

He drew his snubnosed .38, held it casually, the barrel pointing to the floor.

"Like I said," continued Rourke, "I don't want to talk to you about what you've done, I—"

"What's that?!" interrupted Martin.

"It's a gun," said Rourke. "Just a gun. You're not afraid of a gun, are you?"

Martin licked his lips.

Rourke raised the gun between them, its muzzle pointed toward the ceiling.

"This is the way it is," he snarled.

"You're smart and you're bold, you're a gambler. But you stack the deck in your favor."

"You can't get away with intimidation!" said Martin. "Or brutality! You'll blow your case!"

"What case? I told you: I don't want to talk to you about anything you've done."

"People will know—"

"What people?"

Martin's eyes flicked toward the mirror.

"You think there's somebody back there?!" shouted Rourke.

He snatched a metal folding chair with one hand and threw it through the mirror. The mirror exploded. Through a jagged, gaping hole surrounded by chunks of dangling glass, Martin saw the observation room was empty.

"There's nobody there!" screamed Rourke. "No way out! These are soundproof rooms. No microphones hooked up! It's just you and me."

"In court . . ." stammered Martin. "In court you'll have to perjure yourself, you'll—"

"My word against yours, and I'll be telling the truth. I'm not asking about any murders you've done."

"I won't tell you anything!"

"You think you got the odds," said Rourke. "You think you can cut your losses and beat the system. Maybe you can. But we're not in the system anymore. No plea bargaining. No technicalities. You're in a room the size of Maryland's execution chamber. With me."

Rourke pointed the gun at the floor by his left foot, pushed a button on the side of the pistol. The revolver's cylinder swung open toward Rourke. He filled his hand. The cop held something with his thumb and forefinger, then flicked his hand toward where Martin sat trembling.

Cartridges landed on the open ledger book; light glistened off rolling brass cases.

"Look!" commanded Rourke.

Martin stared at him as he held a bullet up.

"There's five cartridges on the table!" said Rourke.

Snap went the gun's cylinder. Rourke held the pistol in the air.

"And one in here."

The cop thumbed back the revolver's hammer; spun the closed cylinder with his free hand.

"You know how it is," said Rourke. "You play the odds.

"You never figured on getting caught. You have been. Other cops will play the system with you. They'll start from scratch, and you might even beat them. That's between all of you."

"You and me," said Rourke, gesturing with his gun, "you and me are in a whole other game.

"I only care about one thing: You've got a hired gun out there. He won't get Thel, but he might get somebody else.

"This isn't business. Business would be enough for some guys, but not for me. This is personal. This game you started cost me a chunk of my guts and heart. I've got a friend out there your killer wants to murder. It's all on the line. I want him. I want him and we're running out of time."

"I . . . I won't talk."

"You're through deciding when it's your turn to play."

Rourke moved next to the table, gripped the pistol in both hands and aimed it at Martin's chest.

"This is . . . this is crazy! I don't—"

"You have a choice," said Rourke. "You saw me make the odds. Five to one. Every time you don't give me what I want, the odds change. Who knows? Maybe you've only got one chance.

"There's no other way I'll get what I need in time to save my friend. We've got you either way. You don't matter to me. If you don't help me right now, then you're worthless. And you've already pulled the trigger on one of my friends.

"Don't think I can't kill you: a murderer who went nuts during a preliminary investigation, tried to kill me, even broke the two-way mirror trying to escape."

Rourke thumbed back the hammer on the revolver.

"You're one creep I believe in capital punishment for!" said the cop. "And I'm willing to throw the switch. We're playing for your stay of execution.

"Who's you're gun? How do I find him?"

"You're just—"

Snap!

The hammer hitting on an empty chamber startled Martin. He jerked back in his chair, his eyes wide.

"You pulled the trigger!"

"Convince me to stop."

"Look, I don't . . . We can work a deal—"

"Negotiations are closed."

"I don't . . . ! I won't work it like that! I won't tell you any—"

Snap!

"Three to one, gambler," said Rourke. "How does it feel?"

"You're crazy!"

"I believe in doing the best I can, in right and wrong, and good and evil, justice. I have no time to figure another way. You've been too clever. The only way I can win is if you help me. It's all out of my hands now."

"You've got the gun!"

"And I'm pulling the trigger!"

"You can't! Don't! This is—"

Snap!

Martin screamed, fell to the floor, spun in circles like a child suffering a fit. His hands covered his ears. When his circles stopped, he lay still, his eyes pressed shut as he sobbed, moaned.

Slowly, carefully, Martin moved his hands from his face. He opened his eyes; looked up.

Saw the policeman standing above him, saw the gun's black bore staring back . . .

"All right! Okay! I'll tell you! Only . . ."

The policeman cocked the revolver.

"I don't know who he is or where he is or anything! I put a coded ad in the *New York Times* classifieds. He wrote me in care of a postal box with the number of a Baltimore pay phone. I went there. He called, bounced me all over town from pay phone to pay phone. Finally we negotiated who, when, all that stuff, and I left him a picture in the booth and Jesus God don't shoot!"

Rourke didn't lower the gun.

"What does he look like?" said Rourke.

"I never saw him. Just a voice on the phone, honest!"

"How did you pay him?"

"Electronic funds transfer to a numbered account in the Bahamas! I don't even know his name! Please, won't you put down the gun?!"

"Where is he now?"

"I don't know! I swear to God, I don't know! After the

garage fiasco, he called twice. I kept telling him I was running out of time, but—"

"How do you stop him?"

"You can't. He's . . . obsessed."

"How can I get to him!!?" said the cop.

"I don't know," sobbed Martin. "I don't know."

The man on the floor shook his head, looked up at Rourke.

"That damn garage!" he said. "That damn basement garage! He should never have tried it there. It's so dark."

"Yeah," said Rourke. He lowered his gun-heavy left hand.

On the way out, he scooped his five cartridges off the table.

Harris relaxed when he saw it was Rourke leaving the room. The lieutenant looked over at a uniformed officer standing nearby, jerked his right thumb over his shoulder.

"We had an accident," said the police lieutenant. "The mirror broke. Escort the gentleman upstairs. Detective McKee wants to talk to him. Advise him of his rights."

"Yes sir!"

Perry joined them. Over Rourke's shoulder, she and Harris saw Ross Martin getting up as the uniformed officer waited.

"Is he hurt!?" said Harris.

"I never touched him," said Rourke.

He turned around, watched Martin being read his rights. When the uniformed officer was finished, Martin focused on Rourke.

"Thank you for your help, Mr. Martin," said Rourke.

Martin didn't reply. The uniformed cop led him down the corridor. Rourke called out to their backs.

"When you're through upstairs with this financial business, my homicide colleagues will want to talk to you. Be sure to bring your lawyer."

Martin didn't look back.

"What went on in there?" asked Harris.

"Nothing I'm proud of," said Rourke. He pulled his gun from his waistband. His colleagues exchanged a puzzled look. "Any word on that rental car?"

"No," said Perry.

She and Harris watched while Rourke flipped open his revolver's cylinder. They stared at the six black holes.

"You went in there with an unloaded gun?" said Harris.

Rourke took five shells from his jacket pocket, one by one dropped them in the cylinder's empty black holes. Then Rourke let his right hand hang below elbow level. He shook his arm. A cartridge fell to the floor. He picked it up, slid it in the revolver's black hole.

"No," he told Harris, "my weapon worked."

69

Elebank. Eyeshaw. Walters.

These are the streets of Baltimore.

Corchran. Woodbourne. Silverthorne.

The Alameda.

Argonne. Crestlyn. Oakridge.

Where are we going? wondered Rachel.

One car separated her vehicle from the killer's as they motored through peaceful residential streets. Since he'd driven off the motel parking lot, she'd followed him as closely as she dared. They spent about 15 minutes on the Beltway, left that interstate for roads cutting toward the center of town. He'd led her through the northern neighborhoods, past St. Mary's Seminary School of Theology, the Cathedral of Mary Our Queen, the Boumi Temple.

Nearer My God to Thee, she thought.

Past the College of Notre Dame of Maryland, past Johns Hopkins University and Loyola College, where students of the 1980s looked back on Rachel's 1960s college days as quaint American history.

What do they know? she thought grimly.

What do you know?

The sky above the budding trees had turned gray with clouds. Rachel fumbled with her car's unfamiliar heat controls. Warm air tumbled over her feet. When she looked up, the car between her and the killer's had vanished; her quarry's car flashed a right turn signal.

Chilton Street.

The purse slid against her thigh as she went around the corner. This was a wide boulevard, with a high school off to the left, and a huge brick and stone open arena on her right.

Memorial Stadium, she read from a green sign pointing toward a stone horseshoe-shaped stadium. *Home of the Baltimore Orioles.*

The killer's car turned onto Ellerslie Avenue, then quickly turned right again through a gate in the chain link fence surrounding the parking lot. The gate's sign read: "Babe Ruth Plaza."

Rachel deliberately got stuck at a red light at the Ellerslie intersection to avoid being spotted. She watched his car disappear over an asphalt hump in the parking lot.

Baseball? she thought as she turned onto the parking lot. *This is all about baseball?!*

By the time she topped the asphalt hump the killer's car was parked a hundred yards away, not far from one of the stadium's arching entrances. Half a dozen other cars sat in the parking lot. A huge blue-lettered, white butcher paper banner stretched across the windowed ticket offices set in the stadium wall to her left: "Good Luck Birds as You Fly South for Spring Training!!"

Doesn't seem much like spring, she thought as she parked her car a hundred feet from the killer's empty vehicle.

Where is he?

His bald head didn't pop up from the front seat.

He didn't see me following him! she assured herself. *He wouldn't have expected that and he didn't see me!*

Want it bad, will it so.

Slowly, she opened her car door. She stepped onto the pavement. Her eyes never left the killer's car as she reached back inside her vehicle, took the Duck's gun from her purse, and shoved it in her jeans. She zipped her leather jacket only enough to hide the gun from a casual observer.

Where are you?!

Rachel closed her hand around the butt of the gun.

Aware of each step, she walked to the killer's car.

Closer.

Closer.

She heard the distant *whump whump whump* of a helicopter, but didn't take her eyes off the car windows. Her heart slammed against her ribs. The cold wind blew through her open jacket, pushed against her shirt.

The car windows reflected the stadium, her approaching image, the distant trees.

Ten steps away.

Five.

She stared through the glass at the empty seats, the floor where no one hid. Exhaled deeply, and leaned against the metal.

Where are you?! What are you doing?!

The stadium.

She walked along the curved stone wall. Glanced up. High above, like the lip of a bowl, the stadium rim met the gray sky. The fingertips of her left hand glided over weathered brick, while her right hand stayed wrapped around the gun butt. She slowly followed the curve toward double doors set inside an archway.

One door was a few inches open.

A hole was punched through the door's glass front just above the inside push handle.

Vandals, she thought. *Kids*.

Sure.

The fingers of her left hand crept round the brick edge, gripped the corner.

Quickly, she ducked her head around the corner—too fast to see anything before she darted back.

Nothing happened.

Slowly, carefully, she peered round the edge.

Through the glass doors she saw a long, dark tunnel sloping up until it ended in a shimmer of gray sky.

This is insanity.

For the first time since the Aquarium she felt the strength of the world. The brick pressed against her back. The crisp air made her skin tingle. She smelled damp spring, saw a helicopter flying across the cloudy gray sky.

What are you doing here? She shook her head. Felt reason reenter her mind like a lightning bolt.

And felt fear.

Don't go down that tunnel!

Whatever he was doing, he'd come here, to that tunnel.

Don't go down it!

There'd be a pay phone nearby. Call Devlin. Call anybody!

But two hundred feet of open parking lot separated her from her car. If he were in the tunnel, if he walked down it while she was crossing that shelterless lot . . .

She had to look. She had to be sure. Enough time had elapsed so that he'd be far from the door. Once inside, she might find a phone, a security guard.

She turned the corner again.

Saw nothing but the black tunnel.

Can't see off to either side. Must have branches.

She stood in front of the doors, waiting for the bullet to come crashing through the glass.

Nothing happened.

She opened the glass door.

Nothing happened.

What's in there?

No one answered her silent thought.

Just a few steps. Enough to see. To be sure. To be safe.

She stepped out of the shaft of sunlight, her hand gripped tight around the gun butt. The cement floor was hard.

Like the garage.

The floor sloped up. She could make out an intersection of a corridor ahead, one that no doubt circled around the stadium. The darkness was eerie, silent.

Two more steps, darkness surrounded her.

Squinting, she tried to make out the details of the corridor.

Pain erupted in her right kidney and she gasped, her ability to scream blown away by his fist.

Her knees wobbled as he grabbed her leather jacket's collar. She stumbled two steps, his grip never slacking. He slammed her face first into a brick wall. Whirled her around.

Something hard and cold shoved into her gasping mouth —her lips reflexively closed tight around it to protect her teeth. The taste was tangy, metal, and her tongue found the round hole before he twisted it up and pressed it sharp against the roof of her mouth. The back of her head knocked against the brick.

His face was a giant moon looming inches from hers; the outline of his bald head showed jutting ears and twin fires for eyes. His breath was rancid. As he hissed, spittle flecked her cheeks.

"You've got one chance to live!" lied the killer.

His gloved right hand groped over her body. Her bladder let go, the warm urine rapidly cooling as it soaked through her jeans. She felt him jerk the Duck's gun from her pants, drop it in the pocket of his army coat.

"Rachel Dylan!" He hissed like a hoarse demon. "Rachel Dylan!"

He grabbed her throat with his free hand. She wanted to choke, to vomit. All the terrors of the universe roared through her.

"We're going to talk," he hissed. "Just you and me. If you give me trouble, you'll die."

He jerked the gun from her mouth. She barely had time to open wide and save her teeth. He threw her to the cold cement floor. Kicked her in the stomach so she doubled up on all fours like a dog.

The killer kicked her in the butt, kicked her forward until she crawled toward the light at the end of the tunnel.

Devlin was driving home, headed north on Calvert Street.

Nowhere else to go, he thought. *Nothing else to do.*

Harris was there. Waiting by the phone. Perry was seeing her mother. Rourke would relieve Harris, give him an hour, maybe two.

And I'll wait for the phone to ring.

On the seat beside him, his police radio squawked.

"Foxtrot calling Command."

Foxtrot: the police observation helicopter.

"This is Command, Foxtrot."

"On that wanted rental vehicle, we have a possible sighting, car deserted."

Devlin grabbed the radio before Command could reply.

"This is Lieutenant Rourke! Foxtrot, where's your sighting?!"

"Memorial Stadium parking lot, lieutenant."

Great place to ditch a car, thought Rourke. He radioed: "Anyone in the vicinity?"

"Negative, lieutenant. A few cars in the lot, but we see no one."

"Lieutenant, this is Command. Do you want units dispatched?"

"Negative. I'm only a few blocks from there. I'll check it. Keep the area clear. We don't want to spook anybody."

Rourke took two minutes to reach the stadium parking lot. He drove slowly over the asphalt. Saw no one. He parked 10 feet from the suspicious vehicle. Radio in hand, he walked to the driver's door.

Right make, model, and color, but not the license plate of the rental car.

He looked in the front seat: a woman's purse.

Never saw Rachel with a purse.

He radioed headquarters for a check on the car's license plate. While he waited, his eyes roamed over the huge stadium, the few other cars in the lot.

Why are all the other cars parked over by the front office and these two parked over here? he thought, looking at a second car parked about a hundred feet away.

Headquarters radioed that the information on the license plate didn't match the car.

Probable cause, thought Rourke. Gingerly, trying not to smudge any prints, he opened the car door. The purse was empty. In the jockey box, he found a rental car agreement made out as a company disbursement to Christy Macy—right car.

His pulse quickened.

Go easy. Go slow. No mistakes. No more mistakes.

With one radio call, he could flood the area with troops. But he might spook her away. Any trail she'd left might be lost under the squeal of anxious police cars' rubber. Maybe she'd just dumped the car here. Maybe it wasn't even Rachel who'd scammed the car. Until he eliminated a few maybes, he didn't want to disrupt the police net he'd spread over the city.

The car parked a hundred feet away bothered him. He walked to it. Nothing inside seemed suspicious.

Why would anyone park here?

He looked toward the stadium. An arched doorway in the curved wall not far from this car seemed the only logical reason for the car being parked here.

He walked to the doors.

Found a hole punched in the glass, the door unlocked. Switched the radio from his right to his left hand.

Saw nothing inside but the long black tunnel.

The tunnel pulled at him like a magnet. He knew he should radio for assistance, yet something even stronger told him he'd walked too far over the line; this was personal, not business.

That's crazy! he told himself.

That's the way it is, his self replied.

He stepped inside the tunnel.

No choice now but to go through it to the end.

The stadium smelled of dust, of cleaning fluids and sawdust sweeping compound, of dried beer and popcorn. His heart raced along a razor's edge, propelled by an irresistible dread yet certain that this was the ultimate and proper moment. He walked softly up the slope, his shoes making no sound as his ears took in the void of the empty corridors and his eyes strained to see the walls amid the blackness.

The tunnel opened in the bleachers high above the Orioles dugout, between home and third base. As he walked into the light, he saw first the empty blue bleacher seats across the field, then the outfield, the brown grass of last summer.

Rourke stepped out of the tunnel.

And found them.

Ten yards away. The killer had forced Rachel into the sunshine where he could see to work. He'd handcuffed her hands over her head and around the top bar of the black iron railing leading down the stairs toward the field. The handkerchief from her back pocket gagged her mouth. She knelt on the concrete steps. The killer's back was to Devlin as he bent over Rachel: beating her—barely controlling the burning rage in him that wanted to rip her to shreds *now* without any thought to the answers he needed. Rachel tried to keep her head tucked between her upraised arms. The killer punched her, slow methodical blows that echoed through the deserted horseshoe arena.

Rourke drew his .38 and raced down the stairs. He couldn't shoot from where he was: Rachel was behind his target. If Rourke missed, if the bullet went through the killer . . . He'd get as close as he could, then kill the son of a bitch. If he could, he'd jam the gun barrel against that goddamned bald *head,* pull the trigger until he ran out of bullets.

The killer heard *something,* whirled and saw *cop* charging down the steps, gun hand forward. The killer had holstered his weapon to beat Rachel, so he swept his foot in an arching roundhouse kick that knocked the gun from the cop's hand. Rourke's .38 clattered off, lost in seats four rows away.

Rourke high-tackled the killer, knocking the man backward so that they crashed on top of Rachel, flipping over her, falling in a twisting, fighting heap to the concrete steps.

Searing blackness engulfed Rachel when the two men crashed on top of her. She groaned through the gag, tasted the salt of her own blood from her cut lips and tongue. She twisted as much as her hands cuffed over the railing above her head allowed.

Saw Rourke. And the killer. Punching, biting, clawing at each other as they rolled back and forth, sliding ever lower down the concrete steps.

Whenever one would lose his grip, the other would gain a hold. They traded blows—Rourke had a bruise swelling beneath his left eye. The killer's nose bled, and his shaved head was scraped raw from sliding on the concrete steps.

Rachel shook her head. There, on the steps below her: Rourke's police radio.

She lunged for it—was jerked short by the handcuffs.

The killer kneed Rourke—missed his groin, but got his stomach. The cop hung on.

Rachel looked everywhere for help. Found none. She stared at the railing above her head: a single black steel bar with its ends sharply angled and bent down, sunk into the floor. If only . . .

Rourke tried to push his thumbs through the bald man's eyes, but the killer was quick enough to sweep his arm like a windmill between them, knocking Rourke's hands away and causing the cop to fall on him again. The two men slid further down the steps.

Rachel crawled and bounced down three concrete steps, her handcuffed wrists sliding along the steel railing. She reached the step where the radio lay.

The killer smashed his elbow into Rourke's neck. Rourke jerked backward as an electric jolt of pain shot through his body. His feet missed purchase on a concrete step, his knee banged into another. He didn't lose his grip on the killer's coat. When the bald man cocked his arm for another blow, Rourke jerked the man off the stairs, the one direction the killer hadn't braced against. The killer's blow went wild. The two men tumbled to the landing at the top of the last section of seats.

Rachel used her feet.

Tried once.

Twice.

Again.

Fourth time, she gripped the radio between her shoes.

As quickly as she could, she hopped on her hips, her handcuffed hands gripping the steel rail and lifting her body off the concrete, setting her down so she could slide her grip up the rail for the next move. Then again—desperately careful on each hop not to lose her foot grip on the radio. Five steps above her, the steel railing bent to the floor. She could slide her hands down with it, pick up the radio, take off her gag . . .

The two men were on their feet. The killer swung an uppercut, palm heel blow toward Rourke's chin which would have broken the cop's neck—except Rourke stumbled backward. The killer was off balance, too. Rourke caught the bald man's arm with one hand and hit him above the heart with his other. The killer's vision burned; he fell toward the cop.

Two more steps, thought Rachel. Sweat mixed with the blood from a gash above her eyebrow trickled into her eyes, but she blinked it clear as she scooted on her butt. *Two more steps.*

The two men crashed onto the roof of the Orioles dugout; the orange and white team lettering needed repainting.

One more step.

The killer was on his back, Rourke straddling him crossways. The bald man kicked his right leg through the air. The force and leverage of his motion spun him around, over and free of the cop.

Rachel slid the handcuffs over the bend in the railing, collapsed to the concrete.

Rourke grabbed the killer's ankle as that man tried to stand, jerked it, and again the bald man crashed to the roof of the dugout. Rourke held on to the ankle—and he felt a gun strapped just above the man's foot. He tried to push the man's pants over the holstered gun.

The radio was four feet from Rachel. She stretched, hook kicked it with one foot—but it skidded in an arc away from her.

The bald man jerked his leg the cop held and kicked at the cop's hands with his free foot.

Rachel's foot covered the radio. She pulled it across the concrete, rolled away, reached toward it—but the vertical pole kept her fingers inches from its black plastic. She could hear routine reports squawk over the airwaves. She saw Rourke jerk a small gun free of the bald man's ankle holster—and saw the bald man kick Rourke: in the head, then in the hand. The pistol skidded across the orange and black Oriole logo, fell into the dugout.

Rachel rolled her body on top of the radio. She curled into a ball, pulling the radio toward the railing with her. When she rolled away, the radio was within reach. She twisted her face to her hands, pulled the handkerchief from her mouth.

On top of the dugout, the killer had regained his feet. Rourke hugged the man's thighs.

Rachel's grabbed the police radio with her manacled hands, turned it over, her fingers frantically seeking the buttons the Duck had taught her so few days before.

Rourke used his grip on the killer's thighs to pull himself up. The bald man kneed Rourke in the chest. The Baltimore policeman staggered to his feet, stumbled backward. The killer smiled. Blood ran from scrapes on his bald head, from his nose. He yelled wordlessly as his hand darted under his army jacket to where the Browning waited in his shoulder holster. Rourke dove off the roof, scrambled into the dugout—frantically seeking shelter, remembering after he hit the rubber-matted concrete that down here somewhere was a gun.

Rachel pushed the button on the side of the radio. Immediately, the sounds of static and other radio calls ceased.

"*Signal 13!*" She yelled into the radio as loudly as she could. "Signal 13! The man who shot the Duck is shooting Rourke in the baseball park. Signal 13! Inside the baseball stadium!"

Baltimore's citizens work hard, believe hard. They have many faiths and one religion: baseball. Their denomination is Orioles. Baltimore Orioles. Baltimorians expect the grassy fields of heaven to be chalked into diamonds for games where the ninth inning never comes. Baltimore's cathedral is Memorial Stadium. Its pews seat 54,062 worshippers. At the start of every service, Caesar is given his due by the singing of his anthem—usually solo by an unseen voice over a loudspeaker. The jam-packed crowd stands.

A splendiforous moment comes near the end of the song when the balladeer sings:

> *And the rockets' red glare,*
> *the bombs bursting in air,*
> *gave proof through the night,*
> *that our flag was still there.*

At the next syllable, thousands of the faithful roar their prayer to the heavens, a resounding, irresistible, overwhelming . . .

"O!!!!!"

For Orioles. For themselves. For sheer love of life.

That shout shakes the stadium, its echo rocks the city. The like of it had never been heard in Baltimore.

Until that day.

Rachel's Signal 13 sounded on every police radio.

Captain Ted Goldstein heard it as he sat talking to the deputy chief in headquarters, a radio on the desk between them.

Gary Harris heard it from the radio next to the telephone on Rourke's desk as he played solitaire, Sam curled at his feet.

Susan Perry heard it as she cruised down Greenmount Street with her mother in the task force's confiscated TransAm.

Hundreds of other policemen heard it—on foot, on scooters, in cars. An extra 47 cars were on patrol that day, filled with volunteer officers looking for a cop killer.

They all heard Signal 13.

And they hit their sirens. From the freeways to Druid Hill Park, from Cedonia Avenue on the east to Powder Mill Lane on the west, from Lake Avenue on the north to the Inner Harbor, Baltimore exploded with screaming police sirens. Clerks and customers broke off arguing. Pedestrians downtown ducked, sought cover for what must be nuclear war. Schoolteachers halted in midsentence, and their pupils wailed with fear.

We're coming! said the sirens. *We're coming!*

Foxtrot heard the Signal 13 in the air four miles west of

the stadium. The pilot banked in a 180° turn—heard the sirens below him drown out the *whump whump whump* of the helicopter's blades.

Captain Goldstein grabbed the radio off the deputy chief's desk, yelled into it, "Get him!" A needless command, for a split-second later he heard the sirens, too, heard them from cars racing away from headquarters in grim disobedience of the dispatcher's frantic efforts to send only the requisite number of backup units.

Harris grabbed his radio off Rourke's desk, ran out of the apartment without his suit coat. He didn't notice Sam ran right behind him. Harris ran as he had when he was a boy and St. Paul Avenue where Rourke lived was an easily acceptable hike away from the home of the fabulous Orioles. Harris was so excited he ran right past his car parked out front, a grim-faced man in tie and shirtsleeves, clutching a police radio, handcuffs, and a .38 bouncing on his belt and a dog running at his heels as he raced through the streets of Baltimore, a chorus of sirens urging them on.

Before Rachel finished her Signal 13, Susan Perry mashed her foot down on the cherry red TransAm's gas pedal and jerked the muscle car out of slowly moving, two-way down-town-bound traffic. The car shot over the center stripe toward the intersection. Inertia threw her mother back in her seat. Susan saw cars from all four streets screech to a stop. The TransAm sped into the intersection. She slammed her shoe on the foot brake, pulled up the emergency brake, and cranked the wheel. The TransAm skidded sideways into a tire-crying 180° bootlegger turn while pedestrians scrambled to safety. Susan released the hand brake, straightened the wheel, and stomped on the gas pedal, headed back toward Memorial Stadium as sirens all over the city wailed. Her mother grabbed the dashboard and screamed at the top of her lungs: *"Go! Go! Go!"*

And for the first time in history, Baltimore's Memorial Stadium rocked from a manmade roar that came from *outside* its walls.

Standing on the roof of the Oriole dugout, Browning 9mm in his hand, the killer heard those sirens echo off the empty horseshoe walls around him, and he knew that the gates of hell were open.

He fired two quick rounds into the wood beneath his feet.

The cop was down there, scrambling, no doubt looking for the
.25 automatic. A puny gun, but weapon enough at this range.

Keep him scrambling, ducking, busy! thought the killer.

He whirled, found Rachel in the stands, still cuffed to the
railing. He aimed at her. She twisted as much of her body as
she could behind a row of seats as he fired twice. Both bullets
shattered the blue plastic protecting her, but no lead cut
through her flesh.

The killer fired a fifth round through the dugout roof,
jumped to the infield, firing into the open dugout. That bullet
buried itself in the wooden bench where star first baseman
Eddie Murray usually sat, but the cop was nowhere to be
seen.

The killer shot into the dugout again. He trotted backward over dead grass toward centerfield, where two score-
boards and giant billboards (one for America's Coke, one for a
Japanese imported car) rose from a chain link fence at the
mouth of the arena's horseshoe. There'd be an exit there. He'd
have time to reach it—if he kept the cop pinned down until he
was out of range of the .25 automatic. Not far. The bald man
pulled the police revolver he'd taken from the woman out of
his pocket, fired two rounds from it into the dugout.

Stay down, you son of a bitch!

He still had a chance. A good chance. He could get to the
field fence, find an exit. Get to the parking lot. Get away! The
hell with witnesses! From the pitcher's mound, he fired two
more rounds into the Oriole dugout.

Matt Davis and his partner, J.J., were patroling half a mile
away when they heard Rachel's Signal 13. Newly assigned as a
violent crimes suppression unit, they patroled with a hungry
eye out for the woman and man who's likenesses they had
taped to the dashboard of their cruiser, right next to the
specially issued VCSU shotgun.

J.J. saw his partner suddenly pale into his white dress
shirt, then immediately flush red. Davis hit the siren and
lights a second behind Susan's crosstown reaction. The cruiser
with the two uniformed cops surged forward.

"Matt!" yelled his partner. "Easy! Easy!"

Matt pushed down on the gas pedal.

A dump truck rolled into the intersection ahead of them.

"Matt!" screamed J.J. He braced himself, closed his eyes
as Matt swerved toward the gutter. The cruiser jumped the

sidewalk. Matt didn't touch the brake. The cruiser knocked half a dozen garbage cans set outside a store into the air, shot off the sidewalk and around the end of the panicked teamster's truck, roared toward the stadium.

"Slower, for chrissake!" yelled J.J., looking over his shoulder in horror as the shopkeeper scrambled outside, shook his fist at their wake.

Matt fed his cruiser more gas.

In and out of traffic, dodging cars, trucks, vans; bouncing off a city bus; busting red lights and leaving squealing near-accidents behind them, they tore through Baltimore. They *passed* two other police cars also racing to respond to the cry for help.

"There's the stadium!" yelled J.J. "Park in front of the— What the hell are you doing!?!"

Matt cut ahead of another cruiser that was almost at the parking lot entrance. He never slackened his speed. The cruiser hit the asphalt wave; shot off the ground and flew ten feet before the tires bounced onto ground again. The bounce knocked the hats off the two cops. J.J. landed sideways on the seat, his eyes two fearful white dots against his ebony skin.

Their cruiser shot along the side of the stadium, past the corporate offices, past the main entrances. Matt had been coming to the stadium since he could walk. When he reached the end of this leg of the arena's horseshoe, he whipped the wheel to the left, sent the cruiser speeding *away* from the chain link fence surrounding the home of the Orioles.

"What are you doing?!" screamed J.J.

Across Babe Ruth Plaza, supposedly safe in Waverly Elementary School, Seth Galanter ran to stare out the windows of his fourth grade classroom while his teacher yelled for him to get back to his seat and for the other kids to quit screaming—the sirens meant everything was *all right*! Seth pushed up his thick glasses that kept slipping down his nose. He saw a police car racing straight toward his school from the parking lot across the street. Seth didn't move.

Matt cranked the steering wheel. The cruiser groaned, turned in a wide, careening curve and shot back toward the stadium.

Toward a closed, locked chain link fence.

"What are you doing?!" screamed J.J. and Seth at the same time.

The cruiser hit the chain link gate going 54 mph. The impact ripped the lock free and the gate flew open. The cruiser slowed to 49 mph. Matt stepped on the gas, pointed the now dented white car hood straight at a corrogated aluminum garage door set in the stadium's stone wall.

The door was down.

"*No!*" screamed J.J.

Both cops ducked beneath the dashboard.

The cruiser smashed into the aluminum door, knocked it off its hinge rollers and punched a jagged 10-foot hole through the metal. The edges of the hole smashed in the windshield, ripped off the antennae and mirrors, tore a section of the roof loose. The cruiser pushed the garage door through the vehicle tunnel beneath the left field bleachers. Sparks flew as the metal door screeched against stone. The cruiser ran over the ripped metal door. Three tires blew, but the car still shot forward. Matt never let go of the steering wheel. Shattered glass fell from his back as he sat up in time to steer the wobbling machine past the Oriole bullpen. The cruiser lumbered into left field, rolled fifty feet, and skidded to a stop.

The killer had reached second base, far enough to risk Rourke popping up from the dugout to shoot at him with the .25 automatic. The bald man had just turned his back on the dugout, started to run, when he heard an awful crash coming from left field. He didn't slow his pace. There was a terrible screeching, glass breaking, metal rending, and suddenly a battered police car rolled onto the outfield.

The cruiser's driver's door flew open. A blond man rolled out, his policeman's white shirt flecked with blood from a hundred tiny glass cuts. The killer saw the cop cradled something, saw the cop roll, whirl up to his knees, something pressed against his shoulder.

The killer fired two rounds from the Browning toward the cop.

Missed.

Matt Davis squeezed the shotgun's trigger. With a roar, buckshot slammed into the bald man's chest and blew him off his feet as sirens surrounded the stadium; *whump-whumping,* Foxtrot cleared the arena's rim, Rourke looked up from the dugout, and Rachel gazed out over the site of America's favorite sport.

70

Thirteen days after the Ward Building massacre—three days after the shootout at Memorial Stadium—the killer's body had been photographed, fingerprinted, and autopsied. He'd been backtracked to the motel where Rachel found him. He'd carried a badge taken from a San Francisco police detective murdered while investigating a vice ring. The killer's baggage contained an arsenal and four sets of false I.D.s. The lab found no telltale laundry marks in his clothing. Although 23 police departments expressed interest in the dead man, none of them could add to what Baltimore discovered. He became a suspect for homicides in half a dozen cities. Interpol and the FBI turned up nothing about the killer. No trace of his electronically shuffled fee was uncovered. The CIA reviewed all the information generated by Baltimore's police but wouldn't answer any of the cops' questions. In a nation where thousands of computers log trillions of bytes of data about every citizen, no machine knew anything about the hired gun who'd come to Baltimore.

He was nobody.

He was anybody.

He was dead.

He was buried in a pauper's unvarnished pine coffin. Chiseled in the concrete tombstone was his death date and "John Doe 109."

"Think we'll ever find out more about him?" the deputy commissioner had asked Rourke as that detective and Captain Goldstein sat in his office that Friday.

"Not unless Martin starts cooperating," said Rourke.

"How did you get Martin to tell you about the hitter in the first place?" asked the D.C.

"Persistence," said Rourke.

"And?" asked the D.C.

Goldstein shifted uncomfortably in his chair.

"And what?" asked Rourke.

"And how did that two-way mirror get broken?"

"Mirrors are fragile," said Rourke.

"Martin's lawyer complained about brutality," said the D.C.

"If he presses charges," said Rourke, "he'll have a hard time proving them. Who'd believe Martin over me?"

The D.C. stared at Lieutenant Rourke for a long time. Captain Goldstein stared out the window.

"Couldn't you have done this tidy?" complained the D.C. Rourke shrugged.

"The headlines are great," he said. "Nobody cares about questions buried somewhere at the bottom of the stories."

"There's always *somebody* who cares, Rourke," said his commander.

"The mayor's office has nothing to complain about."

The D.C.'s face turned gleeful: "That son of a bitch Sonfeld had to *personally* deliver the mayor's congratulatory letter! I loved it!"

"And, of course, we did solve a major crime wave," added Captain Goldstein.

"Oh, yeah," said the D.C., dismissing that analysis with a wave. He glowed again. "And we shoved it right up Sonfeld's ass!"

The D.C. drummed his fingers on his desk.

"What about Thel Chang?" asked Goldstein.

"The prosecutor cut a deal with her," said the D.C. "Her testimony about Blake's murder and the Kiting scam gets her 20 years."

Thel Chang spent five years in prison staring at the barred window of her fourth tier cell. She wore shapeless gray prison dresses. Kept her hair cropped short. One May afternoon, as her level left their cells for the exercise yard, she calmly climbed over the catwalk rail and stepped off the edge. She broke on the cellblock floor without a scream.

"By the way," said the D.C., "the prosecutor, the mayor's office, building inspectors . . . It's been decided not to tear up the garage for Blake's body. That might strengthen our case, but it will definitely weaken a downtown skyscraper."

"What?!" said Rourke.

"The Chang woman gave enough evidence for us to assert

it's there. *Corpus delicti* means basic element of the crime—but not necessarily the dead flesh.

"The big question is whether Martin gets gas. We'll nail him for the embezzlements. The prosecutor will press Blake's murder, too. The contract hits . . . Well, if we lose on Blake or decide to push his execution, we'll try those. The link is harder to prove."

The D.C. stared at Rourke. "You should have got him to confess on the record and within his rights."

"Can't have everything," said the cop. "We're just going to leave Blake's body in the garage floor?"

"Gives the citizens something to think about," said Goldstein, "every time they see that black glass tower."

Martin served 19 years for multiple counts of fraud and the murder of Jackson Blake. He was never prosecuted for the four other Ward Building murders. While in prison, he contracted cancer of the colon, was paroled after his diagnosis, died 14 months later in a charity ward of a Baltimore hospital.

The financial empire of cards Martin built collapsed the day after his arrest. First one bank, then two savings and loans, then half a dozen other financial institutions went into receivership. Two hundred forty-five investors lost their money. Thousands of Marylanders found their savings accounts frozen until the legislature, governor, and a consortium of New York banks bailed out the Maryland institutions. Dozens of people lost their jobs in businesses that went bankrupt under the collapsing cards. Construction on a shopping center ended; unfinished brick walls and foundations stood like monuments for two years. Eventually, the state condemned the land for highway expansion. None of the bankers who willfully or foolishly participated in the scam were ever prosecuted, though many lost their jobs. The state recovered $4 million of the approximately $9 million stolen. The total direct and indirect cost to the public topped $30 million.

Plus the murders.

"What about our guy who blasted the gunslinger?" asked the D.C.

"Matt Davis?" said Goldstein. "He's not doing so good. Got the shakes. Got ghosts."

One week later, Matt Davis resigned from the Baltimore

*police force on a ten percent medical disability. After a year of
psychotherapy (paid for by the department), he took a job at
his father's auto parts store. His girlfriend left him. When he
was 41, still handsome though his blond hair had turned gray,
Matt married a motherly 23-year-old woman who came to
work at the store. They never had children. Until he died, his
hands would sometimes shake.*

"By the way," said Goldstein. "I'm not retiring."

"What?!" said the D.C.

"My wife won't let me," he said. Smiled.

"But what about her heart?"

"There's lots about hearts doctors can't prescribe," answered the captain.

"I don't understand," said the D.C.

"Doesn't matter," said Goldstein. "I never filed the papers, the regs say I can stay. You're stuck with me."

"This is going to screw up a lot of flow charts."

Goldstein shrugged. *So what?*

"And I'd just as soon not leave homicide," said Rourke. He quickly added: "Sir."

"We've already got one lieutenant in homicide! What would you do there?"

Rourke shrugged. "Something will come up. I'd rather hang my hat there, keep my feet in the street, than park behind some desk."

"You saying desk work isn't good enough for you?" said the D.C., who spent his hours seated behind one.

"I'm saying I'm not good for desk work. Or for dealing with guys like Sonfeld. I act crazy when I work with them too long. That would turn out to be bad," said Rourke. He paused dramatically. "Bad for everyone. For the department.

"You wouldn't want that, would you, sir?" he asked.

The D.C. glared at him.

"You took rank, you accepted its responsibilities. I can assign them however I see fit."

"Yes sir," said the lieutenant. "I'm just trying for the best bargain for everyone."

"You're making me a problem, Rourke."

"A small one," said the lieutenant. "And I'm helping you avoid an even bigger one."

"So you say."

"Yes sir."

The D.C. drummed his fingers on his desk. Stared at Goldstein—who nodded back.

"All right," said the D.C. "We'll try it. For awhile."

"Thank you, sir."

"Just don't screw up, *lieutenant*. Now, what about your witness?"

"Rachel Dylan," said Goldstein.

"She's fine," Rourke told him. "A couple cracked ribs, minor concussion. She'll stick around for the grand jury, get her story on the record."

"And then?"

"Then . . . Then she's free."

"Where do you have her now?" asked the D.C.

"With me," said Rourke.

"I've got a couch," he added.

"That's your business," said the D.C. "Just don't let it smudge your badge."

"No sir."

"You look awful."

"My girlfriend's been taking care of me."

"Sounds like she's too beat up to be nurse," said the D.C.

"That's Rachel, the witness. My girlfriend's name is Julia."

The D.C. shook his head.

"You lead a complicated life, Rourke. One more thing.

"Sergeant McKinnon left a will. About a million dollars—don't speculate about where it came from. You know that dog he had?"

"Sam?" said Rourke.

"That's the one. The Duck left the money to him. Some kind of trust fund. After the dog dies, it goes to the police fund.

"And," said the D.C., "he left Sam to you, Rourke."

"What?!"

"You now own a millionaire dog."

"I don't want a dog!"

"You want to disappoint the Duck?"

Rourke didn't reply.

"I thought not," said the D.C. "Congratulations."

"Thanks," said Rourke.

The D.C. shook his head, said:

"Hell of a man, the Duck."

"Yes," said Rourke, "he was."

Rourke and Goldstein left the D.C.'s office together.

"I feel like I shed 30 years," said the captain as they rode the elevator to the garage.

"And I feel like I picked them up," said Rourke.

"Maybe you did," said his boss and friend.

"Ah, but I was so much older then, I'm younger than that now," sang Rourke.

"Does anybody understand you?" asked Goldstein as the elevator shuddered, stopped, and the doors slid open.

"I think so," he said.

"Where you going?" asked Goldstein as they stepped into the garage.

Exhaust fumes made them wrinkle their noses. A grizzled uniformed sergeant walking past them grinned and wrinkled his nose back at them sarcastically.

"I'm going to see my girlfriend," said Rourke.

"Julia?" asked Goldstein.

"That's who I mean."

"Do you think she'll like your surprise?"

"That's the question," said Rourke. He walked away from the Captain, said again, "That's the question."

He called Julia from the lobby of her building.

"Come downstairs," he said, "there's something I want to show you."

"Devlin?" said Julia. "Is something wrong?"

"Come downstairs."

"I'm *frantic*! I'm trying to write a press release about our position on the Blake Fund scandal and the newsletter hasn't gone out yet, my secretary has announced she's pregnant and that's supposed to make me happy for her but means—"

"Put all that aside. Come downstairs."

"Devlin! Sometimes I don't think you understand anything."

"Yes I do. Come downstairs."

"Is she with you?"

"Who?"

"Your new best friend."

"I'm alone, Julia," he pleaded. "Please come downstairs."

She stormed out of the elevators and through the lobby like an angry queen. Her brown hair swayed behind her like a mane, and her perfect breasts bounced beneath her white blouse. The burgundy skirt she wore was part of a suit; she'd left her jacket at her desk. Over her shoulder, Devlin saw a man in a three-piece suit and carrying a briefcase turn to stare at her twitching hips; the man didn't stop walking as he ogled her, and he bumped into the wall.

"I hope this is important!" she told Rourke. Her cheeks were flushed, her full lips set in a grim line. She frowned.

"Why are you wearing that sports jacket?"

"I like it," he said. "I've had it for years."

"I know," she said, "it's so—"

"Come outside," he told her. "I've got something to show you."

"What is this Devlin? Some kind of joke?"

"No," he said, "just the opposite. Come outside."

Reluctantly, she followed him out the revolving doors. He led her up the street to the corner, where a renovated midnight blue '66 Mustang sat gleaming in the sun. The car's only flaw was a star dented in its rear window.

"How do you like my new car?" he said, with a sweeping gesture to the Mustang. "I bought it this morning."

"Wha—Devlin . . . I . . . This isn't what we talked about!"

"It's not what you told me to do, no."

"Then why . . . Devlin, it's—"

"It's a great car!" he insisted.

"But it's so . . . immature!"

The day was warm, beautiful. Sidewalk traffic flowed past them: men in suits, women in skirts and dresses, construction workers in hard hats and blue jeans, college students dressed in corduroys, a uniformed waitress from a nearby cafe. A jackhammer chattered two blocks away.

"Julia," said Devlin, with a sad smile, "this is me. This jacket is me. This car is me. I belong out here in the street with a badge in my pocket and a gun on my hip. That's who I am. That's what I love. Maybe you think that's—"

"What is this?" she whispered. "What are you telling me?"

"You live up there, Julia," he said, turning his face to stare up toward her office window. "Surrounded by acceptable opinions in a structured room where—"

"You're wrong!" She barely breathed. "We love each other!"

"I know who I am, Julia," he told her. "I'm not someone to make over or change. I am who I am. You can dress me up, you can take me out, but it's still me. I try to be anything else and I'll be living a lie. We can't change who we are."

"It's her, isn't it?" said Julia. She was crying.

"Rachel's got nothing to do with it," said Devlin. "It's me. It's you. It's us."

"What's wrong with us!? What's wrong with me?!"

"Not a damn thing is wrong with you, Julia. Not one. You're wonderful. You're a dream woman and a great person. And nothing is wrong with me, either. But I'm not who you want me to be and I won't ever be. And since you don't want me as *who I am*, want me to change, you can't be right for me. That's what's wrong with us."

She turned away from him; hugged herself tightly. He didn't reach out to comfort her.

Two, three minutes. Half a hundred stares from curious strangers walking past.

She turned back to face him. Her cheeks were slick, her eyes wet. Tear stains dotted her white blouse. She looked incredibly lovable.

"What are you going to do?" she whispered.

"The best I can," he said.

"What about me?"

"You're going to be great," he said.

"Was it . . ."

"It was close," he said.

"Yes," she told him, "I guess it was."

She turned, walked back into her building.

Rachel was sitting on the front porch with Sam when he drove up to his apartment building, parked. She stood slowly, gingerly. She walked to the car, peered inside it, grinned.

"Hey fellah, great car!" she said when he joined her on the sidewalk.

"Thanks," he said. "I thought you'd like it."

"What did it cost?" she asked.

"A little money," he said, "a lot of blood."

"Doesn't everything?"

"How do you feel?"

"Ribs ache, but my insides don't feel so knocked around. Your shiner is going down."

Sam barked.

Rourke reached down, petted his head.

"Come inside," he told her. "I've got a lot to talk to you about."

As they walked to the door, she asked, "Anything new?"

They talked for five days.

Five nights.

Rachel spent an hour with the grand jury. When she left, she was finished with the law in Baltimore. The rental car company even agreed to not press charges; in fact, one of the supervisors hinted she could have a job. Rachel smiled sweetly, thanked them for their mercy, and declined their generosity.

They saw a lot of Susan Perry and Gary Harris. The Goldsteins had all of them over for dinner.

On the sixth day after Devlin bought the car they sat in the afternoon sunshine streaming through his bay windows—he in his desk chair, she on the couch. Sam lay on the floor between them.

"Are you sure you want to do this?" he asked her with a frown.

"Is anybody ever sure about anything?" she replied, her smile wistful.

"Then we better get on with it," he said.

"Guess so."

The Mustang was parked out front. When they emerged, the day was so gloriously bright with sunshine, green trees, and early flowers they had to smile, and that smile made them laugh. Rourke tossed her bag in the back seat. Sam, the richest dog in Baltimore, leaped in after it, sat up, and made himself comfortable.

They rolled all the windows down. Rourke slid the Mustang into St. Paul's traffic while Rachel tuned in the oldie-goldie rock 'n roll radio station. They knew all the songs the deejay played, and they sang along, never missing a word or a beat. The Mustang dodged all the chuckholes, drove steady, sweet and true. The warm wind blew over their faces and the world seemed wonderful.

The plastic sign hanging above the double doors on the old brown brick building read "Bus Depot." With Sam at their heels, they walked through the double glass doors, ignoring the glare of an old lady in an orange polyester pantsuit. Sam sniffed, not enamored with odors the pine-scented disinfectant couldn't blot out. To the left were rows of turquoise, plastic bucket chairs, bolted to the floor. To the right was a woman in a ticket booth. Ahead of them was a wall of glass doors leading to a courtyard carved out of the alley. A dozen yellow lines on the pavement made parking slots for buses beneath route signs: NEW JERSEY NYC ATLANTIC CITY; BOSTON NEW ENGLAND; WASHINGTON, D.C., RICHMOND CHARLESTON MIAMI; WEST—PITTSBURGH PHILADELPHIA CHICAGO.

"Why don't you take Sam outside while I buy my ticket?" asked Rachel.

"I can get it for you," said Rourke. "Just tell me where you want to go."

She smiled, shook her head.

He took Sam out to smell the three buses parked between the lines. The diesel fumes didn't please him.

"All set," she said when she joined them five minutes later. "Ten minutes."

She wore her leather jacket over a snap button denim shirt given her the night before by Gary Harris. In her jacket pocket was Mrs. Goldstein's favorite Somerset Maugham book. Susan Perry had given her a new pair of sneakers and a pair of jeans she'd only wore once before she'd "outgrown" them. The Goldsteins, Detectives Harris and Perry, had hugged her; Susan also gave her tears. Standing in front of the buses while drivers loaded and unloaded strangers' bags, Rachel's blue eyes shone, too.

"Wish we could have gotten you more witness money," said Rourke.

"Doesn't matter," said Rachel. "I never expected much from my government."

"Except saving your life," said Rourke.

"Yes," she said, "except that."

"Not a bad deal."

"Not bad at all. And you delivered."

"Yes," he said, "it did."

His stomach felt like it had no bottom, his heart like it would burst.

"This isn't like before, you know," she told him.

"What do you mean?" he asked.

"After all we've said, you know. I'm not just on the road anymore. I'm not just leaving, drifting. I'm going somewhere."

"Where?"

She shook her head *no*.

"This is a pretty good place," he said.

"As bus depots go," she whispered, and they both laughed.

"How 'bout the city?"

"It's great," she said.

"Got some nice people in it, too."

"The best."

"Maybe you should—"

"I can't!" she whispered. "Not . . . Not now. Not yet. There . . . there are things I must do."

"Maybe you could use some help," he said softly.

"Oh God!" she looked away; sniffled. Looked back. "Oh God can I use help. But I've got to do so much myself."

"*Westbound bus leaves in three minutes*," blared the loudspeaker. "*All aboard!*"

Neither of them spoke for a moment. Strangers trickled out of the depot, began to climb aboard the bus to Devlin's left.

"West, huh," he said.

She shrugged.

"One of my favorite directions," he said.

"But you're home," she told him.

"Yeah," he said after a slight hesitation, "I guess I am. But it's not . . . You . . ."

She pressed her fingers to his mouth, stopped his words.

"Hush! Don't say anything. We know what we can't say. What was it you told somebody? We can't change who we are."

"Maybe—" he said, the word escaping from her fingers.

"Maybe can't count for us!" she said. "Maybes and somedays would be cruel. We could never be cruel to each other.

"And . . ." She swallowed. Forced the words out. "And if you don't want to be cruel to me, don't lay your life on my shoulders. Go on. F-f-find a woman who's already home. Someone who's got no yesterdays to finish. Someone who can give tomorrow."

He tried to speak again, but she pressed her fingers harder. Finally he stopped trying.

She bent, took Sam's head in her hands.

"You take care of him, you hear me Sam?" she told him. Sam whined, barked. She kissed his head.

Walked toward the bus.

The driver turned toward them.

"Going with me?" he said.

Neither of them spoke for a moment.

"Look," he said, "you're either on the bus or off the bus."

Rachel took her bag from Devlin, handed it to the driver.

"I'll put that in a rack above a seat for you," he said. Climbed on board.

She turned and faced Devlin.

"I never gave you a going away present," he told her.

"You gave me everything," she said.

He reached in his jacket pocket, pulled out a pair of sunglasses.

"It gets bright on the road," he said. "You might need these."

"They were the Duck's."

She stared at the glasses in her hand, winced; closed her fingers over them and pressed her hand to her chest.

"Don't say goodbye," he told her.

"All aboard!"

Slowly, tenderly, she reached up. Her fingers brushed his cheek. He bent forward. For the first time, their mouths pressed together.

The sun brushed his lips. Then she pulled away.

She turned, climbed up the one silver step . . .

Then whirled, dove into his arms, found his mouth with hers again. Their arms pulled each other tight. Their kiss was passionate, hungry. Fire.

"Let's go!" yelled a voice inside the bus.

Rachel pushed herself out of his arms. Her face was slick with tears.

She ran up the bus steps.

The pneumatic doors closed.

The bus backed slowly out of its slot. Rourke saw her sitting on the other side of the smoked glass window. Her sunglasses stared back at him.

The bus pulled forward, rumbled out of the alley, turned right and was gone.

"Shit," said Rourke.

Sam didn't respond.

They stood alone in the terminal alley for five minutes.

"Let's go," he finally said.

They went for a drive. They saw Harbor Place and lines of tourists. A sign said: "Aquarium Reopened!" They cruised through downtown, saw business as usual—though a few banks had chain locks on their doors. Their route led past the Empire Cafe. Past the Red Moon. Past Memorial Stadium. They drove through quiet streets of flat-faced, marble-stooped rowhouses, past a high school. Classes were letting out. Rourke saw a group of teenagers, adolescents in adult bodies laughing and posturing as they stood next to a row of parked cars they wished could take them somewhere special. One of the boys reached up and without interrupting his story he pulled a strand of black crepe paper off a car's antenna. He opened his hand. The strand of black floated to the ground, drifted away.

The Mustang took them to the Beltway, where they could go round and round the city, spin off on a freeway toward any point of the compass. When he looked in his rearview mirror, he saw his eyes and the star dented in the back window.

The deejay on the radio talked about *gone from the charts but not from your hearts*.

Rourke took the next exit. Stopped at the first roadside pay phone. Dialed the number he got from information.

"Eighty-six-X," intoned the receptionist. "Today's hot one."

"Can I speak to Terry?"

Music from his car radio drifted to him while he waited on hold. He looked past the midnight blue Mustang to the cars whizzing by on the highway. The Ward Building's black-mirrored tower sparkled on the skyline.

"This is Terry," she said. "Can I help you?"

He smiled, said: "Want to go for a ride?"

ROBERT LUDLUM

These hammering bestselling superthrillers by Robert Ludlum prove why he reigns as the world's master of intrigue, conspiracy and suspense.